Her
Darkest
Hour

BOOKS BY SHARON MAAS

Of Marriageable Age
The Lost Daughter of India
The Orphan of India
The Soldier's Girl
The Violin Maker's Daughter

THE QUINT CHRONICLES
The Small Fortune of Dorothea Q
The Secret Life of Winnie Cox
The Sugar Planter's Daughter
The Girl from the Sugar Plantation

SHARON MAAS

Her Darkest Hour

bookouture

Published by Bookouture in 2020

An imprint of Storyfire Ltd.
Carmelite House
50 Victoria Embankment
London EC4Y 0DZ

www.bookouture.com

ISBN: 978-1-83888-664-6
eBook ISBN: 978-1-83888-663-9

Prologue

Christmas Day, 1933. Château Gauthier, Alsace

Marie-Claire knew the precise moment she fell in love with Jacques Dolch. They were both fourteen, she slightly older. It had been snowing all night, and a soft thick blanket of white covered the undulating hills around the chateau. She had risen early: the sun had just made its full and glorious appearance above the horizon, flinging a cloak of golden light over the land, and everything was sparkling and pure, as if the world was alive with a silent joyous song, so that she, too, felt sparkling and pure and full of joy. Village rooftops, just visible in a cleft between the hills below, and the meadows and rows of vines that combed the hills, all glistened as if with a million tiny diamonds; and the branches of the bare trees, silhouetted against the brilliant blue sky, were all etched in white; and life was whole and full of splendour. She opened the front door to all this, laughed out loud with glee and stepped forward, into the untouched snow.

She loved the sound of thick, pristine snow crunching beneath her boots. She loved being the first to leave footprints in the virgin whiteness, breaking the deep silence of a winter morning. She welcomed the new day with a little dance of joy, and then she hurried back inside, summoned back by the book the *Christkindl* had brought her last night. She had spent most of the night reading, and it was pulling her back with the strength of a mighty magnet. It was a delicious love story, just the kind of book to wrap itself around her and sweep her away to a faraway world, a world of ballrooms and beautiful dresses – and, of course, of heroines swept off their feet by charming and handsome swains.

Maman had already lit the *poêle en faïence,* or *Kachelowa,* as they called it here in Alsace, the wood-burning stove that provided heat for the entire ground floor, and the *salon* was filled with a delicious warmth, the kind of saturating warmth that sank into your being when you came in from a crisply cold day, the kind of cosy warmth that made you want to do nothing more than curl up with a good book. Marie-Claire was the reader in the family, and Maman had delivered gold with this particular book. She couldn't wait to get back to it.

And so, curled up in the massive armchair just next to the *Kachelowa,* was where Jacques found her hours later. She had even skipped breakfast, so absorbed had she been in the story.

'Marie-Claire! You're wasting the morning away! Come on out – we're going to have a snow-fight, and we need one more person to even up the teams. It's boys against girls!'

He made to grab her book, but she pulled it away just in time.

'Oh, Jacques, no! Go away! You really are a nuisance!'

Jacques was not a reader, so he could never understand. Nobody understood. In her family, they were all energetic, outdoorsy people, and nobody knew the magic of a good book. The nearest anyone came to understanding was Juliette, Jacques' sister, who also read, but a different kind of book: factual books, books about *things,* not people. And there was still hope for Victoire, her little sister and the youngest in the family, who was slowly learning; Marie-Claire had given her a novel suitable for seven-year-olds last night, and she had seemed genuinely pleased.

Jacques and Juliette Dolch were not only their best friends and nearest neighbours: their mother had died at Juliette's birth, and their own maman had played the mother role all their lives. Thus, they were like siblings to the four Gauthier children, and, as always, had celebrated Christmas with them last night. Their father, Maxence Dolch, was a good friend of their mother, as well as her winemaker, and the six children were in and out of each other's homes. She had never thought of Jacques as anything but a brother, along with her own two brothers, Leon and Lucien. A quite annoying brother at that. Like now. He would not take no for an answer.

'Come on, don't be a boring spoilsport!' He grabbed at the book again, and this time he was able to pull it from her hands and slam it shut, and hold it above his head, high up, so that she, considerably shorter than him, could not reach it, no matter how she jumped and tried to grab it back.

'Now you've gone and lost my page! Jacques Dolch, I hate you!'

'No you don't. You know it'll be fun once you get out. The book won't run away, Marie-Claire. Come on! It's beautiful outside. Look, here's your book. Sorry I lost your page.'

He handed it back to her. She took it, and leafed through it looking for the place she'd left off and, finding it, settled back into her comfy chair.

'You're really going to spend all morning there?'

'Yes, of course, and what's it to you?'

Jacques shrugged. 'I just thought you might enjoy being with us, that's all. But if you're quite sure…'

'Yes, I am, thank you very much.'

She drew up her legs and, curled into a ball, began to read again, ignoring Jacques, who shrugged, turned and walked towards the door.

Marie-Claire read a few more paragraphs but discovered that she couldn't get back into the flow of events. Jacques had made her lose not only her place in the book but her place in the story. She was out of it, and couldn't get back in.

In the end she gave up. She placed the piece of red silk ribbon that served as a bookmark between the pages, closed the book, stood up and stretched. She might as well go outside now.

The snow-fight on the meadow in front of the chateau was in full swing, all the children laughing as they zigzagged around the field, pitching hastily formed lumps of packed snow at each other. Marie-Claire bent down, picked up a lump of snow in her mittened hands, packed it into a ball and charged at Jacques, who had to be punished for the unforgivable crime of pulling her out of her book. Her missile hit him smack in the face; he laughed out loud and soon it was a one-on-one battle between the two of them.

And then it was just as Jacques had said, girls against boys, for Leon and Lucien came to Jacques' rescue, and Juliette and Victoire rushed in to defend Marie-Claire, and the clamour of laughter and screams was enough to bring the grown-ups – Maman, and Tante Sophie, outside, to stand before the chateau's door and laugh with the children, egging on the girls, who seemed so frightfully disadvantaged by the sheer size and strength of the boys.

And then, disaster. Marie-Claire, twisting around to avoid a particularly large snowball fired by Jacques, fell and, when she struggled to get back on her feet, cried out in pain. Maman, though wearing only slippers on her feet, rushed forward to help.

'I can't, Maman, I can't walk!' whimpered Marie-Claire as Maman tried to help her to her feet. 'I think it's broken!'

'Nonsense! It's probably just a sprain. Nothing a bit of rest and an ice pack won't heal. Come on, arm around my shoulder. You can limp back.'

Standing now on one leg, Marie-Claire gave a little hop, one arm around Maman's neck, but lost her balance and fell again.

'Let's make this easy,' said Jacques.

He bent over and scooped Marie-Claire into his arms as if she were a child of three rather than a quite solid fourteen-year-old. Holding her aloft, he marched across the field to the front door. 'I'm not too heavy?' Marie-Claire asked.

'You're light as a feather!' Jacques replied, and grinned down at her.

He had lost his cap during the fight and a lock of dark hair hung forward over his eyes, and his grin was cheeky and his eyes sparkled in a way she had never noticed before; and being carried like this, by a boy as handsome and, yes, as charming, as Jacques – well, it was something very special indeed, a pivotal moment in her life. Only this morning, in the very book she was reading, something like this had happened to the heroine, a girl not much older than she herself, and even with a name, Marianne, similar to her own. And the girl had fallen head over heels in love, and it was the most delightful and moving scene in the book up to now.

And it was happening to her – just like in the book.

Later, many years later, Marie-Claire was to look back to that moment of euphoria and pinpoint it as the trigger for the whole disaster. But that was after the war.

Right now, in Jacques' arms, her heart soared, opened up and folded around him.

Chapter One

1940 Alsace, France

Juliette

They came at dawn. She heard them through closed windows: the perfect rhythmic thud of marching boots, the clip-clop of horses' hooves, sinister against the early-morning stillness. Sounds that chilled the soul.

Juliette leapt from her bed to fling open her upstairs bedroom window. She leaned on the sill to watch. Across the street, up and down, other windows in other houses opened, other men and women, and some children, watched silently. The watchers glanced at each other and some gave slight waves to their neighbours, but mostly they simply watched the seemingly endless column of goose-stepping Germans, slate-grey-coated soldiers in perfect lockstep, left-right, left-right, arms stiffly swinging, rifles on shoulders. An occasional officer on horseback. A break in the column as a tank rolled in, or a jeep. Slow-moving motorcycles ridden by helmeted soldiers, escorting a long black car like a hearse, its windows blackened.

Juliette jumped as she felt a hand on her back, but it was only Grandma Hélène, still in her nightdress, like Juliette. She moved aside to make room. No words spoken. Arms around waists, they only watched.

And then the voice, strident through the megaphone, in German and in French: '*Citizens of Colmar. Your city is now under the jurisdiction of the German National Socialist Government. When leaving your homes, you must carry identification papers with you at all times. Your curfew starts at 8 p.m. and ends at 5 a.m....'* And so on and so forth.

Finally, they were gone. The empty street repossessed its stolen dawn silence. Juliette closed the window and turned to Grandma. They said nothing, not out loud. There was no need. Their eyes, locked together, said all that needed to be said, wordlessly. Then as if driven by a single impulse they fell forward, clasped each other, stood in shocked embrace for a few seconds before pulling apart, to stand, holding hands, gazing again at each other. Finally, it was Juliette who broke the mute wall of shock.

'You must leave, Grandma,' she said. 'Immediately. You cannot stay here.'

'No. I will not be chased from my home. I will not be driven away by a pack of thugs.'

'Grandma. Be sensible. Strasbourg was evacuated; now it's Colmar's turn. This is no time for pride. I can't stay with you, you know that, and you can't stay alone. I'll help you pack. I'll take you to Papa. You must stay with him until it's safe to return home.'

'It's sweet of you to worry, *chérie*, but completely unnecessary. If anyone is in danger it is you: a young, beautiful girl. They won't harm an old woman. It is you who must go.'

'Grandma! You know I am leaving anyway, back to university. But I'm not going to leave you here alone. I just won't. Papa will agree with me. I'm going to get dressed now and run out as soon as the post office opens and ring Auntie Margaux. She'll inform him and come and get you.'

Hélène tried to protest again, but Juliette, normally a soft-spoken, willingly compliant girl who went out of her way to avoid conflict or argument, was adamant, the inner steel that she kept concealed, ready for emergencies, finally emerging full-blown to assert itself, to stand tall at full height. It was Grandma's turn for compliance in a reversal of roles.

Juliette and her grandmother enjoyed an unusually close relationship. When Juliette's mother died in childbirth it had been Hélène who had dropped everything and rushed, husband in tow, to her son's cottage nestled within the hillside vineyards near Ribeauvillé to take over the care of the baby. When Juliette came of school age, the three of them moved back to the family home in Colmar, this very house in which Hélène herself had grown up, leaving Juliette's older brother, Jacques, with his father, the winemaker Maxence Dolch.

Thus, the Dolch family was split into two branches: Juliette and her grandparents, Jacques and Maxence, with Juliette flitting between the two, spending all her holidays with her father and term-time with her grandparents. She might call Hélène Grandma, but for all practical purposes she was a mother, a real mother. Grandpa had died two years previously, in 1938, and now it was just the two of them. With Juliette growing into maturity, her role was changing, and more and more her responsibility for her grandmother's well-being came into focus. Grandma may have managed well on her own in this rather grand Colmar house, but now, with Nazis swarming through the town, it was unthinkable.

As soon as she had bathed, dressed and had her morning coffee, Juliette emerged into the street, identification documents tucked into the pocket of her jacket. The post office was a fifteen-minute walk away; it necessitated passing the town hall. It was now mid-morning, but already its façade had changed. Huge long banners hung from the upstairs window of the building: a black swastika on a white circle against a red background. Three jeeps were parked outside the building, all with swastika signs pasted onto the doors. Soldiers, proudly bearing swastika armbands, marched briskly in and out of the main entrance. Already they owned the place. Soldiers everywhere in the town square, pasting swastika posters to lamp posts.

She stopped and stared. Marie-Claire worked here, at the *Mairie*. Marie-Claire, the daughter of her father's employer, Margaux Gauthier-Laroche. She and Jacques had grown up with the Gauthier children; Marie-Claire, and even more so Victoire, the youngest, were as sisters to her.

Bile rose in her throat. Where was Marie-Claire? Was she safe? And the mayor, a good friend of her grandmother – where was he? All the *Mairie* employees? Across the square she spotted Madame Bélanger, another member of Hélène's wide circle of Colmar friends. She dashed across the square.

'Bonjour, Madame! How are you?'

'I am not well, *chérie,* who could be well on a day like today? This cursed war has finally come to Colmar.'

'Yes – we watched them marching in, Grandma and I. It was shocking.'

'I never thought I'd witness a day like today. Not after the last war. I thought humanity had learned its final lesson. I was wrong.'

'Yes, but, Madame, do you know what happened, here at the *Mairie?* My friend Marie-Claire works here, and…'

But Madame Bélanger was already shaking her head.

'The Nazis took possession of it even before the soldiers marched in. I don't know how they got inside but they did. They simply swarmed through the place and owned it. Later when the employees began to arrive, one by one, they were sent home. They were told to return tomorrow. I know this because my nephew also works there. They will all lose their jobs, including your Marie-Claire. Colmar will now be a town administrated by Nazis. You can see how they have already decorated it in their stirring colours.'

She gestured towards the building, not looking.

'I can't even bear to look at it. Our beloved *Mairie*, festooned in swastikas. It's a tragedy. So Marie-Claire will have returned home?'

'I expect so. But what about you, my dear? Your grandma?'

'I want her to leave, to go and stay with Papa. She doesn't want to go, but she can't stay here alone.'

'Quite right. I'm glad you're looking after her. It's different for me: I will stay, my whole family is here, my husband and sons and daughters. We will keep Colmar alive and French. But Hélène should go back to Maxence. You are at university, aren't you?'

Juliette nodded. 'Yes. But I must move on – I'm just on my way to the post office to ring Tante Margaux and ask her to come and get us.'

'Give her my regards, and your father, when you see him.'

'I will. *Au revoir.*'

They parted, and Juliette moved on. She couldn't help it, however; she looked once more at the *Mairie* and shook her fist at it, a gesture of utter disdain and defiance. Which did not go unseen.

She had not taken five further steps before two officers in greatcoats stepped into her path.

'*Guten Tag, Fräulein;* where are you headed?'

Absolutely none of your business, she thought, but pride must now take second place to sagacity. There was no point in invoking Nazi ire. The words she spoke, clearly, confidently and curtly, were:

'To the post office. To make a telephone call.' No wasted words. Eyes glazed, looking straight ahead, not down, not meeting theirs.

'Papers.' A gloved hand, held out. She pushed her own hand into her coat, brought out her ID card, student card. Shoved them into the black glove. The officer took it, read it, looked up. Looked down, at the photo, and up again. It was a good likeness, but he pretended to doubt. This time she did meet his eyes, but made sure hers gave nothing away. No emotion. No fear, no irritation. She held his gaze, and he looked down again at the papers.

'You live in the rue Courvoisier?'

'Yes.'

'With your family?'

A slight nod. 'My grandmother.'

His eyes narrowed, and dropped to the thick plait that fell over her shoulder, long and black. He reached out and gave it a flick with his fingers.

'Such dark hair. Are you Jewish?'

'No, I'm not.'

He shook his head as if doubting her, then finally handed back the papers. 'You may proceed. Do not loiter.'

She retrieved her documents without a word and only a slight flare of the nostrils, turned away, walked a few metres and spat on the ground. Hurried onwards.

'Fräulein!' She stopped abruptly. Pushed her hands deep into her pockets because they were trembling furiously, uncontrollably. Did not look back. Held her head up. Waited for the officer to stride up from behind and once again plant himself in front of her on the pavement. She met his eyes with a cold stare.

'I will have you know,' he barked, 'that I have the authority to arrest any citizen who does not comply with my orders, or who in any way resists allegiance to German authority. You have been warned. Go on your way.'

It took all her strength to hold back the retort straining at the tip of her tongue, but she did. She nodded, and since he did not budge but simply stood there blocking her path, she walked around him. Her pocketed hands still trembled and did not stop shaking until she reached the post office.

There was a long queue for the telephone booth; it seemed that many Colmar citizens had similar needs to hers. The waiting people spoke among themselves in hushed voices. Snippets of conversations reached her ears.

'Do you think…?'

'Did you see…?'

'We are leaving as soon as we can.'

'…the next train. Down to…'

Many of them greeted Juliette with a friendly word.

'*Bonjour,* Juliette, how's Madame Dolch?' said M. Bordeleau, her grandfather's former tailor, as he joined the queue behind her.

'She's well, but I think it's better she leaves Colmar. She's on her own now so she'll go to live with Papa.'

M. Bordeleau nodded. 'That is a very good decision. Colmar is no longer what it was. France is no longer what it was. Seeing as how *les Boches* simply marched into France and took over... well. Terrible times. And now they are here in Colmar too.'

'Living as we do on the border to Germany, it was only a question of time,' put in Madame Coulon, who had just joined the queue to stand behind Juliette.

'So much for the Maginot Line,' said M. Bordeleau. 'The Boche simply ignored it.'

'Well, they might think they own Alsace but they don't. They never will. Alsace will stay Alsace.' Juliette's voice was defiant.

'There's Alsace *Français,* and Alsace *Allemand,*' said Madame Coulon. 'Back and forth, back and forth. A tug of war, which has now literally come to pass. You of course are too young to remember the last time we were German. Do not underestimate the damage that can be done. Why, your own name, Mademoiselle Dolch, is a testimony to that, a German name. When the Germans come they mean business. Everything will change: our names, the language, everything.'

Juliette merely nodded; she'd heard it all before. She was now at the head of the line; the person inside the booth was shouting into the mouthpiece, gesticulating as he spoke as if the person on the other end could see. Juliette rapped sharply on the glass, pointed to the long queue behind her, shrugged a question mark. The man understood. He slammed the receiver into its holder and stormed out of the booth.

Juliette entered, dialled Margaux's number. She picked up right away.

'Juliette! Thank God... are you all right? We heard the news on the wireless. I hoped you'd call... How's Hélène? What's going on?'

'We are all right, Tante Margaux, but Grandma's a bit shaken as you can imagine. I think it's best she move in with Papa for the time being.'

'But of course! It's what I've been saying all this time. And you want me to come and get her?'

'Yes, if you have the time.'

'For you, always; I just hope the traffic isn't too bad. I've heard everyone's fleeing Colmar, and the roads are packed.'

'But the roads coming *in* to Colmar should be free, don't you think?'

'Who knows? It is terrible, terrible.'

'But it was only a question of time, wasn't it. If they can take Paris, they can take Strasbourg and Colmar. We are just small fry after Paris.'

'Not at all! Colmar and Alsace: they are precious to Hitler and to Germany. It's more than just a small town in their eyes, *chérie* – for the Germans, Alsace is the crown jewel of France. But we will discuss all that later. I'm going to look after the animals and as soon as I'm finished, I'll come for you both. *Adieu, ma petite.*'

'*Adieu,* Tante Margaux, and thank you.' She hung up the phone, left the booth, nodded goodbye to M. Bordeleau and Madame Coulon as she walked past them – many more had by now joined the queue which now snaked out into the street – and headed for home.

Tante Margaux was, of course, not her real aunt; she was, in fact, her father's employer, but more than that, a good old friend of the family. Margaux's vineyard Château Gauthier-Laroche produced possibly the best wine in all of Alsace – an arguable estimation, the subject of many rigorous discussions in many a public house in all the Alsatian towns and villages between Thann in the south and Strasbourg in the north.

But a wine is only as good as its winemaker, and it was Juliette's father Maxence who worked the magic that transformed Margaux's Riesling, Pinot Gris and Gewürztraminer grapes into the wine people called nectar of the gods. Once, half of the Gauthier-Laroche vineyards had actually belonged to Maxence, but Max was a bad businessman and hard financial times and sloppy accounting had forced him to sell – on condition that he remained as winemaker. Margaux had been only too happy to form that alliance, because if her wine was indeed nectar of the gods, then Maxence was the magician whose wand performed that divine miracle of transubstantiation.

But to Juliette, Maxence was simply Papa. Her adoration was complete, and it was mutual, and as a child she had loved nothing more than returning 'home' in the school holidays, to frolic behind her father up and down the rows of vines; to learn from him, to cuddle on his lap of an evening while he read her to sleep beside the fireplace or, in summer, beside the outdoor fire he and Jacques made and on which they roasted their sausages and potatoes. Life on an Alsace vineyard was idyllic.

But close behind Maxence and Jacques, and Grandma and Grandpa – the Dolch clan – came the Gauthier family: Tante Margaux and her brood of children: Marie-Claire, Lucien, Leon and Victoire. They had all grown up together, in and out of each other's homes, all the parents and grandparents parenting all children, all the children like brothers and sisters.

Adolf Hitler was a living threat to all that. For years the province had lived under fear, fear of the looming menace just across the river, behind the Maginot Line and the River Rhine. Of what would happen should Nazi boots cross the Rhine and the Line. And now they had.

On the walk home Juliette noticed that already every single lamp post carried a swastika poster, and even more tanks were lined up outside the town hall. Even more soldiers walked smartly in and out of it, carrying briefcases and boxes and an aura of brisk efficiency. They had wasted no time in claiming ownership of her hometown. She walked past them all with her head held high, but bristling internally.

She arrived home, to the terraced house on the shady street she had played in as a child, only to find that there was no escape. The Germans were here too. Her front door stood open, and as she walked up the drive the very same officer who had stopped her earlier in the day, who had demanded her papers and asked for her home address, that very same officer stepped out.

'*Ah*, Fräulein Dolch!' he said as he saw her. 'Good that you have returned. We have decided that this house and all its furnishings shall be requisitioned by the German Army. Ten officers have been billeted here and shall be moving in by 6 p.m. today. You and your grandmother are free to stay, or to vacate. It is entirely up to you.'

Chapter Two

Margaux arrived a few hours later; by that time several army vehicles, all liberally plastered with swastikas, were parked along the street so that she had to park the van around the corner and walk back to the house. It swarmed with soldiers, the front door wide open, men in uniform walking in and out as though they owned the place. Margaux, striding into the hall, ignored them all.

'Coo-coo! Juliette! Hélène! Where are you?'

Juliette returned the call. 'We're here, in the kitchen!'

Margaux pushed open the kitchen door and entered. She found Hélène sitting at the central table calmly sipping tea; Juliette, who had been marching back and forth, unable to contain her nervous energy, rushed towards her, grabbed Margaux by the hand.

'Tante! Thank goodness. We've been waiting *ages.*'

'Sorry I took so long – Marie-Claire came home in hysterics; they've invaded the *Mairie*, chucked out all the staff... what's going on?'

'They're throwing us out! Out of our home!'

'Not quite true.' Hélène's voice was calm as she rose to her feet to greet Margaux. The two women kissed each other in greeting. They were an incongruous pair: Margaux, tall and strong, buxom, even, with a dishevelled head of pepper-and-salt hair, dressed for farm work in tired overalls and a bulky pullover, her face carved with lines drawn by life; Hélène, petite, elegantly attired, now, in a prim grey woollen skirt and a dusty-pink cardigan buttoned up to the neck, not a hair of her neat chignon out of place, her face porcelain-smooth (not without the help of an expensive cream or two), her lips finely drawn and accented with a discreet pink lipstick, perfectly matching her cardigan. A single string of pearls circled her neck.

Hélène shrugged, and gestured towards the four packed suitcases standing against the wall, along with several baskets packed with food. 'They gave us the option of staying; I could have kept my bedroom and shared facilities – bathroom and kitchen – with them. I'd have been happy to do so. These thugs don't scare me and I won't be thrown out of my own house. But I suppose my will doesn't count. *She* wouldn't allow it.' She gestured towards Juliette.

'Oh, Grandma! It's nothing to do with me *allowing* you or not. You know very well you can't live in a household of – well, thugs you said, and thugs they are. Tante Margaux – she can't possibly stay here, can she?' Her eyes pleaded with Margaux. *Support me, agree with me! I've been arguing with her for hours!*

'I should think not,' said Margaux briskly. 'But I don't understand. Why *you*? Why *this* house in particular? I don't see them in any of the other houses?'

'That may happen yet. It's my fault. I think I annoyed one of the officers this morning and it's a sort of revenge.' She related the incident on the way to the post office. 'I suppose provoking them didn't help. They must have come straight here. I had to give him my address.'

'That was a silly mistake, *chérie*. But you are young; you do not yet know that it is easier to catch flies with honey than with pepper. You will learn.'

'You should have seen them, Tante, marching in lockstep, right past the house. It was horrible, horrible! I wanted to kill them!'

Margaux placed an arm around her waist, hugged her close. 'We all want to kill them. But tell me – have they yet discovered the cellar?'

'Not as far as I know,' said Juliette. 'I haven't seen them go down. They've been up in the bedrooms, mostly, carrying up boxes. It looks as if they're going to be setting up offices as well as accommodation. Why?'

'Well, you know what is down there! Do I have to spell it out?'

Hélène shrugged. 'Who cares about a few bottles? They've got the *house*. My family home, the house I grew up in. It can't get much worse than that.'

'What sacrilege! It's a good thing your good husband isn't around to hear those words! But, you know, it has gone quiet outside – let me check.'

Margaux cautiously opened the kitchen door, peered around it. Seeing no one, she stepped into the hall, walked to the front door, opened it a crack; opened it wide, stepped out onto the front porch, looked left and right, up and down the street, and hurried back inside.

'*Vite, vite, ils sont partis.* They've gone. I'll go and get the van. Juliette, Hélène, run down and prepare a few crates. We'll save as much as we can. They'll get my best wine over my dead body.'

Hélène shrugged again, but did as Margaux requested, and walked towards the cellar stairs; why not save what one could? Juliette understood better; she sprang down the stairs ahead of Hélène and by the time Margaux returned with the van the two of them had packed several crates of Maxence's wine. Saving the best wine was a futile gesture of revenge, perhaps, especially as it must go unnoticed if it were to be effective, yet still it granted her a small prick of satisfaction. A tiny notch of one-upmanship, a minute victory.

The three women hastily loaded the van with wine crates and suitcases. Juliette slammed the front door shut with a resounding bang. She had no idea, nor did she care, whether or not the invaders had a door key. She and Hélène climbed into the cabin, and Margaux edged herself in behind the steering wheel.

'*On y va!*' she said. 'Let's go!' The van stuttered a little before jumping into activity. Margaux slammed down the accelerator, and they roared off as if a tiger was behind them.

*

It took almost three hours to cover the twenty-five kilometres between Colmar and Margaux's chateau, nestled in the hills behind Ribeauvillé. It seemed that many other people had the same idea: the roads out of town were like snakes of metal, vehicles almost touching as they crawled along at a stop-and-go pace as the townspeople sought refuge in the villages or further afield. Juliette brought Margaux up to date on the events of the day, Hélène filling in some of the details.

'I have to say, that for Germans, they were extremely polite,' she said.

'Polite thugs? Tell me another!' scoffed Juliette. 'In the end, they told you they're moving into your house, throwing you out. Try saying that politely.'

Hélène shrugged. 'You are young and impetuous. We older ones are not so easily thrown off balance. We've been German before, before you were born, right through the great war. How do you think Grandpère got that awful name, Dolch, dagger?'

'I know, Hélène,' said Margaux. 'Maxence has told me that story, many times. Max thinks it's funny.'

The family name had been Coûteaux, a traditional French surname, but the Germans responsible for renaming the citizens mistook it for Couteau, knife; Dolch was the German for dagger.

'We should have changed the name back after the last war, when Alsace became French again. We have been French ever since and we will remain French no matter what our name or how many Germans invade. They can throw us out of our homes but they will never make us German.'

Juliette said: 'You're putting on a brave face, Grandma, but you were just as upset as me when they marched in this morning. You cried. Don't deny it.'

'Yes, I cried a bit because it's hard to believe that after the thrashing they got last time the Germans are at it again, that they have not learned their lesson. It was hard for me to understand that they are back. It was a terrible time, Juliette, the Great War. You cannot imagine. And I am desolated that you might have to live through something similar. Let us only hope that it won't last long. Not like the last time. But whatever happens, we must be calm and strong and not be cowed. I would have preferred to stay in my own home, even if I have to share it with Germans. It seems to me defeatist to run away.'

Juliette squeezed her grandmother's hand. 'You are stubborn, and strong, Grandma, but you could not have stayed there alone with them. You must see that.'

Hélène sighed, and returned the hand-squeeze. 'I do. I suppose I do. It would not have been pleasant. But it feels like a defeat already, running away like this. Like when the Germans marched into Paris and the French government just ran off, tail between the legs. Capitulated. It's a disgrace.'

'The most important thing now is for us all to be safe. Even at the cost of our pride. Juliette is right, Hélène. The future for us all is unknown. It's a new chapter opening on us and nobody knows how it will develop. Perhaps it will all be over in a few months. I am glad you are going to Maxence. He must be worried out of his mind – he will have heard of the invasion over the wireless but I have not been able to drop in to let him know you are coming. He will be so relieved to have you with him. And you, of course, Juliette!'

'I haven't been home for ages! I can't stay long, but it'll be wonderful to see him.'

'How are your studies? What's happening with your university? Max told me you had to evacuate?'

'Yes – like all of Strasbourg. They've relocated the university to Clermont-Ferrand, near Vichy. I'm just on a mid-term break. Luckily I could be here for Grandmère.'

'Well, I am just happy that I get to see you unexpectedly, even if the circumstances aren't good. You come so rarely! Victoire will be delighted. You must come to the chateau as soon as possible.'

Juliette smiled. 'Ah, Victoire! How is she?'

'She misses you desperately. As you can imagine! She treasures your letters.'

It was a curious thing with Victoire. She was only fifteen, five years younger than Juliette, yet from the beginning Victoire had clung to her, Juliette, with all the devotion and admiration due an older sister. Even though she had an older sister of her own, Marie-Claire: Marie-Claire, who went her own way, and had no time for a little sister always at her heels. So Juliette had grown into that sisterly role.

Now that Victoire was becoming a young woman herself, mature beyond her years, that five-year gap seemed to grow less and less, on the cusp of disappearing altogether. Out of sisterhood genuine friendship was emerging; they would travel the world together, they had decided, visit England and Italy and maybe even Asia one day, and South America. Life had been so full of promise, so full of excitement and romance and adventure. Until now.

Margaux shrugged, pressed the horn sharply to get the car in front to move on. 'That idiot – is he sleeping at the wheel or what? Look at the gap in front of him! At this rate we'll be here all night. What were you saying? Ah yes, Victoire. Well, you know her. Restless as usual, following the news as best she can over the wireless, frustrated, anxious, worried.'

'And the others? Marie-Claire?'

Margaux launched into a tirade about Marie-Claire: 'That girl lives in the clouds! You know, I got her a job in the Ribeauvillé *Mairie* last year; better than moping around the house. She actually did quite well, so agreed to take a secretarial course and was promoted to the Colmar *Mairie*. But she still thinks she's too good for it. Too good for Colmar. We're all too provincial for that girl. Wants to run off to Paris to join her father.'

'Well, why doesn't she?'

'Run off to *Paris*? Are you mad? People are running *away* from Paris, not *to* Paris!'

'But Marie-Claire always dreamed of Paris, even before the war. Why didn't you let her go?'

Margaux pressed on the horn again, this time letting it blare for a full ten seconds before responding. '*Imbécile!* Sleeping at the wheel! What was that? Ah yes – Marie-Claire. I wouldn't let her go because that father of hers has no idea what to do with her and I am not letting a daughter of mine run wild in Paris. She has him wrapped around her little finger; he would say yes to anything she wanted, just for an easy life. *Papa, can I join the Folies Bergère and do the can-can? Yes of course, my little darling!*

'He spoils her rotten and it is my job as her mother to delay the inevitable until she is of age. She has a few more months to go before she's twenty-one and then she can run off to Paris – if Paris is still standing in a year, if it has not been flattened by the Germans – and do as she likes. She fell in love with the place when she was thirteen and we spent Christmas there. She thinks all her dreams will come true in Paris. Now it's all Paris, Paris, Paris. Papa, Papa, Papa. Over my dead body. But she has improved since she got that job and it gets her out of the house, doing something useful. And now they've chucked out the *Mairie* staff, goodness knows what's next. She's quite distraught. Even though she thinks it's all beneath her, she thought she could work her way up to Paris. Work in some grand couture house or something. Why couldn't she be nice and sensible and responsible and clever like you?'

'That's not fair, Tante – don't compare. Every child is different and everyone has their own weaknesses and strengths.'

'I haven't seen your weaknesses yet, nor her strengths.'

'Well, they exist, I assure you. So, enough of Marie-Claire. I do like her a lot but I know she is a headache for you. What about the boys? Are they back yet?'

Leon and Lucien had run off to fight for France after the invasion; they had been captured and were now prisoners of war somewhere in Germany.

Margaux sighed. 'No. Goodness knows when Hitler will send them back. It's all a disaster, from beginning to end.'

'And Jacques? I haven't heard from him in ages.'

'Your brother has absconded. He's in Strasbourg. Ran off just after the *vendange*. We haven't heard from him since.'

'In Strasbourg? That's not like Jacques. What's he doing up there?'

'I think the less we know about what Jacques is up to, the better. He always had a political bent, and ever since the Nazis took Strasbourg he's been on a mission.'

'You don't mean…?'

'I said, the less we know, the better. Don't you get involved.'

'But I have to go to Strasbourg anyway. I might as well visit him. Do you have an address for him?'

'He left a telephone number with Maxence. For emergencies. Not for social visits.'

'But—'

'He was quite clear about it, Juliette. Only for emergencies. Stay away from Jacques.'

Juliette fell silent. She understood perfectly. She knew her brother well. If he was in Strasbourg, it could only mean one thing.

Eventually they arrived at La Maison des Collines, Maxence's home at the end of Chemin des Sources, the winding lane that passed by Château Gauthier. As its name implied, La Maison des Collines nestled between gentle hills, mounds that eventually rolled up to the Vosges mountain range that separated Alsace from Lorraine and the rest of France; softly undulating hills, striped with the inevitable ranks of grapevines characteristic of the region, vines now brown and bare, stripped of fruit and foliage. Here, nature was so close it wrapped itself around a person, each season coming and going with unmistakeable gestures, familiar signs.

Now dusk was approaching, a grey November dusk with a low-hung sky and a hint of drizzle. As the van drove into the cobbled front yard two dogs leapt forth from behind the house, barking, which turned into yelps of delight as Juliette descended from the van's cabin. She bent over to fondle their heads, crouched down to accept their excited writhing, stroked their sleek wriggling bodies, laughed at their slobbery kisses.

'Gigi! Rififi! How I've missed you! You lovely, lovely creatures! Calm down, calm down, you will both get your share of hugs! Where is Papa?'

'Here I am, *chérie!*'

A man, dressed as a farmer in torn and faded dungarees and a sloppy, over-large gabardine coat and black rubber boots, emerged from the barn-like building adjacent to the house. Dark strands of hair flopped forward over a gnarled, weather-beaten face lit up not only by a broad smile but by eyes that shone with love. Maxence Dolch, tall, gaunt, wiry, strode towards the group of girl and squirming dogs. Juliette abandoned the dogs and leapt towards him, flinging herself into his arms.

'Papa! Papa, it's so good to see you!'

'And you, *ma petite!* And when will you stop growing? I still cannot believe you are so tall! Let me look at you…' he held her shoulders and pushed her back, took her in, then drew her back into his embrace. '…more beautiful than ever. You look good, my darling, in spite of the terrible news. I heard it on the wireless and I've been worried all day. I've been trying to get hold of Margaux for news – I knew you'd call her – and went over this afternoon.

Victoire told me she'd gone to pick you up, so I've been waiting here and worrying. Hello, Margaux. Thank you for bringing them. Maman! So it took a German invasion to drag you back home!'

Max let go of Juliette and stepped forward to embrace both Margaux and Hélène, exchanging cheek kisses, folding his mother into his arms.

'Maman, you are so thin. You are like a feather. I'm going to have to feed you up.'

'I'm not staying long, Maxence. Only until that bothersome Boche has retreated out of Colmar so that we can get on with our lives. Hopefully not more than a week or two. At the most, a month.'

'You haven't even heard the worst of it, Papa! They requisitioned our house and threw out Grandmère!'

'What! Really! Hopefully they did not harm you? Come on inside. I have prepared a nice soup for you all.' Maxence ushered the three women towards the house and in through the front door. The hallway was cold; Maxence hurried them into the large square kitchen, warmed by a pot-bellied cast-iron stove on bowlegs, and gestured for them to be seated around the heavy oak central table.

'The child exaggerates,' said Hélène. 'They did not throw me out. I volunteered to go. Or rather, given the option of staying – which I would have been perfectly happy to do – I decided after all that I prefer your company for a while than to share my home with a bunch of uncouth, uncivilised brutes.'

'I should think so! Here, sit down, the soup is still warm but I think I'll heat it up a bit. And there's some bread to go with it – slightly hard, but the soup will soften it.'

He placed a large and apparently heavy pot onto the range, opened the stove door to feed the smouldering fire, stoked it and shut the door again. The stove gave off a pleasant, cosy warmth and the smell of burning wood lent to the atmosphere a sense of homely comfort; the delicious, distinctive feeling of home wrapped itself around Juliette and she hugged her father once again.

'It's so good to be back!' she said.

'Well, you know – nobody chased you away. You're welcome to stay here all the time.'

'Papa, you know I have to study, get a degree. I can't do that here.'

'I don't see the point of it. Why didn't you do like Jacques – he didn't bother with all these nonsensical school qualifications. It just goes to people's heads, makes them think they're better than us uneducated morons.'

'Oh Papa, don't say that! And don't compare me with Jacques. Jacques is a born winemaker like you, with an instinct for his work. I can't very well become a vet just by instinct.'

'But I miss you. I want you here. I wish you would come more often.'

'You know how it is, Papa. Grandmère needs me and between her and my studies, well, there's not much time left. I miss you too. But – here I am!'

'Well, we need to make the most of it. I would be happy for you both to stay here forever. All of us living here, Jacques too. Families need to stick together. Promise me that if the war comes to Alsace you will move back home, Juliette. The people might have returned to Strasbourg but it's still dangerous. Your safety is more important than your studies.'

After the declaration of war on 3 September 1939, all 120,000 Strasbourg citizens had been evacuated and relocated to southern France, like other border towns west of the Rhine River separating the two warring nations. For ten months the city had been completely empty except for garrisoned soldiers. At the arrival of the Wehrmacht troops in mid-June 1940 most of the citizens returned – but to a city now occupied by Germans.

'I won't. I haven't told you yet, but – the university is not returning to Strasbourg. It will remain in Clermont-Ferrand. I happened to be in Colmar, with Grandma, only because of a study break.'

'And the war has already come to Alsace, Maxence. That's why we're here now, isn't it. Nothing will be the same again. But hopefully the British will come in and drive the Boche from our streets.'

'I wouldn't count on it.'

For the first time, Margaux spoke, and she and Maxence looked at each other.

'*Non?*' asked Maxence, holding her gaze. 'You think we are in for another long war, like the last one?'

Margaux nodded. She stood up and stepped over to the stove, opened the lid of the pot, peered in, stirred the soup. 'I do. My useless husband does have some skills, besides business. He's kept in touch with the major politicians in Paris. He says that we are in for a long, long war. It will be just as brutal as the last one or even worse.'

'It can't be possible!' Maxence exclaimed. 'What are our leaders thinking! Haven't they learned from the last war?'

'Nobody wants war except that madman Hitler,' said Margaux. Her voice was calm, as if she didn't care. She stirred the soup. Around and around and around. 'He's the one agitating for bloodshed. He's the one who wants to expand and expand until the whole world is German.'

And then, without warning, she banged on the edge of the pot with the wooden spoon, and her voice was a cry, a rallying cry. 'But over my dead body! They'll have to shoot me and all of my children before we submit! We will never surrender, never!'

'Shhh, Margaux,' said Maxence. 'It's not going to come to that. Come, the soup's finished. Bring the pot. We're all starving.'

Chapter Three

Two days she spent at home, one day with at the chateau with Victoire and Margaux. On the fourth day, Juliette managed to tear herself away her father's overprotective affection, her grandma's overzealous attentions, her best friend's over-devoted neediness, excuse herself tactfully and escape back to Colmar, a city now decked in swastikas. As she hurried through the cobbled streets of the old town towards the *Pharmacie* Blum, her heart began to beat faster, and a dialogue with herself ran through her mind. *I hope he's there. No, I don't. Let him be there, dear God.* Taise-toi! *Shut up! But I hope… no, he won't be…*

He – that was Nathan Levi-Blum, the pharmacist's son, who had graduated just a few months ago and now worked at the pharmacy full-time, alongside his father or alone in the large storeroom behind the shop, filled with countless shelves stocked with bottles containing mysterious substances: liquids, tablets, capsules.

Juliette had known him when they were children; as they both grew older she had seen him from time to time when she went to collect prescriptions for her grandmother. In his final years of secondary school he had worked there after school as an assistant in the shop, greeting customers, supplying them with over-the-counter remedies, taking their prescriptions and passing them through the hatch to whichever pharmacist was on duty, and Juliette had often found herself calculating his work hours so as she could coincide with them on her medicine-collection errands.

Then he had gone off to university, and she had seen him only during the holidays. She had nursed a secret hope that once she, too, became a student they'd meet up at the university; the truth was, she could count on one hand the times she's seen him at the Strasbourg campus, and then only from a distance. Sometimes, even, she'd wished she'd chosen pharmaceutics instead of veterinary science as her discipline – but no; she invariably dismissed that thought. She'd always known she'd be a vet, and not even the soulful dark eyes of Nathan Levi-Blum could change that.

Nathan, in his final year of studies, had often worked at the pharmacy alone during the *vacances*. He took on night and weekend shifts, and it was during the weekend daytime shifts that their paths sometimes crossed. Or rather, didn't cross. They barely spoke. Juliette would ring the bell on the counter that summoned him from the storeroom. He'd come through the door in his white lab coat, like a doctor; her heart would skip a beat, and there was nothing she could do to stop it, or to stop her eyes from seeking his, searching his.

His face! Long, dark, sallow, with an inevitable strand of black hair falling over his forehead: it seemed to contain a sadness, an enigma she longed to solve, and his eyes spoke volumes but in a language she could not understand. She tried to read them, but couldn't. But the act of trying to read them meant that she'd gaze into them for a moment too long; she knew she shouldn't but she did it anyway because – well, because his eyes were magnets and she could not look away.

She'd hand him Grandma's prescription, held by those eyes. They'd exchange a few words, if need be, but most often he'd glance at the prescription – he was always the one to break contact – nod and walk back through the door to the storeroom with it. She'd wait, heart pounding, breath shallow, for his return, browbeating herself with the internal commands: *Stop it! Breathe normally! Don't stare when he returns! It's nothing, he's nothing, just stop it!*

She loathed this weakness of hers. This sense of her knees turning to jelly when he reappeared, this inability to make normal small talk

with him: *normal!* That was the element missing! Why couldn't she
just be *normal,* her normal cool, calm, sensible self, when in this
shop, when in the presence of this perfectly *normal* young man who
obviously cared less than two hoots for her and probably couldn't tell
her apart from the other customers, who knew her simply (probably!)
as the girl-who-brought-the-prescription for Madame Dolch.

The year she had first joined primary school, she had been a sheep
in the nativity play, and he had been Joseph for a few rehearsals. Just
for a few. Then his father had stormed into one of the rehearsals,
grabbed him from the makeshift stable, railed at the teacher and
stormed out of the school with Nathan in his arms. They'd had to
find a different Joseph. So tall, so dark, so brooding; he'd been a
perfect Joseph. But he would never have noticed a stupid little sheep.

But *she* had noticed Joseph, noticed *him;* she remembered.
Even then, he had made an impression on her, and in later years,
as they both attended the *lycée,* she'd always noticed him. But it
was perfectly hopeless. She had since learned that he was Jewish,
but that mattered not one bit; she might be officially Catholic, but
surely Jesus was Jewish; she didn't see what difference it made, and
this whole hullaballoo going on in Germany, with Jews somehow
being the target of hatred and acts of violence – it flummoxed her,
and placed her irrevocably on the side of the victims. That was her
nature. It was why she loved animals and was studying to be a vet.
She'd always be on the side of the innocent.

Sometimes there would be other customers in the pharmacy
before her, and Juliette would have to wait. She noticed that he
was quite different with other customers. He might chat with
them as he took their prescriptions, or even crack a joke. He'd be
relaxed, and even smile; he *never* smiled at her. Not even when he
handed over the little bottle of drops or the box of tablets; he'd
give her any information with a serious face, glum even, and his
eyes would burn into hers (that was, of course, just her imagination – in reality they'd just be *normal;* it was her eyes that weren't

normal): *twice daily, after meals, on an empty stomach, with water.*
Occasionally, the customer before her would ask detailed questions
and Nathan Levi-Blum would discuss the case with him or her,
and Juliette would listen to his voice and that would be in itself
so deeply satisfying: such a rich, resonant, slow voice! She herself
hardly spoke a word beyond a thank-you; she dared not, for fear
she might stutter, fall over the words.

Juliette, to all who knew her a confident and knowledgeable and
impressive young woman who could hold her own in any conversation, reduced to a blushing, stammering mass of shyness by this
one man. How had it happened? She didn't understand it herself.
She just knew that in his presence, something happened to her and
she wasn't herself, and now she'd been away too long. She longed
for his presence and that state of jelly-bellied discombobulation as
much as she dreaded it. It was bad enough, that visual contact over
the counter when her eyes would meet his and she'd try to force
herself to look away but couldn't – always, they'd linger too long,
as if trapped by his gaze, and she'd try to push away, but fail, that
sense of being almost hypnotised – no, that wasn't the right word.
Too clinical. *Spellbound.* Dazed. Mesmerised – those were the words
that sprang to mind but again, they were dangerously explicit, and
explicitness was a thing she couldn't handle. Bad enough, those eyes.
She could never handle speech. Push it all away, she thought, just
push it away. He doesn't even see you, except as a loyal customer.

Today she had no prescription for Grandma. But there was
always a need for aspirin, wasn't there, and any excuse would do.
The closer she came, the more her feet seemed to hurry of their
own accord and her heart seemed to beat faster, audibly so, and
again that mental agitation, that hovering desire to see that face
again, those marching thoughts, a prayer, almost: *let him be there.
Let him be there. No, don't. I can't bear it.*

She turned into rue Berthe Molly: and her feet came to an
abrupt stop.

Chapter Four

Across the shop window, partly blocking the neatly arranged display of beautiful stoneware jars large and small, an ornate antique apothecary scale and decorative bottles containing seeds and dried leaves and berries, was pasted a huge paper strip displaying, in bold, black letters, the word *FERMÉ*. She stared at it for a moment and then drew nearer and tried the handle of the door next to it. It did not budge.

Closed? The shop had *closed?* But why? The *pharmacie* Blum was an institution in Colmar – Grandma said that even when she was a little girl, there it had stood. Juliette had a dire suspicion, a suspicion so ominous all coyness, all her customary nervousness, melted in a second. There was no help for it. This was not the time for bashful wariness and tongue-tied reserve. She knew that the Levi-Blums lived in the apartment above the shop, and that the heavy wooden door on the other side of the shop window was the entrance to that apartment. She placed her thumb firmly on the well-polished brass doorbell set into the wall beside the door and pressed. Through the open window in the half-timbered wall above her she could hear the chime; she looked up, and just a second later a head emerged through that window.

It was him.

'Oh!' he exclaimed with palpable shock, and then, more calmly, *'Attend... je viens.'*

Through the door, descending footsteps thudded on wooden stairs, and then the creak of a key and a cautious opening and there he stood, in the doorway. It was all she could do to stop from flinging herself at him; but the moment of greeting was short and brisk.

'Juliette!' he said, a sharp cry of astonishment; but in the next instant, almost simultaneously, he had grasped her upper arm, pulled her into the darkness of the stairwell and shut the door behind her. They stood staring at each other in the dimness of the hall at the bottom of the stairs, and only now she realised how foolish a move this had been.

'What are you doing here?' he said, and she felt all the more foolish. She didn't even know him, not really. What on earth had she done? And how did he even know her name?

'I-I saw the sign. On the shop. I wanted to know – what has happened? When will you open again?'

'You should not have come.' He spoke more calmly now. 'It is dangerous for you – though actually, I was... But now you are here, come upstairs.'

He led the way up the narrow steps, their wood shiny and worn away in their centres through the weight of footsteps over a century or two. All her shyness had returned by now; she felt ridiculous.

At the top of the stairs he ushered her through a door and then turned to her, his eyes searching, kind, haunted. 'I'm sorry I addressed you in a familiar way, Mademoiselle Dolch. I was just so astonished to see you. What is it? Does your grandmother need some urgent medicine? I'm afraid the shop is closed, as you can see, but I could—'

'No,' she interrupted. 'I don't need anything...' She remembered the aspirin she'd have asked for and abandoned that excuse. 'I came because, well, I have been away and I thought, well, I thought... and then I saw the sign and I was worried. Very worried. And please call me Juliette.'

They were in a parlour at the front of the building, with several narrow casement windows opening to the street. He gestured towards an oval table of polished oak.

'Do take a seat… Juliette. What can I bring you? I'm afraid we haven't much, no coffee, but I can make you some tea?'

'No, thank you, nothing. I—' She was interrupted by the opening of a door at the back of the room. A woman, middle-aged, her face gaunt and bearing an expression of deep concern, entered the room.

'Nathan? I heard the bell and— oh!'

Seeing Juliette, the woman started and stared; but only for a moment. Her face broke into a welcoming smile.

'It's Juliette, isn't it! Juliette Dolch! I would recognise you anywhere: you are the spitting image of your mother, Colette. Colette Roussel. She and I were in the same class, long ago, before we were married – we were such good friends! Your mother – she was such a wonderful friend. I was devastated when… when I heard. Welcome to our home, Juliette.'

Juliette smiled and placed a hand on her sternum, fingered through the cotton of her blouse the little pear-shaped sapphire pendant she always wore. It had been her mother's, a family heirloom; touching it always made her feel safe, protected by the mother she'd never known.

Madame Levi-Blum continued: 'I didn't know you were friends with Nathan. Why didn't you come to visit before, if so? Why wait until such terrible times?'

She sighed at those last words, pulled out a chair at the table next to Juliette and repeated, this time in a whisper: 'Terrible times. *Terrible, terrible.*'

'I was just about to tell her,' said Nathan. 'I promised her some tea – you tell her, Maman. She wants to know why we closed the shop. I'll be back in an instant.'

He left through the same door his mother had entered by; Juliette could see a corridor leading into the back of the building. All these timber-framed buildings in the centre of town had a similar layout: a staircase leading to the upper storeys, corridors leading to the back of the house and further rooms. Presumably, he had gone to the kitchen to make her tea. She should have insisted that she didn't want tea. She just needed to know.

She turned to Madame Levi-Blum. 'What has happened, Madame? Why have you closed the shop? I just returned to Colmar today and I saw the sign.'

Madame Levi-Blum shook her head sadly and laid a hand over Juliette's.

'Then you will not have heard... It is so awful. We have had this shop for generations. We have lived here all our lives, above the pharmacy. We mind our own business. We attend the synagogue and obey the tenets of our religion. We do no harm. We are friendly to all and polite. But now these – these Nazi *salauds* have said we must leave. They are sending us away, Juliette! We are not allowed to do business here. They have forced us to close down the shop, as you can see. And now we all must leave. Leave Colmar.'

'But-but-where to? Where will you go?'

'All Jews are being sent to Vichy France. That is what they tell us, the Boche. They are in charge now and they want to make Alsace, Colmar, free of Jews. *Judenrein.* We hope it is true that they are sending us to France and they are not in truth sending us in the opposite direction, into Germany. But we have no choice in the matter. No choice at all. Because if we do not go – well, I did not call them *salauds* by accident. We all know what they are capable of, if you have heard the stories coming out of Germany. We tried to delay it. We hoped it would not come to this. But the signs were there from the start, weren't they. This is not a good time for Alsatian Jews. For any European Jews.'

Juliette had, indeed, followed the news; her brother Jacques had kept her up to date. A year ago, before the war, there had been about 20,000 Jews living in Alsace and Lorraine. At the declaration of war in September, the French government started a precautionary evacuation of all Jews, and had managed to relocate about 14,000 of them to Périgueux and Limoges in south-west France, far from the German border. About 5,000 more Jews fled to southern France after the German invasion of France the following May. It had been a slow, stealthy culling of the Colmar Jewish population; one by one the families had left, her friends had left, sometimes coming over to say goodbye, sometimes just disappearing into the night. The Levi-Blums had held out till the last.

Madame Levi-Blum sighed. 'And so now, we too must leave. We have delayed it long enough. We always had hope, such hope – that the war would be over in a few months, that we could stay, keep our home, our livelihood, our lives. We held out as long as we safely could.'

'But now the Nazis have come to Colmar and it is not safe,' said Nathan, re-entering the *salon*. He placed a steaming teapot and two cups on the table, served the two women their tea, sat down opposite Juliette. She tried not to look directly at him because the anguish in his eyes was so very palpable. Never had she seen eyes as eloquent, eyes that spoke so loudly, as Nathan's; they flummoxed her. What exactly were they saying? Was she misinterpreting something? They were so candid – but she feared what she saw, drew away, and at the same time was drawn back again and again. Now, Nathan turned to his mother and said:

'Maman – where is Papa? Is he still in bed? You must get him up. It's not good, this broodiness of his. It's not healthy. You must get him up and he must face reality, help you to pack.'

Madame Levi-Blum shook her head as if in resignation. 'Yes – he is hiding away in the darkness of the bedroom. He finds it hard to accept the truth and leave it all behind. But you are right. I must.'

She sipped at her tea, replaced the cup.

'It is too hot. I will go and fetch Papa, and by the time I am back it will have cooled down. I will drink it cold if need be. *Excusez-moi,* Juliette – it was a delight seeing you and I hope that once this is over we will all see each other again and celebrate France's victory over Germany.'

She stood up, and so did Juliette. The older woman clasped both her arms and drew her close, kissed her on both cheeks. Whispered in her ear. 'I was so very fond of your mother, *chérie*. Such a tragedy. But I am glad you came, glad that I was able to meet you. Take care, little one, and do not be bowed by what is happening here. We will survive, we will win in the end.'

Tears swelled in Juliette's eyes as she whispered her goodbye, touched at the woman's poignant words. Such a pity that this first meeting with her might very well be the last – she was another link to her mother, and Juliette never tired of such links. She might never have known her mother, but the stories she heard of her brought her close, so close, brought her alive. Madame Levi-Blum turned and walked away, back through the door she had entered by. Juliette was alone with Nathan. And now it was not possible to avoid those eyes.

'Juliette. I— sorry. I'm so glad you came. I was thinking of you…'

'Of me? Really? I didn't know… think – but why?'

'…of you, and your brother Jacques. I need to see Jacques, urgently. Where is he?'

'I didn't know you knew Jacques!'

'We were classmates in secondary school. Friends, even. You didn't know? I lost touch when I went to university and he stayed to help run the vineyard. But we were friends, and, well, I need to see him, now, today! Where is he?'

'I don't know, exactly. He's in Strasbourg, but I don't have his address.'

'Can you get a message to him?'

She shook her head, 'No, not really. He left a telephone number, but Papa doesn't have a telephone. Though I could ask Tante Margaux to help. But he said we should only call if it's an emergency. Why do you want to see him? Sorry. I suppose it's none of my business, but—'

'This is an emergency,' interrupted Nathan. And then he paused, as if deliberating what and how much to say next. Their eyes locked; in his were a thousand questions, a thousand doubts and fears, all hovering there, unformulated, reaching out to her; and more than that, something else, something intimate, personal, a question meant only for her.

'Juliette – I'm sorry. I'm being so rude. But when I saw you, standing at the door, it was like a miracle that you had come – because, like I said, I'd been thinking of you. It is like an answer to a prayer.'

'Because you need to find Jacques?'

'No… yes – no. I wanted to see you, too, but you have been gone for so long. I had no hope – and yet I hoped. And then you came. And there you were! On my doorstep!'

'But—'

'I know it's not the time or the place but I need to tell you, now, before it is too late, now that you are here and nobody knows the future and – well, here you are and before you go again, I need to say it – that I think of you all the time, Juliette. I do. Every day, every minute. I don't know how it came about. I just do. And now, now it is too late. I wish I had said something, earlier, when you used to come every week—'

'Every day!'

'Yes, you came often, very often, with your grandmother's prescription, and sometimes I thought, does she really need so much medicine, or is it…'

He hesitated, and she nodded. 'Yes! It was just an excuse! To come here. To see you!'

They beamed at each other across the table. Hands reached out, clasped each other, his fingers firm but gentle around hers; long, elegant fingers, long, sensitive hands that sent a multitude of silent but unmistakeable messages into hers, messages that all channelled into one wonderful, miraculous, unequivocal declaration that told her all she needed to know.

Now he sighed. 'We have been so foolish, haven't we. Wasted so much time. I have had such... *feelings* for you, Juliette, but I hesitated to confess them. And now... now time has run out. The train to Vichy is tomorrow, at dawn.'

The moment of intimacy, so precious, had passed. He frowned, and a cloud of despair seemed to fall upon him. His eyes, so eloquent with feeling just a moment ago, now turned opaque with distress; but a second later that anguish, too, had transformed, morphed into something else, something she could not at all interpret. An urgency, an overpowering sense of emergency flared into them, sweeping her up in its power. His grip tightened around her hands and his voice, too, filled with that desperate urgency.

He leaned forward.

'Juliette – I'm not going anywhere. I'm not getting on that train and I won't let my parents get on it. I don't trust the Nazis. They say they're sending us to France, but what if it's all a lie? What if they're sending us to the east, into Germany, and maybe even Poland? You must have heard the rumours? I don't trust them one bit. That's why I need to see Jacques. That's why I said it's an emergency. And I need you to help. I must see him – today!'

'Then I must ring Tante Margaux. She'll know how to find him.'

'But nobody else must know, Juliette. It has to be utterly secret. I am only telling you because you are his sister but otherwise it is too dangerous. I am going to ask his help.'

'I think he'd help you. And, Nathan, I'll help too. You know that.'

'I'm sorry, Juliette, I'm so sorry for involving you in this. Because I'm putting you –and Jacques – at risk and that's the last thing I want to do.'

'There's no question. I know Jacques will help, and I will too.'

He squeezed her hand in gratitude. 'You see, Jacques and I talked of this before. I know he would understand, he would help. Years ago, before the war, when we were at school, he and I spoke of it, what we would do. Even then, the spectre of war hung in the air and people were speculating that the Boche would invade any day and Alsace would be put under German rule yet again. And most of the boys just shrugged and said, so what? Alsace has been German before and if it becomes German again, so what? – it would mean we are kept out of any war.

'Jacques was the only one who said no. He predicted that Germany would want Alsace above all else and he swore he would never accept that. He swore he would fight the Boche to the death. And I listened to him back then, and I said, *moi aussi*. I too would fight them. And that is what I have to do now, Juliette. Fight, not flee! I have to! But now that they are sending Jews away, it is precarious. My parents expect me to flee with them but I cannot. I need to find a solution before tomorrow. I've thought about it long and hard. I need to find safety for my parents. And then – Juliette, this is my home, my homeland. I must fight. I must go underground and fight this thing. That is why I must see Jacques. I remember the fire in his eyes. I remember his passion. And I want to be a part of that.'

At those words he ran out of breath. Now it was Juliette's turn to squeeze his hands.

'Oh, Nathan!' she breathed. And then, 'I will find out where he is, and I will take you to him.'

And then, after a pause, '*Moi aussi.* I want to be a part of it too. I want to fight this thing too.'

Chapter Five

Victoire

'No, *chérie*. Decidedly no. I will not allow it.'

Margaux slammed the lump of dough onto the kitchen table, turning it upside down as she did so. She had managed to procure some precious flour from the Ribeauvillé baker, Monsieur Martin, yesterday, in exchange for a fine bottle of *vin crémant*, sparkling wine. She pressed down into the dough with strong gnarled hands, kneading it, stretching it with her knuckles, folding it, kneading it again, stretching and folding it again.

Tonight, there would be bread for supper, along with fresh eggs from the hens scratching in the backyard and goats' milk butter she had made herself, from the goats romping in the fields behind the house. Rationing might be ever more severe in these hard times, but they were lucky here at the chateau. Bread, butter, eggs, not to mention crates of apples and pears from their own trees, potatoes, carrots, turnips and cabbage from their own garden, from the greenhouse. Not to mention wine; an endless supply.

Enough, not only for them but to share with some of the villagers, those with no farms of their own, no man to provide for them. Old women, young women; old widows and war widows, single mothers whose menfolk had gone away to fight a war they could never win, been captured by the Boche and were still prisoners of war somewhere in Germany. Margaux was lucky: both of her sons had been captured, not killed, like so many of their friends and comrades. Yes, they were prisoners in Germany, but at least they were alive. Hopefully unscathed by the experience except for the trauma of having fought for their lives, escaped death by a hair's breadth. Yes, she was fortunate. Her children were all alive, and two of them were at home and sitting at her table. But both of them nagged, for one reason or another. It was exasperating. This one, for example, right here at the table and doing nothing useful.

'But, Maman…'

'No *buts* about it, Victoire. You are not going to join Jacques. *Absolument non.* That is my last word and there's no use bringing it up again tomorrow and the next day and the next. I am sick of your nagging. Now get your useless little backside off that chair and fetch a bucket of apples from the cellar. There is enough flour to make an apple pie as well as bread. I will send one to Madame Flaubert – the poor woman, she is still grieving for her fallen husband and she has those three small children. And then you will chop the apples to prepare. And then you can take it over yourself, later on, when it is finished. That's the way you can help. None of this underground nonsense.'

Victoire sighed and stood up. There was no use arguing with Maman; she was always right, and never gave in. She made her way to the door, but stopped in her tracks as a telephone rang. Not the usual telephone; this was the private one, connected only to the gatehouse, and it was not in the hallway but fixed to the wall above the sideboard, and it had a different ring: strident, somehow, urgent, demanding. It had never rung before.

Margaux immediately stopped her kneading. Victoire stood still in her tracks. But only for an instant.

'It's Papa, from the gatehouse!' gasped Margaux as she dashed from the breadboard to the sideboard, wiping her floury hands on her apron during her sprint. She grabbed the receiver.

'*Allo*, Papa? What is it?'

She listened. And then; '*D'accord.*' She replaced the receiver, turned to Victoire and said, 'You're quicker than me. Run upstairs;

Leah's doing the rooms. She must hurry, down to the hideout. *Vite, vite.* She and Estelle. They must hide. The Boche is here.'

'Merde!' yelped Victoire as she sprang out the door – a forbidden word, forgivable in the circumstances. Margaux herself ran to the front room, to the window overlooking the front of the property. There, a hundred metres away, a soldier in the grey-green uniform of the German Wehrmacht was getting into a jeep; he had obviously just opened the gate, the gate that was now always kept shut for just such an eventuality – a delaying tactic. Next to the gate was the lodge, the little gate-cottage occupied by Margaux's father. He himself stood outside the cottage door, watching.

Margaux's heart began to pound. Breathlessly, she ran back to the kitchen, to the window above the sink, just in time to see Victoire, Leah and little Estelle vanish into the barn behind the house, across the cobbled farmyard. They had been quick; the plan was working. Now it was up to her. She returned to the kitchen table, coated her hands once more with flour and began her kneading again. And then it was no longer her heart that was pounding but a demanding fist on the front door.

She took a deep breath. Walked leisurely across the kitchen, down the hall to the front door, stood behind it.

'Who is it?' she called. A voice called back:

'Machen Sie auf. Deutsche Wehrmacht.' Open! German Wehrmacht!

Though the command came as no surprise, it was Margaux's term to utter *'Merde!',* but under her breath. This was it, the moment she had been anticipating ever since the day the Nazis had marched into Colmar. Expected, but worthy of an expletive nevertheless, and ones far more explicit than *merde*. She had practised for this moment; the most important thing was to stay cool, relaxed, not to get hot and flustered. She took another deep breath, walked to the front door as slowly as she could, taking her time to once again wipe her white-dusted hands on her apron.

'One moment, please!' she called through the door. Only then did she twist the latch that would unlock the door, and open it. Two smartly attired officers stood before her, both wearing the slate-grey jodhpurs and shiny black knee-high boots she had seen in photos in the daily newspapers, and both with swastika armbands. One was older, maybe in his mid-fifties, with a slightly egg-shaped head and portly figure: the other young, tall, square-jawed.

The older and obviously more senior of the two, his lapels and collar decorated with a plethora of medals and obscure insignia, clicked his heels and, strangely, inappropriately, Margaux thought, smiled. It wasn't a proper smile. It was a stretching of the lips; there was something slimy, almost sinister about it. Margaux had been dealing with smiles all of her adult life; she received them often and judged them always. She automatically sorted them into smiles that were a true expression of a person's smiling soul, and those that were pasted on. This one was decidedly the latter. She did not return it. His eyes bulged, by dint of which they seemed to contradict his lips, so thin as to be simply lines beneath a pencil moustache, a combination that set off an itch of irritation in Margaux's mind. It was instant antipathy.

The officer now removed his black-visored cap and gave a slight bow. In German, he said, 'Good morning, *gnädige Frau*. I am *SS-Ortsgruppenleiter* Otto Grötzinger, 19th Division, *Kommandant* in the Haut-Rhin region of Alsace. I am responsible for the supervision and organisation of the Colmar region of Alsace, and as such, I have arrived to inspect your property, make an inventory of your wine cellars and record all members of your household, both family and staff. I am here to request an immediate interview with the head of the household.'

Margaux, who spoke three languages, understood every word, but simply stared blankly and smiled sweetly. She said in French: 'My apologies, sir. I do not speak or understand German.'

Grötzinger looked up at his companion, nodded, smiled again and said in an oily voice that set Margaux's teeth on edge, again in German, 'If you have language comprehension difficulties, my companion, *SS-Obersharführer* Mendes, speaks fluent French and will translate.'

The officer at his side translated simultaneously and exactly; at the words *SS-Obersharführer* Mendes, he pointed to himself, as if to make it clear that there was not a third officer, yet invisible, perhaps hiding in the bushes next to the door. Grötzinger continued, in German, Mendes translating:

'May I request that you very quickly acquaint yourself with the German language, as it is to be the official language in Alsace henceforth. I shall make allowances today but regrettably, this will have to change. In future, speaking French will incur a penalty of five Reichmarks. German from now on is the compulsory language of Alsace. You understand?'

Margaux nodded. Grötzinger flicked his tongue over his lips and bowed slightly, obsequiously. He pulled a small notebook out of his jacket pocket, looked at it and said, with Mendes again translating: 'Very well. Now down to business. This vineyard is registered under the names of Jean-Pierre Laroche and Margaux Gauthier-Laroche. Is that correct?'

'*Oui.*'

'Surely at least you know the German word for yes. *Ja?*'

She nodded slightly. '*Ja.*'

'I thought so. I'm afraid, *gnädige Frau*, your previous reply, in French, leads me to believe that you are being deliberately obstinate? If so, I would remind you that it is in your best interests to comply with my instructions; I do not want to have to fine you or, indeed, arrest you for non-compliance, which I am authorised to do. I am, as you can tell, addressing you in a perfectly polite and civil manner and I would request that you respond in kind. Now, to business. We cannot stand here on the doorstep all day. I request entry into the house.'

Margaux stood aside and waved the two men in with an exaggerated bow and sweep of her hand. Now, they all stood in the hallway in a small cluster with Margaux slightly apart from the two officers. Grötzinger said, looking around, 'A very imposing chateau you have here. Nevertheless, we must proceed; we have already wasted too much time. As I said earlier, I am here to conduct an immediate interview with the head of the household. I request that you summon him.'

Margaux said, 'I am the head of this household.'

He looked at his notebook again. 'No. Jean-Pierre Laroche – he is your husband?'

'*Ja.*'

'Is he at home? My interview must be with the head of the household.'

'I told you I am the head of this household.'

'No – it says here…' tapping the notebook, 'Jean-Pierre Laroche. Your husband.'

'Yes, my husband. We are joint owners of the vineyard but I am the head of the household. This is my house. My house alone.'

Grötzinger looked flummoxed. He scratched his forehead and licked his lips once more.

'But where is your husband? I want to speak to him. I understand this is a wine business. Where is at least the manager?'

'That would be me, sir.'

'So you are manager of the business as well as owner of the house?' His eyes practically boggled. 'How can that be? Where is your husband? I need to speak to him.'

Margaux straightened her back. 'My husband lives in Paris. Indeed, I am the head of the household and the manager of the business, as well as its joint owner,' she said. 'What can I do for you?'

'You? A *woman?*'

The officer looked at her, slowly letting his eyes wander down from her unruly hair tied back with a faded headscarf to the stained apron, the still-floury hands and arms, the scuffed boots she always wore, whether inside the house or outside it. He looked more uncomfortable than ever, like a man in his smartest suit finding himself up to the knees in a swamp. Margaux decided on the spot to play into his discomfiture.

'Indeed. And I would be happy to talk to you. Oh dear, where is my hospitality, keeping you standing here in the hallway like this – do come into the *salon*. Can I offer you a cup of tea? A glass of wine?'

Instead of translating, Mendes snapped: 'This is not a social visit! We require chairs and a table to write on.' He turned to his superior and translated that into German. Grötzinger nodded approval.

'Then do come into the *salon*. You may sit at the dining table.'

She opened one of the doors leading from the hallway and, once again with an exaggerated gesture, ushered them into the *salon*, the room set aside for formal entertainment, part dining room, part sitting room; unheated, and quite chilly. Grötzinger sat himself down at the head of the table and his partner took a seat beside him. At a gesture from Grötzinger Mendes handed over a smart leather briefcase. Grötzinger opened it and removed some files and a heap of papers.

Margaux pulled out a chair and sat herself further down the table. She interlinked her fingers, placed them on the table before her. She had left the door to the hallway open; with some relief she heard the back door open and close again. Victoire had returned. Good. Leah and Estelle were safe.

Grötzinger shuffled his papers, removed a black fountain pen from a pocket in the briefcase, laid a clean sheet of paper on the table before him and started with his inquisition.

'I will need some details. You said earlier that you are joint owner of this vineyard?'

Margaux nodded. 'Yes.'

'And it is called the Château Gauthier-Laroche?'

She nodded again. 'Indeed, that is the name of the *domaine*.'

Mendes barked, 'Confine your replies to the words *ja* or *nein*, which you can say in German, if such are required, or to direct answers of the questions. I do not need opinions or explanations.'

He looked at Grötzinger for approval, which was given with a curt nod.

Margaux said, 'Very well.'

'Now, I need a list of all persons currently living in this household, including servants and other employees. Starting with yourself and your husband. You said earlier that your husband is currently in Paris. Is this a permanent or temporary sojourn?'

Margaux shrugged. 'That is entirely up to you Germans, sir. We have been told that all non-Alsatians must leave the province. My husband is a non-Alsatian. He is originally from Paris and he spends much of his time there.'

'I see. Children?'

'Four.'

'Their names and dates of birth?'

Grötzinger wrote down the names and birthdates as Margaux slowly dictated them. She could see, from her position lower down the table, that he wrote solely and meticulously in the jagged and rather ugly German Sütterlin script.

'The occupations of these children?'

'Leon and Lucien are prisoners of war in Germany. Marie-Claire works at the Colmar *Mairie*. I mean she worked there, past tense. You Germans have taken over the *Mairie*, so evidently, she has lost her job; she has been told to report there tomorrow and I assume she will be dismissed along with all the other staff. *Tant pis*. Never mind. Today she went into Colmar to look for a new job. Victoire still attends school – she is only fifteen. However, the school is going through a readjustment period and has temporarily closed, except for a few essential classes.'

'Ah yes, indeed. All schools in Alsace are going through the readjustment process from French to German; no doubt they will soon reopen with the required German teachers and German curriculum. French teachers must be re-educated in Germany.'

Margaux shrugged. 'So we have been told.'

'So what is Victoire doing for an occupation?'

'She stays home with me and helps on the farm.'

'You have a farm? I thought this was a vineyard.'

'A small farm. A few goats and fowls. And a cow and a pig. We grow our own vegetables – we have a greenhouse. Victoire looks after it.'

'You will show me afterwards. All farm produce and livestock must be listed separately; it will be assessed for requisition.'

'What? You can't just—'

'Silence, please.' Grötzinger bestowed on her another oily smile. 'Your opinion is not required, *gnädige Frau*. Let us proceed. How many employees are working for you on this farm?'

'None. I do all my work myself, in the house and on the farm. At present with Victoire's assistance.'

'So you are now alone in the house?'

'Alone, with Victoire. I believe she is in the kitchen. I was making bread when you interrupted me; hopefully she will finish it or the precious flour will be wasted.'

'Any Jews?'

'What?'

'You heard me. Are there any Jews on the property?'

'Of course not. I have already listed all my family members. None of us are Jews.'

'I must inform you that it is a criminal offence to harbour Jews in an Alsace household, to hide them, to in any way support them. Contravention of this law and conviction will lead to imprisonment and in some cases even to execution. You are aware of this?'

'I have heard of this. It does not apply to me.'

Grötzinger leaned forward and said in a voice that was both slimy and conspiratorial: 'Frau Gauthier-Laroche, you must now tell me in confidence: do you know of any Jews living in the vicinity? Do you know of any Jewish businesses, or of any Alsatian citizens who harbour Jews in their household? You must inform me if you do. It is your duty.'

Margaux shrugged. 'I do not.'

'Nevertheless, I require of you that you be extremely vigilant and report back to the German authorities immediately if you become aware of any Jews hiding in the area. It is required by law. All Jewish residents of Alsace have been ordered to register and leave the province and they have all been sent to the south of France – but we have heard of some stragglers who resisted, and they must be caught and punished. I am making you aware of this. Now...'

He removed from the briefcase a small book.

'It is required by law that all residents of Alsace change any French names they might bear to German names. As an exception, due to your valuable contribution to the German economy through your position as a winemaker, you and your family members will be allowed to choose your names, within reason. Christian names as well as surnames must be changed accordingly. This is a small book with approved German names. I will leave this book with you now, and I expect you to register your new names at the Ribeauvillé *Rathaus* within a week. Is that clear? Generally, it is advised to choose names that are the equivalent or similar to the existing French names, or at least to bear the same first letter. Unless the name is already taken, we will accept any combination of German Christian and surname. Is that understood?'

Margaux managed to suppress, under great tribulation, the retort that was dangling on her lips. She merely pressed them together and nodded.

Grötzinger's tongue passed over his lips again as he regarded his notes. 'Now, let us backtrack a little. I see that you have two sons, young men, in your household. Leon and Lucien. Where are they?'

Margaux shrugged. 'I already told you. They are in Germany. Prisoners of war, captured by the German army when they fought for France during the invasion earlier this year.'

Grötzinger stroked his moustache and glanced at his notebook, nodded, scraped back his chair and stood up.

'So,' he said, 'I now request to be shown around the premises – the house and outbuildings. In particular, I want to see your wine storeroom as we will be requisitioning most of your produce. All Alsace wine is now German wine and belongs to the German state. Is that understood?'

Margaux suppressed the urge to scream. She pulled in her lips, nodded and stood up. Grötzinger said, 'Very well. Let's go. My men will search every corner of the property, including any cellars.'

Chapter Six

Margaux had no words left; they had all drained away, evaporated. The fighting spirit with which she had flung open her front door and ushered Grötzinger into her house, the fire that tickled the tip of her tongue – all were gone, leaving her a ghost of herself. Silently, limply, she led the way back into the hall, into the kitchen, where Victoire had just covered the mound of dough with a damp cloth. Victoire looked up; their eyes met, and Victoire's opened wide in alarm. It was not often her mother was defeated, but when it happened it was complete; when Margaux lost a fight, her eyes declared her downfall more eloquently than words ever could.

Victoire mouthed, 'What's the matter?' Margaux merely shook her head and shrugged.

'…and this door leads to the outbuildings and, I presume, your wine stores?'

Grötzinger was already drawing back the bolt, opening the door, leading the way into the cobbled back courtyard. Margaux made to follow after Mendes, but Victoire grabbed her elbow and whispered in her ear, 'Maman, what's going on? What happened? You look—'

Margaux wrestled her arm free, frowned and fiercely whispered back: *'Taise-toi!'* I'll tell you later. Are Leah and Estelle safe?'

'Yes. But—'

'Stay here. I'm going with them.'

The interlude with Victoire had given her back some of her spark. She strode ahead to catch up with Grötzinger, who was making a beeline for the long low buildings where last year's wine was stored in ceiling-high wooden vats. She entered the building behind them. The air within was tinged with the scent of musty fermentation, pungent and somehow intoxicating. A door led into a storeroom where crates of older wine sat stacked and ready for delivery to Colmar, Strasbourg and further afield. In the past, Margaux's wine had travelled mostly south and west into France; she had achieved good prices for her best wine. But since the German occupation of France, prices had fallen dramatically, for Germany set the prices for French wine, and the wine had now to be sold to Germany, not France.

Grötzinger asked questions. Margaux answered them, her replies curt, her voice bland; Margaux, who could speak with passion and devotion on the subject of wine, now gave dull explanations to this, that or the other query.

A staircase led down into the cellar. A black hole yawned before them. Grötzinger turned to her. 'You first, *gnädige Frau*. I assume you know where the light switch is.'

She nodded and led the way down. At the bottom she flicked a switch and a grimy bulb hanging from a cord in the ceiling flickered light into the gloom. In the dimness, stacks of crates loomed into the cool dank space, reaching into the shadows. Margaux led the way forward and now, at last, she found her voice.

Reaching into one of the open crates, she removed a bottle. It was dusty with age; she swiped at the label with a cloth she pulled out of her overall packet, and said, 'This is one of our very best wines; it's a Riesling from the year 1910, perhaps the best year ever. You know about wines, *mein Herr?* If so, you must have heard of that vintage? Alsatian wines were particularly superb that year, and of course, mine were the best. You must have heard?'

Grötzinger nodded, but even in the darkness Margaux could read the doubt in his eyes. She knew the look of smug uncertainty. She'd seen it on the faces of people keen to be considered wine connoisseurs, though they had no inkling whatsoever. Encouraged by the revelation that he knew nothing at all, Margaux talked on. Walking around the cellar, she removed one bottle after the other from its crate, describing each in poetic terms. Grötzinger hung onto her every word; he asked no questions now, because Margaux left no space for questions; she was, in fact, selling this wine to Grötzinger.

But even as she talked, even above her own words, Margaux could hear her own heart pounding away and her ears were poised for sounds, sounds that didn't belong in that dank dark cellar. A stifled cough, a muffled sneeze. A careless whisper. A silent breath. Because, just beyond a door concealed by a moveable pallet on castors, a door built into a false wall she and her family had built as a precaution many years previously, was the equally dark and dank room where Leah and her daughter were hiding. Behind Margaux's seemingly enthusiastic accolades was this: the lurking fear of discovery. And her breath was short; as were, finally, her homilies to her very *best* wine.

Because it was *not* her very best wine. Even as she waxed lyrical, Margaux's spirit gradually returned; anyone who knew her would have noticed the devilish glint that now lit her eyes, even in the cellar's gloom; would have known she was up to something.

That false wall built so many years ago had been constructed not to hide Jews but for another, far more mundane purpose. To hide wine. To hide the really very *best* wine. The aged and aging wines that were the true fortune of the chateau, its treasure. These wines on display had been deliberately sorted from the cheapest stock. The labels had been removed and replaced with labels that showed an older and more noble vintage; and the bottles had been covered in carpet dust – dust recovered from the bag of Margaux's vacuum cleaner, in which each new shiny bottle had been rolled, one at a time, until it truly looked old and worthy and venerable. The Germans would never know the difference, Margaux had said, and, having met *Ortsgruppenleiter* Grötzinger, she knew it now. His palate was unschooled. He could not tell good wine from bad, and he was welcome to claim the entire bounty of this cellar for himself and his army colleagues. None of them would know.

And she, Margaux, and her family would relish a very private victory. As she did now.

'Well, Frau Gauthier-Laroche,' said Grötzinger as they made their way back up the cellar stairs, 'that was all very interesting. But, unfortunately – as I informed you previously – all Alsatian wine products now belong to the German government. We shall allow you to keep the cheaper quality in your storeroom; I realise that you need an income and far be it from me to deprive you of your maintenance. But the wine in our cellars – we Germans do appreciate a good wine and it has been most agreeable to find such a good source so close to hand. I shall send some recruits over tomorrow to make a full inventory of your cellar, and in a day or two it shall be collected and delivered to Colmar.'

Grötzinger was not finished. He insisted on a short tour of the farm; he made a note of the number of goats that Margaux kept behind the house, the two cows, the chickens, the rabbits.

'We do not need these animals immediately,' he told her, 'but please know that they, too, all belong to the German government, and will be requisitioned as required.'

They returned to the house; Grötzinger insisted on returning to the *salon* so that he could make his notes. The other officer was sent out to wait in the vehicle. Margaux returned to the kitchen, where Victoire had in the meantime cleaned up and was waiting anxiously for her mother.

'Pour me a glass!' she exclaimed. 'I need a drink. And to sit down. Those bullies!'

She pulled out a chair at the central table and plopped herself into it. Victoire poured a glass of Pinot Noir and placed it in front of her mother. Margaux kept shaking her head, still overwhelmed by the invasion of her property, an accurate reflection of what was happening all over France. She gave Victoire a summary of all that had been spoken.

A sharp rap on the kitchen door interrupted the conversation. The door opened; Grötzinger filled the doorway.

'I have finished making my notes, *gnädige Frau*, and I will now take my leave. Tomorrow, German officers will come to assess and remove the wine slated for requisitioning, and the animals; the German army has to be fed. Don't worry, we will leave you enough for your own use. *Auf Wiedersehen, gnädige Frau, gnädiges Fräulein.*'

He bowed slightly towards Margaux, towards Victoire, then turned away. Margaux rose to her feet, almost toppling the wine bottle on the table as she did so. Victoire caught it in time, set it upright on the table. Grötzinger marched down the hall, Margaux hard on his heels. He opened the front door.

'Oh!' he yelped, and tumbled backwards, catching himself at the last moment.

Chapter Seven

Marie-Claire

Marie-Claire stood on the porch, fumbling for her keys in her precious Coco Chanel handbag, sent by her father from Paris two years ago and much treasured. Startled by the sudden opening of the door, she looked up.

Marie-Claire did justice to her reputation as the beauty of the family. She possessed that natural *je ne sais quoi* that drew male glances; with her wavy blond hair, now elegantly coiffed into a chignon, perfect skin, symmetrical features and svelte figure, she could easily be mistaken for a Parisian young lady stepping down the rue du Faubourg Saint-Honoré. Marie-Claire's image was carefully managed and enhanced. While her mother and sister cared not one whit for fashion and chose to spend their days in men's trousers and old jackets and boots, Marie-Claire's hankering for Paris haute couture meant that she was always dressed to the nines. It was a predilection endorsed and supported by her father. He, using some of his connections in the world of Paris businesspeople, and gratefully accepting his wealthy mistress's cast-offs of fashion, make-up and perfume, took great pleasure in supplying his older daughter with whatever the chic young ladies of the capital deemed *en vogue*. Of course, that supply had diminished drastically since the invasion last June, but nevertheless, Marie-Claire could well boast of being the best-dressed young lady in the region; possibly better-dressed than anyone in Colmar, and – who could tell – perhaps even more well-dressed than anyone in Strasbourg.

It was not only her clothes: Marie-Claire's blond hair was at all times beautifully styled, never a single strand out of place. Her cornflower-blue eyes were framed and made even more seductive by a subtle but expert application of shadows and liners, her lashes long and fluttery with the aid of mascara, her lips reddened, not with beetroot juice like the hoi polloi of Colmar, but with real lipstick, sometimes just left-over stubs gleaned from Papa but gratefully accepted by his daughter; Marie-Claire was not a snob when it came to hand-me-downs from Paris. The porcelain skin of her face was enhanced by fine powders. Other women might use the ubiquitous beetroot juice to attain a winning blush for their cheeks, not so Marie-Claire. *Her* cheeks – already well-accented by nature – were enhanced by *real* rouge. And her shoes. Never the wooden clogs French women of wartime reluctantly shoved their feet into; Marie-Claire's shoes were of real leather, and they came from the best couture houses. She even had a pair of silk stockings, which she hoarded for special occasions; for everyday wear, she stained her legs to imitate stockings and drew a black line up the backs of her legs. Not for nothing had Papa been moving among the rich and famous of fashion's world capital. Wine went with fashion, commercially speaking, as well as it did with cheese, gastronomically speaking.

Sadly, Marie-Claire had little opportunity to actually put all these very special gifts on display. There were no balls, no parties, even, in the wine country of Alsace. Back in the good old days, before the war, there had been the occasional concert or formal function in Colmar – but then she had been too young to go unescorted, and her mother refused to take her. What was a well-dressed girl to do? So Marie-Claire wore some of her best clothes to work. She might have only a lowly secretary's position at the *Mairie,* but at least it got her out of the house, and at least she could strive to be the best-dressed woman in the building, in the town. It was an accolade she treasured.

Now she had lost that job, apparently, and so, day after day, put on her best attire to go job-hunting in Colmar. Sadly, today's hunt had been once again unsuccessful.

Now, standing on the porch of her once-stately, now neglected chateau home, the golden November sunlight falling around her almost like a spotlight, she was a vision, an apparition.

'Oh!' she gasped, almost in unison with Grötzinger. They gaped at each other. And then Marie-Claire looked beyond him, to her mother, and said, 'Maman, what's going on? What's that German jeep doing in the driveway? Who is this?'

She gave an offhand flick of her wrist towards Grötzinger. He, caught off-balance for the first time that day, soon recovered his usual aplomb. Giving a slight forward bow, clicking his heels, touching his cap, and an obsequious smile on his lips, he said: 'May I introduce myself, *gnädiges Fräulein,* if I may be so forward. I am *SS-Ortsgruppenleiter* Otto Grötzinger, of the Haut-Rhin region of Alsace. And you, I believe—'

Margaux barged forward between the two, grasping Marie-Claire by the elbow and pushing her past Grötzinger into the chateau.

'My older daughter, Marie-Claire. And now, if you'd please excuse us...'

Still pushing Marie-Claire gently forward, she edged past Grötzinger. Marie-Claire glanced up at him as she walked past. 'What's going on?' she said again. Grötzinger called after her: 'Ah! The daughter who works at the *Rathaus* in Colmar, am I right? Well, I'm sure you've heard that all the former staff have been invited to attend a meeting tomorrow at the *Rathaus.* Attendance is compulsory. And—'

'Auf Wiedersehen.' Margaux slammed the door shut.

And then they were gone, the German intruders. Margaux wiped the sweat from her brow.

'Maman, what's going on?' said Marie-Claire for the third time, impatience lending a peeved undertone to her words. She threw her hat over a hook on the hat stand, her handbag onto the sideboard, and bent over to tear her shoes from her feet. 'These things are *killing* me!' She set the shoes together carefully on the shoe-stand and straightened up, smoothing her skirt along her thighs and patting her hair into place.

'Nobody forces you to wear them,' Margaux retorted, 'and no, they won't *kill* you. And if I were you, I'd be less flippant about using that word when your country is at war.'

'But you're *not* me, are you, and I haven't seen much of any war. It's getting quite boring out here in the sticks. But again, who was that officer? Why was he here?'

'He came to find you and lock you up,' said Margaux, 'so you don't get too bored.'

'*Now* who's being flippant about war? Where's Victoire? She'll give me some proper answers.'

She strode past her mother towards the kitchen door. Margaux gave herself an internal slap. She'd done it again: succumbed to her own cynicism, let her tongue run loose needlessly. The bickering between mother and daughter had become so habitual that it now seemed almost impossible to hold a normal conversation, ask or answer a normal question; and Marie-Claire's question *had* been normal, and deserved an answer. Margaux was self-aware enough to note that she let her basic irritation at Marie-Claire's vanity distort every little everyday exchange. She had to put a stop to it. She had to overlook Marie-Claire's casual snobbishness and simply try to *love* her daughter. She *did* love her; Marie-Claire was her firstborn, how could she not love her? She just did not *like* her very much, and she let that dislike show.

She took a deep breath, straightened her shoulders and followed Marie-Claire into the kitchen, filled now with the calming fragrance of a baking apple pie. Victoire, busy sweeping flour from the floor, looked up. 'Maman!' she cried. 'You were gone for ages – I was so worried! Did they… Oh, hello, Marie-Claire!'

'Yes, it's me. And I just wish someone would tell me—'

'They came to see what's what here, stomp around, throw their weight around a little and show who's boss,' said Margaux, her tone now softer. She looked at Marie-Claire with what she hoped was a reconciliatory expression. 'We've got a German administration now and they're taking an inventory of all the vineyards and farms. Requisitioning things. Houses and livestock and harvests – and even people.'

'People? What do you mean?' Marie-Claire sat herself down on a kitchen chair, hitched up her skirt, and placed her right perfectly formed calf over her knee. Massaging her right foot, wriggling her toes, she stared at her mother with wide-open eyes. 'How can they requisition *people?*'

'Not you,' said Margaux, holding back a sarcastic (and not so witty, considering the circumstances) '*thankfully*'. She had to stop it. She had to be a better mother. More loving. More kind. Kindness was what would help Marie-Claire the most. A kind mother. A *kind* mother might diminish that obsession she had with her father.

'Jews,' she said. 'They are looking for Jews.'

'Well, thank goodness we aren't Jews,' said Marie-Claire.

'But Leah is, and—' Victoire, drying her hands on a ragged towel next to the sink, began, but stopped abruptly when Margaux, standing behind Marie-Claire, narrowed her eyes fiercely and mouthed, 'Shut up!'

'It has to be top secret between us,' Margaux had told her. 'Just you and me, and maybe a few other select allies. The fewer people who know, the less chance there is of someone blabbering out of turn. Marie-Claire especially. You know how she likes to gossip.'

'…and I worry about her,' Victoire finished lamely now. 'All right, I'm off. The chickens need to be locked up.' She left the kitchen through the back door, leaving her sister to Margaux.

Marie-Claire, sitting at the table and carefully rolling down her stocking, said, 'Well, I do feel sorry for her – I like Leah – but surely she should have left Alsace long ago, when the Germans first marched into France. Everyone knows that now the Germans are in Alsace they'll do one of those Jew-clearing manoeuvres they've been doing in German towns. So Colmar will be Jew-free as well. What a bore. I would have left, if I were Jewish. You just pack your bags and go. She's only herself to blame.'

'How can you be so glib about it, Marie-Claire? What about the Zuckermanns, and the Cohns? They are our friends!'

'Yes, I know, Maman, and it's a bother, but these things happen in wars. She can still go somewhere else in the south of France for a while and return when the war is over. That's what people in the *Mairie* are saying. It's perfectly all right.'

'Easy for you to say, Marie-Claire.'

Marie-Claire, immune to her mother's criticism, only shrugged, and changed the subject. 'Anyway, you said they requisitioned the wine. Not all of it, surely? Not…'

She gave her mother a conspiratorial smile.

Margaux returned the smile. 'No, not *that*. That's well hidden.'

'Good,' said Marie-Claire. 'Papa will be pleased to know. It was a brilliant idea of his, to build that wall and secret cellar. At least the best wine is safe.'

Margaux bristled. 'It might have been his idea originally but we all built that wall and helped to hide the wine. We worked as a team, if you remember.'

'Yes, I remember, and I also remember you calling Papa a fool because he warned that Hitler would start a new war. He said that years ago and nobody believed him. And as you can see, Papa was right. I remember very well how you used to argue that there would not be a war. But Papa knew it, even back then.'

'You don't have to bring that up every single time, Marie-Claire!' said Margaux. 'We are living in perilous times.' It was her turn to change the subject. 'By the way – how did your job-hunting go today? Any luck?'

Marie-Claire shook her head.

'Nobody's hiring. The situation is just too precarious. Nobody wants a lowly secretary. I went to the people you told me to and everyone said no. So it looks as if I'm going to have to mope around here again. Unless…'

'Unless what, Marie-Claire?'

'Well, we've been told there's a staff meeting tomorrow. You heard what that awful man, the *Ortsgruppenleiter*, said. We've all got to turn up at the *Mairie* tomorrow. I suppose he's going to officially fire us all. But there's a rumour they're going to keep a few of us.'

'But you wouldn't want to work for the Nazis anyway.'

Marie-Claire shrugged.

'A job's a job, isn't it? Why not?'

'Marie-Claire! I can't believe you said that! Who in their right mind would work for the Nazis?'

'Oh, for goodness sake, Maman. I'm just a secretary. It's not as if I'd be planning bomb attacks or… I don't know. To invade England or Spain, or inviting Hitler and serving him wine, or something.'

'Any kind of collaboration with the Germans is abhorrent. You should know that.'

'Oh, Maman. You do exaggerate. But anyway, I'm not at all interested, so you don't have to worry. What I've been thinking, on the other hand, is that this is a good time to move to Paris after all. I'm sure I could get a good job there, and…'

Margaux glared at Marie-Claire. 'You. Are. Not. Going. To. Paris. Get that into your pretty little head. Not before you're twenty-one and can do as you like. And anyway, Paris is not the Paris of your fantasies. Paris is in Nazi claws now.'

'Paris will always be Paris,' said Marie-Claire. 'It's a certain… *je ne sais quoi*. Not even the Nazis can destroy that.'

'Don't underestimate the Nazis,' said Margaux. 'Pure evil is contaminating. But…' she took a deep breath and straightened her back. 'But good will win in the end. And Marie-Claire…'

She paused. Marie-Claire, massaging her left foot, which now rested on her right knee, looked up at the pause.

'Yes?'

'I think you and I should call a truce. All this squabbling, all this tension between us – we have bigger things to worry about now, and we all need to pull together as a team, as a family. You and me, we're not enemies. We've got a real enemy at our doorstep and we need to focus on that – together, united. I don't want to be fighting *you* as well.'

'You wouldn't have to fight me if you'd just send me to Paris,' said Marie-Claire. 'But… well, I suppose you're right. In his last letter Papa said Paris is not what it used to be. You can't even go out at night because of the blasted curfews and everything is rationed.'

She sighed. 'I suppose I'll have to wait till the war's over. Such a bother.'

'So then – a truce? You and me?' Margaux held out a hand. Marie-Claire took it. Their eyes met, and then Margaux gave it a great yank, pulling Marie-Claire to her feet, drawing her close, into a hug. Marie-Claire stiffened, and then relaxed, allowing her mother to embrace her, but not returning the hug.

'I do love you, you know!' whispered Margaux. 'You're still my daughter, my eldest child, and we need to get along now in these terrible times.'

'Yes, Maman. We should. But now…' Marie-Claire wiggled her way out of the embrace. 'Now I need to go upstairs and get out of these clothes and have a bath. Excuse me.'

She pecked her mother on the cheek, bent down to pick up her shoes, and a second later, she was gone, leaving Margaux alone in the kitchen.

'Marie-Claire, Marie-Claire, Marie-Claire.' Margaux slowly shook her head in frustration as she repeated her daughter's name. She cleared away the rest of the apple pie, and said aloud, 'Well, at least we called a truce.'

Chapter Eight

Marie-Claire coasted down the last hill before the straight stretch of road into Ribeauvillé, and pedalled into the village. It hadn't been easy, at first, riding a bicycle wearing two-inch heels, but she had taught herself a trick: tuck the pedal into the ball of the foot, just in front of the heel, and after that everything was easier. Luckily, so far November had been mild, and she didn't mind the cool air on her bare legs; but winter was just around the corner and one day, reluctantly, she'd have to switch to boots, and they'd be ugly, now that Papa's supply of Paris footwear had run dry. Once she reached the village, she'd catch the bus to Colmar; another futile day awaited her. This staff meeting was such a useless waste of time. She didn't have a hope in hell of keeping her job.

Initially she'd fought Maman, who had forced her to find work, but that had been a matter of principle; in truth, she'd welcomed the opportunity to get out of the stifling chateau and away from her mother's endless nagging and the boredom of being without an occupation. But then she'd grown to love her job, which had brought more and more responsibilities with it. She'd been the only secretary in the Ribeauvillé *Mairie* who was perfectly bilingual in French and German. Since the declaration of war over a year ago her translation skills had become more and more in demand, and while everyone in Alsace knew *some* German at least, Marie-Claire was the only one of her colleagues – apart from the mayor himself – who was equally proficient in both: a German-speaking nanny and bilingual schooling in Colmar had seen to that.

Thus had come the promotion to a job at the Colmar *Mairie*. They had sent her on a four-week secretarial course earlier in the year, so as to bring her bilingual typing skills up to scratch.

And so Marie-Claire was not only the best-dressed woman who worked at the Colmar *Mairie:* she was also the most-promoted, most in-demand secretary. Her dreams of a possible move to Paris had taken a more realistic turn. Admittedly not the Paris of her long-cherished dreams, not the City of Light that had captivated her those long seven years ago, breathed itself into every cell of her body, held her mind and heart hostage.

Wartime Paris was a shadow of its true self. A German Paris: it didn't make sense! Paris, adorned with swastikas, its streets patrolled by soldiers! She imagined Panzers on the Champs-Élysées, troops goose-stepping along the rue de Rivoli (Papa had kept her well informed), and shuddered. No, a thousand times no!

But it would not be forever. Whether Germany won the war or not, the spirit of Paris was indomitable and would reassert itself and she, one day, would be there, basking in the limelight (admittedly, of her imagination). That future role was still quite vague, but Papa would see to it. Make sure she met the right people, was seen at the right places, made the right connections. One day she would shine, possibly as the wife of some famous person. Wives were important to important people, and she'd be married to one of those: perhaps a famous writer, or a director of the Opera, or even a statesman. Her imagination knew no bounds.

Arriving at the bus stop in Ribeauvillé, she leaned over her bicycle to lock it. Hopefully she'd not have a long wait, but the bus was very seldom on time and she was resigned to standing there along with several other villagers who worked in Colmar. It really was time she found lodgings in town. If she were lucky enough to find a job, it definitely had to be done before the winter. She knew these villagers; all were friends of her mother, and all enjoyed a little chat early in the morning. Since the invasion, the chat had all been fearful; nobody knew what was happening and, her being a former employee of the *Mairie*, they turned to her for answers. But she had none. Her answers were curt, dismissive; she knew no more than they did, and her future, too, was uncertain.

On the bus, Marie-Claire sat by herself, brewing in anxiety. She gazed out of the window as the bus trundled through the undulating countryside, curling around hills where the vines were now bare parallel lines hugging their contours.

Just a few weeks ago, these very vines had been covered in plump and succulent grapes: dry, white Riesling and Pinot Blanc, fruity Muscat and Gewürztraminer and light, red Pinot Noir, basking in sunlight as they ripened in late summer glory. And then the harvest; she herself had been out there picking on her mother's hills; the *vendange* was her favourite time of year (wasn't it everyone's?) and time off work was guaranteed to every employee in the region. It was almost like a religion; in fact, for many Alsatians, the *vendange* was more than religion; it was a ceremony of joy and great celebration. Now, the *triste* landscape – for the day was grey with drizzle – was a reminder that joy and celebration were relics of the past, and no one knew what lay ahead. Trepidation nipped at her heart. The Germans had invaded the *Mairie* – what would it mean for her, her job, her long-term plans?

Colmar, as usual these days, was clogged with armoured vehicles, jeeps, cars festooned with swastikas. And soldiers, soldiers, soldiers. Soldiers everywhere. When the bus arrived at the stop she descended into the street, pulled at the hem of her tailored jacket (soon she'd have to wear a coat), slung the straps of her handbag over her shoulder and walked the short distance from the bus stop to the *Mairie*.

A few metres from the heavy front door she hesitated. Both wings of the door were adorned with swastika banners. Two soldiers stood guard; at the moment they seemed to be questioning one of her colleagues, Yvonne Duvall, another secretary. Yvonne was nodding; one of the soldiers handed her back a bundle of papers, and she walked up to the *Mairie* doors. That was the signal for Marie-Claire to approach, and she cautiously stepped nearer. The soldiers turned to her.

'Papers.' A gloved hand held out. She fished in her handbag, produced her ID and placed it in the hand.

'You work here?'

'Yes. I am a secretary.'

The soldier inspected the document, handed it to his colleague, who also looked closely at it as if making an internal recording of its details. He frowned as he inspected the photo, looked up at Marie-Claire as if comparing her face to the one in his hand. He then unfolded a paper of his own; Marie-Claire glimpsed a list, probably of names. The soldier scanned the list, looking, apparently, for her name. Once satisfied, he handed her back the card.

'Very well. You may pass.'

She nodded and was about to step inside when the sound of someone calling her name made her swing around. A car had pulled up right behind her, beyond the pavement.

It was similar to the car that she'd seen yesterday blocking the driveway of her own home – or perhaps even the same one – a long black bulky thing with a small swastika flag flying from the Mercedes-Benz emblem at the crown of the hood. The same driver stood obsequiously holding open the back door... and the same man who had blocked her entry into her home yesterday, now pulling himself up straight, tugging at the hem of his jacket to straighten it, called out to her. In two long strides he was by her side on the top stone stair, his hand held out in greeting.

'*Guten Tag,* Fräulein Gauthier! I am delighted to meet you again. Let me escort you into the building.'

The two guards stepped forward in unison, opening both wings of the door. Grötzinger placed his hand lightly just above Marie-Claire's elbow, and all but thrust her through the entrance.

Chapter Nine

Marie-Claire

Grötzinger, standing at the front of the room, looked at his watch. Behind him, in a straight line, their hands linked behind their backs, all with their feet the same distance apart, chins up, blank stares into nowhere, stood five uniformed aides. The *Mairie* staff sat in uneasy silence, watching, waiting, in several rows of chairs.

Grötzinger coughed, shuffled the papers he held in his hand, looked at his watch again in obvious impatience. He turned around and, in a low but audible voice, said to one of the stiff-backed soldiers behind him, 'He's late. I'll have to begin without him – I have other appointments.'

He cleared his throat, turned back to face the room and then said, in German, while an aide simultaneously translated:

'As some of you already know –' here he glanced at Marie-Claire '– I am *SS-Ortsgruppenleiter* Otto Grötzinger, 19th Division, *Kommandant* in the Haut-Rhin *département* of Alsace. I would like to announce that, as of today, the *Mairie* will be run by a German administration of the Third Reich. We will install our own staff who will all be from Germany or at least fluent in German, replacing most of you. The *Kreisleiter* for the Haut-Rhin district, Herr Dietrich Kurtz, will be joining me any minute now...' He paused here to look at his watch again. '...so I'll just start with the preliminaries, to get them out of the way. We will be needing a few natives of this locality to stay on as staff, so there are going to be interviews this morning. Please will all those of you who are fluent in German step forward and announce your name. The rest of you may go home; you will not be needed. You will be generously paid your whole November salary, even though it is only mid-November, in lieu of notice.'

Marie-Claire and her colleagues, seated in rows in the assembly room, looked at each other, some frowning, some leaning close to their neighbour to whisper a few words. All shuffled in their chairs, crossed and uncrossed legs, fidgeted with fingers. Nobody said a word. Nobody rose from their seat, nobody stepped forward.

Marie-Claire bit her thumbnail, a habit she had had since her childhood, had managed to curb during the last year for vanity's sake, but which now seemed to have suddenly returned with a vengeance. Noticing what she was doing, she pulled her hand from her mouth and sat on it, firmly. She, too, did not rise from her seat. No, she would not work for the Germans. It was too high a price to pay for retaining her job. It was out of the question.

'So, then, nobody speaks fluent German? *Niemand spricht Deutsch?* That's very strange.'

He scanned the faces, pale, anxious faces staring blankly at him from the three rows of chairs. His gaze came to rest on Marie-Claire.

'But, Fräulein Gauthier – I believe you are the exception? Didn't we speak German together earlier this morning?'

Marie-Claire squirmed in her seat. It was true. It had all happened so quickly since meeting Grötzinger on the *Mairie's* doorstep this morning. As they entered the building he had made some small talk, and then nominated her as his messenger, telling her to go through the entire building requesting that the staff gather here in the assembly room. There had been no time for the usual early-morning gossip and exchange of news, or even of greetings. It had been all, '*Vite, vite,* we're having a meeting'.

But: he had spoken to her in German. She had understood, replied in kind, and this had revealed her to be one of the bilingual members of staff.

Now, she mumbled, in German: 'Yes, I do speak a little, but…'

'Well then. I hope this does not mean you would be disloyal to the administration of Colmar. It will all be much better if we have the cooperation of everyone. So, now: anyone else? This is the perfect chance for you to retain your employment. We need bilingual staff. Please raise your hands if you are eligible.'

Marie-Claire looked behind and around her. Pale, stony faces stared back at Grötzinger. Not a single raised hand.

'Well, then, I will have to interview you all one by one. First of all, though: which of you is the mayor?'

Involuntarily all heads turned to look at Monsieur Tailler, who sat in the middle of the first row; he was a pleasant, grey-haired but balding man in his mid-fifties. He had once been a jovial, pot-bellied charmer of a fellow, a popular mayor, but the last years had wiped the joviality from his face and demeanour and written lines of worry into his face. He had aged ten years in two. Now, after a short pause, he raised his hand.

'Stehen Sie auf, Herr Bürgermeister!'

Obediently, M. Tailler rose to his feet.

'So, I see you do understand German,' said Grötzinger, in German. 'What a surprise. And yes, that was ironic. Now, *Herr Bürgermeister,* I want you to address your colleagues, or should I say former colleagues, and tell them that as of today they are all expected to speak German; German is now your native language as Alsace is now a part of Germany, just as it was before the previous war. The province was stolen from us in an act of despicable, not to mince words, *legalised looting* as a punitive territorial measure imposed by our enemies in that fraudulent document known as the Treaty of Versailles.

'Now that Alsace is back where it belongs, in German hands, certain measures are imperative in order to sustain loyalty and patriotism among the people. Later on I'm going to distribute a small booklet with the most basic words and useful phrases, and they must take it from there. They must inform their fellow citizens.

'Also, a German teacher will be sent to each village to give classes for those unfamiliar with the language, and to help others perfect it. Alsace is now a part of the German state of Baden, and full integration is required. All the schools will of course be re-programmed. The children will be taught in German and the German school curriculum will be introduced. There will be a short adaptation period, after which speaking French will be an offence that will incur a fine. Furthermore, all citizens of Alsace must now adopt German names and register them here next week once we have got the system running. Also, all male citizens of Alsace under the age of thirty-five must register in Colmar for potential active military duty.'

Nervous shuffling went through the gathering; this order would affect all the men present except the mayor himself; and all the women certainly had husbands, sons, brothers who might now be called up.

Grötzinger had by now warmed to his topic and forgotten entirely the original purpose, the weeding-out of non-German speakers in the gathering. Clearly, this was a man who liked the sound of his own voice, a man who saw himself as something of an orator, inspired, perhaps, by the German *Führer* himself.

'I see some long faces,' he boomed, 'what is *wrong* with you people? Clearly you are lacking both in a knowledge of history and in patriotism. Alsace will always be German; you should be proud of that fact, proud to be citizens of the greatest and most powerful nation of all time. We have already swept through France and won full capitulation. We are all looking forward to a German Europe, a better Europe, a Europe, and indeed a world, led by the most forward-thinking, the most progressive, the most powerful, the most culturally advanced race the world has ever seen. Let us look forward to Europa Germanica – a continent united by a common language, a continent designed to rule the entire world…'

On and on he blustered, becoming more passionate with each sentence, each word. Marie-Claire watched in fascination as drops of spittle spewed from his lips as he spoke, and his face turned as red as gammon, and his eyes narrowed to slits, and his forehead grew shiny with sweat. She suppressed an inappropriate giggle – the man was, really, a caricature of the leader he was quite obviously trying to emulate. But then, this wasn't a giggling matter. He also, quite obviously, believed in his own bluster – and what if it were true?

Marie-Claire had never quite taken the war seriously up to now. In spite of her mother's warning words and her father's actually lived experience in a Paris invaded by the German army, she had somehow managed to maintain the belief that it all wasn't real; that this was all just an annoying interruption, and life would soon return to normal and she, at last, could escape to Paris. Nobody had been able to convince her otherwise. After all, no bombs had dropped in Alsace. No artillery had taken up positions in the idyllic hills surrounding her home. The nightmare people spoke of – it was so far away, conveyed to them all by disembodied voices over the wireless. Her mother tuned in each evening – illegally – to the BBC but the newscasts telling of the German threat – well, it all seemed so far away.

But now here it was, in tangible, human form; yesterday on her doorstep, today in her place of work. With this spitting, ranting, beast Grötzinger the war had caught up with her at last. And with that realisation the giggle she had tried to suppress turned into a sob, one that could not be withheld, one that, against her will, emerged as an awkward and very audible gulp.

At that very moment the door at the back of the room swung open. A man entered: straight, tall, wearing the light brown uniform – jodhpurs, high black boots, tunic and visored cap – as well as the swastika armband of the Nazi Party. Unlike Grötzinger, this interloper exuded authority. Bluster was not part of his make-up. He strode to the front of the room, nodded coldly at Grötzinger and turned to the captive audience, clicking his heels together and giving the hint of a bow.

'*Guten Morgen, Herr Bürgermeister*, staff, of the Colmar *Rathaus*.
I am *Kreisleiter* Dietrich Kurtz. I apologise for my late arrival but
I trust *Herr Ortsgruppensleiter* Grötzinger…' here, a slight bow in
Grötzinger's direction '…will have brought you up to date with the
changes to be made in this *Rathaus*. Thank you, Herr Grötzinger.
I will take over the meeting now. How far have you informed the
staff of the changes to come?'

Thus from the moment he entered the room, the *Kreisleiter*,
though considerably younger than Grötzinger, demonstrated his
superior rank. The latter did all but grovel – a clear indicator that
true authority derives not from age and not only from rank, but
from personality. Kurtz exuded authority. Dominance radiated
from him like a magnetic force, impossible to resist. Even his
outer appearance demonstrated that here was a man not to be
trifled with. His uniform – the brown jodhpurs and tunic with a
wide belt at the waist – was impeccable, unsullied by even a speck
of dust, stiff as if newly starched. His knee-length boots, black as
ebony, were polished to a high shine, and even the silver buttons
down the front of his tunic, the braiding above the visor of his
cap, glistened. Beneath the cap, blond bristles covered the back of
his head, as if he had been shaved down to the scalp and his hair
was just growing back. The same blond bristles formed a pencil
moustache above thin lips that looked as if they'd never once
smiled. His head itself was bullet-shaped, resting on a thick neck
only slightly narrower than the face itself, straight up from neck
to skull at the rear. A formidable man.

Grötzinger replied in German and they continued in that
language.

'Ahh-ahm – I have tried to identify the German speakers, ahh…'

'And who are they?'

Grötzinger pointed at Marie-Claire. 'This young lady, Fräulein
Gauthier, for one, has identified herself as a fluent German speaker.'

Kurtz turned to look at her. She quivered under his gaze; it seemed to dissect her, pull her apart into small pieces to assess her worthiness. At last he spoke, still in German, addressing her directly.

'What are your skills, Fräulein Gauthier? Can you type? Do shorthand?'

Like Grötzinger before her, Marie-Claire could only stutter a reply.

'Y-y-y-yes, *Herr Kreisleiter*, I h-h-had secretarial training.'

'Excellent. And typing – what are your speeds?'

She told him, regaining a little confidence. She had excelled at her shorthand and typing course in Colmar last May, the best in the class, and on the job she'd only improved. She had initially balked against her mother's decision for her to take up a job, but in the end had seen it as a good thing – a possible exit manoeuvre out of the home and into the big wide world. Colmar was just a stepping-stone; they'd surely need secretaries in Paris, even in wartime.

Without being asked, she added, 'It was bilingual secretarial training, *Herr Kreisleiter*.'

'Indeed! Do you know the *Einheitskurzschrift,* German short-hand, so that you can take dictation in German?'

'Yes, *Herr Kreisleiter*.'

A hint of a smile flickered on the thin line of his lips, and he nodded in approval. 'Excellent, excellent. I'll see you later. As for the rest of the staff – who else is fluent in German?'

Unlike Grötzinger before him, he put this question in that language, and this time the response was impressive. Several hands rose, hesitantly, their owners furtively glancing around to see who else had made the admission; to ensure that those who should confess had done so; to ensure that nobody among them escaped the dilemma they all faced: lose one's job, or work for the hated enemy, a traitor to France.

Marie-Claire suddenly felt deep, hot shame, felt the blood rising to her face and knew she must have turned beetroot red. Why had she done that? Why had she added that last bit of information, as if this was a desirable job she was eager to assume, as if she had not, with those words, identified herself as a *collaboratrice,* willing, perhaps even eager, to work for the enemy? The words had jumped from her lips almost without her permission; almost as if some subconscious voice within her had spoken out against her conscious will. She hadn't meant to say them, didn't want to work for the Germans. Yet she'd now put herself forward, and would have to deal with the consequences.

Kurtz spoke again, in excellent French, his voice an authoritative boom that did not allow for dissent.

'All those who did not raise their hands may now leave; your salaries for this month will be paid as usual, in full, but for the last time. You are dismissed. In addition, all men who raised their hands may leave except you, *Herr Bürgermeister; I'll see you later.'*

Staff, most of the women and all of the men, began to stand up, make their way towards the door, watched in silence by Kurtz. Marie-Claire hung her head. She could not bear to watch this culling of her former colleagues; she knew instinctively that today she had done something that would make her the subject of village gossip for months to come, whispered among the housewives: *'She always was a bit snooty, wasn't she? Always thought herself a cut above the rest of us. A bit too ambitious, I always thought. No wonder she wants to work for the bloody Germans. Putting herself forward like that! Her mother should be ashamed of her.'*

Her mother. Word would get back to her mother, most definitely: word that she'd made a spectacle of herself, showing off in front of the Germans in order to bag a job working for the despicable enemy. *Traitor! Collaboratrice!* That's what they'd all call her, and Maman would be furious.

Just when she'd believed they were about to make peace, she had done this thing. It was one thing to have been selected, against one's will, to work for them; what she had done was practically to *volunteer*. She should have bitten off her tongue rather than speak those disloyal words. She noticed one or two women whom she knew to be fluent in German leaving with the rest. That was what she should have done, instead of boasting that she was bilingual; practically begging for the job.

Kurtz was speaking again: 'The rest of you ladies, you can return to your usual desks. I'll be interviewing you one at a time for the rest of the morning. Fräulein Gauthier!'

She snapped to attention as he barked her name, and gaped at him.

'Ja, Herr Kreisleiter?'

'I'll be interviewing you first in the former *Bürgermeister*'s office, wherever that is. Be there in fifteen minutes. *Herr Ortsgruppenleiter,* let's go there now. I want to have a preliminary word with you.'

Kurtz's command was absolute. People fell into line when he opened his mouth. They obeyed. They collapsed. She, too, Marie-Claire noticed, had collapsed, and, right now, so did Grötzinger. It was extraordinary. The only other person Marie-Claire had ever met who possessed that gift of authority was her mother, but even Margaux's inherent bossiness – as Marie-Claire would describe it – faded into mediocrity against the sheer power of Kurtz's personality. His dominance radiated from him as the pull of a magnet. It was not a question of liking or disliking him, or what he stood for, or which words he spoke: it was *him,* the man himself, who possessed that domination, and Marie-Claire found it at once terrifying and fascinating. She couldn't help staring at him. Everyone did.

Chapter Ten

On the dot Marie-Claire turned up at M. Tailler's former office and knocked on the door.

'One moment,' came the call from within. She waited beside the door. And waited. After ten minutes, it opened and a red-faced Grötzinger emerged, stripped of his own authority. She stepped aside. He glanced at her and said, 'You may enter.' She did.

There were two men in the office. One was M. Tailler, who stood before the bookcase on the wall behind the big oak desk in the middle of the room, removing his personal books, packing a crate that stood on the floor at his feet. M. Tailler turned as she entered, gave Marie-Claire a nod and a half-smile; sadness weighed heavy in his eyes. Marie-Claire wanted to say something, commiserate, make some remark about how terrible these changes were and how upset she was to see him go, but she couldn't because right there in the chair behind the desk sat her new chief of staff, *Herr Kreisleiter* Kurtz.

Kurtz did not look up as she entered, did not in any way acknowledge her presence. He was speaking on the phone; or rather, listening on the phone, nodding every now and then while uttering a *ja,* completely ignoring both M. Tailler and, now, Marie-Claire. Now and then, an outraged *das ist ja Unsinn!* That's nonsense! He slammed down the phone, picked up the receiver, dialled again. 'Yes, I'm ready,' he said, nodded several times while listening intently, the telephone receiver in his left hand. With his right hand, he picked up a rather ornate fountain pen, moved it slowly across the open page of a large ledger, and his eyes fixed on that page, murmuring, *ja, ja,* as he wrote.

Marie-Claire, uncertain as to what to do, did nothing. She stood before the desk, hands fidgeting behind her back, waiting for her presence to be acknowledged, or even noticed. She watched the hand moving across the paper, slowly, deliberately, the thick fingers like sausages.

She tried to read the words the *Kreisleiter* was writing, but not only were they upside down, she was too far away. They were neat, though, each letter meticulously penned with surgical precision. Once, instead of *ja*, he said: 'Can you spell that for me?', after which he slowly and precisely copied down what was obviously the dictation of a series of letters. And now and then outrage crept into his voice and he spluttered, *Unsinn!* Nonsense!

M. Tailler placed a few framed photos into the box. Kurtz still being engaged on the phone, M. Tailler nodded once in his direction, once in Marie-Claire's, bent down to pick up the box, cradled it to his waist and walked to the door. Once there, he turned back as if to take leave of his successor of the office, but even now Kurtz did not raise his eyes from what he was doing. He did, momentarily, raise his hand from the ledger, though: he gave it a quick flick, as if to say, *be gone.* M. Tailler was out the door, leaving Marie-Claire alone with the *Kreisleiter.*

Finally, Kurtz spoke a few words of thanks and dismissal into the phone, replaced the receiver onto the body of the apparatus, blotted the page of the ledger he had been writing on, and closed it. He slowly and deliberately slid the blotting paper into a shallow drawer on the underside of the desk, picked up the ledger and placed it to the left side of the desk, screwed the cap onto the fountain pen and put it carefully in an upright pen-holder, which he placed in what seemed like precisely calculated alignment with the position of the ledger, then placed the telephone in equidistance to the other items on the desk. Each movement was slow, precise, meticulously executed, without a single glance at Marie-Claire.

At last, he was finished. He looked up, straightened himself on his chair as he drew it closer to the desk, placed both hands on the desk in front of himself, fingers and thumbs touching.

His gaze as he met hers was stony and penetrating and Marie-Claire found herself involuntarily shivering, but not from cold.

'Fräulein Gauthier,' he said. 'You may take a seat.'

Marie-Claire looked around for a chair and saw that the two that in M. Tailler's time were habitually in front of the desk were now shoved against the back wall. She gestured to them as if to ask permission to fetch one of them, and Kurtz gave her what she could only interpret as a nod of impatience. She fetched a chair, placed it before the desk with her back to the door and sat down, all of this watched closely by Kurtz.

'So, Fräulein Gauthier, I have already made my enquiries and have been informed that you are not only a competent secretary, you are the daughter of one of the most prominent winegrowers in the region. Is that correct?'

'Yes, sir. My mother owns the vineyard Château Gauthier-Laroche. It produces one of the best wines of the area.'

'Please only reply to the questions asked. If I need further information, I will request it.'

'Very well, *Herr Kreisleiter.*'

'Well, your credentials seem to be in order, though of course there will be some necessary security checks you will be subjected to, as with all French employees in German administration units. Your work here will be absolutely confidential. That is the first thing you must know. Nothing may be removed from this building, and you will be searched by a German guard at the end of each workday. I have already decided that you will be my own personal assistant, which carries with it an increased level of confidentiality. You may not discuss your work here with anyone, not even your own mother. Do you understand this?'

She nodded. 'Yes, *Herr Kreisleiter.*'

'I understand that your mother's chateau is somewhere in the region of Ribeauvillé? How do you get to work each day?'

'I cycle to Ribeauvillé, *Herr Kreisleiter,* and I take the bus to Colmar from there.'

'I understand that winters here can be quite severe – how do you get to work when there is heavy snowfall?'

'I-I was not working in Colmar yet last winter, but my mother has said that in the winter months I can stay in town and live with my great-aunt.'

He nodded. 'Very good. In fact, it would be better if you moved in there already – immediately. I insist on absolute punctuality, and this business with bicycle and bus – it's too unreliable. You can return home for Saturdays and Sundays, if you so wish. Now, the next subject I need to discuss with you is that of your name. It must be changed. I believe you have already been made aware of this.'

Marie-Claire gulped. 'Yes. I have been told this.'

'And have you as yet decided on your new German name? I believe Herr Grötzinger left our booklet of approved names at your home? We do, if possible, allow Alsatian citizens to choose their own name, and only interfere with duplicates. Have you yet selected a name?'

'No, *Herr Kreisleiter.* I haven't seen the booklet.'

He bent over to retrieve the leather briefcase from the floor next to his chair. Holding it on his knee, he groped around within it until he found what he was looking for. He held up a thin booklet.

'Here it is. Let's make it simple: a German female name beginning with M. There are many of them: Maria, Manuela, Margarethe, Martina… pick one.'

'I-I don't know, I…'

'We haven't got time to waste; if you can't decide I'll do so for you. Margarethe: my sister's name. Now you need a surname, but I expect your mother will have to choose that for the whole family. Something beginning with G. I'll give you a day to speak to her and tomorrow I expect you to register your full new name first thing in the morning. So that's settled. Now, let's move on to other matters. That's your desk.'

He pointed to a much smaller desk adjacent to his own. On a corner of it stood a typewriter, now protected by a dust cover. When this was the mayor's office, an older woman, Mademoiselle Leprince, had worked at that desk, taking down shorthand, typing out letters here sometimes but more often in the typing room with the other girls. Marie-Claire had seen Mademoiselle Leprince walk out of the *Mairie* during the earlier culling of staff – even though her German was perfect. Once again, she felt shame; she had practically volunteered to work here: a betrayal of her family, her country. She was a traitor.

Though there were some Alsatians who would welcome the invasion. Despised by Margaux and almost everyone she knew, these were the *Allemani* – descendants from an ancient tribe of ethnic Germans, still proud of that heritage. And wasn't it true that there were people, older people, mostly, who had shrugged their shoulders at the German annexation of Alsace? 'They come and they go, the Germans,' said these older ones. 'sometimes we are French, sometimes we are German. But always, we are Alsace. What difference does it make, as long as we can live our lives in peace.' Secretly – she would never reveal these treasonous thoughts to Margaux, and even less so to Jacques – Marie-Claire was one of them.

Marie-Claire didn't have a political bone in her body and had not really kept up with developments. She knew, of course, that Hitler was the villain in this story – everyone said so – but she never listened to his speeches over the wireless and even less did she listen to her own mother's tirades against the *Führer* and the occupation of Alsace. She knew it was all *bad* in a general sense; war was always bad, and there was a war on; but war had not yet arrived at their door, and hopefully never would. There was no artillery on her doorstep, no bombs falling, and nobody she knew had been killed or driven from their home. It had all been so far away. Until today.

Marie-Claire was not a rebel, not an activist. Her main source of news was her mother, but Marie-Claire wasn't interested in her mother's opinion on politics, or on anything for that matter; she was more likely to take an oppositional stance to anything her mother said.

If Marie-Claire was at all anti-Nazi, it was because of two people. One was her beloved father, who for years had warned against the Nazis and predicted war, predicted that Germany was a formidable enemy and that when – not if – they came, France would face great peril. Her father was decidedly anti-Nazi.

The other person was... Jacques. She couldn't even *think* of Jacques without a sense of hollowness, a sense of the emptiness and futility of her life here in the backwoods of France. If only... but Jacques hardly took note of her existence. She had once tried to remedy this. She could not think of this one attempt to win him without acute embarrassment.

They had both been sixteen at the time; as was often the case, Jacques was staying at the chateau after a wonderful September day of harvesting. There had been a party; wine flowing; song and dance and flirting and fun well into the night. But Jacques wasn't the dance-and-flirting kind of boy. He had slipped away without anyone noticing – except her. Jacques had always had his own room in the chateau; he came and went as he pleased, and Margaux treated him as a third son. She, Marie-Claire, was in a state of heightened excitement; Margaux had turned a blind eye, for once, to her adult friends when Marie-Claire, bright-eyed and charming, had seduced them into 'just a little sip'! Several little sips had probably added up to a full glass, and Marie-Claire felt not only more charming and beautiful than ever, she also felt adventurous, daring – and seductive.

She edged up behind Margaux – deep in conversation with Jacques' father, Maxence – placed her hand on the wine-glass-holding arm, leaned in and whispered in her ear, 'Maman, I'm tired. I'm going up to bed.'

'*D'accord!*' replied Margaux. 'A bit too much to drink, I suspect. Drink a glass of water before you go upstairs. *Bon nuit, mon petit choux.*' Back then, she and Margaux had had a fairly amicable relationship. Papa was often at home, and Paris already burned as a beckoning light in her heart. The pestering of her mother to actually move there had not yet started.

Instead of a glass of water, Marie-Claire had slipped into the kitchen and helped herself to a glass of Riesling from an open bottle standing among the clutter on the sideboard. For courage.

She'd gone up to her bedroom, taken off all her clothes and slipped into a silk dressing gown her father had given her for her last birthday – there was a nightie to match, but Marie-Claire didn't need a nightie for tonight's adventure. She wrapped the soft folds of the dressing gown around her, tied its waist belt into a bow, slipped out of the door and padded, barefoot, to Jacques' room. She knocked on the door and without waiting for an answer, opened it and entered.

The room was dark except for a circle of diminishing light at the head of the bed; Jacques lay there, propped up on a few pillows, reading. He looked up, startled.

'Marie-Claire! What are you doing here?'

She giggled; her hand reached for the switch and light flooded the room. She stepped forward. 'What do you think, Jacques! Visiting you, of course!'

With one flowing move she pulled at the bow at her waistband and lowered both her arms (she had practised in her room: she knew what would happen), turning her body in a slow, dramatic pirouette. The dressing gown slid in soft billowing folds to the floor, like a rippled flow of water, forming a silken pool around her feet from which Marie-Claire stood in a silent, sultry glory, a water nymph, perhaps, one foot slightly in front of the other, knee bent, hip slanted, hands holding her luxurious mane of golden-blond hair aloft. She narrowed her eyes, opened her lips slightly and gazed at Jacques with a look that left no questions open.

'Marie-Claire!' Jacques' angry shout cracked the spell. He leapt from the bed pulling a sheet behind him, wrapped it around her.

'You silly, silly girl! What on earth! Are you drunk?'

Marie-Claire blubbered, 'Jacques, you don't understand! I want to… Jacques, I love you! Don't you understand! I always loved you! I wanted you to-to know, to see… I-I…'

And she began to cry, to sob. Jacques held her around her waist and led her to the bed, holding the sheet in place around her shoulders. He turned her around and pulled her down to sit, and sat down next to her, his arm still around her waist. With his other hand he gently dabbed at her tears with a corner of the sheet. His anger had left him; now he spoke in gentle, soothing tones.

'Marie-Claire, don't cry. It's all right. You had too much to drink, didn't you – I saw you, you know! It's all a big mistake, this. It's all right, don't worry.'

'It isn't a mistake!' she sobbed. 'I just want you to see me, to notice me! You don't even know I exist! And I love you, I always loved you, and – and you're a man, and everyone says I'm so beautiful, but you don't even notice, you don't even see me at all, and I thought, I thought…'

Jacques stroked the back of her head.

'Oh, Marie-Claire. Of course I see you, of course I love you! I've known you all my life; how could I not love you! But that's the thing, you see – you're like my sister. I can't think of you in any other way, and you need to see me as a brother as well. It wouldn't be right, Marie-Claire, what you're proposing. I think you mistake the love you feel for me. You think it's romance, but it isn't, it's just sisterly love, and it's fine that way, and it wouldn't be right to – to change that. We're brother and sister, don't you see. We're all brothers and sisters together, you and me and Victoire and Juliette and Leon and Lucien. We all grew up together, one family—'

'But we're not! We're not even related and I've always, always loved you and I always vowed I'd marry you and now it's all over and – and I hate myself and I feel like a stupid idiot now and it's so embarrassing!'

'You're a little bit tipsy, Marie-Claire, and everyone does silly things when they drink too much – it's why I never drink more than a glass or two. No need to feel embarrassed. I promise I'll have forgotten it all by tomorrow and so will you.'

'I'll never forget it, never! I can't believe you rejected me! I thought—'

'Shhh, Marie-Claire. You thought wrong, that's all. Tomorrow you'll be a bit hungover and you won't remember a thing.'

But she *had* remembered. The embarrassment was seared into her memory, a mishap she'd never forget. She pushed it away but every now and again she'd recall the burning mortification of that rejection; it was a pivotal moment in her life. She'd never recover. From that day she had avoided Jacques' company; leaving a room as soon as he entered, and never saying more than a few formal words of greeting or farewell, never meeting his eyes, not even at family dinners around Margaux's table.

But Jacques had obviously forgotten. He didn't even seem to notice or to care that she avoided him; at those family dinners he was irritatingly casual, smiling when he greeted her without ever dropping a hint that it was all awkward and damaged between them. He was even less aware of her now than ever before; all he ever spoke of was the Resistance to the Nazis, and she was little more than a footnote. It was that memory, that embarrassment, that humiliating rejection that pushed her all the more towards Paris. It was Jacques she had to forget, Jacques and that most ridiculous, most humiliating moment.

Paris was the very antithesis of Jacques; Paris was the antidote to Jacques. Paris was couture and culture; Jacques was mountains and forests. Never the two would meet. Yet she knew: in a heartbeat she would turn from Paris and live with Jacques in some mountain hut in the Vosges forests.

If he would have her. But he wouldn't. And so only Paris remained: the cure.

Jacques hated the Nazis, and if she were Jacques' woman, Jacques' wife, she'd certainly hate them too; but now all she could feel was the embarrassment at having accepted this plum job with the enemy. And yet; and yet. New thoughts nibbled at that vague shame, swirled in her head, an idea she'd never before entertained. Personal assistant to the *Kreisleiter*... what a step up the ladder! From Colmar to Paris wasn't that big a leap. If she could do well here, perhaps, just perhaps – a transfer, one day?

But even to think such ambitious thoughts seemed selfish, traitorous – what would Jacques think? He'd be horrified. No wonder he rejected her. She was not worthy of him, not noble enough... and one word from him, one sign that he wanted her, and all this would be as nothing. Paris would be nothing. But such a word, such a sign, was an impossible dream. Better to just take the job.

'This is as of now *my* office,' said the *Kreisleiter* now, jolting her away from her self-recriminations. 'Herr Grötzinger will be the new *Oberbürgermeister,* district mayor, and he will be given a smaller office across the hallway. You may not use this office on your own. Once a week, perhaps more often, I shall be here and I will use this office, and employ you as my secretary for the letters I'll dictate, translating them into French where necessary. You may not use this typewriter – there are enough machines in the communal typists' room. I'll be away a lot of the time as I'll be inspecting conditions and upholding laws all over the region. When I am in the office you'll be taking shorthand notes of letters I'll dictate to you, or minutes of meetings, and typing up reports in the general office with the other girls. Do you understand?'

She nodded. 'Yes, *Herr Kreisleiter*.'

'Right now, I want you to leave; there's work to be done. Your first job will be to make a list of all the bilingual secretaries waiting to be interviewed. Take the name booklet and make sure they choose their German names by the end of the morning, and that those names are recorded by the registrar. This office has to set an example.

'I'd like a new list with the new names as soon as possible. By then I should have finished the interviews – I doubt they will last long, I only want to test the level of German fluency, and in addition make my own subjective assessment of each girl. Obviously, I require absolute reliability, absolute confidentiality. You will be going through a security check later today, as well as all the staff provisionally employed. Make sure all the staff members know of this. I can't have gossips working here – this is serious work, and German efficiency is to replace the French lackadaisical attitude that I understand has been the order of the day until now. Do you understand?'

'Yes, *Herr Kreisleiter*. I understand.'

'Good. Then go.'

Chapter Eleven

She was right: Maman was furious. 'Nobody in my family works for the Nazis! Have you no shame, girl? No honour?'

'Maman, I had no *choice!* I had to!'

Yet she blushed as she said those words, remembering how she had, indeed, made a show of her qualifications. But Maman couldn't know that. Unless... she'd find out. *Of course* she would. Maman knew everyone and at least two of the women who had walked out even though they were bilingual were her friends. They'd tell her. The only way for Marie-Claire to retain a smidgen of pride now was in defiance.

'Well, at least I still have a job now, unlike half the other secretaries! A good job at that!'

'I refuse to allow it. You're still underage; you need my permission to get a job.'

'Maman, I'll be twenty-one in four months' time! It's hardly worth it, to forbid me!'

'In four months' time they won't need you any more. You think you're so important that they'll wait? For you? Ha!' Margaux chuckled wryly and shook her head in disdain, which annoyed Marie-Claire all the more.

Victoire, sitting next to her at the dinner table, placed a placatory hand on her mother's wrist.

'Maman – please!' she whispered. It was always Victoire's role to calm the stormy waters between her sister and her mother, and it was always her mother who needed a restraining hand.

Margaux's passions tended to run away with her; she could be the most wonderful, generous, kindest person in the world but once her ire was provoked, she would say things that could never be unsaid. Especially where Marie-Claire was concerned. Now, she shook away Victoire's hand and was about to launch into a new tirade, but Marie-Claire had already sprung to her own defence, shouting the words, red in the face, her eyes blazing with anger.

'They want me, Maman, because I'm good, and you really don't want to anger the Nazis, you know! You don't have to collaborate—'

'—unlike you!'

Marie-Claire shrugged and continued, now in a calmer voice: 'You don't have to collaborate, but you don't have to *demonstrate* your hatred. Denying me the job – a job I *want* to take! – would be an act of rebellion and you'll only make a personal enemy of them. Do you really want that? You really want to make a fuss? You really want to set yourself up as an enemy?'

The truth of Marie-Claire's words left Margaux without an argument. She glared at her daughter now, searching for more words, words that would hurt, words that would cut.

'Well, let me tell you this, girl: not in my house. I won't have a *collaboratrice* living under my roof, eating from my table. Find somewhere else to live.'

Marie-Claire gasped. Was her mother, *her own mother,* actually throwing her out? Was what she'd done that bad? She straightened her shoulders and glared back.

'So you're throwing me out. I don't care. In fact, I was told I have to move to Colmar anyway, so as not to be dependent on buses. How convenient. I'll move in with Tante Sophie. I'll pay her rent – I'm sure she'll be happy to have me.'

'She's welcome to you. Little traitor!'

Marie-Claire threw her spoon down into her half-finished soup and scraped back her chair.

'Maman, you're really a bitch! And you know, if I *really* wanted to be a traitor there's a lot more I could do! I know a lot of things the Nazis would be happy to know but guess what, I do have some honour and I won't tell them a thing, but I *know*, don't I, and you'll always wonder, won't you! You and your precious *wine!*'

She fled to the door, and a moment later it slammed behind her, and her footsteps pounded up the stairs.

Margaux sat at the head of the table, deflated. Those last words were a knife twisting in her back; she knew exactly what Marie-Claire was alluding to. Because *of course* Marie-Claire knew her big secret. Marie-Claire had helped construct that wall in the wine cellar, behind which the most valuable bottles were stored. If Marie-Claire chose to hit back at her mother, that knowledge was ammunition enough.

Victoire said, soothingly, again touching her mother's arm, 'Don't worry, Maman; she won't tell them about the wine. I know Marie-Claire. She's a bit flighty but she's honourable, deep inside. I know it. She won't betray us. The wine's safe.'

Margaux slumped in her chair. 'Why oh why do I let myself get so riled up by that girl? I guess my nerves are all on edge. I don't really think she'll betray us; but, you know, it's not so much the wine I'm worried about. Victoire, did you ever tell her, or even hint, about hiding Leah and Estelle?'

Victoire's eyes widened. 'No, Maman, I didn't tell her. Nobody knows except Jacques. She just thinks Leah's gone.'

'Good. Because hiding Jews is enough to get us both executed. You know that.'

Victoire gulped and swallowed.

'I know it, Maman. And I promise you I've told no one else. I never would. But, Maman – you really need to make up with Marie-Claire. Maybe she really didn't have a choice about taking the job, and you've just made things a lot worse. You can't throw her out just like that.'

Margaux nodded. 'You're right – I let my anger run away with me. I'll go and talk to her. As soon as I finish my soup. And I'll warm up the rest of hers and take it up to her. That girl is too thin – she can't afford to miss meals. Pass the bottle, will you.'

Victoire refilled her mother's glass. Margaux took a sip, and immediately felt better. Bad enough having the Germans as an enemy on her doorstep, she couldn't afford to be at war with her own daughter as well. But it was true: her nerves had been rubbed raw by all that had come to pass since the Nazis had marched into Colmar, and she was constantly on edge. Marie-Claire's behaviour didn't help, but it wasn't enough to make an enemy of *her*, too. Marie-Claire knew too much. Not that Margaux thought that her own daughter would betray her… but one could never be too careful.

'Damn!' she said and emptied the glass. She stood up, walked to the stove, warmed up the remains of Marie-Claire's soup, added some more to it from the pot and carried it upstairs as a peace offering.

Chapter Twelve

A month later

Victoire pulled on her boots – a size too big; they were actually Margaux's cast-offs – slipped her arms into the sheepskin jacket hanging near the back door and stepped out into the dawn. She picked up the bucket of kitchen scraps from yesterday and walked across the cobbled courtyard to the chicken pen. The two hens heard her, and waddled across the yard in a medley of excited squawking and flapping of wings, making far more noise than you'd expect from only two. Once, they'd had over twenty hens, and it had been mayhem just walking into the centre of the pen to distribute the scraps. A mayhem she'd enjoyed. But most of the hens had been taken by the Nazis, leaving just these two. At least that gave her the chance to name them: Millie and Chloe were their names, and she'd grown very fond of them.

'Good morning, girls!' she said as she emptied the bucket in a wide circle around the pen, and the hens returned her greeting with yet more squawking and scraping of the ground and fluttering. She watched them fondly for a minute, walked over to the coop to check for eggs – there weren't any; there were seldom eggs in winter – then let herself out of the pen with the empty bucket. There were still the goats to feed and milk and the rabbits to look after, after which it would be back to the kitchen, breakfast to prepare for everyone, and then out again and across the yard to the winery, with fresh water and yesterday's bread for Leah and Estelle. The poor things, they hadn't seen daylight for weeks now – what must it be like, hiding in an underground cellar, knowing that simply emerging for a few moments of fresh air and autumn sun, a few rounds of the courtyard to stretch their legs, would be risking their lives? She had pleaded with Margaux to allow them out just for a while each day but Margaux had shaken her head.

'No. I understand how tough it is but remember how it was when Grötzinger came that first time? How they returned without warning to steal our wine and our produce, how they keep coming back without warning to make sure we haven't stocked up again? They don't trust us, we don't trust them. Grandpa isn't always capable of warning us. We have to be absolutely vigilant, and that means never letting our guards down, ever. Sorry, Victoire, but that means Leah and Estelle have to remain as virtual prisoners for the time being.'

Now, she pulled away a wheeled pallet loaded with several cases of wine. Behind it was a door, quite indistinct against the stone cellar wall as it, too, was cladded in stone. Victoire reached for a large key on a ledge above the door, turned it in the lock and entered the doorway, bowing down to pass under the low lintel.

'*Bonjour! Le petit déjeuner est arrivé!*' she called. The cellar was dark, but not black, for a dim dusty light bulb glowed in the arched stone ceiling – Leah and her daughter did not have to live in total darkness. Leah had a clock, so as to keep pace with the rhythm of life outside, and now, from the back corner that they had all outfitted in a semblance of homeliness, Estelle rushed forth.

'Victoire! *Bonjour!*' she cried, as she leapt into her visitor's arms. Victoire laughed, holding the basket with breakfast up higher and clasping the little girl around the waist. 'Careful!' she said, 'we don't want your food to fall on the dirty ground, do we!' She set Estelle back on the ground, and hand in hand, they walked over to Leah, who was sitting on the cot she shared with her daughter.

'…and look, Estelle – I've brought a new book for you!'

'A storybook, or a schoolbook?' Estelle's tone was sceptical; she loved the picture books Victoire brought from time to time, gleaned here and there from families she and her mother sometimes visited in Ribeauvillé and Colmar, exchanging them for farm produce. But Leah was also giving her daughter school lessons, and Estelle wasn't so keen on such books.

'It's a storybook. Look – it's about penguins. Do you know what penguins are?'

'Of course I know! I'm not stupid! They live in the snow and look like men in black suits and white shirts going to a ball!'

'That's right. Well, here you are. Your maman can read it to you.'

'No! I can read by myself now!'

'Can you now! Clever girl! See, those schoolbooks are useful after all!'

'But I learned to read with storybooks, not with stupid schoolbooks!'

They talked for a little while longer, and then Victoire said her goodbyes and left them. She'd be back in the afternoon with more food. As she left, she picked up the bucket that served as a toilet and checked the water level in the wooden vat that served as a water reservoir; Margaux had created an ingenious piping system through the wall that allowed those on the outside to turn on a tap to feed the basin so that Leah and Estelle could wash themselves. Now and then, Victoire removed their soiled laundry for washing, and returned a clean little pile. They had to be careful never to dry the child's clothes on the line – questions might be asked.

Back in the kitchen, preparing breakfast now for herself and her mother, Victoire thought about the situation of their guests. It couldn't go on like this. What if the war was to last a year longer? Several years – two, three, ten years – longer? They had to find a solution. Jacques had once mentioned a route over the mountains and down to the south of France, but had been too busy in Strasbourg to actually work something out. The next time she saw him, she'd raise the subject.

It was frustrating, being only fifteen years of age, too old for the insouciance of childhood, too young for the responsibilities of adulthood. It was the latter she hankered for, yet here she was, relegated to the role of her mother's domestic helpmate and farmhand. She had no particular function, nothing to fight for, no conflict to resolve, no risks to face or dangers to overcome. Even Marie-Claire was better off. Marie-Claire, now, was of an age where she could do anything at all she wanted: almost an adult. But Marie-Claire, far from joining the Resistance and putting up a fight, was practically working for the enemy. Had she no pride at all? No sense of loyalty? What a waste of an opportunity.

Marie-Claire claimed openly to be as neutral as Switzerland and, now fully ensconced in the *Mairie,* didn't at all appreciate her unique position at the hub of Nazi power in Colmar. If she, Victoire, had had that chance, she would have *done* something. There must be *something* one could do if the *Kreisleiter* was one's immediate boss; even a lowly secretary, surely? She, Victoire, would have found some way to work against her *chef.* She'd have been a spy. But Marie-Claire, it seemed, just sailed through life obeying orders and not caring. What a waste of a job.

As for Jacques: Victoire knew exactly what he was up to. Immediately after the *vendange* Jacques had gone underground to fight the Nazis, had disappeared into the shadowy world of the *maquisards,* guerrillas fighting for France, men and women who had escaped into the mountains to avoid conscription into Vichy France's *Service du travail obligatoire*, Compulsory Work Service, to provide forced labour for Germany. He had come home for a few days last week and, as ever, had taken time for her. So had it ever been with Jacques: he was closer to her than her own brothers, never dismissing her as a child, always including her in his projects and plans. But not this time; this time she was too young, the project too dangerous.

'No, Victoire. I'm sorry. You cannot be a *Maquis*.'

'Just because I'm a girl! I heard that lots of boys my age are fighting the Germans. Why can't I?!'

'They are playing a dangerous game in Strasbourg, those boys. Throwing grenades into shop windows and running away. They are brave boys and I have full respect for them. But I'm not going to let you join them.'

'Because I'm a girl!'

'Because it's reckless. Brave, but reckless, and I worry about them. They're all below the age for conscription so they're under the Nazi radar, but still, I fear that sooner or later they'll be caught, and it's for nothing. It's not enough to throw grenades and run. To truly defeat the Nazis takes more planning, a more mature approach. And I promise you, Victoire, I'll find a role for you. Later. Something you can do well, and which will be essential to our work. Just wait.'

So that was what she had to do: wait. Fulfil her duties, the same tasks, morning and evening. Look after the hens and the rabbits and the greenhouse, not to mention Leah and Estelle, morning, noon and night. Margaux constantly reminded her that looking after their fugitive Jews was important and dangerous war work, but Victoire found it hard to see it that way; where was the *adventure* in looking after a woman and a child? She longed to be out there, like Jacques, *doing* things. Killing Germans. That was real Resistance work.

Another day passed by, a day filled with domestic and farm duties, not to mention school. Once the kitchen was in order after supper she put on her coat, lifted the torch from its hook on the wall next to the back door and sallied out into the night. There'd probably be frost tonight; winter was breathing down their backs and she had to make sure the greenhouse door was closed and the plants were protected.

Pushing her hand into her coat pocket, she felt something: paper. She remembered: today at school a woman had visited and invited pupils to take part in a special First Aid course sponsored by the Red Cross. There'd be a course starting in January, in Colmar. It sounded mildly interesting. Something to do, something more than looking after house and home for Maman. A start. A First Aid course might not have the same stature as joining the *Maquis,* but it was better than school. Particularly now that all classes had to be delivered in German. It was simply grotesque, and so unfair.

Victoire sighed as she walked across the cobbles to the greenhouse. Being the youngest, with no skills at all except the care of plants and animals, she was by default regulated to the boring domestic duties that everyone depended upon, but no one appreciated. A nobody.

Chapter Thirteen

Marie-Claire

There was a knock at the back door. 'Who would come at this time of night!' said Tante Sophie. 'And knock at the back door!'

'I'll get it,' said Marie-Claire. She put the *Vogue* magazine she'd been leafing through on the floor beside her armchair and got up. She had managed to develop a comfortable relationship with her great-aunt, Grandpère's sister, whom she called Tatie; of an evening they sat together in the parlour, beside the fire dancing in the hearth, Tatie knitting a scarf for her, she leafing through all the old magazines her father had sent in the previous years. She had over the last few weeks discovered an unlikely ally in Tatie, who had never married and who had, in her day, enjoyed some local fame as a clarinettist, but had never been close to her niece, Margaux; there had, it appeared, been some family disagreement between the two.

Tatie had received her with open arms, welcomed her into her home, told her she could stay as long as she wanted, and over time they had talked, and grown close; and though she had never quite understood the reason for the estrangement, she knew now that it had nothing to do with her or any of her siblings; it was all between Margaux and her own mother.

'It's no use chewing it all over again,' Tatie had said, 'but you and I can start from scratch.' And so it had developed into this: cosy evenings by the fire, a sense of homeliness Marie-Claire had never known in a house dominated by her mother's personality.

'Be careful, *chérie!*' Tatie said now as Marie-Claire walked towards the door leading to the kitchen and back door. 'Check who it is first.'

'Of course, Tatie,' said Marie-Claire. She proceeded through the kitchen. At the back door she drew back the curtain over the little window that allowed those inside to view those outside and speak to them. But it was too dark to recognise the face that loomed in the blackness of the courtyard.

'Who is it?' Marie-Claire called. 'I can't see you.'

'It's me. Jacques. Can I come in?'

She gasped, and immediately opened the door.

'Jacques! Come in! What are you—?'

He didn't let her finish.

'Marie-Claire, I need to speak to you. Is it possible? It's very important.'

'Yes, yes, of course – but Tante Sophie – she's in the parlour, and—'

'Yes, of course I will go and greet her first. But I need to speak to you alone. It's terribly important.'

'Come with me.'

She led him back into the parlour. She noticed that he was dressed all in shades of black and grey, like a burglar in a back alley; his face was long and gaunt as if he had not had a good meal in weeks, and his clothes looked old and worn. But he was still, beneath it all, *Jacques,* and the moment she'd recognised him her heart had started that unwanted and involuntary mad thumping that was its customary reaction whenever Jacques was within touching distance. It was as if that terrible, inexcusable, painfully embarrassing scene had never happened.

Jacques greeted Tatie with such enthusiasm and seemingly genuine warmth he might have been her own nephew; and yet he was quick to excuse himself and pull away.

'I'm so sorry – I'd love to stay for a chat and a glass of wine, Madame Gauthier, but I have only a few minutes and I need to discuss a small matter with Marie-Claire – may we be excused?'

'But of course! I know all about such small matters. Go in the kitchen and take as long as you like.'

'Then I'll say *au revoir* now; I'll come for a longer visit when I get the chance.' He stretched out a hand to her; she took it in both of hers, pulled his face down to her and kissed him on both cheeks.

'You were always a good boy, Jacques, just like your father. A pity, such a pity—' She stopped abruptly then, and let him go with a farewell nod.

Jacques nodded at Marie-Claire, and she led him back into the kitchen. They stood, facing each other. Jacques' eyes seemed on fire.

'Marie-Claire…'

'What is it, Jacques?'

Her heartbeat, her breathing, had returned to normal. She knew this visit was not to be the one where he finally capitulated and confessed a burning love he'd finally become aware of; the confession she still, after all that had happened, dreamed of. She could tell that the fire in his eyes was not one of passion.

'Marie-Claire – I need your help. I hope you can give it. We must defeat the Boche by all means at our disposal and – well, Margaux has told me you now work for the *Kreisleiter* at the *Mairie*. That you are his personal secretary.'

'His personal assistant. Yes, it is so.'

'Then, Marie-Claire, you must help! You are in such an excellent position – surely you know, surely you want to help?'

'If you are asking me to spy on my boss, Jacques, the answer is no. How could you ask me such a thing? Do you not realise the danger? The danger to me? I and all of the staff at the *Mairie* – we have gone through rigorous security checks. We are trusted. It would be so dangerous. I can't possibly—'

'It is for France, Marie-Claire. For Alsace. There are things we need to know.'

'But, Jacques, I know nothing that could be of interest to you. I am really only a typist, and the things I am given to type – they are nothing that could possibly be of interest to you. Anything confidential – anything to do with the military, anything to do with the annexation – that is not my job. He types his own confidential reports and keeps them in a safe and I don't know the combination. I'm sorry, Jacques. There's nothing I can do to help and even if I could, I don't think I would. It's just too dangerous.'

His shoulders slumped. 'It's just – there are things we need to know. Locations, movements of military instalments. It would be so useful. But if you have no access…'

'I don't, Jacques, and I don't want to go sneaking about in drawers or fiddle with safes or anything. I can't risk it! Why, they would execute me if they thought I was a spy, execute me probably even without a trial!'

'If you can say that, Marie-Claire, then you know. You know how dangerous they are. You know that they're your enemy too and that they've brought the Nazi poison to Alsace. The only reason to work for such a despicable enemy is to defeat him. Have you no conscience at all? Maman used to say that all the time: Marie-Claire is as shallow as a crêpe-pan; and I used to laugh it off and tell her she misjudges you. But I see now she was correct.'

'Jacques! I—'

'I understand. It is too risky for you. I won't try to persuade you to do anything that will put you in danger. It's disappointing, but there it is. But, Marie-Claire – if you ever change your mind…'

He hesitated.

'I'm telling you this in complete confidence. Because somehow, I believe you do have a conscience, tucked away somewhere in the depths of your soul. And I believe that sooner or later you will wake up and want to help. Once you *see,* once you open your eyes and truly realise what we are up against. And when that day comes, we already have someone in the *Mairie* working for us. She has only a humble role, that of cleaner, but she is intelligent and dedicated to defeating the Nazis. Madame Guyon is her name. If ever you change your mind, let Madame Guyon know. She cleans the offices in the evening. You will find a way to let her know and I will take it from there. *Salut,* Marie-Claire. I will go now. I wish you well.'

He leaned forward, kissed her on both cheeks, and then he was gone; a ghost in the night, slipping out of the back door and into the darkness.

Marie-Claire stood alone, eyes closed, hands on her cheeks, as if to protect forever the place where his lips had warmly touched her.

She quickly settled in, quickly lived up to her role as head secretary, personal typist to the mayor, personal assistant to the *Kreisleiter* whenever the latter should deign to put in an appearance. This was, approximately, once a week. In he would stride, up the stairs and into the ex-mayor's office, always with some new development that needed urgent attention. Marie-Claire would be summoned through the in-house telephone, rushing in with pencil and pad in hand, and with coffee, made to his specifications in the tiny *Mairie* kitchen.

She'd bring it up to him; tap cautiously on the door, wait for his bold *Komm herein!* before gently easing it open and as invisibly, silently as possible, slip through, trying not to make a sound as she tapped across the polished wood floor, bearing the coffee cup as if it were a fragile ornament to be placed before a king. Kurtz never looked up when she entered. He was a man of minute detail and it was she who attended to those details. It was she who refilled his fountain pen at the end of each day, she who sharpened his pencils, she who wound the clock, she who emptied his ashtrays – for he smoked incessantly, a trait that did not quite mesh with his otherwise controlled and meticulously ordered lifestyle, for surely smoking indicated a certain neediness, a lack of inner discipline? But it was not for her to question his habits or his predilections. So he liked her to do these little things for her – so be it. She would perform them to the best of her ability, and not complain, and not question.

She spoke only when spoken to. He was a silent man. He spoke only to give orders, except on the telephone, which he would bark into, punctuating his tirades with his favourite expletive: *Unsinn!* Nonsense! Once, he summoned her to command her to put fresh logs on the fire that burned constantly in the grate. Once it was to tell her to draw the curtains; the winter sun gave off a certain glare at certain times of the day.

Always, she obeyed with no more than a *Ja, Herr Kreisleiter.* She did as she was told, gliding in and out of the office, the only one of the four secretaries with permission to enter. Soon she had gained such familiarity she could come and go as she wished, bringing him papers from the lower offices to sign, keeping the flames in the fireplace dancing, fulfilling his every need. Three little knocks on the door, his call of *herein,* and she could walk in with confidence, coffee cup or file in hand.

He would be either sitting at the huge mayoral desk perusing documents or writing long-hand notes in a ledger. The items on top of the desk were all meticulously laid out – low heaps of papers precisely aligned with the edge of the desk, a small clock symmetrically placed at the other corner of the desk, bottle of ink and blotter in perfect constellation above the large leather writing pad he leaned over, pen in hand, blond-stubbled head bowed.

Or sometimes he sat at the smaller desk, tapping away at the typewriter; in such cases, Marie-Claire had to suppress a smile for the fact that he typed with two fingers somehow diminished him, removed a layer of dignity from the impregnable veneer of inaccessibility he wore as an armour. What was he typing? It was obviously far too confidential to involve her or any of the other professional secretaries.

Even Grötzinger did not use that typewriter. Whatever it was, it was not for her eyes and she respected that. Like everything Kurtz did in this room, it was secret, possibly of the highest significance for the success of the Nazi regime in France and all of Europe. It gave Marie-Claire a certain thrill to be so close to all these secrets. It gave her a sense of her own importance. What a pity, though, that nobody respected her for it; quite the opposite. They despised her. Most of all, Jacques.

Kurtz had had a safe built into the wall next to the fireplace. Everything he dealt with, all the paperwork, all the self-typed whatever-it-was, was concealed in that safe. Only he, apparently, knew the combination. What a treasure trove, Marie-Claire thought, for Jacques! If only… but no. She dismissed the thought even before it took form. She was a responsible employee, loyal to the bone. None of this patriotic disobedience Jacques had tried to instil in her. But if there was one thing she could do to win his favour, banish his censure… but no. Never. And so Marie-Claire grappled with herself and her guilt and her loyalty and her neutrality and her longing, deepest yearning, to win the approval of the one man on earth whose approval meant something to her. (Her father's approval, after all, was guaranteed; she did not have to *earn* it. It was always there, whatever she did.) That safe was the receptacle of all the power that kept Alsace a vassal state to Germany. Its secrets were sacrosanct. *Verboten*.

Yet, objectively, Marie-Claire knew: if she wanted to, she could. Once, she had seen him standing at that safe, twisting the lock back and forth several times to lock it before striding back to his desk and closing the open ledger. A hasty glance had shown her, just before it snapped shut, a number written on the inside cover of the ledger. It was the combination code; she was convinced of it. That ledger was kept in a locked drawer of the desk. And all she had to do was… but no. Never. She was neutral and she was loyal. And she feared Kurtz. He struck a certain kind of terror into her heart that she had never known before – a kind of inner immobility, a chilling sense of *complete and utter obedience.* She would never betray him. Not even for Jacques.

When Kurtz was absent, she worked for the former *Ortsgruppenleiter* Grötzinger, now the district mayor, in his office across the hallway. His style was quite different, his desk covered with heaps of papers untidily strewn about its surface. Several newspapers in a heap on the floor beside the office chair – Grötzinger, it seemed, read every word. A radio blared from a shelf against the wall – news reports of Germany's victories, its unchallenged crusade to become the undisputed single power in Europe. *England is being decimated!* Marie-Claire learned. *German bombs are flattening London! We must celebrate as Germany marches across the continent, westwards and eastwards, consolidating power!* Sieg Heil! Sieg Heil! Sieg Heil!

Grötzinger himself loved to talk, over and above the radio. He informed Marie-Claire of Germany's superiority over France and how it was a *good thing* for Germany to be in charge; it was a superior culture and France should thank Germany. He gloated at the way France had laid itself down on its back, submissive as a dog, and complained that England did not; but England would one day capitulate. He assured Marie-Claire of the rightness of it all. She merely nodded to everything he said and got on with the job.

Letters to write, reports to type, new regulations to impose. The entire French staff, those who had been kept on, had new, German, names; Marie-Claire, the book of names in hand, had helped some of them choose their names and, that done, everyone in the whole of Alsace had to be renamed. Her own name was now Margarethe Gauss, the surname chosen by her mother (who refused to use it) for the simple reason that the first three letters aligned with their French surname. Now Marie-Claire was, officially, Fräulein Gauss.

The streets in Colmar and all the surrounding villages also had to be renamed, new plaques with the new names commissioned, the old street signs replaced; and for this task, too, Marie-Claire found herself the main organiser.

Lists. Lists of farms and businesses and who ran them and what could be requisitioned from them. Billets for the officers; several houses that had once homed Jews were now empty, to be filled by German officers. Bakers and butchers instructed as to what they could and could not sell, and to whom. Schools! Alsatian teachers sent off to Germany for training, German teachers brought in to replace them and to introduce the German language and script to the pupils.

Marie-Claire was at the hub of all this work, work that piled up. More and more, she became the nucleus of the changeover from a French to a German administration; more and more, her new employers depended on her. More and more, she won authority in the *Rathaus*; more and more, she enjoyed her work, tedious as it mostly was.

She enjoyed the busy-ness of it; the sense of being important, valued, a sense of being indispensable to the new regime, a sense of worth, and new confidence, fulfilling tasks that nobody else in the building could, or would; either because they lacked the knowledge of Alsatian language and infrastructure (Germans) or because they resented the changes (Alsatians). Marie-Claire just did it, without judging.

'But dear – surely you feel some sense of *guilt?* Working for the enemy?' Tante Sophie put variations of this cautious query to her again and again, those winter evenings when the two of them sat before the dancing fire, Tatie knitting or embroidering, Marie-Claire leafing, as ever, through old copies of *Vogue* or reading a German novel 'to improve her vocabulary'.

Marie-Claire would shrug. 'Not at all, Tatie. I'm just doing a job. I maintain a sense of neutrality. I don't judge, I don't condemn. Society changes; sometimes there are great upheavals, as we all in Alsace know. This is just one of them. We were French, now we are German. It has happened before. *C'est la vie.*'

'But, *chérie – Hitler!* The war! Doesn't it all alarm you? Don't you ever discuss the war at work? You and your colleagues?'

She shook her head. 'No, of course not. We are kept up to date on what is happening by our German superiors. Germany is winning the war – that much we know. What is the point of resisting or even objecting? What's the point of getting upset about a thing I, as a single person, can't change anyway? It is as it is. Alsace will stay safe – the province is precious to Hitler and the war will never come here.'

'And you don't care about others caught up in it? In Poland, Russia? The bombing of London? It's dreadful! People are dying from German attacks! Surely you care! What about those English friends you had, the girls who stayed with you for years, their mother? You were all so close! Don't you wonder about them?'

Whenever Tatie brought up such ideas Marie-Claire would shrug externally and cringe internally. She didn't care because she didn't *want* to care. Because she could not allow herself to care. *I'm just doing a job,* she told herself, again and again.

And yet. Sometimes she touched her cheeks, put her hands gently against them and closed her eyes. Sometimes she remembered. And sometimes, a little twinge of guilt filtered through the armour of neutrality. Guilt, carried on Jacques' voice: *The only reason to work for such a despicable enemy is to defeat him.* Jacques, the only person whose good opinion of her she cared about. Jacques would not condone these arguments, put forward to Tatie so boldly, as if, deep down inside, she truly believed them.

She could hear his condemnation: *'Have you no conscience at all? Tante Margaux used to say that all the time: Marie-Claire is*

*as shallow as a crêpe-pan; and I used to laugh it off and tell her she
misjudges you. But I see now she was correct.'*

Sometimes that accusation would tap on the edges of her guilt-
free shield, the shield that protected her conscience. Tap insistently,
annoyingly. But invariably she would push away the tapping, silence
it with self-assured denial. It didn't matter what Jacques thought.
His opinion of her was of no consequence, because he did not
want her. In fact, there was a certain *Schadenfreude* in her denial;
a certain sense of revenge, for Jacques had cruelly, humiliatingly,
rejected her. Why should she live up to his hopes and expectations?
No: she was doing the right thing. Of that she was confident, and
would defend her actions to the death. She would.

Chapter Fourteen

One evening she happened to be the last to leave the building – apart, of course, from the armed security guards who kept watch day and night beside the *Mairie's* front door. Grötzinger had been dictating all day, and the typing of reports had taken her an hour into the early evening. Just as she was coming down the main staircase, she met a portly woman in a headscarf walking up. A woman with a bucket in one hand and a mop in the other. The woman stopped on a lower step as she saw Marie-Claire.

'Ah – Mademoiselle Gauthier! I recognise you though you are much older – you won't remember me. I am Madame Guyon. I used to clean for your mother. You were fifteen at the time but who could forget that face! As beautiful as ever.'

Marie-Claire murmured a hasty *bonsoir* as she stepped past. How impertinent for the cleaner to address her in such familiar terms! She was secretary to the German administration in Colmar, after all!

'*Bonsoir,* Mademoiselle, and *vive la France!* I believe Jacques has told you about me. Remember – if ever you feel the urge to stand up straight, I am here!'

Marie-Claire did not reply. She quickened her step and fled the building. Madame Guyon had spoken French, and used a French name. Even responding to such a person would be against the rules of her employment. In fact, as a good employee she ought to report the woman.

But she wouldn't. She knew she wouldn't, and it troubled her.

*

Marie-Claire had not slept a wink, and it was long past midnight. She tossed and turned and worked the sheet into a knot around her legs, and the eiderdown had fallen to the floor three times, leaving her freezing cold in Tatie's unheated attic room. Unravelled, tangled thoughts bothered her, prevented her from sinking into contented oblivion. It was getting worse by the day. It seemed that, while it was fairly simple to push away one's nagging sense of guilt during the busy day, night-time, when all was quiet and no new task cropped up to distract one's thoughts from returning to that little nub of agitation, left one completely exposed. And sleepless. The more she tried to push away the agitation, the more it seemed to knead at her being.

Outside, a giant yellow moon hung in the velvety night sky, centred in the dormer window she could see from her bed, and casting a gentle silver glow into the room. She stood up, wrapped the woollen bedjacket Tatie had knitted her for Christmas around her shoulders and padded over the icy bare floorboards to the sideboard, where she poured herself a glass of water from the jug, her feet well protected in the bedsocks that matched the jacket. She had never known a grandmother, and it was good to have Tatie in that loving role. Not so good the knowledge that Tatie, without ever letting it show, was deeply disappointed in her. As was every single person who had ever cared for her. Maman's disapproval was, of course, palpable, had been from the beginning. Maman never minced words. Victoire's was more cautious, expressed more in loaded questions tempered with smiles: *do the Nazis expect you to* Heil-Hitler *them? Did you have to make a vow of allegiance when you started the job?*

Papa's disapproval was expressed in postal silence. She had told him all about the new job soon after she'd started, let him know that it was not a sign of collaboration but the first step on what she hoped was a path leading to Paris, to him, whether or not the war lasted longer than they all hoped; which seemed absolutely possible. *You see, Papa, otherwise I'm just stuck at home waiting for it to end so I can finally make the move; but even then, what would I do in Paris? This job will open doors for me, and I'll be with you all the sooner!*

But Papa, whose letters of reply had always been prompt, had not deigned to respond. She knew what that meant. Papa was proudly French, and if there was one thing he and Maman agreed on, it was that the Germans were unwelcome and any cooperation with them was treachery.

And then there was Jacques, and that was the worst of all. Jacques, whose words still reverberated in Marie-Claire's head: *The only reason to work for such a despicable enemy is to defeat him. Have you no conscience at all? Tante Margaux used to say that all the time: Marie-Claire is as shallow as a crêpe-pan; and I used to laugh it off and tell her she misjudges you. But I see now she was correct.*

Of all the people close to her, it was Jacques' opinion that hurt the most, his censure that kept sleep at bay. His proposal that squirmed and wriggled against all the self-justifications that made up her inner armour. *If ever you change your mind, speak to Madame Guyon,* he had said. Now that she'd met Madame Guyon there was no excuse.

Loyalty towards your nation's enemy was not loyalty. It was betrayal.

She was squandering a chance. To make a strike, however tiny, for France.

To even *agree* to do so would be a step forward. It would, at least, ease her conscience. Moreover, even if there was nothing she could do, to agree to help would surely win Jacques' approval, and there was nothing in the world she craved more – not even Paris. Paris would be, at most, a consolation prize. She would drop it all for Jacques; for a kind word, an approving word, from Jacques.

What if…

She couldn't help thinking about it, picturing the *Kreisleiter* as he turned the safe's combination lock back and forth, following a series of numbers. Five times, or maybe six.

That glimpse she had had of a number written in the inner cover of the ledger, five numerals, or maybe six. That was the code. She was sure of it.

What if she 'worked overtime' again? Managed to sneak into the office, got hold of the ledger, tried the code, just to see if it worked, and if it did, what was in the safe. It would be papers, of course, all red-stamped CONFIDENTIAL.

And if it did, what then? She couldn't very well tuck the papers in her handbag and leave the building with them. Every day, when she left the building, she was given a cursory search by the security guards at the entrance. Nothing serious – she had to open her coat, allow them to peek in her handbag; that was it. They were unsuspecting, and lax, and lazy. And they were only human; over time they had all, every one of them, grown more familiar, interspersing their superficial searches with a few words of conversation, or admiration, mild flirting. She could, she was sure, wrap them around her little finger simply by dint of being female, and beautiful. Yet still: to walk out with a bag full of papers was ludicrous.

No. This would take planning. First, a trial run, to see if the numbers actually worked. And if they did, if she managed to open that safe, then a talk with Jacques, to let *him* decide what to do. Just letting Jacques know that she was, after all, willing to help – oh, the relief!

A weight fell from Marie-Claude's heart. She would do it. She would! She smiled to herself, tucked the eiderdown more tightly around her, and promptly fell asleep.

*

The decision once made, Marie-Claire could not wait to put her plan into action. It was not difficult to invent work that would force her, once again, to stay on in the building once everyone else had left, and the following day saw her typing furiously, in German, some overdue reports on the Germanisation of schools in the rural areas of Alsace.

One by one the other typists tidied their desks, stood up, pushed in their chairs, hung their handbags over their shoulders and walked out to retrieve their coats, hats, scarves, winter boots from the wardrobe area near the door.

Marie-Claire had managed to build up, by now, a reasonably civil relationship with the German secretaries. As for her Alsatian colleagues: the initial resentment she had been confronted with had gradually melted over the weeks. After all, they were all equally guilty of collaboration and needed each other's support in the increasingly hostile atmosphere outside the building. Marie-Claire's rapid ascent to head secretary, and in particular personal secretary to the *Kreisleiter,* had at first been deemed suspicious, especially in view of her consistently stylish appearance, but once it had been established that there was nothing extracurricular going on between her and the senior officers and that she really was diligent and efficient at her job, the petty remarks and resentful glances had stopped. Now, as they walked past her desk, most of her colleagues granted her a smile, a farewell wave, a casual comment.

'Who's a busy bee!' said one.

'Don't work so hard!' said another.

But most just glanced her way and gave her a half-smile, and at last they were all gone. She waited some more. The building had to be empty. She had ascertained it was empty. The door to the typists' room didn't actually have a door; it opened up into the hallway, and so Marie-Claire could see the stream of officers and other German employees as they hastened out for their *Feierabend,* their leisure time. She could hear their footsteps as they descended the wooden staircase. She heard their farewell greetings, wishing each other a pleasant evening, their see-you-tomorrows. And then, at last, all was silent.

Marie-Claire left her typewriter just the way it was, a page half-written in the carriage, and slipped out of the room and over to the manager's office. The hallway light still burned, but the manager's office was in darkness. Light from the hallway illuminated the key safe. There, on the wall, was the small wooden cupboard where all the keys to all the doors hung; when she left, she'd lock that door and hand the key over to the security guards – a task always left to whoever was last to leave.

With any luck— there! It was there. Hanging from a hook labelled *Generaldirektion*. The key to the *Kreisleiter's* office. Before she had time to think Marie-Claire whipped it from its hook. Earlier in the day she had deliberately left a small notebook in one of the drawers of the smaller desk; in case she was unexpectedly discovered entering the room, she had to have an excuse. Such a surprise was, however, unlikely; the key safe was full, all the keys hanging from their respective hooks, all the offices locked up for the night.

The stillness was unnerving. She could hear her own breathing, her own heartbeat. Her thoughts seemed to echo into the darkness, louder than actual shouts. Was she truly doing this? *Spying*. That's what she was doing. Spying on her employer. Spying on the Nazis. If she were caught… she held no illusions as to what the result would be. There would be no excuse, no reprieve. The Germans were merciless – that much she knew. She would be tried as a spy and the punishment would be execution.

Marie-Claire was not a person of great moral courage. Rather, she let things be and allowed others to make the decisions; as long as they left her alone to live her life. She enjoyed luxury, good food and lovely clothes and had to accept that, for the time being, she was obstructed from realising her goals because of this blasted war.

Then there was Jacques. Marie-Claire couldn't explain it, but given the choice between all the worldly goods and glamour she so craved on the one hand, and Jacques, only Jacques, on the other, she would choose Jacques. Every time. She was doing this for Jacques, because Jacques wanted it. And Jacques was the source of her courage right now.

She found the ledger. It was in the top right-hand drawer of the main desk. She opened it. There, on the inside cover, was the string of numbers she'd seen. Six numerals. She read them, committed them to memory and walked over to the safe.

By now her heart was thumping so loudly she was sure the security guards downstairs could hear it. But that was nonsense. Of course it was. Her heart trembled as, one by one, she entered the numbers.

Nothing happened.

Perhaps she'd got the number mixed up. She walked back to the desk, checked again, tried the safe again. And again, nothing happened.

Disappointment flooded through her. So much build-up, and no result! There had to be something, some little thing, she could do… She sat down at the desk, leafed through the ledger. It seemed innocuous, more a sort of diary of day-to-day goings-on, nothing that Jacques could remotely be interested in. How silly she'd been. Of course a senior Nazi officer would never do something as careless as write a code into a ledger and leave that ledger accessible! It had been a stupid idea from the start.

She heard the footsteps on the hall floor outside just seconds before the office door flew open. Too late to do anything but shriek and spin around to face the intruder.

Chapter Fifteen

Marie-Claire stood frozen as the door opened, and even her brain seemed frozen as she scraped through it, trying to find a reasonable excuse to be here, at the desk.

There was none. There was no reason on earth for her to be in the *Kreisleiter's* office after office hours, sitting at his desk. There was no reason for anyone to be here except for something nefarious, something underhand, something anti-Nazi, and no excuse she could ever think up would be enough. And so her brain stayed in that state of frozen immobility – blank.

The person behind the door stepped into the room and the relief flooding through Marie-Claire was so immense she almost fainted.

'Madame Guyon!' she breathed.

'Yes, it's me. And I am supposed to be here – but you? You, Marie-Claire? You are not supposed to be here. Not at all. Unless… unless?'

She stood there in front of Marie-Claire, mop hooked in one hand, bucket in the other, and stared at her. Marie-Claire gulped, swallowed, but said nothing, just stared back.

'Marie-Claire, is it possible that you have changed your mind? That you will, indeed, help us? What are you doing here?'

Marie-Claire gulped again, and managed to stutter a few words.

'Yes, I-I thought, maybe, maybe…' She pointed to the safe, 'I thought maybe I had the combination but I was wrong. I'm sorry. I should not be here. I will go home now.'

Madame Guyon carefully set down the bucket. It was full, and a few drops of water sloshed onto the floor. She smiled and took a step closer to Marie-Claire, patted her arm.

'You did well, Marie-Claire. Even if there is nothing to show for your effort, you did well in that you decided to help, to do the right thing. Now, you can continue in that vein. Jacques is desperately in need of an informer within the *Mairie;* I am useless without such a one. You can be that, Marie-Claire. You are a clever girl – you will find a way. Of that I am sure. But now you must go.' She winked. 'Remember to flirt with the guards when you leave. You must disarm them. That is much easier for a pretty girl than for an old hag like me. But, you know, even old hags have their uses. We are the last people to come under suspicion. They think we are too stupid. But now – go.'

Marie-Claire muttered a thank-you, and fled.

Two weeks after her failed attempt at espionage, the *Kreisleiter* summoned Marie-Claire to his office through the direct telephone line. This was happening more and more often these days, increasingly to fulfil little tasks that, in her view, he could easily perform himself. What was it now, put more logs on the fire, rattle the grate? She sighed, stood up and made her way upstairs. The office was, as usual when he occupied it, filled with a smoky fug; she could hardly breathe. If only he would occasionally demand that she open a window! But he never did. She closed the door behind her.

'How can I help, *Herr Kreisleiter?*'

He was sitting at the typewriter desk in the far corner, and at first did not reply as he typed out a few final words. That done, he ripped the page, together with the sheet of black carbon paper and the duplicate page, from the typewriter, separated the sheets and placed the original and the copy on two separate heaps, the carbon, ready to use again, back in the flat box lying next to the machine. Only then did he look up, his eyes as blank as ever, impenetrable. That done, he picked up the cigarette smouldering in the ashtray at his side, took a long drag and replaced it. Smoke billowed from his nostrils.

'The typewriter ribbon needs changing,' he said as he stood up. He picked up the two piles of typescript and walked over to the main desk. 'It's so faint now it's almost illegible. You should have seen to this already.'

'I'm sorry, *Herr Kreisleiter* – I would have, but—' She wanted to say that she'd been told the typewriter was off-limits, but he interrupted.

'No excuses. Just do it, now. The maintenance of this machine falls within your remit. You must check that everything is in working order.'

'Very well, *Herr Kreisleiter*. I'll just go and fetch a fresh tape.'

'And hurry up. I've more work to do.'

'Very well, *Herr Kreisleiter*. I won't be a minute.'

She left the room, hurried downstairs as fast as was possible while still retaining the dignity of her position as assistant to the *Kreisleiter*, as fast as her heels allowed her. She headed for the storeroom at the back of the building. It was a room far longer than it was wide, with a dividing wall containing shelves stacked with various office supplies. At the front of the room sat the young storeroom manager, Tobias Heller, young enough to be called by his first name, the only employee in the entire building to be so addressed. He was a pleasant lad, with floppy hair hanging over his forehead, a native Alsatian of Germanic roots.

'Hello, Tobias. I need a new typewriter ribbon.'

'Coming up – for which typewriter?'

'The *Kreisleiter's*. Up in the *Mairie's* old office.'

It was possible to use words like *Mairie* and the occasional other French word with Tobias, he being, like her, fully bilingual. He grinned at her. She liked him; he was the only male in the entire

Mairie who ever smiled. Women did; women, she conjectured, always helped to raise the ambience in any office because not only did they provide a decorative function, they also smiled. Even in wartime. But Tobias smiled too.

'I meant, what make is it? Remington, Smith-Corona, Olympia?'

'It's an Olympia 8.'

'Ah! I might have guessed that the *Kreisleiter* would use a German model.'

They exchanged a look that stopped just short of being a roll of the eye. Both knew what the other was thinking, if not speaking: 'German quality' was a phrase often bandied about, the insinuation being that everything German-made was, by definition, head and shoulders superior to anything produced anywhere else; in fact, everything else was more than often met with a nose-in-the-air sniff: shoddy quality. Tobias stood up and walked along the partition shelves. He stopped, and rummaged in a box.

'Yes. We secretaries still use Remingtons.'

'As do most people in France. But of course, only the best will do for the *Kreisleiter!* Here you are.'

Tobias handed her a new spool.

'Tobias! Be quiet!'

He grinned and winked. 'The walls have ears, you mean? Well, between you and me…'

He stopped and shrugged, pulled out a large book and opened it at a page half-filled with writing, wrote the date and next to it *Olympia Ribbon* and *Margarethe Gauss.*

'I nearly wrote your real name there!' he said with another grin. 'Now, if you'd just sign here…'

She bent over the book and signed.

'I forget my name, the new one, often enough!' she said.

'Lucky me, to have always had a German name. I used to hate it – now I suppose I can call myself fortunate.'

'Tobias! Ssshh! You shouldn't say those things aloud.'

'Don't worry. I know who I can say them to.'

'Anyway, thanks. I'll see you again, no doubt.'

'Au revoir, Marie-Claire!'

'Tobias!'

His grin was wide and cheeky as he gestured goodbye.

She returned to the *Kreisleiter's* office, knocked and entered at his *herein.* She said nothing as she walked across to the typewriter and set about replacing the old spool with the new. It was quickly done. She coughed for attention and he looked up. She held up the old spool.

'What do I do with this?' she asked.

'What do you think, girl? Throw it in the rubbish.'

She opened her mouth to speak, and shut it again, holding back an astonished *Really?* Because right at that moment a light went on in her brain, and she knew exactly what she would do. It came to her in a flash of insight. A method of espionage that would, she surmised, make of her a hero – at least in Jacques' eyes, and that was all that mattered.

She chucked the used spool in the wastepaper basket, emptied the full ashtray into the fireplace, added a log to the same and left the room, lighter than she'd felt in weeks. Feeling smarter, much smarter, than one's boss tended to have that effect on a lowly secretary. Especially one generally treated as a menial dogsbody to a Nazi's every whim.

Chapter Sixteen

Marie-Claire could hardly wait to discuss her plan with Jacques. Not only would she be dependent on his material support, she couldn't wait to see the light of approval in his eyes. Nothing hurt more than the knowledge of his condemnation of her. *Marie-Claire is as shallow as a crêpe-pan…* it hurt, oh how it hurt! The words were pinpricks of shame, constantly piercing her heart; though she had done her best to turn away from the insult, had launched herself body and soul into her work in order to forget Jacques' throwaway remark, still it was always there, under the surface. It shamed her, and at the same time it was a goad. Hadn't he, that night, expressed the hope that she could change; that she could do better; that she was, after all, not *that* shallow?

And she wasn't. Under the surface, the goad had been working. It had prompted her, a few days ago, to try the code for the safe's lock. It hadn't worked; but she had *tried,* and she would try again, and this time, this time, oh it was brilliant, her idea! And Jacques needed to know. He would not only approve; perhaps, just perhaps, there was the tiniest chance that his approval would grow into something bigger. Erase all the previous disappointment, raise her in his eyes; she would be his co-conspirator, and surely, as such, he would see her as something more than a sister?

One could only hope. She had to talk to him.

Over the last few weeks her relationship with Margaux had once again mellowed. It had always been that way. Maman would explode in an outburst of fury, throw Marie-Claire's faults and misdemeanours in her face, exaggerating them beyond reason, say the sort of thing a mother should never, ever, under any circumstances, say to a child, not even in a temper… Marie-Claire would stomp off in a cloud of hurt feelings, vowing never, ever, under any circumstances to forgive her mother. And then, a few days later, it would all be back to normal, normality being a sullen tolerance on both sides.

So it was now. Marie-Claire found living with Tatie stultifying, and needed a regular escape back home, to the chateau, with its solid core, Maman. Maman accepted her back home every weekend with no mention of the work she was doing or who she was working for. Though disapproval hung heavy in the atmosphere, it was never brought up in speech, Marie-Claire was never again accused of treachery and life continued as ever, as if nothing had changed, every Friday evening through to Sunday.

But now, something *had* changed, and that Saturday, after a hearty lunch of the sort she could never expect at Tatie's, Marie-Claire casually said, 'Maman, how is Jacques? Do you know where he is?'

Margaux's reply was gruff and dismissive. 'How should I know? Am I his keeper?'

But afterwards, once Margaux had gone off on one of her wine-delivery errands, leaving the two girls to clear the table and the kitchen, Victoire said, 'Why did you ask about Jacques, Marie-Claire? Do you need to speak to him?'

Victoire had an antenna for the unseen, unspoken things; Marie-Claire had always envied her this capacity, but now she was grateful for it.

'Yes – I really need to see him. Do you know where he is?'

Victoire hesitated, and Marie-Claire noticed it.

'Look, I know you all disapprove of what I'm doing, where I'm working, and I know Jacques hates me for it…'

'Marie-Claire! Jacques doesn't—'

'Shhh, I know he does. Hate might be a strong word but that's what it is. You all hate me. But – but you have to give me a chance and I really, really need to speak to Jacques. It's important!'

'We don't hate you, Marie-Claire, we really don't. You mustn't think that. You're—'

'Victoire, I don't bloody *care* if you hate me or not! That's beside the point! The point is, I need to speak to Jacques! It's urgent! Is there some way you can let him know?'

'Well… I suppose…' She hesitated.

'What do you suppose?'

'He left a telephone number, a Strasbourg number. But he said we should only use it in emergencies. We can leave a message and he'd call us back, he said.'

'Give me that number.'

'I can't, Marie-Claire. Not without telling Maman. I can't do it behind her back.'

'Oh, Victoire! Still the good little mama's girl, I see!'

Victoire's eyes flashed with ire.

'No, Marie-Claire. It's a matter of trust. We're living in a time of war and we can't just do as we want, break the agreed rules. Maman needs to know if we contact Jacques. It's a pact. I'm not at liberty to break that pact. Jacques is doing important work, and—'

'Oh, shove it. Very well, I'll be a good girl and ask Maman's permission but I warn you, if she won't allow it because she doesn't think it's emergency enough, it's on your head. And Jacques won't thank you either.'

'If you'd just tell me what it's about! I know you and Jacques…'

'What do you know about me and Jacques?'

'Well – I do know you had a crush on him for a long time, and…'

'How do you know that? Did he say something?'

'Calm down, Marie-Claire. No, he said nothing. I have no idea what passed between the two of you but it was pretty obvious that you were mad for him, and he, well, he didn't reciprocate. We all knew that.'

Marie-Claire felt the red spreading to her cheeks.

'I didn't know…'

'It doesn't matter, Marie-Claire. I mean, I'm much younger than you but even I could tell, but it doesn't matter, but you see, that's why I can't just use the emergency contact line for something that might be…' She paused, searching for the right word. 'Frivolous.'

Marie-Claire struggled to hold back her irritation and took her time replying.

'Victoire. I assure you, I promise, it's not frivolous. It's vitally important, and Jacques would want to know as soon as possible. It's vital. You see, Jacques came to see me a few weeks ago, and asked for help, and… well, I want to help.'

Victoire's eyes lit up. 'You do? You want to help? Really? Oh, Marie-Claire, that would be the best news ever!'

'So you'll help? You'll contact Jacques for me? Without asking Maman?'

Victoire hesitated. They looked at each other, eyes locked in an exchange that was of an intimacy the two of them had never shared as sisters. An exchange of trust, of confidence, one in the other, a linking of something nebulous, unsubstantial, and yet strong, so strong – the forming of a bond that had never before existed between the two. And in that linking, Victoire knew.

'I'll do it, Marie-Claire. I'll get a message to Jacques.'

Chapter Seventeen

Victoire

Jacques. She wondered if Marie-Claire had made the phone call yet. She wondered what it was all about. Marie-Claire had seemed so serious yesterday; she, Victoire, hoped she'd been right to trust her and give her the number and the code: *The Citroën broke down last Saturday.* That would be the sign for Jacques to call back as soon as possible; it indicated an emergency, but Victoire had no inkling how serious Marie-Claire's purpose was in seeking out Jacques. She hoped it was, indeed, nothing romantic – Marie-Claire had promised it wasn't, but her judgement sometimes had to be called into question. Yesterday Victoire had decided to trust her, yet a few doubts lingered.

In any case, it was done. Sooner or later Jacques would call back. Perhaps then she could mention the escape route for Leah and Estelle. Now *that* was what she called a developing emergency.

It might be silly, but she wished for an emergency of some kind. Everyone else seemed to be engaged in actual war or Resistance work of some kind, or had the potential to: Jacques, and Maman, and now Marie-Claire; and, she was sure by now, Juliette, who had disappeared off the face of the earth after running off to see Jacques in Strasbourg last November. They were all in the thick of the action, even if that action was working in a Nazi office as Marie-Claire did. They all had responsibilities. And she – she was just a youth, not yet fit for anything serious, delegated to do the background work of looking after animals, plants and refugees. Not that those tasks weren't important, she was quick to correct herself, and she was happy to do them; but she longed for something with a bit more – *bite*. Something that would truly challenge her, something exciting, something adult. She hated being fifteen.

There were exactly two eggs in the ceramic egg-basket back in the kitchen. She'd boil them, and with a slice of old bread and last year's strawberry jam, that would be breakfast. She knew they were lucky to have even that. Many, if not most, people in Colmar and the surrounding villages had to make do with much less; she knew it, because, of course, much of the produce had come from the chateau. All of the surrounding farm, farms much bigger than this one and actually dependent on their animals and produce, had been decimated, ruined. The Nazis invariably left only enough for personal use. Two hens. One goat. One rabbit. They'd manage. Other farms wouldn't.

The egg water was boiling. She watched it for a few minutes and then fished out the eggs, doused them in cold water to make the shelling easier. One she wrapped in a cloth for Maman. The other one she placed on a plate for herself, still musing about her own predicament.

She walked over to the crockery cupboard, moved aside a big bowl, revealing the wireless Maman kept hidden, switched it on. It was permanently tuned to the BBC, and the crackling it emitted gave her a pleasant sense of connection to the outside world. She sat at the table and cracked open the egg.

She finished the egg and had started on the bread-and-jam when the pips denoting the top of the hour and the news made her stop chewing, stop ruminating and listen.

The news was devastating. Yet again, London had been targeted for carpet-bombing. Whole districts had been obliterated. Thousands were dead and dying. The emergency services and hospitals could hardly cope.

Victoire's eyes brimmed with tears. The tears spilled over, ran down her cheeks; she choked on her bread, rushed to the sink for a glass of water.

Here she was, feeling terrible because her life was so mundane, wishing for more excitement, when people were losing their lives, their families, their children, their homes, bleeding to death in the streets and under rubble! How callous, how selfish, to envy those caught up in war! To wish for a more thrilling life! She was lucky, fortunate, that she was safe and protected, that no bombs were likely to fall on Alsace as they were on London, that she wasn't being herded onto cattle trains to be sent to a darkness in the East, as in Germany. She was lucky, so lucky, and should count her blessings… but no. That wasn't right either. Counting her blessings was smug and just as selfish.

She needed to *do* something. She had to. It was a necessity.

The BBC announcer was describing now the situation at Guy's Hospital, which had been evacuated to the south of England. It was then that it hit her. She knew what she had to do. It was the perfect solution, and even Maman could not object.

She would become a nurse.

The moment she had that thought it was as if she rose up on a wave of elation. Of course! That was it! Nursing was a vital profession in a war; it would not only give her the skills needed to actually engage herself in something important, it would also give her the confidence of knowing she was making an important contribution. She'd go off to Colmar as soon as she could and train. There must be a demand for nurses at this time.

There was a small problem, though: Maman needed her here on the farm. Someone had to feed the animals, look after the greenhouse plants and tend to Leah and Estelle. But she quickly countered that argument – which Maman was sure to raise – in her mind. There were so many young women like herself, stagnating at home. In the villages, in Colmar. Maman had so many trusted friends. She was sure to find one, someone, with a daughter, like herself, who could take over. The work was easy. She could be replaced. She was not needed here. Not really.

A shrill screech torpedoed the measured voice of the BBC announcer. Victoire jumped out of her ruminations. The telephone. She hastened into the hallway to answer it. Grabbed the receiver.

'Hello?'

''Hello. Victoire?'

'Jacques! Yes, yes.'

'I got a message. What's the emergency?'

'I don't know, Jacques. It's Marie-Claire. She says she needs to see you.'

A slight pause followed. And then:

'*Bien*. I will come down as soon as I can.'

'While you're here, Jacques, there's something else…'

'An emergency?'

'Well, not exactly, but…'

'Then it can wait. I'll see you in a day or two.'

'Jacques! I—'

But he was gone. The receiver buzzed rudely in her hand. She sighed and replaced it on its cradle. It was always that way. Nobody took her seriously. Oh, to be an adult!

Chapter Eighteen

Marie-Claire

'I've decided to help, Jacques.'

An untrimmed beard covered his chin. A curved moustache almost entirely concealed his lips. His hair was almost shoulder-length, while a greasy fringe hung in dank tendrils over his forehead, past his eyebrows. As for his clothes, they stank of old male sweat and looked like weeks of wear, hanging on his skinny frame as on a scarecrow. The soles of his boots laughed at her through a wide toothless gap.

Had she met this man as a stranger in the streets she'd have given him a wide berth.

But beneath it all was Jacques, and there was nothing she could do to quiet the pounding of her heart, the shortness of breath when she spoke, to stop the yearning from permeating her gaze. Her recoil had been instinctive but brief; after all, there was nothing about his physical appearance that a good bath and a haircut and shave couldn't fix. Jacques was Jacques, the being behind the form, and it was this *being* that held her in its sway, it was this *being* that seemed impervious to every effort she'd made to charm it, bring it under *her* sway. It worked with almost every other eligible male she came into contact with. All her male colleagues before the Nazi takeover, and now all the officers who occupied the *Rathaus*. The unspoken admiration leaping into the coldest blue eyes, the slight nod of the head, the tiny adjustment of voice. It was something she was proud of. A secret power, you could say.

But it didn't work with Jacques. His words continued to sting.

'You're like my sister.'

'As shallow as a crêpe-pan.'

'Everyone does silly things when they drink too much.'

He didn't want her, and it hurt.

But now, tonight, it would be different. She had something more to offer, more than just the animal appeal she'd always been able to bask in when it came to the opposite sex. She had something he *did* want. She could see it, now, in the way his eyes lit up.

'You've decided to help? Marie-Claire, that's wonderful!'

He opened his arms and stepped towards her for an embrace. They'd often embraced in the past: exchanged kisses on the cheek, hugged each other; and always she'd known it meant more to her than to him, but anything was good enough. Now, though, she instinctively stepped back – no matter how much she longed for his arms around her, she was still too fastidious to hug a gutter-bug.

'Jacques, no! You're filthy! And you stink!' She laughed. 'And I bet you've got lice!'

He stopped in his tracks, scratched his head and laughed too.

'You know, I think you're right! Sorry, Marie-Claire. I'll try to keep a distance from now on.'

He pulled out a chair and sat on it. 'So, you want to help. That's wonderful. Is there a specific way you can help? Tell me what you can do.'

She told him. About the typewriter on the little desk in the corner, the one that he alone used. The one he used for his most confidential letters and reports, the ones hidden away in his safe or taken off to important Nazi meetings. The one he hunched over for hours, his fingers like missiles hammering secrets onto paper through the medium of keys and ribbons. The machine she alone serviced with new ribbons.

'He can't even change his own ribbons! He can't do anything on his own, not empty his ashtray, not put a log on the fire. I do it all. And so…'

She told Jacques of her proposal.

'I need to change the ribbon after it's been used once, just once, top and bottom. Before it's gone back and forth a hundred times and all the letters are obliterated. But after one use, the letters are clear – imprinted on the ribbon.'

'So – if we get hold of those, whatever is written could be deciphered.'

'Exactly. But the thing is…'

She told him about the storeroom, about Tobias who managed it, about having to sign for everything she took out.

'I'd need a steady supply of unused spools. I'm not sure how long it would take to cover a ribbon once, top and bottom, with writing, but it won't take long at the rate he writes. So I'll need you to keep me supplied.'

'I'm sure that can be arranged.'

'I'd give the used spools to Madame Guyon.'

'And she'll give you new ones. But you need to tell me the make of the typewriter so we can get you the correct spools.'

'Here. This is an old one, obviously unusable as it's been typed over a million times. But this is the spool I need.'

She handed him the fully used spool, the one the *Kreisleiter* had told her to throw away.

'You smuggled this out?'

'Of course!'

'They don't search you when you leave the building?'

'Oh, they look in my handbag. But those security guards – they're just boys. It's easy to distract them. Women know how it's done.'

'Marie-Claire, you're a goddamned vixen!'

She laughed, and her heart soared. It was the greatest compliment Jacques had ever paid her. And now, when he stepped forward to wrap his arms round her – that was not the embrace of a brother, surely?

Chapter Nineteen

Marie-Claire

Marie-Claire removed her shoes, picked them up and tiptoed across the office. The *Kreisleiter* – he had been in the office yesterday; he had hammered away at the typewriter for thirty minutes (she had witnessed this; he had called her up to bring him a cup of coffee), sat at his desk entering data into the ledger he always kept in his briefcase, called up the *Dienstleiter*, the *Landesinspekteur* and the newly appointed *Ortsgruppenleiter*, his subordinates by order of rank, for a discussion, made several telephone calls, then announced that he would be in Strasbourg for the rest of the week. Marie-Claire had been in and out of the smoke-filled office all day, attending to his demands. As for the mayor, *he* was at a meeting downstairs along with several military officers; it was likely to go on for at least an hour. This meant the office would be free for the foreseeable future.

Yet still, her heart was galloping, her breathing grew shallow and her nerves were at breaking point as she slipped the cover off the typewriter, opened the bonnet for the spool cavity, lifted the unused spool to check how much ribbon remained. She did this as often as she could, whenever she found a free moment, anxious not to miss the return point, when the ribbon would reach its end and automatically reverse, deleting the single line of typed letters, or part of it. Marie-Claire had to be quick on the ball to prevent this; finding the optimal point near the end of the ribbon, yet not leaving too much unused. She had no idea how much typing it would take to create one full line of used ribbon, thus the necessity to check again and again, as often as she could. When the top half of the ribbon was as full as possible, she would turn it round to use the bottom half.

Now, she eased the right-side spool out of its case as gently as she could. More than half of it had been used, wound now on the left spool with every word the *Kreisleiter* had typed over the last ten days since she'd changed spools. Every word, every secret, every bit of confidential information was stored on that left-hand spool, and more was to come. Pride surged in Marie-Claire's breast: what a brilliant idea she'd had, and how Jacques would be grateful, appreciative, beholden!

She was doing this for Jacques. Risking so much for him. Not only her job: if she were found out, she'd be guilty of espionage, and the consequences for that crime were dire, probably deadly. This much Marie-Claire knew. But she would do it for Jacques.

It was hard to gauge how much ribbon would be used at the next sitting. Sometimes the *Kreisleiter* typed for over an hour, hammering away with his two-finger method, which was remarkably fast. Sometimes, he only needed ten minutes. She replaced the spool. She'd give him another day, and then turn the ribbon. A full spool of top-secret writing: Jacques would be ecstatic. Hopefully.

A week later, and the ribbon was almost full, top and bottom. It was time to remove and replace the spool. She carefully threaded the new spool, delivered by Madame Guyon the week before, and placed it in its slot, ready for use the following day, or whenever the *Kreisleiter* chose to return.

The full spool in hand, she walked over to the window. Thick green velvet curtains hung on both sides, now open. She stooped down, lifted the hem of the right-hand one, found the spot where the stitching had been cut open for a few centimetres. She slipped the spool into the gap; it fell to the bottom of the hem.

Later, Madame Guyon would ease it out, hide it in the gusset of her underwear, where the security guards would never think, or dare, to search.

'Isn't it uncomfortable, there?' Marie-Claire had asked. Madame Guyon only cackled.

'What we women will endure to rescue France; it is truly *extraordinaire!*'

Chapter Twenty

Juliette

She stood at the edge of the forest, a black shadow herself in a forest of shadows, black against black. Beyond her, crowning a wide hilltop, the blackness yielded to an open space lit only by a moonless night sky, a wide barren expanse curved across the hill's gentle crest. Between her and this broad summit, a wire fence, high and barbed. Beyond the fence, the mountaintop had been reclaimed. No longer a soft rounded mound, it had been carved and churned, chunks of it removed. Bare earth lay before her, bare earth cut into wide terraces hugging the downward slope of the mountain. Terraces, obviously prepared for yet more building work, a project in its infancy. Orderly rows, like a giant's stairway down the mountainside.

The moon was bright tonight, almost full, and Juliette could make out in the distance, near what appeared to be the front of the wired-off space, shadows that moved slightly, shadows of human shape.

'Guards,' she whispered to herself. 'Sentries. Soldiers. But why?'

Something was going to be built here, and Juliette, who had always scoffed when Victoire spoke of intuition and sensing things that had no factual reality: she knew. She knew that here, right here, an evil thing was brewing.

The entire scene seemed shrouded in menace; or maybe that sense of menace was her own creation, a feeling of foreboding that had grown steadily over the last hour's slog through the forest.

Juliette had always loved the Vosges mountains that had formed the backdrop to her childhood and youth. Jacques had often taken her up into the forested hills; they had camped here together, with their Gauthier-Laroche friends and others. Not, of course, *this* particular mountain; but those closer to home were surely no different and never had they evoked fear and antipathy within her, this sense of creepiness and, yes, *evil.* The intuitive notion of wrongness. And here, now, before her was the vindication for her sense of trepidation. No, she was not fearing ghosts; her unease was not a delusion. The cause was real, and it was here in front of her. The enemy was here, concrete and visible and solidly present in the mutilated mountain, and her instinct had not deceived her. A shiver went through her, and it was not from cold. The November night might be chilly, but this particular chill came from within.

She had seen enough. She turned to go home. Not *home* home: Juliette, now in the Resistance, lodged with a farmer in the nearby village of Natzwiller. It was her first mission: Jacques had reports of unusual and suspicious Nazi activities here on Mount Louise, and he had sent Juliette to investigate.

'Something is going on there,' he'd told her. 'See if you can find out what.'

Juliette had applied for a waitress job at the *Gasthaus Zum Schwarzen Ochsen*, a country public house just outside Natzwiller; after a short interview with the owner, a stocky, bull-necked man with a ruddy pockmarked face called Herr Heck, Juliette was immediately employed. They were, apparently, short-staffed. Alsatian girls, it seemed, did not want to work there and German girls would have to be imported. Difficult, to get them to come to the back of beyond.

She had quickly proved an asset to the *Gasthaus*; the Nazi officers were happy to be served by a pretty young Alsatian woman. It meant, however, walking the fine line between politeness to the over-flirtatious punters and rejection of the same. She kept her eyes and ears open, but had learned nothing in the first few nights. And so, on her one night off, she had gone out to investigate herself, walked uphill through the forest – and had found *this*.

Jacques was right. Something was going on here, on Mount Louise. She was no closer to knowing what, exactly. But this: an enormous building site, excavations on the crest of the mountain; this was vital information. It was news enough, urgent enough, to report back to Jacques.

Chapter Twenty-One

Victoire

Once again it was vegetable stew for dinner, mostly cabbage. She carried the steaming pot across from the stove and placed it in the middle of the table. She called into the hallway: 'Maman? *À table!* Dinner's ready!'

'Coming!' called Margaux through the open door of her office. 'Just let me address these envelopes, so that Pierre can take them to the post tomorrow morning.'

Victoire busied herself with cleaning up the used utensils and setting the table for the two of them. Her mother appeared in the doorway, walked over to the sink to wash her hands, then scraped back a chair and sat down at the table.

'You look worried, Maman. Is everything all right?'

'Not too good. Now that we are forced to sell our wine in Germany instead of France, it is impossible to run this business. Everything has slowed down. Germany has its own vineyards already producing excellent wines. And they are established. We are just a new upstart company in their eyes. And French, which makes it worse.'

'But I thought French wines were the best? Especially from Alsace?'

'That's what they say – but not in wartime. It's like they believe we have poisoned the wine. So many rejections. Too many.' She shrugged. 'We will make do. We always do, don't we, and we must still count our blessings. Many Alsatian businesses have folded. People just don't have the money. Not for new shoes, or new clothes, or new hats. I have seen one small business after the other in Colmar go bust. We are fortunate that our market is large and not just local. People will always want wine.'

Margaux talked some more about the business, and then she looked up.

'You are very silent today, *chérie*. Is something the matter?'

'Yes, Maman. There's something I must tell you.'

Margaux looked at her and raised her eyebrows.

'I'm listening?'

'I'm leaving school, Maman.'

'You're leaving… No! You must not, you cannot, not without my permission!'

'Then you must give it.'

'Good schooling is essential – one day the war will end and—'

It wasn't often that Victoire interrupted her mother, but she sensed a lecture coming on and had to nip it in the bud; once Margaux raised her voice there was no stopping her, and that point was coming. There was nothing for it but for Victoire to raise hers, and almost shout:

'Maman, I have a plan! Just listen!'

That did it. A moment's silence, then, from Margaux, 'A plan?'

'Yes, Maman. Today after school I took the bus into Colmar. I went to the Red Cross headquarters and signed up for a six-month course in nursing. I need to do something useful and this is it. There's a war on and nurses are always needed in a war.'

'How can you sign yourself up? You are only fifteen! You need my permission! Which, young lady, I am not prepared to give!'

'Maman, I'm sorry, but I told them you'd come in later to sign the permission. Please, Maman, please sign. Don't make a fuss. Let me do this. I need to do something besides looking after the animals and the greenhouse and… and cooking and cleaning!'

'All of those are honourable and vital occupations. What would happen if there were nobody to do them? And what about Leah and Estelle?'

'You know what I mean! I mean something – something a bit more…' She shook her mane of curls, as if trying to shake out the word she was searching for. *'Challenging.* Please, Maman!'

Margaux scraped a chair back from the table, dropped herself onto it, placed her head in her hands. Victoire immediately squatted down next to her, placed a hand on her back.

'Please, Maman!'

'I thought-I thought I could keep you safe! I thought I could keep you, the last of my children! One by one, I have lost them. Marie-Claire, Leon, Lucien – they are all dropping away.'

'Oh, Maman! That's not true. It's not as if they've… died, or something! Leon and Lucien will surely be back soon. And Marie-Claire isn't far away, you see her all the time!'

Margaux looked up, met Victoire's gaze with eyes brimming with apprehension.

'Yes, but I have lost that girl's soul, and that is just as bad. She is consumed by that den of yellow monsters; she is no longer my child.'

'Don't say that, Maman. I think, maybe, if you were to reach out to her, try to understand her…'

'What is there to understand? The child has cotton wool for brains. Do you know what she said to me last time she was here? She said, "Maybe the Germans aren't so bad, they're just people like you and me." Imagine that. But… we are talking about you. *Chérie,* please don't believe that you are useless. And your list of what you do is not complete. You also take care of Leah and Estelle. Is that not important, vital work? Is it not risky enough for you?'

Victoire sighed, stood up, walked to the sink and filled the kettle with water. She placed it on the stove.

'Being a nurse is not really risky. It's not like being a soldier, is it! And the war has not even come to Alsace, not really. Maybe it never will; both sides want to keep it intact.'

'If you are a nurse employed by them they can send you wherever they want. That's what it is, to be an employee. They can send you into the thick of things, to the front line. Do you want that, Victoire? Do you know what that means?'

She squirmed, and nodded. 'Yes, Maman. I'm not stupid. I'm just asking you to understand. I cannot sit here at home safe and sound when the world is blowing apart out there.'

Margaux shuddered. 'Don't use words like that, they are terrifying. Think of your brothers. Think of Jacques – who knows where he is, what he is up to? I only know that it is all so dangerous.'

'It is Jacques who is my inspiration. It is Jacques who I want to live up to.'

At that moment the kitchen door flew open and Jacques walked in. 'Did someone just mention me?'

The two women sprang to their feet, cried out his name in delight. 'This calls for a special wine!' declared Margaux. 'It's been ages, Jacques! Two months, at least! I've been worried sick!'

'Worried, about me? What a waste of worry. It's all right, Tante. I have a way of landing on my feet.'

'What brings you here? I thought you were in Strasbourg!'

'I was. As for what brings me here – actually, now that they've invaded Colmar I'll probably be working here more and more, around Colmar. It's my home, after all. But specifically, why I'm here, now, at the chateau...' He turned to Victoire. 'It was to speak to you, Victoire. I want your help.'

A light flickered in Victoire's eyes; hope, mingled with doubt. 'My help? Yes, yes, of course! In any way! Maman and I were just talking... what can I do? Is it for the Resistance?'

'Everything I do, everything we all do, is for the Resistance, Victoire! But yes, you are right, I have a small role for you. For you, and Tante, and I hope you agree. But first, tell me – how are Leah and Estelle? Are they well? How are they making do in that dark room?' He looked from one woman to the other.

'Victoire looks after them – business has taken over my life, now that the Nazis are in Colmar. She will tell you.'

'They are fine, Jacques. Yes, it's horrible and dark down there but they do come out once a day to stretch their legs and get some fresh air – don't worry, we are very careful about it. Estelle is learning to read, which keeps them both occupied. But of course it is very frightening to have to hide, and also very boring.'

'We have to get them down to the south of France. I'm working with some people to figure out the route, and anyway, snow is on the way and it's not a good time to cross the mountains, which is what they will have to do. I am going to be training a young man – his name is Eric – to escort them, and future Jewish refugees. And that brings me to the task I foresee for you. For you and Maman, that is.'

Again, he enclosed them both in an enquiring gaze, meeting their eyes, silently questioning.

Both Victoire and Margaux nodded, encouraging him to go on.

'It is this. I am working now with a Jewish organisation that is creating a network of safe houses for Jews, from the German border in Rhineland and Baden through Alsace and then over the Vosges to the south of France, to Vichy. I have figured out the best and safest route would start right here, in Ribeauvillé. There are people, Jews, coming from Germany, through Kehl, to Strasbourg and then down to here. So I need a safe house to collect them and send them on their way. And of course, Tante, I thought of you. Because of what you are doing for Leah.'

'Jacques, you silly boy! Why do you even have to ask? Of course I will do, *we* will do it. Victoire is just raring to do something – we were just talking about it. *N'est-ce pas,* Victoire?'

Victoire beamed back at her, then at Jacques. 'Yes, Jacques, yes, of course!' She turned to Margaux.

'But I'm still going to do that nursing course.'

Margaux sighed. '*Mes enfants, ils sont tellement têtus!* These headstrong children of mine!'

Chapter Twenty-Two

Marie-Claire

Christmas that year fell on a Wednesday, a fortuitous day as it meant that the *Mairie* closed down for that full working week, bookended by two weekends. Which meant that its staff could enjoy an extended holiday, allowing the Germans to return to their homes and families. A skeleton staff kept vital affairs running, but Marie-Claire and her colleagues were excused.

A day before the long break began, the *Kreisleiter* paid an unscheduled visit to the office, striding into the building with his usual air of absolute command. Secretaries scurried out of his way, low-ranking male clerks stood around uncertainly in his path and Grötzinger hustled behind him as he strode across the hallway to the office, Marie-Claire in his wake, summoned by a click of his fingers. She had learned to read his body language, his signals. Now he flicked his wrist at the mayor, with the same hand movement reaching into his pocket for his cigarettes.

'Herr Grötzinger, I don't need you. I have work to do. Fräulein Gauss, I have something to discuss with you; stay.'

'Yes, sir,' stammered Marie-Claire as Grötzinger hastily retreated, his face as red as gammon. She and Kurtz entered the office and Marie-Claire closed the door, then walked to her chair and stood before it hesitantly, looking up at him in expectation.

He, meanwhile, lit his cigarette, took a long drag, placed it on the edge of the ashtray, then busied himself with rearranging the permanent items on the desk and placing them with geometric precision around the large leather writing pad: clock, pen tray, calendar, ink-bottle, stapler, brass container for paper-clips. Opening drawers and removing other items: a wad of blank paper, a French–German dictionary. From his briefcase he removed a single item: a thick book whose title, Marie-Claire could read upside down, was *Mein Kampf.* Whereas the other paraphernalia he had produced or rearranged was familiar, part of his regular routine of re-settling into the office after an absence of several days, this last thing was new; she had never seen the book before, though she had heard of it.

To her astonishment, his face, too, now turned an unaccustomed beetroot red. He coughed, produced a neatly folded handkerchief from his inner jacket, wiped his forehead, coughed again, picked up the cigarette, took another drag and, standing across the desk from her, spoke:

'Fräulein Gauss… aaaahhm… I have to say I am extremely pleased with your work here at the *Rathaus.* You have been attentive, thorough, hardworking. *Eine fleissige Frau.* A diligent woman. That's what you are. The kind of young woman the Third Reich appreciates and supports. You have been an indispensable assistant to me as I attempt to instate the new German order into this region – a Herculean task, let me tell you, which I could never achieve without your indefatigable support, and sometimes, even, as a native French speaker, advice. Yes, I am very pleased.'

At this point he dropped abruptly onto the office chair behind him so that the cushioned seat emitted a light puffing sound, which, under other circumstances, would have produced a giggle from Marie-Claire, resembling as it did a light breaking of wind. But the seriousness of the speech precluded any such hilarity, and she managed to keep a straight face, gazing at him with focused intensity. Inside her, she felt a swelling of pride at his words. Nobody, ever, had spoken words of praise to her; at least, not so far as her memory informed her. Nobody, not even her mother.

She did not include her father; his flattery, of course, was more paternal ego-massage, with the sole aim of retaining her adoration. She recognised that, even while basking in it. This was different. It was genuine.

At the same time she felt a twinge of guilt. If he only knew! Only two weeks ago she had delivered the first spool to Madame Guyon. She was diligently – she smiled to herself, because diligence, he claimed, was one of her main strengths – keeping watch on the next band, ready to turn it over at the best possible moment for the bottom row to become the top, for a second row of highly confidential material. If he only knew…

But he didn't, and now he continued.

'And, *gnädiges Fräulein,* I was thinking that it would do you good to also educate yourself. You have exactly the characteristics the Third Reich exalts as necessary for the perfect woman. The only thing that is lacking, I fear, is education. Yes, you do need to educate yourself for the new world order as ordained by our great Führer, in order to understand what is going on and to fully support the revolution in ideas we have started. A revolution in thinking, in insight and in motivation. History is being made, and it is vital for a young woman like you to stand on the right side of it. A human being needs a great idea in order to develop to his maximum potential. I believe you have not yet reached this maximum, and thus I have brought this book…' he pushed the *Mein Kampf* volume across the desk towards her… 'for you to take home and read over the Christmas holiday. Please read it carefully and with all your attention: it is an important volume that will have as much impact on society as the Bible, eventually surpassing that book in its effect on global politics and societal improvement. Go on, pick it up.'

Marie-Claire did as requested. She picked up the book.

'Take it home and read it. Let your heart imbibe its wisdom, absorb it to the fullest. Self-education is imperative. As I said, history is in the making, a new world order is being created, and it is vital that your thinking is correct.'

He fell silent, as if re-gathering the lost strands of his previous personality, the reins of his authority. When he spoke again, his voice was the usual bark.

'That will be all, Fräulein Gauss. I have some typing to do; if I need any help from you for the remainder of the day, I will send for you.'

He laid his cigarette back in the tray, removed a ledger from a drawer and opened it.

Having regained whatever equilibrium he had temporarily, and uncharacteristically, lost, his dismissal of her was as abrupt as that of Grötzinger before her. She nodded, clasped the volume to her stomach and fled the room.

Chapter Twenty-Three

Marie-Claire sighed, and clapped the book shut. She couldn't. It was impossible. She'd tried, the last two nights, but never made it past a few pages. There were passages that she simply couldn't stomach, or didn't understand, or found, simply, shocking. She had started at the beginning, and had then taken to opening the book randomly and just reading, here and there. And, slowly, a chill spread through her as she read the words.

> *The very first essential for success is a perpetually constant and regular employment of violence.*
>
> *Humanitarianism is the expression of stupidity and cowardice.*
>
> *Through clever and constant application of propaganda, people can be made to see paradise as hell, and also the other way round, to consider the most wretched sort of life as paradise.*
>
> *The great strength of the totalitarian state is that it forces those who fear it to imitate it.*
>
> *The receptivity of the masses is very limited, their intelligence is small, but their power of forgetting is enormous. In consequence of these facts, all effective propaganda must be limited to a very few points and must harp on these in slogans until the last member of the public understands what you want him to understand by your slogan.*

These, and other passages, disturbed her deeply.

She had from the very beginning done her best to take a neutral stance, deliberately closing her ears and her mind to the passionate arguments of her family members against the Nazi regime. She had been determined to remain objective, to avoid their obvious bias. People had strong opinions about Hitler, yes; but surely, in the end, everyone strove for self-preservation; for maintaining the best possible outcome for him or herself, his or her family. She could understand that. She understood that her mother, her sister, Jacques, all wanted nothing to change, and that this Hitler was changing their world. France was going to be ruled by Germany. Thus the invasion. *So what,* she'd thought. What did it mean for them, personally? Alsace had been German before, and nobody had minded. Had they? They'd been German, and then French, and then German again, French again, and life as everyone knew it had simply continued.

She did not believe in war, and violence, of course. Nobody of any sense did. And nobody should be killed. That much was obvious. And Jews – what exactly did Hitler have against them? Marie-Claire liked Leah and her daughter – what had they ever done to Hitler, to the Germans, to evoke such hatred? She'd tried valiantly not to believe what her family was saying – that Jews were being persecuted in Germany, killed, even – that their lives were in danger. Surely it was all an exaggeration?

Maman had come to collect her and Great-Aunt Sophie that morning, drive them home, to the chateau, for the Christmas celebration. Marie-Claire had finally agreed to come, reluctantly – she'd been perfectly willing to stay behind in Colmar, celebrate a lonely Christmas all on her own. She hated these family festivities, and was not in the mood for forced jollity. She and her mother might have called a truce, but there was no denying the suppressed conflict. Christmas tended to bring such matters to a head, to release all that was pushed out of sight.

But Margaux was adamant. She had simply not accepted Marie-Claire's sniffy, offended rebuttal. It was Christmas. A time for family, for healing old wounds, putting aside differences, for coming together in peace. As always, Tatie was invited for the festive days, and *of course*, Marie-Claire must come too. Grandpa would be there from the gatehouse, the Dolch family – what was left of them – would be there, and tonight, a few other guests, neighbours or colleagues – as always. As tradition demanded.

'Of course you must come. It's Christmas. Run along and pack your bags. The van's waiting. Are you ready, Tatie? See, Marie-Claire, Tatie's ready, why aren't you?'

And like the respectful little girl she'd once been, Marie-Claire had obeyed. And now she was home, back in the comforting warmth of the chateau, where the walls had wrapped themselves around her like a loving mother's arms; and the floorboards, the curtains and the wooden kitchen table all seemed to breathe their welcome, seemed to whisper *we missed you.* She couldn't help it; the nervous tension that had gathered over the weeks had slowly started to dissolve. But there were changes; disturbing ones.

For a start, Leah and her daughter seemed to have disappeared. There was another girl who came to do the cleaning and laundry, Aimee, a girl from the village. What had become of Leah and Estelle? Nobody told her anything, she realised with some resentment, and she was too proud to ask, hadn't enquired into their well-being, presented a front of complete indifference to anything to do with Hitler, war and Jews. Taboo subjects, never to be raised, and everyone seemed to have signed a mutual pact of non-mention.

Until dinner. That had been a catastrophe for Marie-Claire, and she'd fled at the earliest opportunity, retired to an early bed amid the cries of *'stay, stay, the evening's just begun!'* But those cries had come not from family, not from Maman, but from strangers, invitees, neighbours, friends of Maman, who knew nothing of the awkwardness hovering like a ghost in the shadows. So here she was, in bed, pillows puffed up behind her, the bedside lamp casting a yellow glow on the pages as she turned them, desperately searching for some spark of enlightenment to leap out at her, draw her in.

Instead, this required reading – it sent shock-waves into that carefully nourished placidity of non-alignment, that state of diligently cultivated neutrality, requiring a not-so-neutral shutting-down of natural curiosity and interest in the world around her. That world was changing far too quickly for her liking, disrupting all her carefully laid plans and enthusiastic dreams for her own future. But she had carefully, methodically, rearranged her strategy, shelved her needs and dreams for the time being, while trying to outsmart the Germans by playing along with them, placating them, playing the role required of her, in order to achieve what, in essence, were her own private goals. That had been her long-term plan; the very reason for acquiring a job in the Nazi nest at the *Mairie.* Her decision. Justifiable, even in the face of family objection.

The only fly in the ointment, of course, was her love for Jacques. No matter what she did, how much she fought it, it would not recede. It was simply there; a virus eating at her being. While all else in her life was meticulously cultivated and executed, there it was, illogical and deeply annoying: she loved him. She'd push it away, and it would rise up through all the layers of refusal and rejection and negation and repudiation, burst into her consciousness with a shout of acclamation: *here I am again! I love him all the same! Do what you will!*

It was hopeless, and she was helpless against it. And so, as a sort of last-ditch attempt to win his approval, she had done this thing, this dreadful thing, this betrayal of her employer.

But now, reading this book, shaken to the core by what she read there, a new insight began to creep through, emerge into the broad daylight of her conscious mind:

Jacques was right. They were all right. Her mother, her sister. Leah was indeed in danger. (Where *was* Leah?) Her friends of long ago, the Lake sisters and their mother, in England – would they be bombed? How could she live with that knowledge, that guilt, if so? How could she work for the enemy, work *with* the enemy, enable the enemy? How could she be a cog in that malevolent wheel of conquest and brutality? She shuddered.

At that moment, a knock on the door caused her to gasp, jump and quickly shove the book under the bedclothes.

'Y-y-yes? Who is it?' she called, but the door had already opened and Victoire, wrapped in a rather threadbare dressing-gown, stepped across the floor towards her. Marie-Claire pulled herself up in bed, leaning against the wooden head-rest, pushing a pillow up behind her back.

Victoire, smiling, held out both hands as she came.

'I just wanted to say goodnight!' she said. 'You slipped away from the dining table; anyone would think you're trying to get away from us!'

It was true. Margaux had invited some guests from the neighbouring vineyard, the Sipps, as well as her old friend and winemaker, Maxence Dolch, and the conversation, fuelled by wine, had been animated, livened by harmless disputes centred on exactly those topics Marie-Claire was struggling with: Hitler, the war, the Jews. She couldn't deal with it, had nothing to say herself, and so, while Victoire had been in the kitchen, had said a quick goodnight and made her escape.

Now, here was Victoire, the bright little sister she had so often ignored but who had always, always, treated her not as a distant alien to whom she had no connection, but as someone whose self-constructed barriers did not exist. Victoire was by her very nature warm and loving, and it was becoming ever harder to shut her out – especially in these strange times when Marie-Claire's own indomitable self-confidence was on a journey through the wringer.

So Marie-Claire smiled.

'Hello, Victoire. Sorry I didn't come to say goodnight. I had a bit of a headache – it must be the wine. I don't drink often, down in Colmar, and I think I had a glass too many.'

Victoire laughed, and plonked herself down on the bedside. 'Well, tomorrow's Christmas Eve and there'll be even more wine, more guests. Better prepare yourself.'

Marie-Claire groaned. 'Do I have to? I'm not really feeling all that sociable these days.'

'I noticed you hardly said anything at all at dinner.'

'Well, I don't have much to say.'

'I hardly think so! You're actually working with the enemy – I'm sure you have a lot of stories to tell, and some opinions! What are they really like? That awful Herr Grötzinger – do you have to take orders from him? What's it like?'

Marie-Claire made a face. 'I hardly think that's a good topic for dinner conversation. They'd all jump on me and berate me for working there in the first place.'

'Not true. Even Maman has accepted it, that you just wanted to keep your job and earn some money. It might not be the most pleasant workplace, but we understand you had to do it. As long as you're not actively *collaborating,* people understand and are forgiving. I certainly don't blame you.'

'Maman does. She puts on a neutral face but deep inside, she wants to kill me.'

Victoire swatted the air. 'Oh, Marie-Claire! Don't exaggerate. Of course not! Of course she wasn't happy for you to work there but I promise you, she understands and just wants us to have harmony in the household. I do wish the two of you could act – well, normally. Like mother and daughter. And we could be sisters. It's what I always wanted.'

'You never wanted me. You had Juliette.'

'Juliette and I are close but you're my sister. It's just that you're so – different. So apart. I just think that in these hard times we should all stick together, no matter what our differences.'

'It's not something I can force, Victoire. I am the way I am and that's just the way it is.'

'Families should make the effort to draw closer together in times of war, like now. It's what I always wanted – a big warm loving family, with you and the boys and Juliette and Jacques. And now we're all apart – oh! did you know that Jacques is coming tomorrow? For Christmas?'

Marie-Claire tried to hide her interest.

'Oh?'

'Yes – just for a day. It's all a bit rushed but he'll be here for dinner and then leave the next day, back to Strasbourg.'

Marie-Claire pretended to yawn. 'Well, it'll be nice to see him again.'

Victoire grinned, and shook her head.

'You can't fool me. I know you and he have some secrets you aren't sharing. I know you're doing something for the Resistance – I contacted him for you, after all. But I know it's all top secret so I won't ask any questions. And no, Maman doesn't know, but if she did she'd be so proud of you. I think you should—'

'Victoire! Stop it now. I don't want to talk about Jacques or the war or the Nazis or anything. I'm really tired.' She yawned ostentatiously.

'But you were reading when I came in. Don't deny it. I saw you shove the book under the bedclothes. What was it, some naughty love story full of sex?'

'Don't be disgusting.'

'I bet it was. I bet you think I'm too young for books like that. But I'm not. I do know the facts of life, you know, and I have to because I'm going to be a nurse. You can even let me read it afterwards. What was it?'

'Victoire, shut up and mind your own business!'

'The more you deny it, the more curious you make me! Go on, show me the book! I promise not to tell Maman. Or laugh. Does it have them kissing on the cover, or something? Where did you hide it?'

She began to grope along the top of the blankets, patting up and down.

'Ha! Found it! Here it is!'

Marie-Claire, protesting, had reached out to push away Victoire's probing hands, but she wasn't quick enough to stop them whipping away and diving beneath the blanket. Out they came, holding the volume of *Mein Kampf*.

Never had a face converted from glee to horror with such instantaneous speed. Never had Victoire taken the Lord's name in vain.

'Good God!' She dropped the book as if it were a live red coal. As if she would catch fire from it, or some violent, deadly disease. She leapt to her feet. The book fell to the floor. Marie-Claire sprang from under the covers, dived down to retrieve it.

'Victoire! It's not what you think! It's—'

'It's poison, it's evil! How could you bring that thing into this house! How *could* you, Marie-Claire!'

'Wait! Don't go! Please, Victoire, let me explain – it's…'

But Victoire had already reached the door, was out in the hallway; the door slammed shut behind her, and Marie-Claire could hear her footsteps fleeing along the wooden floorboards.

The next morning, Marie-Claire woke late after a night of tossing and turning. The book lay discarded, sprawled upside down, on the floor beside the bed, and she stepped round it with a shudder. A sinister aura seemed to radiate from it – she couldn't bear to touch it, to pick it up, put it away. But she'd have to, before emerging from the refuge of her room to go downstairs and meet the family again. Had Victoire told them all? Would they all look at her with hate and rage boiling in their eyes? She washed and dressed herself, and hesitated at the door. She couldn't leave it there.

She walked back to the bed, picked up the book as if it were covered in filth, gingerly at the end of its spine, opened her wardrobe and threw it in. There. Done. Discarded.

She took the stairs down to the ground floor slowly, dreading whatever confrontation was waiting for her, gathering the courage needed to face them all, look them in the eye, if need be, with defiance. *I am Marie-Claire. I have chosen this path, and nobody can pull me down.* She repeated the words to herself, silently, and with each repetition the courage gathered within her. She was prepared.

Just as she reached the bottom step, the kitchen door opened and Victoire emerged. Marie-Claire stiffened, prepared for a new onslaught of abuse. Instead, Victoire rushed forward, arms open, eyes alight.

'Marie-Claire! There you are at last! It's almost midday and I was wondering if I should—' She broke off, having reached Marie-Claire. Stretched out her arms, grasped both of her sister's hands in her own.

'Oh Marie-Claire, I'm so sorry, so sorry for the scene I made last night. For thinking the worst of you, for not listening to your explanation. For judging you! I hardly slept a wink, I felt so terrible! It was such an emotional reaction, and I'm sorry and I beg your forgiveness. I'm sure you can explain. Please, please forgive me and let's be friends!'

Marie-Claire lifted her chin and slowly withdrew her hands from Victoire's loose grasp.

'Have you told anyone?'

'No! No, of course not! I went straight to bed. Maman and the Sipps and Uncle Max were still downstairs, I could hear them laughing and talking, so I did not go back down. You know what Maman is like after a glass too many! So I went to my room and thought about it all and felt immediately sorry. I overreacted. Now come, come with me and have some breakfast. I will make you some good coffee and I baked some fresh bread today, Maman has real flour! And strawberry jam from the garden, also made by me. You must eat, come.'

And Marie-Claire let herself be drawn into the kitchen, let herself be seated at the table and served, and allowed the process of slowly melting into the comforts of home to be continued. It was Christmas Eve. Not even the spectre of *Mein Kampf,* and the threat it contained, could spoil the sense of goodwill that every year, on this day, seeped magically into the atmosphere and laid its embrace around them all.

One thing Victoire had said last night plucked at her heartstrings like a persistent tune longing to be heard.

Jacques was coming. Tonight.

Chapter Twenty-Four

The day had edged past, and Marie-Claire had cautiously manoeuvred herself through it, avoiding her mother when at all possible, making strained conversation with Victoire and, all the time, every moment, waiting, waiting. She hoped to catch him alone, before the others flung themselves at him, claiming him for themselves. Jacques was far too well-loved, more popular than was good for him; it forced him to be polite and friendly to all, and gave her little opportunity to have him for herself, for just a few minutes. Add to that the fact that he thought her as shallow as a crêpe-pan – well, it made things difficult.

She didn't understand it. He was a man; why did he not react to her as other men did, even the horrible Nazis she worked with, from the security guards right up to – well, not to the *Kreisleiter,* but he was immune to feminine charms for his own probably nazified reasons. She had learned to easily recognise the spark that leapt up into a man's eyes when he laid eyes on her. It was instinct.

But not Jacques. Jacques had said that it was because they had grown up as siblings, but that couldn't be everything – surely not. She was a woman now, not a child. She wondered, as she had done many times, if Jacques was turned 'the other way'. He was so different, so aloof from ordinary humans, and, after all, now that he was in the Resistance, he knew only men, and perhaps *that* was the cause. He preferred men to women. In the past his indifference had irked her, offended her, humiliated her, even – but now, now, it goaded her. At their last meeting he'd been different, because *she'd* been different, offering herself up as a major spy in the *Mairie*. Perhaps that would be the chink in Jacques' armour. Crack him open.

All these thoughts ran through her head as she prepared for dinner. She had not yet decided what she'd wear. It had to be special; it was a pity that the other women in the family – that would be her mother, her sister and Tatie – would all be dowdier than ever, even on Christmas Eve, because none of them had anything festive to wear – that she knew from previous festivities. They just didn't care. It was as if they weren't women at all, but half-men, clothes regarded as nothing more than coverings for nakedness and cold. That was the kind of thing that gave the impression that she alone was shallow, because she alone *cared*, knowing that people judged each other according to their appearance.

She judged them and they judged her; but because this was rural France, the back of beyond, she was the one dismissed as shallow. In Paris it would be quite different. There, the right clothes would secure one's position in society. They were all so *backward* here… And yet she knew, whether others were conscious of it or not, a well-turned-out woman always won the room. Won the men. She *would* win Jacques. She could not let the previous humiliation stand. She'd been drunk, immature, at the time; this was different. Marie-Claire had matured into a sophisticated young woman. She knew what she was doing, and she'd finally won Jacques' approval. The time was right.

Her skin still moist and warm and glowing from the long bath she'd indulged in followed by expensive body-cream she'd gently massaged into her body with slow, sweeping motions. She stood, naked beneath a warm woollen housecoat, before her open wardrobe. A dozen dresses hung shimmering before her, silk and satin in a variety of colours, sent to her over the years by her father from Paris. There had been no new dresses over the past year. The war had come between her and couture. Yet here it made no difference because, there being little opportunity for evening wear, they were all practically new, new to her, new to everyone.

She removed them, one by one, from their hangers, regarded each one, assessing it, remembering the joy she'd felt when first unpacking it, and the disappointment of knowing the lack of opportunity she'd have to actually wear it publicly. Now, she had to make a choice. As she held each one up, placed it against her body, swung it back and forth, frowned, assessed, she imagined herself in it, making an entrance into the sitting room – she'd plan it so that she was, indeed, the last to appear – slender and slinky, walking in with just the right amount of *je ne sais quoi*. A woman. *Shallow as a crêpe-pan.* She gave a wry chuckle. Deep inside, they'd all be either envious or desiring. Juliette and her grandmother would be there tonight, as always at Christmas; they'd be well-dressed, as always, but with traditional sophistication rather than allure. She was different.

She wished there'd be more men. Men who would demonstrate to Jacques how a man should react to a beautiful woman. There was just his father, Uncle Maxence, who did know this, who would, as ever, whistle under his breath, compliment her, act the gallant swain; but Uncle Maxence was old, and everyone knew that he was actually in love with her mother, for all her frumpy looks. It was aggravating but couldn't be helped. She gave a grunt of annoyance as she made her choice – a red silky sheath – slammed the wardrobe door shut, flung the dress across the bed and dug into her lingerie drawer for suitable but useless and unappreciated underclothes. There would be, tonight, only one man she wanted to impress, as ever. And he would not be impressed. What a waste of a lovely dress.

Chapter Twenty-Five

Victoire

The kitchen door opened, and Jacques walked in. Victoire gave a scream of delight and flung herself at him.

'You came! I don't believe it! I was certain you'd ring to say you couldn't make it!'

He laughed, and pulled her arms from round his neck. Her hands and forearms were covered in flour – she was making her mother's traditional *tarte flambée*, with mostly substitute ingredients, but at least they'd managed to get hold of flour – but she'd kept them aloft, embracing him round the head with her elbows. He kissed her on both cheeks.

'I'm here, my little Victoire, and I've brought a guest. I hope there's enough for one more!'

'Any friend of yours is a friend of ours, Jacques! Welcome!'

She turned to the man who'd entered the kitchen behind him, and blinked.

He was not what she'd expected. Or rather, she hadn't had time to expect anyone in particular, but a young man hardly older than herself was not typical of those who, in the past, had swirled in Jacques' entourage: they were usually older fellows, slightly dishevelled, mostly, with beards, and smelling of stale sweat. Jacques brought them for a bath and a clean-up and a good meal – sometimes they hadn't eaten properly for weeks, and Margaux's doors were always open for such. As long as they were fighting for France, they were welcome. Baths and food and a bed for a night, and some clean clothes. Every *maquisard* had such needs from time to time. But this was not a man. He was a *boy*, with a milky face that had never been touched by a razor.

'This is Eric,' said Jacques. 'He recently joined us and I thought I'd bring him along. He has nowhere to go for Christmas.'

Victoire smiled, and held out her hand. 'Welcome to our home, Eric! Sit down, both of you! Can I offer you some tea? No coffee at the moment, *tant pis.*'

'I feel bad, barging in on your Christmas festivities,' said Eric as they shook hands. 'I didn't want to come, but Jacques—'

'I insisted,' said Jacques. 'As I said, he has nowhere to go. His family is from Lorraine and they have all been evacuated down to Poitiers. He did not go with them as he wants to fight for France, here in Alsace. He's a good lad. I thought you and he might get on, Victoire; you're about the same age.'

'Yes? You are only fifteen?'

'Sixteen, actually,' said Eric. 'And I'm sorry, very sorry. Jacques, you should not have brought me here, this is a family home, family time – Christmas – let me go again!'

'Go – where, exactly?'

'Back to Strasbourg. I do not need to celebrate Christmas.'

'But you will be just twiddling your thumbs in Strasbourg because everyone is on a Christmas break for the next few days.'

'But the family – they will not want a stranger…'

Victoire said: 'I said you are welcome and I mean it. Nobody who fights for France is a stranger. Everyone who resists the Nazis is a friend, a family member. Now stop objecting and take a seat and I will make you both some tea. And then you will both go upstairs and have a bath – you stink! Put your dirty clothes in the laundry basket and Aimee will deal with them tomorrow. Jacques will find you clean clothes from Leon and Lucien – I'm sure something will fit. Isn't that right, Maman?'

Margaux had just entered the kitchen, bearing a basket full of apples.

'Is what right?'

Victoire introduced Eric, and told her mother why he would be their dinner guest tonight. Margaux smiled at him, set the basket on the table and held out her hand.

'Welcome, Eric, and of course you must join us for Christmas! Any friend of Jacques is a friend of ours. You say your parents were evacuated?'

Eric nodded. 'All Metz residents were sent down to Poitiers after the invasion. But I fled to Alsace because I wanted to help fight and I heard there were boys in Strasbourg who were organising.'

Jacques nodded. 'They call themselves the Black Hand. They are very brave; I'm friends with their leader, Marcel Weinum. I took Eric under my wing as he has no family in the city. And I think I have a job for him to do, right here in Ribeauvillé.'

'Really? What job?'

'Victoire, this is not the time to be discussing jobs. Have you finished that pastry yet? No? Then get on with it. Come, Eric, I will take you upstairs and run you water for a bath and find some clothes for you. You too, Jacques – follow me. You can share Leon's room tonight.'

Margaux hustled Eric and Jacques out of the kitchen. Victoire sighed, and plunged her hands back into the pastry bowl. Jacques' words itched within her. It sounded as if Eric was already a legitimate *maquisard* in his own right. And he was only sixteen. He must have started when he was fifteen, like her. Yet Jacques had constantly rejected her for the *Maquis*. Because she was a girl, too fragile for Resistance work. *Too precious,* Jacques corrected her again and again whenever she argued for more involvement. *Women are precious. We cannot risk their lives with dangerous work. Your role is a different one, and just as essential.*

And so here she was, kneading pastry, when Eric, not much older than her, had been singled out for some no doubt vital role in the Resistance, right here in Ribeauvillé. A role that *she* could have had.

Chapter Twenty-Six

Marie-Claire

She turned before the full-length mirror – the only one in the house – looked over her shoulder to see just how the smooth silk of the dress wrapped around her behind. Turned back for a final frontal critique, hands on hips, chin up. Her hair was in an elegant chignon, her *maquillage* perfect, considering the meagre collection of powders, crèmes and pastes she had to work with. Her favourite lipstick, just a left-over knob of an expensive brand her father had managed to salvage from the woman she suspected was his mistress, matched her dress perfectly; a seductive red, not bright enough to be considered vulgar, and yet strong, vigorous, providing the perfect contrast to the porcelain-white of her face. She smiled at herself. She was ready.

No. Just one final touch… She stepped across to the vanity table, littered with the detritus of the last hour, picked up a small perfume bottle. L'Heure Bleue by Guerlain. Her favourite. Another salvage from her father's mistress, sent to her more than two years ago and used sparingly, on special occasions like this one. Just a fingertip behind the ears and in the crease of her elbow was enough. The perfume was elegant and mysterious all in one, capturing that precious moment of dusk, the bluish hour before the first stars make their appearance in the sky, a celebration of dusk, when a woman is at her most seductive. *Now* she was ready.

The fire in the hearth of her room was slowly dying, so there was a slight chill in the air, but nothing like the icy blast that greeted her as she stepped out into the upstairs hall. She wrapped the woollen shawl she'd selected earlier tightly around her shoulders, moved as quickly as her admittedly uncomfortable shoes would allow her (another salvage from her father) and scuttled down the stairs. Reaching the sitting room door, she paused, took a deep breath, let the shawl fall to her elbows, pressed the handle and made her entrance.

She'd timed it perfectly: they were all gathered, and she saw him immediately, standing next to the fabulous *Kachelowa*. Tonight, as at every Christmas, the *Kachelowa* was, quite literally, the imposing centrepiece of the home. An object of antique beauty, it was a tiled ceramic stove typical of the region; here, in the *salon*, it was a massive object, ceiling-to-floor, protruding from the wall and entirely covered in embossed tiles, alternately concave and flat, a rich, dark green in colour, each tile a square edged with an intricate abstract pattern and a similar, larger design in its centre. Hot air circulating behind the tiles heated the entire construction, top to bottom, and radiated into the air, emitting a cosy warmth that filled the entire room and spread through the open doors to the dining area.

Through its back, where the kiln had its entrance door, it heated the kitchen as well, and provided space for dishes and plates to be kept warm. This magnificent structure was only heated for special occasions in winter; even though it was economical in the burning of wood – one load of wood burning for hours – the family had never seen the need to heat the entire downstairs; the kitchen was heated by a smaller cast-iron stove, and that was sufficient. This was not a family that had the leisure to sit around all day in a warm room, reading books (with the glaring exception of Marie-Claire) or playing the piano or entertaining guests. This was a working family, and the kitchen was its hub. But not at Christmas.

There they all were. Gathered around it like worshippers around the altar of a benevolent god: Maman and Victoire sitting

on the wooden bench that surrounded it, their backs soaking in
its delicious warmth, Grandpère and Tante Sophie and Juliette's
grandmother, Tante Hélène, sitting in comfortable *fauteuils* facing
it, Uncle Max standing behind them, a pipe in his hand. Jacques,
standing to one side, smoking. Jacques…

Jacques had cleaned himself up. This was not the vagabond
Jacques she had last seen in Tante Sophie's kitchen, his beard so
unkempt she couldn't even see his lips, his hair long and greasy, his
clothes partly grime-encrusted, partly torn, wholly smelly. (How
could she, so meticulous about every aspect of her appearance, even
begin to love such a man? How was she not repelled, appalled, by
his outward appearance? But you cannot help whom you love. You
just do. You just love.)

Now, though, as she could tell at a glance, he had shaved off
his beard, cut and washed his hair. Not as neatly or stylishly as
she would have done it, had he asked her – this was probably
Victoire's work – but at least it was clean, and short. His clothes
(Leon's, actually) were not new (nobody but she wore new clothes
these days), but were at least fresh, and though they were not
well-fitting, for Jacques had grown painfully thin, they emphasised
his loose-limbed lankiness. There he stood. One hand was spread
against a flat green tile as if plugged in and drawing heat from
it, his weight pressed against it. A cigarette hung between the
fingers of the other hand.

His eyes, as she entered, or, actually, *made an entrance,* the one
she had planned, were lowered, fixed on Margaux and Victoire. He
appeared to be listening to their conversation, as everyone was (and
who was that other fellow, vaguely hovering in the background?).
She stepped in and, just as she had known they would, all eyes
rose to receive her. She posed before the door for a few seconds,
all the better to be appreciated, knowing that despite themselves
admiration would leap into those eyes – yes, there it was, that little
spark of wonder that could never be suppressed, wonder at feminine

beauty at its best (best under the circumstances, which were less than best), and on display. Marie-Claire could never understand the female modesty that seemed to inhabit all the women in her family and close acquaintanceship. Her mother, Victoire, Juliette, even Aunt Sophie – they all pretended not to care. But of course they did, deep inside! Surely their indifference was pretence! Yes, deep inside, they envied her.

Now, during that first silent moment, they all drank her in. Frowns (of envy) on the women's faces, except for Aunt Sophie, who moved her head slowly from side to side as if in disapproval. A grin across Uncle Max's – he could always be relied upon to show appreciation. Sheer awe on that young stranger's – who on earth was he? And on Jacques' – what? She could never read Jacques' expressions, a thing that had always annoyed her, from childhood – that she could never get Jacques right. That her feminine instincts as to what a man was thinking, how he regarded her, so infallible in other instances, stalled and broke down with Jacques.

Now, he looked straight at her, meeting her gaze with candour, revealing nothing of his inner thoughts. A simple acknowledgement of her presence, a nod of his head, then a smile as she broke the moment of silence with a 'Good evening, everyone!' and approached them all, arms held out as if she really, truly, was delighted to see each one. Faces lit up at her approach, as if in relief that the statue of beauty contained an inner soul after all.

Margaux and Victoire stood up to take her hands, as if they had not seen her earlier that day, as if she had metamorphosed into a new human needing a new greeting.

'*Bonsoir, chérie!*' murmured Maman, while Victoire simply said her name, and then added, 'How elegant you look!'

Marie-Claire nodded and moved on, through Tante Sophie, Tante Hélène, Grandpère, Uncle Max – whose cheek-kisses and praise were particularly exuberant – to the young stranger she'd never seen before.

'This is Eric!' said Victoire as she approached him. 'He's Jacques' friend, and we've invited him to celebrate Christmas with us. Eric, this is my big sister Marie-Claire.'

She nodded as she greeted Eric, but quickly dropped his hands – they were a mite too warm and sweaty – to turn, last of all, to Jacques, who, in the meantime, had extinguished his cigarette in an ashtray on a narrow ledge halfway up the *Kachelowa,* and now turned to her, arms open.

She fell into them. 'Jacques,' she murmured.

'Marie-Claire,' he replied, and, 'it's so good to see you. You look splendid.'

Still in his arms, she gazed into his eyes, and gave him a smile she hoped was enigmatic, full of veiled promises, a smile she had practised before the mirror. Something she interpreted as admiration lit up his eyes; certainly, he did not take his gaze from her. She basked in that gaze; she could feel his admiration. *Shallow as a crêpe-pan,* indeed! This time, this night, she would win him.

'Jacques,' was all she said, and then she raised a hand and brushed a lock of hair out of his forehead, a gesture that would give him a good whiff of the L'Heure Bleue secreted in her elbow; Guerlain and the mysterious scent of dusk would, hopefully, destroy his last defences. She would win. She *had* to.

Part of the art of seduction was not to give in too easily. Men needed the chase; it excited them. Jacques was no exception. His explanation that he regarded her only as a sister was ridiculous. Of course he didn't – it was just a convenient excuse to suppress his natural instinct and avoid a relationship that might be awkward, considering his involvement in her family. An armour she would break through; a challenge. She too enjoyed the chase. She didn't like men who fell too easily; she needed to win.

And so it was Marie-Claire, knowing the rules of the game and confident, now, that she *would* win, who extricated herself from this long embrace, peeled herself from Jacques' arms and turned round to look for somewhere else to place herself. Uncle Max was accommodating. He drew a leather *fauteuil* into the circle, gave her an elaborate bow and said, 'Do sit down, Marie-Claire. We've been waiting for you!'

'Actually, we've been waiting for her so we can start dinner,' said Margaux briskly, already on her way to the door that led directly into the kitchen. 'Come, Victoire, help me serve.'

Chapter Twenty-Seven

Victoire

'I really miss Juliette this year,' Victoire remarked later to Jacques. 'I know it's all top secret, but – well, I miss her. It's the first Christmas without her!' She sat between Jacques and Eric; Jacques was at the head of the table next to Margaux, who, having divided the *tarte flambée* into into equal pieces and served them all, had turned to Tante Hélène, on her left. Next to Tante Hélène came Uncle Max, already engaged in conversation with Marie-Claire on *his* left. Tante Sophie sat at the end of the table opposite Margaux, and then came Eric, next to Jacques.

Jacques shrugged, and cut off a piece of his tart. 'It's not all that secret. She is in France, at her university; she had to see one of her professors about her dissertation and he invited her to stay to celebrate with his family. It would have been too much of a rush to return at this time. She sends her love.'

He winked, grinned and attended to the food on his plate.

Victoire gave a wry chuckle. 'You can't fool me, Jacques. I know that Juliette is working with you and has no interest at all in her studies right now.'

'In that case, Victoire, you will be as discreet as she is and not ask questions.'

'Huh! Very well, I will only speak when I am spoken to from now on. At least, with you. And never ask another question. Maybe your friend will accept questions.'

She sniffed and turned away in pretended affront, to face Eric.

'Hello,' she said.

'Hello,' he replied.

And then they both just sat there, half turned towards each other; just looking. Eric had the face of a boy on the cusp of manhood. His cheeks and chin had the perfect milky-white complexion of a child, yet his chin was strong and his eyes, a dusky brown, spoke volumes: of things seen that no boy should see, of things beyond the promises of youth. Victoire spoke first.

'So you are from Lorraine?'

He nodded. 'Yes. I grew up in Metz. When the Germans came in through Belgium I joined the French army to fight them.'

'But you were surely much too young?'

'They needed *men* – they did not care about age. I am tall and strong enough to pass for eighteen, and inside I am already a man.'

He flexed his arm as he said this, and through Lucien's best blue sweater Victoire saw the bulge of a bicep. She resisted the urge to touch it, feel it, and only laughed.

'Your face doesn't match your body, though!' Again, she resisted the urge to touch him, stroke her fingers along his jawline. 'Not a hair!'

'A beard does not make a man. A man is formed from the inside: from his thoughts, his feelings, his sense of justice, his bravery, his need to protect his family, his friends, his country. These are the things that count, the things that define manly strength, *n'est-ce pas?*'

'Indeed,' she replied. *Absolument.* And for a woman, it is the same. A girl becomes a woman when she can summon her strength from inside her, from her heart – it might not be physical – I do admit that men have greater bodily strength – but I think our courage and our desire to fight for justice is in every way equal to that of a man. I may look like a girl to you, but—'

'But inside you are a woman. I know that, Victoire; I can see that, and also Jacques has told me a lot about you.'

'Aha – good things, I hope?'

SHARON MAAS

'Excellent things. He is very proud of you; he thinks of you as a little sister wise beyond her years and with the courage of a lioness.'

'He said that?'

'He did. He told me of all the adventures you had when you would all go with him into the mountains, as children – how even your older brothers feared the noises in the night when you all went camping, but *you* – you were up for anything. And he taught you to use a rifle and you shot your first rabbit when you were just ten, before your brothers. Your aim was perfect, he said.'

'He told you all that?'

'Yes. And, Victoire – he said that you are eager to join us, in what we are doing – but the time is not right. It is not because he thinks you are incapable. Quite the opposite.'

'Well, what is it then? If he approves of underage boys in the Resistance, why not girls?'

'Perhaps he has a special task for you, which does not need brawn, but brains? Maybe he doesn't want to risk your life in some kind of primitive act of pure brawn, but is saving you for something more…' he paused, searching for the right word '…sophisticated? More high-level? How would I know? Ask him!'

'I have, so many times, but he brushes me off. And then I have Maman to contend with, who won't allow me to join him, with the excuse that she needs me here to feed chickens and bake apple pie! It's infuriating!'

'Well, I would curb your impatience, Victoire. I have no doubt at all that one day, your heroism will be tested and there will be no doubt left – I see it written all over you. You are one of us, but in a different category altogether. If I were you, I would trust Jacques, and wait. Your time will come.'

She sighed. 'You certainly know how to flatter a girl.'

'I said it earlier, and I will say it again: you are not a girl, you are a woman.'

And once again their eyes locked, and this time, this time, she felt it: a connection, as if an inner fuse had been lit, a spark, leaping from his eyes to hers to light that fuse; an inner glow. And she knew. It was at that moment of her *knowing* that the kitchen door flew open.

Margaux gave a shout of alarm and leapt to her feet. She had taken the risk of abandoning their 'alarm system', since of course Grandpère sat at the table with them all, meaning that Nazis could barge in at any time. But then again, the front door was locked, so how could Nazis get into the house – thoughts that flickered through her mind in the fraction of a second before she recognised the intruder.

Intruders. *Plural.* Two of them. Two men, in the scruffiest clothes anyone had ever seen. Barging into their feast, with jubilant cries of *'Joyeux Noël!'* and arms flung up and out, striding towards the table, arms now wide open, two pairs of arms, two men…

'Leon! Lucien!' Margaux's cries were louder yet than theirs, and she was locked in an embrace that held all three of them, and all three were weeping, babbling half-finished sentences, almost toppling over in their excitement.

And then everyone else was on their feet, everyone was embracing everyone else, and crying out with joy, and tears flowed, and the cork of a precious champagne bottle popped, and chairs were drawn up to the table, and the second *tarte flambée* produced, and the family, this Christmas, was almost complete, almost, for Juliette was not among them. But Leon and Lucien were back, alive, and unscathed, and it was a time of great rejoicing. And so, this year, they bundled into their warmest jackets at eleven thirty, and jammed themselves into the van, the two older women and Grandpère squeezed in beside Margaux in the cabin and everyone else in the back.

Snow had fallen, and lay in a white layer over the countryside; thankfully, not enough to hinder their progress. But if it had, they would have started earlier, and walked into the village, and taken their place in the family pew for Midnight Mass.

And for half an hour Victoire was removed from the war and the Nazis and terrible fear that had been creeping through her being, slowly and perniciously, erasing all traces of hope and the faith that in the end, all would be well. And as she raised her voice for her favourite carol, 'Minuit Chrétiens' (O Holy Night), for a few minutes her spirit soared, and miracle tears poured down her cheeks, and all was well with the world, and she knew, with every fibre of her being, that one day, deliverance would come:

> Pour effacer la tache originelle
> Et de Son Père arrêter le courroux.
> Le monde entier tressaille d'espérance
> En cette nuit qui lui donne un Sauveur.
>
> Peuple à genoux, attends ta délivrance.
> Noël, Noël, voici le Rédempteur,
> Noël, Noël, voici le Rédempteur!

> Long lay the world in sin and error pining,
> Till He appear'd and the soul felt its worth.
> A thrill of hope, the weary world rejoices,
> For yonder breaks a new and glorious morn.
>
> Fall on your knees! O hear the angel voices!
> O night divine, O night when Christ was born;
> O night divine, O night, O night Divine.

Chapter Twenty-Eight

Marie-Claire

She woke late on Christmas Day, by the chateau's standards, and would have stayed in bed until early afternoon, but she had to get up; it was already almost ten, said the alarm clock on the bedside table. Jacques was in the house, and with him there was no telling when he would run off again.

There had been no time or opportunity to draw him aside last night, neither at the dinner table nor afterwards, when everyone, including her, was rejoicing at the return of Leon and Lucien, and before and after Mass it just would have been inappropriate; even she recognised that. So it had to be today. This morning. A pity; she would never be able to look her best, as she had last night. But hopefully last night he had taken note; she had made an impression, and today they could take the next obvious step.

She yawned, sat up, stretched, wrapped a shawl around her shoulders, wished she could just snuggle back down under the eiderdown, into the warmth, rather than face the bitter cold of her room; but there was nothing for it. She had to get up.

Slipping her feet into her sheepskin slippers, she padded to the window, drew back the curtains. The windowpanes were frosted over, but through the gaps of clear glass she could make out a landscape covered in a blanket of soft white. Marie-Claire had never been the kind of child who would rush out into the snow. She was that child who would seek the delicious warmth of the *Kachelowa* whenever it was lit – and it always was, on Christmas

Day – and play quietly in her pyjamas with the presents she had received the night before, while her brothers and sister, along with Jacques and Juliette, who often celebrated and spent the night with them, rushed out to build snowmen and frolic in the fluffy whiteness. That is, *if* there was snow.

Today, the adult Marie-Claire suppressed her longing for bed. She opened the window, bracing herself against the slap of cold that greeted her, for a better view. She could see a set of footprints despoiling the pristine purity of the snow, leading away from the house, and they could only be from one person. And she could see that one person, just coming round from the back of the house, carrying a spade. Shovelling the drive would take an hour, so she had a little time. He was still here. She closed the window.

Despite the breath of warm air escaping through the vent – the *Kachelowa* would have been lit long ago and was happily spreading heated air throughout the house – her bedroom was still icy cold, and so, wrapping her woollen shawl even more tightly around her, carrying a bundle of the clothes she would wear that day, she made her way into the even colder corridor and two doors down, to the bathroom; which, luckily, was cosily warm thanks to a tall black cast-iron stove, lit earlier that morning but with still enough glow to take the chill out of the room. Who had lit the house fires today, seeing as Leah had mysteriously disappeared, and Aimee had been given a holiday? Maman or Victoire, most probably.

She emerged half an hour later. Today she wore soft woollen culottes, warm as well as stylish, just a hint of lipstick, and her hair down, curling and bouncing on her shoulders. A satisfying glance in the mirror. She made her way downstairs.

She longed for coffee – or at least tea, considering the sad substitute that passed for coffee these days – but decided against stepping into the kitchen. Maman and Victoire would be there, probably Tante Sophie as well, possibly the boys. Maman had driven Uncle Max and Tante Hélène home last night, after Mass, but the kitchen would be brimming with good cheer and Marie-Claire had more urgent needs than breakfast and festive company. She needed Jacques.

Her sheepskin coat – not elegant at all, but good-quality, and warm – hung in the hall wardrobe, as did a pair of leather sheepskin boots, purchased from their Colmar cobbler years ago, perfectly snug round her chilled feet. A woollen cap and gloves completed the outfit; she stepped out into the whiteness.

Oh, the glory of the Alsace landscape blanketed in snow! Marie-Claire, usually indifferent to the beauties of nature, stopped outside the front door and could not but gasp at the magic of a winter morning: the trees with their white-laden branches silhouetted against the cloudless blue sky, the parallel lines of vines etched in white, undulating to the horizon, the backdrop of purple mountains capped in white. The vivid blueness of the sky, the blinding whiteness of the snow, sunlight glistening like silver stars upon it took even Marie-Claire's breath away, and she gasped in wonder, her breath escaping in a mist of white and dissolving into the crisp coldness of the atmosphere.

A metre-wide path had been dug into the snow. The snow itself was a hand's-width deep, the walls of the shovelled channel about twenty centimetres deep. Jacques had made swift progress – there he was, already near the front gate, his dark form briskly shovelling away. She walked towards him. His back towards her, intent on his work, he did not see or hear her approach.

'Good morning, Jacques!' she called, once in hearing distance. '*Joyeux Noël!* Hard at work, I see!'

He swung round. 'Marie-Claire! *Joyeux Noël!* Did you sleep well?'

'I did,' she replied. 'It is good to be in my own home, my own room again!'

'I can imagine. But hopefully it's not too bad at Tante Sophie's.'

'Oh, it's not bad at all and I'm not complaining. A bit small, a bit cramped, but that is the price I am willing to pay for my independence. Still, it's good to come home and enjoy a few home comforts again. And what a beautiful day!'

Jacques slammed his spade into a mound of snow and grasped her upper arms, drawing her close. They cheek-kissed in greeting, then pulled apart. He glanced at the spade, and Marie-Claire got the hint. He wanted to return to his work. Dismissed, already? It couldn't be.

'Jacques,' she said, and paused. He tilted his head.

'Yes?' She was astute enough to understand that this was not exactly the seductive opening or setting she needed. But an alternative was immediately to hand.

'Well – I was hoping we could talk some time, about, well, about what I'm doing at the *Mairie*. If you're satisfied?'

His face broke out into a grin. 'Satisfied? Marie-Claire, I'm more than satisfied! That spool you sent, it's worth gold. Absolutely top-notch information. You couldn't have done better.'

She beamed. 'Really? It was useful?'

'Excellent. You did good work, Marie-Claire!'

'Well. There's more to come. You just have to make sure that I have new spools to replace the used ones.'

'That's not a problem.' He glanced at his spade again. She took the hint.

'So, you want to get back to work. I'll leave you to it – I might go for a little walk. I love crunching into fresh snow, leaving footprints in pristine snow. It's not too deep, I think.'

'No – you'll be fine in those boots. But I didn't know you liked walking in the snow! Or walking at all!'

She gave him an enigmatic smile.

'You don't know much about me at all, Jacques!'

'Well, you've changed a lot. I remember, as a child, nothing would bring you out from the *salon*, next to the *Kachelowa*; you preferred playing with your dolls or reading a book to snow-fights with the rest of us.'

'I'm not exactly going off to have a snow-fight now! Unless you want one?'

She winked, and was rewarded with a mischievous grin. He bent down, digging into the snow with his gloved hand. In playful menace, he formed a tight ball with both hands.

'Well, that's an idea! Why not? Better late than never, Marie-Claire!'

She let out a shriek and ran back down the path, towards the house. The snowball landed with a splat against her back. She swung round.

'Right, that does it!' She dug into the snow herself, made her own ball, flung it towards him, but it missed its mark as he leapt aside. Already he was forming a new ball, and she had plunged off, laughing, to the side of the shovelled path, across the snowed-over meadow, shrieking, stumbling in the snow, bending over to collect another handful of it. Jacques plunged after her, bending now and then to collect a handful of snow, pelting her with sloppily formed balls, most of which missed their mark. She fled, darted away, screeching in mock-terror, zigzagging across the field, stopping just once to bend over for her own ammunition, flinging it at him in retaliation.

She reached the wooden fence and stopped, panting, laughing, against it. Jacques caught up with her, flinging away the last ball of snow. He too was out of breath, also laughing. They stood side by side for a moment, catching their breath, leaning against the fence. Marie-Claire clutched her side.

'And now I've got a stitch, and it's all your fault!' She bent over double for relief.

He chuckled, and gave her a playful punch.

'What's got into you, Marie-Claire? I've never seen you so playful.'

'Like I said, Jacques, you don't know me, not at *all!* You've put me in a little box and you just never made the effort to get to know me!'

'You're right about that – I'm already seeing a few new sides to you.'

'Nobody in the chateau really knows me, Jacques, including you, and it's – well, it's irritating. Everybody hates me.'

He chuckled.

'Don't be silly, Marie-Claire. You're being overdramatic. Nobody hates you. Of course not! You're my sister! Well, almost…'

She did not laugh back. Her eyes no longer twinkled. Her face, just a moment ago rosy with a winter blush and radiant with joy, now a pale and sullen mask.

He held out a hand to gently grasp hers, but she snatched it away, spun round, strode away, towards the closed gate that led into *Chemin des Sources,* her body stiff with snubbed pride, hands stuffed into coat pockets. He hurried to catch up. She opened the gate, slipped through it, and was about to close it behind her, but he was right there behind her, so she left it and walked into the road. The snow here was completely untouched, pristine, glistening in the early-morning sun. She walked briskly away, boots crunching into the deep unblemished whiteness, leaving footprints behind.

'Marie-Claire, wait! What's the matter? Why're you running away? What did I say wrong?'

Marie-Claire finally stopped and turned to look at Jacques. Her glistening eyes caught his in a pleading, almost desperate gaze. He could not meet it; he looked away.

'Jacques: look at me! Just look at me!' she demanded.

He raised his eyes to meet hers. 'I'm looking. What is it, Marie-Claire?'

'You don't know? You really don't know? You don't *feel* it?'

'Feel – what?'

She stamped her feet in frustration.

'Christ, you're so – so dense! Obtuse! Do I really have to spell it out? Jacques, what are you, a robot or what? Have you ever actually *been* with a woman? Do you even know what a woman *is?* Who I am?'

'You are Marie-Claire, and I don't know what the problem is.'

'Yes, you do. You know very well but you refuse to confront it. Yes, I am Marie-Claire, that is who I am, but do you know what I am? I am a woman, Jacques, a flesh-and-blood woman, and you are a man. And I am not your sister, never was, so don't come to me with that rubbish. You did that before, remember?'

He smacked his forehead with a gloved hand.

'Ah, yes. I remember. That night when you got drunk and you played a stupid game of seduction, which didn't go too well.'

'Yes, I was drunk, and you are right, it was stupid and awkward but I was young, just a teenager still, and now I am a woman and I stand before you asking you if you ever really saw me as I am, instead of as a silly child who made a mistake back then. If you cannot see past that embarrassing blunder. If all you are thinking is *zut alors,* silly Marie-Claire, just a little drunk girl who came into my bedroom by mistake one night, and I told her off and that was that, if that's the box you have put me in, if you are so arrogant as to refuse to see that I have grown into a woman, a beautiful woman, then…'

She stamped her foot in exasperation. Her eyes shone bright with fervour, trying to hold his but failing, for Jacques' gaze was fixed beyond her, towards the purple snow-capped mountains of the Vosges. Her words exhausted, silence descended between them as she waited for a response, she watching him, him looking away into the distance, their breath forming white dissolving clouds in the crisp cold morning air.

Finally, he spoke. Slow, calculated words; it was as if in the preceding silence he had weighed each one, chosen each one for its ability to make its meaning clear, unambiguous, while simultaneously not cause offence, a tightrope strung between two mutually exclusive goals, tact and candour.

'Marie-Claire. I understand now. At least I think I do. I am not as – what did you call me? Obtuse. I am not as thick-headed as you think. I had indeed forgotten that incident, and I beg your forgiveness. I did not take it seriously at the time and I never held it against you – to me, it was not embarrassing; we all make mistakes when we have had too much to drink. I am the same, and the best thing to do is to let it be as if it never happened, and that is what I have done, and only now that you have reminded me—'

'Jacques, you are talking too much.'

'Yes, yes, I am. I am very sorry. What I wanted to say is that the slate has been wiped clean. You are my sister as you have always been—'

'I am not your damned sister! That is Juliette!' She cried the words, stamped her feet, pummelled the air.

'You are like my sister, as I said then. I know what you are trying to say. Yes, you are indeed a beautiful woman, and as a man I can appreciate that, but—'

'And I have abandoned all pride and all modesty and am throwing myself at you. I love you, Jacques. Can you not see it, feel it? I have always loved you, since we were children. I have tried to fight it but I cannot. I know we are very different, so very, very different, and I have tried to push my love away, but it only comes back stronger than ever. I am almost the opposite of you and yet still I love you with all my heart and all my being and I don't understand. I don't understand why you can't, why you can't just…'

She paused, openly weeping now, tears leaking from her eyes; she wiped her glove against them, sniffed, and then, with clear eyes locked into his, she whispered the rest of the sentence:

'…just love me back.'

Jacques held the silence that had closed them in. His carefully selected words had failed; but then, words had never been his strength, nor the adequate formulation of feelings. In fact, his words had not just failed, but produced the opposite effect he had hoped for: instead of easing her gently and discreetly away from further intimacy, more confessions, they had brought out this, an unabashed declaration of love – a thing Jacques was totally unprepared for and for which no words could ever be adequate, except the four she was begging for. Now that was embarrassing.

All he could do, now, was speak the truth: 'I-I don't know what to say, Marie-Claire.'

'So it is quite clear, then; you don't love me, except as a bland sister.'

It was a statement, not a question. He answered truthfully, no awkward searching for words this time.

'Yes, Marie-Claire, I love you as a sister, and a friend.'

'What if I said, I don't demand or expect your love, but I would like to give you mine, in every way possible, mind, soul and, especially, body; if we made love, perhaps, you could learn to—'

He could not let her finish. 'No, Marie-Claire, it is out of the question! I cannot, I could not possibly – even the thought of it – just no.'

She cried out: 'I can't believe you are so – so totally *sans passion!* You are a robot, an empty excuse for a man. I bet you're a – a bloody damned *faggot?*'

She almost spat that last word, her mouth distorted into a sneer, her eyes glaring with naked animosity, no longer pleading, no longer begging for love, filled now with a wild, furious loathing, the hideous backside of love, her whole face transformed into an ugly, distorted mask. She swung round then and ran, away from him, up the middle of the snow-blanketed road, boots crunching into the crisp white snow. He made to follow her, again, but she turned and shouted at him: 'Leave me alone! Don't you dare – just leave me!'

So he stood in silence, hands once again shoved into pockets, watching as she ran away.

A woman scorned… he thought, and an inexplicable sense of foreboding washed through him, a sense of evil descending, almost a premonition, an intimate perception of some intangible but awful thing lying in wait, a dark and nebulous creature waiting in the shadows.

He shuddered to shake it off, turned and returned to the chateau.

Chapter Twenty-Nine

Victoire

She was the first to get up and go downstairs, as usual; but then, she had gone to bed early, whereas Maman had stayed up late, after they returned from Mass, to talk to Leon and Lucien, along with Uncle Max, Eric and Jacques. Tante Sophie had gone up to bed with her, and Marie-Claire – she had not even gone to Mass with them. Heaven only knew what was going on in her mind. She had been dressed so inappropriately – didn't she realise, couldn't she see for herself, that it was insensitive to doll oneself up like a Paris mannequin when she knew perfectly well that nobody else had the luxury of new and stylish clothes? Not for the first time, Victoire felt a wave of resentment against her father, who made it so blindingly obvious just which of his two daughters was his favourite. But, ever quick to monitor her feelings, Victoire switched off her own sense of – what was it? Jealousy? A feeling of unease that poisoned the entire family unit? – and returned to the task at hand.

First, lighting all the wood-fired stoves in the house; the tall, thin bathroom stove, the black bowlegged kitchen stove and the magnificent *Kachelowa*. By the time the others woke up and came down for breakfast the rooms so heated would hold a delicious warmth.

She visited Leah and Estelle with boiled eggs for their breakfast, and words of cheer. Then, she was out feeding the animals, letting the chickens and the goats out of their pens; all of them reluctant to emerge because the ground was covered in a thick layer of fresh snow, which had fallen in the hours between their return from church and dawn.

She loved the snow; but when one had a little farm to run, there was no time to enjoy the beauty of the landscape, or indulge in a lengthy morning walk, which is what she would have liked to have done. Hearing a scraping sound, she walked round the house and saw that Jacques had started to clear a path to the gate.

'Good morning, Jacques! Merry Christmas!' she called.

He saluted her. 'Merry Christmas, Victoire! May this be the first and last Christmas under the Nazi jackboot!'

'Let us pray for that!' she called back, and returned to the animals. Jacques had a one-track mind: it was never far away from the disaster that had fallen upon them. Even at Mass last night, she had seen him kneeling at his pew, head bent over clasped hands, and she had known exactly what he was praying for. Jacques had no personal life outside of his self-chosen obligation to expel the Boche. And it was good so.

Stoves lit, Leah and Estelle cared for, animals fed and comfortable, Victoire returned to a kitchen now cosily warm and began to prepare breakfast.

Sometimes, quite often, in fact, Victoire felt that *she* was the head of this household, not her mother. Increasingly, she was the one who ensured that everyone was fed and warm and comfortable. If she knew Maman, that talk with Leon and Lucien and Max and Jacques – essentially, a talk with 'the men' – had been fuelled by bottle after bottle of wine. Indeed there, in the basket next to the sink, were all the empties, waiting to be cleaned and refilled and relabelled. She could well imagine it all: Maman refilling everyone's glass again and again and again, and finally staggering up the stairs to bed, knowing full well that she, Victoire, would take care of everything come the morning.

It wasn't that Maman was lazy, or negligent of her own duties. Maman had a business to run, and did it well, but in her own time and manner. It had been increasingly difficult for Alsatian winegrowers and businesspeople since the coming of the Nazis: Margaux and her colleagues had had to find a completely new market, a German one, and somehow deal with the fact that they could only keep going through transactions with German buyers; by forming pacts with the devil. Margaux had managed to turn this awkward situation round by using it to its opposite effect: the bribing of Nazis in order to undermine their dominance had become her strategy, a ruse by which she had been able to deceive them again and again. A risky game, but one she had perfected. Maman was now a master at twisting Nazis round her little finger. 'They all have a weak point,' Maman said. 'You have to find it.' Catching flies with honey, she called it, a Dolch family motto she'd taken on from Maxence.

But that had meant that Maman's hands were full, and the day-to-day running of the household had automatically fallen to Victoire. Aimee came in once a week to clean the chateau from top to bottom, but now all the cooking, the care of the animals and garden, the heating of rooms and general upkeep fell completely into Victoire's hands. She didn't particularly like it, but it had to be done and it made no sense to complain.

But then she remembered: in January everything would change. She had finalised the arrangements for her Red Cross nursing course, and even found a place to stay, with Evelyne, a friend who lived in Colmar and who had invited her to share her bedroom in her parents' house. It was all coming together. She would play a part in resisting the Nazis. She could not just sit back and watch the disaster as it happened.

She lugged the basket of empty bottles out of the back door, hung up her coat, rolled up her sleeves, turned on the tap over the sink, placed a kettle of water on the hob of the now scalding hot wood burner and set to work to clear up the kitchen from yesterday's festivities. There were dirty dishes piled on the central table and in the sink; pots and pans to be cleaned; and, of course, wine and water glasses. She sighed, and entered the dining room to assess the mess left there. Indeed more glasses, left right there where Maman and the men had sat, philosophising and arguing and bonding into the wee hours.

Well, at least Leon and Lucien were back, and safe. Victoire loved her brothers, though she wasn't particularly close to them, and looked forward to hearing their stories of captivity and eventual release. She also looked forward to feeding them up: they both looked skeletal, and must have been half-starved. She wondered if last night's overindulgence had not been too much for their first night home. But it was Christmas, they were home, and that was the main thing.

'*Bonjour*, Victoire!' She jumped, and swung round. Eric stood in the doorway. Jacques' new friend.

'*Bonjour*, Eric, and merry Christmas! You're up early – didn't you stay up till dawn, with the other men and Maman?'

'No. Jacques and I went up at about one; I felt that it was more of a family reunion and I didn't want to intrude. And besides, I was tired, and so was Jacques – we walked all the way from Colmar, yesterday. But after a good night's sleep, I'm raring to go! Jacques is already up – his bed is empty.'

'Yes – he's shovelling snow on the driveway. You can go out and help, if you want. There are spades in the open shed just outside the kitchen. You can wear my coat – it's an old man's one, it'll fit you.' She pointed to the coat hanging on a hook beside the door.

'I will,' said Eric. 'See you later.' He grabbed the coat and retreated out the back door. Victoire sighed, and emptied the kettle of hot water into the sink, tested the water to ascertain the temperature and collected several empty wine glasses to start with. But then she looked up: Eric was back.

'Seems that Jacques has decided to have a playful pause,' said Eric. 'He's having a snow-fight with your sister – Marie-Claire's her name, right?'

'Yes. But really? This I have to see. It's not like Jacques, or Marie-Claire.'

She walked through to the dining room, and looked out the window onto the front drive. Indeed, Eric was right: Marie-Claire and Jacques were zigzagging around the snow-covered front meadow, laughing, dodging each other's snowballs. Eric came and stood beside her.

'That looks like a massive flirt to me!' he said.

'Flirt? No. No way. They are like brother and sister. We always played together, just like this. Snowballs and snowmen, every winter. There's nothing behind it, just a bit of harmless fun.'

'Well, you are very innocent – and not very observant. Marie-Claire is in love with Jacques. It's obvious – I saw it at once, last night. And I can see it in the way she's playing with him now. It's a flirt, all right.'

'Well, if so, Jacques isn't interested. I know Jacques. He'd never get involved with Marie-Claire. Like I said, we're all like brothers and sisters.'

'But you aren't, really, are you? You and Jacques, brother and sister?'

'No. But it feels that way. Anyway, back to work.' She turned away from the window and walked back to the kitchen, to the sink, pushing her hands into the water to retrieve one of the glasses and a sponge to wipe it with. There was no soap, no suds. Soap was one of the goods it was getting increasingly difficult to get hold of.

Eric looked around, saw a cotton dishcloth hanging from a hook next to the sink. Unhooking it, he stood beside Victoire, waiting. She looked up, and smiled.

'Thank you,' she said, and handed him the glass. He took it, began wiping it dry and continued.

'I asked because I noticed last night, at dinner, that you and Jacques are very close,' he said. 'And he speaks so lovingly of you. I would have thought that if he's interested in one of the two sisters, it's you, not Marie-Claire!'

'Eric! Really, that's such nonsense! Jacques really is a brother to me and I won't have you insinuating otherwise. It's – well, it's disgusting!'

'All right, I'm sorry. So you regard him as just a brother? Even though he's not?'

'Of course!'

'But you already have two brothers… and feelings of love can change and develop over time?'

Victoire snatched the dishcloth and glass away from Eric. She glared at him.

'Really, Eric, that's out of order, completely! You don't know a thing and yet you come here not knowing any of us and making all these wild guesses… Just go away! I can manage the dishes on my own.'

But Eric only grinned, and shrugged sheepishly. 'I'm sorry, Victoire. Please forgive me. I didn't mean to be rude or intrusive. It's just that – well, I wanted to know if your feelings are already taken, because, you know, I find you so very pretty and, and absolutely adorable. I guess I just wanted to know if you were free and-and if you like me. Just a little.'

Victoire could only stare, and when she found her voice it came out as a stammer.

'Me? P-p-pretty? No! Look at me! I'm j-j-just a – well, I'm so ordinary! Marie-Claire is the pretty one!'

Eric threw back his head and laughed. 'See, that's exactly what I love about you! You aren't even aware of how adorable you are! Not in the slightest!'

Victoire did not know how to respond. She just stood there, glass and dishcloth still in her hand. Eric shrugged and turned away, back to the sink.

'So, you prefer to dry? *D'accord.* I'll do the washing-up.'

Chapter Thirty

Marie-Claire

She ran and ran, boots pounding into the pristine snow as she careered up the road, in a lumbering, decidedly inelegant gait. The road now wound gently uphill, through the vineyards, around the white mound that now hid the chateau from sight. Into the white void. Day had seriously broken by now, mild sunshine filtering through the naked trees that lined the road. The sky was brilliantly cobalt. It was a glorious silver-gold-blue Christmas morning, but no glory for her, only abject humiliation, complete and final.

She wanted to howl, to scream, but it seemed obscene to shatter the compact silence of early morning and so she just whimpered as she ran, and let out a subdued wail, and sniffled, and snorted and sniffed at the threatening snot. What a good thing she had refrained from wearing make-up this morning – it would have made a mess of her face, and even now, in the disastrous aftermath of the fiasco with Jacques, and even though she was quite alone, Marie-Claire was mostly conscious of how she must look. Thank goodness there was no one to see her. In particular, no man.

A man had done this to her, thrown her into this state of utter wretchedness. A man she loved, had adored for all of her short life, since childhood, fallen in love with when she was fourteen. A man had thrown that helpless adoration back in her face with the most spurious of excuses. *I think of you as a sister* – that baloney spewed out again, just as he'd done so long ago, when she'd been a drunk teenager with no knowledge of the art of seduction – then, it could have been excused but now, now? No excuse. It was a slap in the face, a stinging slap.

Marie-Claire had always been aware that her power lay in her looks; she had been a beautiful child, and had been accustomed to the adulation that beauty inspired in others; in females as well as males, but in the last few years, particularly in the latter. That adulation had delivered not only confidence, but a certain sense of being exalted enough to keep others at bay. It gave her the power of choice.

'You could have any man you want!' She had been told this at least three times by rejected suitors; men turned humble and doting in her presence, and even in the stilted atmosphere of the *Mairie* she knew that even when they said nothing, her male colleagues and superiors drank her in with their eyes. Except, of course, the *Kreisleiter,* but he did not count as a man – he was a robot in thrall to Nazi ideology, not really human.

But normal men? They were hers, all hers, and not wanting them was her power. *Had been* her power. Because, if the one man she did want did not reciprocate, of what value was that power? What was it worth? What was *she* worth?

Nothing. Nothing at all. She had failed, miserably. She had been flung away as thoughtlessly, as brutally, as a discarded potato skin, something ugly and worthless. What man discarded beauty as recklessly as Jacques had just done? What was she worth?

She slowed to an amble, all the better to think, hands thrust into the pockets of her coat, shoulders hunched. She felt bruised and battered, sawn up and torn apart like a tree that had been axed for firewood. Not physically, of course, but emotional pain could surely match physical pain in intensity. Because that was certainly how it felt. Pulled apart, and how would she ever be put back together again? How would she ever feel normal again, confident, beautiful? Validated? Only a man could do that, but the only man who had that power was the man who had kicked her into this state.

She wallowed in her pain as she walked on, revelling in it almost. Somehow, it felt good to reflect on the deep, deep insult Jacques had dealt her. And the more she reflected on it, the more her pain underwent a sort of transformation; it seemed to be turning into a different thing. A person can wallow in their humiliation only so long; sooner or later, it morphs into anger, and that was what, now, was happening in Marie-Claire's soul. Anger, directed towards Jacques. And a sense of need for retaliation. Revenge.

She had long stopped whimpering, and now she felt herself taking deep long breaths, as if gathering strength, as if realigning her feelings, rediscovering her confidence. She would not take it; she could not take it.

She had been walking now for twenty minutes. The rows of vines were coming to an end; beyond them lay the cottage where the Dolch family lived. Jacques, and his father Maxence, and occasionally Juliette, and now Hélène. Here, she used to play regularly with her siblings and the Dolch children, climbing trees, camping out in the orchard, playing ball games and with the dogs that Jacques and Juliette always had around them.

She stopped, and stared. Just like his son at the chateau, Max was on the driveway shovelling snow. Jacques, obviously, was not at home – she had left him behind to reflect upon his sins. But Max – she used to call him Uncle Max, but had dropped the Uncle years ago at his own suggestion. Max had always treated her like a lady. Max was the first man who had made her aware of her beauty. Max had an innate charm, some of which his son Jacques had inherited; but unlike Jacques, Max was mature, a real adult, a real man, who knew the art of playful but harmless flirting between the sexes, a game that would never lead to anything, but which both sexes enjoyed and women, especially, needed for their self-esteem.

Max had played that game last night. When Marie-Claire had come downstairs and made her dramatic entry into the *salon* her eyes had first fallen on Max, because Max had let out a slow, soft whistle, and his eyes had danced and met hers with a complete arsenal of admiration. *You are beautiful!* those eyes had said. *You are desirable!*

And now, more than anything else in the world, Marie-Claire needed those eyes. Needed that silent message: *you are a desirable woman! I like you! I want you!*

That, more than anything else, would heal those inner wounds. Besides, Max was a man, fully matured, a man who had been married and fathered children, unlike Jacques, who had never been known to be romantically associated with a girl or woman. Max's attention was more valid than Jacques' inattention.

It was an emotional inner reasoning rather than an intellectual one, but it was enough. She straightened her shoulders, lifted her chin. *I can!* she told herself firmly, *and I will.* She ignored a slight twinge of guilt. Max had often played a father's role in her youth. How could she… but no. That was then. Now, she was an adult and the age difference meant nothing at all, and he *wasn't* her father.

She bent down and picked up a handful of snow, spread it over her face, pressed it into her eyes. Wiped it all away. She wished she had a powder compact to check her face. She didn't want her cheeks to be too red, from crying and from the cold snow, but a fresh rosiness would do. She took several deep breaths and walked on. Reaching the gate, she leaned on it.

She raised her hand and waved.

'Bonjour Max! Joyeux Noël!'

Chapter Thirty-One

Victoire

The kitchen and dining room were pristine, the dishes from last night washed and dried and put away, and they had done it together, chatting away as if they had known each other all their lives, as if Eric had been part of that childhood clan that had wrapped her in companionship and warmth and security. He was like another Jacques, just as passionate about defying the Nazis, but less consumed; most of all, he made her laugh, and Victoire needed laughter. Life had been so grim, these last few years, and finding someone who could still laugh – well, it was a balm.

The kitchen was now deliciously warm, heated not only with its own cast-iron stove but with the back wall of the *Kachelowa*. The *salon*, today, would no doubt be in full use, and that too was cosily warm. The others, when they woke up, would come downstairs to a snug and welcoming home.

She had prepared breakfast for them both. Nothing special, because even for Christmas there was just one egg each, and with so many mouths to feed in the house – and now, three unexpected guests, her brothers back from Germany and Eric – one had to economise. They had been saving eggs for days. But the three chickens were as reliable as ever; there were fewer eggs in winter, but still, they delivered. Victoire had found three fresh eggs this morning, and Maman had managed to barter for butter, and so right now two of those eggs sat sizzling in the frying pan.

Eric had already told her his story, about his childhood in Metz and how he had escaped, alone, after his family had been evacuated to Poitiers after the invasion. He had walked all the way from Metz to Strasbourg, crossing the Vosges mountains, foraging for food, sleeping out in the rough. Luckily that had been last summer, before the cold weather set in. And then he had joined the Black Hand, committing small but effective acts of sabotage to disrupt the Nazi machine as much as possible.

'Jacques said he has a new job for you, here in the Haut-Rhin?' she said as they sat down to eat. She poured him a cup of ersatz coffee.

'Yes. It's because of my experience crossing the Vosges. I'll – well, I don't know if he'd want me to talk about it. He's so secretive.'

'You can tell me,' Victoire coaxed. 'All of Jacques' secrets are safe with me.'

Their eyes met, and they gazed at each other across the table for a few seconds. Then Eric nodded. '*D'accord.* In fact, you are part of the job so it must be all right to tell you. I just hope Jacques won't be cross.'

'He won't be, I promise.'

Eric nodded. 'Well, it's this. Sabotage is only part of our mission. What Jacques also wants to do, and in fact is doing, is helping Jews to escape. He's already started that, but, he says, there are some Jews hidden right here, in the chateau. A woman and a child.'

Victoire nodded. 'Leah and Estelle. I look after them.'

'Jacques is going to help them escape, over the Vosges. He already knows a route. He wants me to go with him when he takes them, teach me the route, so that in future I will be responsible for guiding escaping Jews that way while he concentrates on other tasks.'

Victoire gasped. 'He's training *you* to do that? Why not me? I've been begging him for months now to let me do something important, something worthwhile! I would have *loved* that job!'

Eric shrugged. 'I guess he thought it was too dangerous for you.'

'But why? Why is it dangerous for me and not for you? I'm not that much younger than you and perfectly capable! We children were always camping out in the mountains! I know the mountains and forests around here like the back of my hand – he knows that, because he's the one who taught me! I've been that way lots of times with him.'

'Maybe he feels responsible for you? Because you are so young, and you are a—'

Victoire cried out her reply, her face red with exasperation.

'A girl! That's it, isn't it! It's because I'm only a girl, and all I'm good for is looking after the house and cooking for everyone! While you and Jacques get to play the hero!'

Eric, visibly uncomfortable, scratched his head. 'Everyone who works for the Resistance is a hero, Victoire, nobody is more valuable than anyone else. You have been feeding and looking after Leah and her daughter – isn't that important? Isn't it risky and dangerous and heroic? If the Nazis caught you, you'd be in enormous trouble, perhaps executed. Why do you think that it would be more heroic to guide them over to Lorraine?'

'Because – because it's more *adventurous*. I'm tired, so tired, of being at home doing the drudge work for everyone!'

'But without what you are doing, nobody else could do what they are doing. You are basically the backbone of our work. The backbone is invisible, but without it, the body would collapse. Why not see it from that perspective instead of grumbling and thinking your contribution is worthless?'

Victoire had no answer. They ate on with an awkward silence between them. Finally, Victoire looked up at him and said, 'When?'

Eric shrugged, and replied: 'I don't know. Soon. That's the real reason he brought me here. He said as soon as the weather allows it. He said there's going to be snow but probably a thaw and then we can go.'

Victoire nodded. 'Jacques was always good at predicting the weather. So he didn't even tell me that much, but he told you.

But…' She looked up with a new light of hope in her eyes. 'But maybe I can come too? Jacques, me and you. Why not?'

'Well…'

She answered her own question. 'No, I suppose that would be too many of us. And I'd just be a useless hanger-on.'

'Look, Victoire, I wish you wouldn't see yourself like that! What you're doing is important – really important. It's no less important than helping them escape. No less dangerous; in fact, more dangerous.'

'Still. I just wish I could do more. I wish I was a boy. Then he'd have taken me.'

Eric said nothing for a while, and then he said, 'Well, I'm glad you're not a boy.'

'Yes, because you get to have all the adventures.'

'That's not what I meant. I…'

But she was already on her feet. 'Anyway, we can't sit around arguing all day. I have to look after Leah and Estelle. Take them their breakfast.'

'Can I come with you? To meet them? And tell Leah?'

She shrugged. 'If you want to. I suppose you have to meet them if you're taking them over the mountains.'

'And then, afterwards, can we go for a walk?'

'I have to chop wood for the ovens.'

'I'll help you, if you come for a walk with me.'

Their eyes met. And then she shrugged again. *'D'accord.'*

Chapter Thirty-Two

Marie-Claire

Max shoved his spade into a snowdrift and walked over to the gate, grinning broadly.

'Merry Christmas, Marie-Claire! I didn't know you were such an early riser!'

Reaching the gate, he kissed her on both cheeks.

'I didn't sleep well last night so I decided to go for a walk and somehow I ended up here.'

'Well, would you like to come in? Have you had breakfast yet? I haven't quite finished here' – he gestured at the several metres of un-shovelled snow behind the gate – 'but there's no hurry; I'm not expecting visitors. Work can wait – I'd much rather entertain a beautiful woman! Maman is having a long lie-in – yesterday was exhausting for her.'

She had already opened the latch, and was pushing the gate open. 'I'd love to, Max! Thanks. It's true I haven't had breakfast, and walking has made me hungry.'

'Then come in. I haven't got much, just the usual bread and cheese. And an egg. I'll fry it for you. And coffee. War coffee. Sorry about that.'

'I'm used to it by now. Though I can't wait for the war to be over and for my first cup of real coffee!'

'You said it. Real coffee, real everything. Real life.'

They walked side by side back to the house, the two dogs dancing around them. Reaching the kitchen door, Max opened it and gestured for her to enter.

'Ooh, lovely and warm!' She walked over to the cast-iron stove and held her hands out above it, absorbing its radiance. And then she turned round.

'Max,' she said. Her voice was serious now, the bantering tone abandoned. 'There's something I wanted to talk to you about.'

'Of course. Have a seat. Just a minute…'

He cleared the kitchen table, which was cluttered with various items: a basket of apples, a pile of crockery and, incongruously, a skein of wool, with two knitting needles stuck into it, and two inches of what looked like a very badly knitted scarf.

'Maman's teaching me to knit,' he said, as if to excuse the latter. 'She says men need to learn to knit and sew and take care of themselves, especially men who live alone. Like me. And Jacques.'

'I saw Jacques when I came out,' said Marie-Claire. She wasn't quite sure how to start, and felt suddenly shy. 'He's shovelling snow over at the chateau.'

'Ah, yes, he would. He always loved outdoor work, since he was a boy. But – you were saying, you wanted to discuss something? You sounded so serious.' He pulled out a chair and gestured for her to sit. She did so.

'Max,' she said, once she was seated. Max continued to move around the kitchen. He placed a breadboard and a knife on the table, and a knob of bread, and a slab of cheese. She wished he would sit still – his activity made her nervous.

'It's not much,' he said, 'but help yourself. I'll make you a fried egg. Those hens are a godsend – so generous with their eggs!'

Marie-Claire nodded, but did not touch the food. 'Max!' she said again, more firmly.

He turned round. 'Yes?'

'Max – last night, when I came into the *salon*. You remember?'

'Of course I do! Lovely as a picture, you were! As if you had stepped off a Hollywood film! You have a slight resemblance to Greta Garbo, you know! Something about the lips…'

'Thank you. But your son doesn't seem to agree.'

'Jacques?' He chuckled and shook his head as if perplexed. 'Jacques wouldn't recognise a beautiful woman if she turned up naked in his bed.'

'I was wondering about that. Is he – perhaps – you know, the other way?'

He frowned. 'Why do you ask that?'

'Because – well, it's a bit awkward and embarrassing, but, you know, Jacques is such an old friend and I was just wondering why he never had a girlfriend?'

'Oh, that. I wouldn't bother about that. He's just obsessed about the war and the Nazis. Most young men are obsessed about women, but it's hard to hold two obsessions in your head at once. Jacques is normal, Marie-Claire. A normal red-blooded man. Once the war is over and we have chased out the Nazis, he'll find himself a nice girl and settle down. I'm sure of it.'

'And you, Max? You've been a widower for so long and you never seem to have a girlfriend.'

He threw back his head and laughed. 'A girlfriend? Which girl would even look at an old codger like me?'

'Well, then, a woman.'

'Not much chance of meeting a woman, an old hermit like me. I tend to keep to myself. How am I to go out and find myself a girlfriend?'

'But you obviously have an eye for women. The way you looked at me last night – I almost thought, for one minute, that you were, you know, flirting!'

'Marie-Claire, what's going on? Why are you talking about these things? It's a bit, you know, inappropriate? Of course I looked at you in an appreciative way. Women like that. Some women, at least. *You* liked that, I could tell. It's fun, it's a game between the sexes, I like to play it. What of it?'

'Well, yes, I did like it. But I was wondering, Max – you know. I mean, where there's heat there's fire, isn't there? You've got fire,

I've got fire. Everyone else around here seems so, so very, what's the word? Boring. *Sans passion.* But you and me, now…'

'Marie-Claire! Now you really are being ridiculous. What are you suggesting?'

'Why does it have to be a game, Max? Yes, I like being appreciated, by men, by *you.* I think that's normal, and natural. And I think that if there's this attraction, then why not…' She reached out and took his hand.

'Max, I'm a woman, and I enjoy being attractive. It's a natural thing, and I think you're the only man around here who can understand. I wanted you to know that I like you, and to me, you're not an old codger at all. You're a very attractive man, mature and experienced. You can appreciate a woman. I just wanted you to know that I don't mind if you want to take it further.'

She pushed back her chair and stood up.

'Max.' Her voice was soft, seductive, almost a croon. 'I like you, I really do. I…' She took a step closer to him.

Max, initially speechless with shock, almost leapt away.

'Marie-Claire!' he yelped. 'Stop this! Stop it at once! How could you! How could you even think, that I, that we…' He shook his head as if trying to shake off something particularly nasty. 'You're like a daughter to me! I've known you since you were a child… I – Marie-Claire, you'd better go. I'm sorry, but this-this is just ridiculous and so very wrong, inappropriate. Just go, please. I'm truly sorry – it was a-a misunderstanding.' He blushed tomato red and turned away.

Marie-Claire gasped. She saw his face, distorted with anger and embarrassment and even revulsion. She let out an agonised cry of deep humiliation, and swung round and rushed out the kitchen door, back out into the white wilderness, back the way she'd come. For the second time that day running away from a man who had rejected her, brought her shame, she plunged back down the road towards the chateau, as fast as the thick crunching snow would allow, and as she ran she felt something dying within her, engulfed by a red-hot sense of humiliation and embarrassment and complete mortification.

Chapter Thirty-Three

Victoire

It might have been the worst Christmas of her life from a political point of view, not to mention from the culinary perspective, but for Victoire it was the best, the happiest.

She was not a pretty girl. Of this she was convinced. Marie-Claire had always been acknowledged to be a beauty, and she was. She looked like a *Vogue* model or, some said, Greta Garbo, and had times been different, she surely would have had such a career, in magazines or on screen. Victoire had always accepted her place in her sister's shadow. It didn't matter. She was not in the least interested in clothes or shoes, and how would a pretty face have helped her enjoy the things she did enjoy: animals, and walking through the forest, camping out with Jacques and fishing in streams? Jacques had taught her to use a slingshot, and she had once missed a rabbit by a hair's breadth.

And her favourite time of year had never been Christmas, but the *vendange* – the wine harvest, that time of year when the skies are vivid blue and the grapes are plump and bursting with nectar, bathed in golden sunshine, and everyone from the surrounding villages and even from further afield, tramps out and into the fields and moves up and down the stocks with their scissors and baskets, and the baskets fill up and are carried piggy-back to be loaded onto the waggons; and the heart sings and every day is a celebration. THAT was Victoire's favourite time of year.

This year, the second harvest since war had been declared, it had all been subdued; many of the younger men were still prisoners of war in Germany, so that there had been a shortage of picking hands, not to mention the grief for those young men who had been killed fighting for the French army, and the mourning of families and friends and communities. A grey cloud of angst had hovered over the event. There had been no celebration; this year, it had been only duty, and then came the invasion of Colmar and the grey cloud had sunk lower and infiltrated hearts and minds, and the boys, their boys, were still in captivity.

So Christmas, this year, had promised to be a subdued thing, a matter of tradition rather than rejoicing. But then Leon and Lucien had returned, and then, today, there was this: Eric.

Because she was not (in her own eyes) pretty, because of her rather masculine tastes in clothes and pre-war activities (after all, which self-respecting girl would spend her weekends camping in the forests, catching fish!), Victoire had not enjoyed what was seen as a normal adolescence and coming-of-age. Where other girls in her school class and from the village primped and preened themselves, and side-eyed boys, and were side-eyed in return, Victoire had found herself walking alone; not exactly excluded from the groups of girls who had been her childhood friends – for she was a friendly girl, liked and even loved by everyone – but unable to join in their conversations, lacking the necessary interests and enthusiasm. She had often wished she was more like Marie-Claire, more feminine; but on the other hand, she *didn't* wish it, because it all seemed such a foreign world. But there it was: she had few close friends, and her extracurricular activities had been farm and garden work. She knew that one day she'd probably marry some neighbour's son and have children of her own, but it wasn't a future she thought about at all, because, after all, for now she was just a plain freckled farm-girl with a wild, tangled mop of hair.

But today, there was Eric. Eric, a handsome young man just a year older than herself, rugged and strong and brave – he had *walked* to Alsace, over the mountains, all the way from Metz! Hiding from Nazis all the way! And had joined the Black Hand, those daring Resistance boys of Strasbourg – and a friend of Jacques besides, which was saying something, because Jacques did not befriend just anybody.

And this Eric had not only called her pretty (he must be blind, or just kind), he had helped her with the most boring domestic duties, clearing the kitchen and washing dishes, and then they had gone for a long walk together, and they had talked and laughed as if they had known each other all their lives. It was extraordinary, a miracle.

And then they had returned to the chateau and chopped wood together, and brought it in and stoked all the fires so that the house stayed warm and inviting for everyone; and she and Eric had sat together in the window-seat in the *salon* and, just as they had been doing all day, talked and laughed and teased each other, and, yes, flirted. Victoire had never known that she even knew *how* to flirt, but there she was, doing it, and he was flirting back, and she could tell; and her heart was full to bursting and this was the best Christmas of her life. And maybe, just maybe, she couldn't be sure, she was falling in love. And maybe – she was even less sure about this, but that *thing* shining in his eyes – almost a voice, it was, and she thought she could read it, but didn't want to presume anything – just maybe, she dared hardly think it, he too was falling in love. With her.

It was too good to be true. A Christmas miracle.

Chapter Thirty-Four

Marie-Claire

Marie-Claire came home, and went straight to her room. She could not bear to meet anyone, and luckily, she did not have to. As she slipped down the hallway she could hear voices in the kitchen and in the *salon*. Everyone seemed to be having a jolly time, soaking in the Christmas spirit that had always evaded her. She had not seen Jacques on the way back; if she had, she'd have found a way to avoid him. He had finished shovelling the snow, though. The road up from the village was still snow-covered, so it seemed a useless endeavour to have shovelled up to the gate and then left it. Usually everyone would pitch in with a shovel so that the way down to the village was clear – but not today.

Up in her room, she collapsed onto her bed, pulled a blanket over herself against the chill and sank into the deep swamp of self-recrimination, blame-assignment, reproach. *Why* had she made a fool of herself? Twice today, in a matter of hours. Before breakfast. Twice, thrown herself at men who categorically rejected her. Rejected *her*. How was that even possible? Rejection was hers to dole out. It was the prerogative of a beautiful woman to be desired and courted; how could she have been so stupid, been so overconfident she had failed to read the signs?

But then, surely it was *their* fault. Something must be very wrong with Jacques. She did not accept the 'I see you as my sister' excuse. He was surely hiding something. Did he have a secret lover, perhaps? But even then, no real man would reject the opportunity she had offered. It was a rejection not only of her body but of her entire self.

And then Max. Max, the ultimate ladies' man. Yes, Max was a bit rough around the edges, but she had a soft spot for that rugged masculinity he exuded; it was the very thing she liked about Jacques, in fact. Sophisticated men were a dime a dozen, even in Colmar, and they were easy to wrap round one's finger. They bored her. But Max – why on earth would an older man like him (he was surely approaching fifty now, like her mother) not jump at the chance of a young and beautiful woman offering herself on a plate? Her cheeks turned hot at the memory. Oh, the humiliation! The degradation!

How could she ever live this down? How could she ever face either of them ever again? What if they spoke of it to each other, or to others in the family, laughed at her, mocked her? She buried her face in her hands and gave out a low, long moan of utter vexation and mortification. How could she ever, *ever* recover her dignity after today? Hold her head up high?

She threw back the blanket and stood up. Paced the room, her hands tucked into her armpits for warmth. She had to think, do something to recover that lost pride. She could not live with such a humiliating defeat. It was a vital necessity that she recover her self-worth, find validation. Now, immediately. She could not live with this gnawing sense of having been spurned, not only by the man she loved (*had once loved,* for she would now expunge that feeling from her heart, come what may; dig it out, tear it to pieces, never let it take root again!), but by a man of the stature of Max Dolch.

She needed to take action. Today. That lost self-possession had to be regained – she had no way of continuing otherwise. She could not live a single day longer with this sense of having been torn into rags. The only way to put this defeat behind her and stand up straight again was to turn it into a victory. Right now. With someone else.

There were three more men in the house: her two brothers and that boy, Eric. He was very handsome, with his dark hair falling over his forehead, and was in possession of that male ruggedness that had always attracted her. Had she been a few years younger, he a few years older, she would certainly have regarded Eric as worthy of her attention. Not overtly, of course – a clever woman was never overt. But she would have played with him, deployed this little feminine wile or that, to elicit his devotion.

Obviously, he was too young for her, more in Victoire's area, but Victoire obviously had nothing to offer, with her wild, unkempt hair, freckles, too-wide mouth and badly-fitting men's clothes. Eric would be a pushover. Young men were hungry for older women, beautiful older women. Such liaisons raised them up. It would be too easy, really, but in the state she was in, he'd have to do – she didn't have much choice. She had to take what was available. A little harmless flirt, that spark of admiration in a man's eyes. That would be enough to recover, just a little, from this morning's disaster. The rest would be set in motion once she returned to Colmar. In Colmar, men were falling over themselves to court her, and she held all the cards. But in today's emergency, Eric would have to do. A plaster on a bleeding wound.

Apart from that, she was feeling the pangs of hunger. She would go down to the kitchen, see what there was to eat (hopefully, Victoire would be around to fry her a fresh egg or two, and maybe even make her a pancake, if there was any flour left over), and then go off in search of Eric.

It was a plan, and it immediately bolstered her flagging pride. She sought the bathroom and splashed cold water on her face to remove the tear-trails and to return the colour to her cheeks. She regarded herself in the mirror over the bathroom sink: she'd need a lick of make-up. Returning to her bedroom, she fixed her face, changed into a less crumpled set of clothes, tidied her hair and made her way to the stairs. It was amazing how a bit of lipstick and rouge could entirely restore a woman's poise. Miraculous.

The old ladies – Aunts Hélène and Sophie – were in the kitchen when she finally came down, sitting at the central table and laughing at something Maman, standing at the stove, stirring a pot, had just said. They all looked round and smiled at her as she entered. Christmas greetings and kisses were exchanged, questions asked about sleep-ins and hunger and desire for coffee. Marie-Claire behaved as expected, smiled and kissed with the requisite serenity and indicated her desire for coffee. It was as ever: a warm cosy kitchen, good cheer, hospitality, everyone relaxed and without a care in the world – if one put aside that one overriding care, the war, of course, a taboo subject today.

She supposed that was how humans managed to survive through hard times. They simply pushed their cares away and pretended they didn't exist. These three women seemed happy enough, though all three carried a lurking anxiety in their hearts. As for her, she had no intention of showing her own inner pain, which had nothing at all to do with the war.

She sipped her coffee and listened to the banter, not really interested, and certainly not participating. *Where was Eric,* she wondered, but could hardly ask. Jacques had said he'd be staying a day or two. Perhaps he was still asleep, in the room he'd shared with Jacques. Where was Jacques, for that matter? She was happy to note that she no longer felt shame. The last remnants of humiliation had miraculously transformed into something else far more worthy: a hardness like armour, outrage, and the need for vengeance. The table conversation swirled outside her bubble of inner strategising, and only at the third, and loudest, call of her name was she shaken out of her reverie.

'Marie-Claire! Will you come too?'

'Huh? What? Come where?'

Margaux sighed. 'Lost in her thoughts, again! Marie-Claire, one day you will get really lost inside that pretty head of yours, and never come back!'

Tatie said: 'Don't tease her, Margaux. Marie-Claire, we wanted to know if you'll come for a walk to the village. Margaux has made a delicious rabbit stew and an apple pie and she is going to visit a few old widows with a hamper of stew and pie, and pears and potatoes, and of course wine. Hélène and I are going with her. Would you like to come along?'

'Oh! Oh, that's very kind. But – well, no, I don't think I'll come. I-I have a bit of a headache.'

'I didn't think so!' said Margaux to the aunts. 'Well, I'll leave this pot to simmer for a while – Victoire will take care of it when she returns. Let's go, ladies. You'll need long boots, the road down to the village is ankle-deep in snow.'

The aunts both rose and set about preparing the baskets. 'Oh, I love tramping through the snow!' said Hélène. 'It reminds me of when I was a girl. We all would come out and clear the road to the village, and then we children would have snowball fights, and…'

The three older women, busy with the packing of hampers, all began to reminisce about the good old days when they were young and the world was whole, and how growing up here among the vines was the most perfect childhood of all, especially in winter – but of course, no comparison to the *vendange* – and how fortunate and blessed they all were, and what a pity the Nazis had to spoil everything – but – oh, we're not going to talk about war today: one day, one day of not remembering the war…

Marie-Claire drifted away on her own thoughts again, and as the others said their goodbyes, she nodded and conveyed her good wishes to the widows they'd be visiting. 'Tell them I'll visit them soon!' she said, though she knew it was a lie. Yes, visiting and helping the old and frail was a convention and ritual that Margaux had installed in all of her children, but those days were long gone; the only one of the four who still did so, Marie-Claire assumed, was Victoire. Victoire, the goody-goody of the family. The angel, the saint.

When the kitchen was finally empty and silent, Marie-Claire stood up. She was still hungry; she still hadn't had breakfast and nobody had offered to make it for her. She'd have enjoyed a fried egg, or even a boiled one, but the egg-basket was empty, and anyway, she had forgotten how long it took to boil an egg. Maman had taught them all, but without practice – well, one forgets such details. She glanced out of the kitchen window, which looked out over the courtyard. Beyond the shed and the hen-pen, she saw them: Victoire and Eric.

There they were, next to the woodpile; Victoire, in her old ugly duffel-coat, as usual, her hair falling out beneath her cap, wielding an axe, holding it high above her head, and laughing her head off, Eric holding up a thick block of wood, laughing as well, pulling away his hands, the axe dropping and the block splitting into two. Eric clapping, Victoire dancing a jig, as if she had achieved some major victory. It was as if her very name gave her the authorisation to chalk up every little thing that happened in her life as well as some wonderful achievement, a victory.

Now here she was, flirting with Eric. As if she had a chance. Just the way she'd flirted with Jacques, and she hadn't even taken that particular defeat seriously. Victoire and Jacques had always been so close, and that irked Marie-Claire. It irked her that Victoire didn't even begin to hide her admiration and love for him. It had always been crystal clear that she wanted him, and Jacques had indulged her in the most obscene manner. Taking her on camping trips into the forest, and the like. He had never asked *her*, Marie-Claire, to go camping. Had he done so, they'd have been a couple long ago. The funny thing was that though Victoire *had* enjoyed such intimacy with Jacques, and still *did*, she didn't seem to mind in the least that it had come to naught; that he treated her, Victoire, with the same annoying platonic equanimity that he did her, Marie-Claire. Well, that was one good thing, at least. It would have been unbearable had Jacques and Victoire become a couple. Not only was she far too young for him, she didn't possess a fraction of her, Marie-Claire's, beauty, and such an outcome would have been a stinging slap in the face. Nevertheless, she had always regarded the two of them with suspicion – and, yes, a mite of jealousy.

Now here was Victoire, behaving with that same boyish over-excitement with Eric. She had obviously set her cap at this new addition to the household. One could almost pity her, so innocent she was of the ways of women. Still basically a child, in spite of her womanly figure. And yes, Marie-Claire did concede that Victoire's figure was excellent, even concealed as it was beneath ill-fitting men's clothes.

She continued to watch them: Eric, with admiring eyes (yes, he'd be a good catch, if a bit young), Victoire, with deep criticism, tinged with an instinctive rancour she didn't understand and couldn't shake off. Victoire was no *competition,* she told herself sternly. She couldn't be – just look at her, a wild thing without a modicum of allure. Victoire had never once worn lipstick, and had never once asked her, Marie-Claire, if she could try hers, just once, the way any normal growing girl would. Marie-Claire snorted. She felt sorry for Victoire. She'd probably end up marrying some boring winemaker's son, but not Jacques, never Jacques.

But, how quickly she had forgotten Jacques! Look at her now, pretending to attack Eric with the axe, laughing as she did so! Surely that was a heavy flirt! What did she think she was… oh! Eric now grabbed the axe, wrenched it – carefully – from Victoire's hand, and – my goodness, no! NO! – he had grabbed Victoire, pulled her to him! His arms round her now, hers round him – and they were kissing! *Kissing!* Standing in the disturbed snow, fragments of wood all around them, oblivious to the world… standing there. Wrapped together, *kissing!*

What on *earth*…?

Chapter Thirty-Five

1941
Victoire

After the exuberance of Christmas, it seemed the chateau could not wait to empty itself and return to its static state of edgy anticipation, always on the edge, always on tenterhooks. Change had come, but they were changes that lent themselves to the holding of breath, a sense of the shifting of circumstances, the clearing of a theatre stage while the next set of props and actors waited in the wings.

Leah and Estelle were no longer in Victoire's care. Just two days after Christmas there'd been a big thaw and Jacques had immediately arranged for their evacuation. He and Eric had taken them over the mountains, returned three days later with news of their safe arrival at a farm near Saint-Dié-des-Vosges, from where they'd progress on their southward flight to Vichy. The route had all been worked out, an escape from safe house to safe house, escorts from towns to village, forged documents – all had been meticulously planned and Jacques was at the centre of it all.

Marie-Claire had been in a hurry to leave, pestering Maman until she, Maman, had agreed to drive her and Aunt Sophie back to Colmar along with the thaw. Aunt Sophie, Victoire thought, would have liked to stay on for a few days but Marie-Claire, in vintage Marie-Claire fashion, had overnight woken out of the state of bored lethargy she had demonstrated through the festivities and proclaimed the urgent necessity to be back at her job; this, even though the *Mairie* was closed until the new year. But, it seemed,

Marie-Claire was one of the skeleton staff urgently and immediately required. Leon and Lucien had taken the opportunity of a lift to Colmar, intending, they said, to travel on to Strasbourg in search of work.

Jacques and Eric, too, had returned to Strasbourg. She missed them, especially Eric, but Jacques had promised they'd be back, and that he'd have more work for her – soon.

As for Eric: just thinking of him brought a smile to her face. So this was how it felt, to be in love, to be loved! A warm, safe centre, like an inner refuge, a place to retreat to when the worry and the fear and the fury got too much to bear. They had spent five wonderful days together, not counting the three days he'd been gone with Jacques. She'd missed him desperately in that time, but the joy she'd felt on his return made up for the agony of being apart. And the knowledge that it was mutual, that he felt the same, missed her and thought about her day and night – it was a new thing for her, a wonderful thing. She had stumbled into love at a time when she'd least expected it, and it had mitigated the sense of emptiness and uselessness that had plagued her ever since the invasion. Now she was not just a *me*, she was part of an *us,* and that made all the difference. But it had now been weeks since she'd seen him, spoken to him. There could be no contact when he was away; she could just hope and long and yearn for his return.

Fortunately, life had offered her a new beginning, a new direction. The year had started well; she had plunged wholeheartedly into the Red Cross training, and now, at last, she had a sense of contributing something, anything, to history, and her inherent impatience was somewhat stilled. She now rose an hour earlier each day to take care of the animals, walked down to the village and took the daily bus to Colmar – or Kolmar, as it had been renamed by the Nazis. Maman had sighed a little, scoffed a little, but in the end consented and even employed a lad and his sister – Pierre and Jeanette – to help Aimee in the house and the yard.

It was as if the whole household had given itself a good shake, thrown off the old year with all its aches and problems, and had started anew, in a state of cautious and expectant waiting. This year, anything could happen. This year, the war would end. This year, France would surely find its heart and its courage and its allies, and repel the virus that had invaded it. How could it possibly be otherwise? Because 'otherwise', a worsening of circumstances, was unthinkable. The time of togetherness over Christmas had brought with it a sense of optimism, optimism founded on nothing more than the overpowering sense that it just could not be. Alsace could not remain in this state of limbo: no longer France, unwillingly claimed by Germany. It could not be. And every night, Victoire knelt at her bedside, closed her eyes tightly, clasped her hands and prayed with every fibre of her being: *Please, please, let us be free again! I will do anything!*

The hallway telephone was ringing. 'I'll get it,' Victoire called to Margaux, who as usual was in her study buried in paperwork. The transition from business dealings with retailers in France to those in Germany was proving more difficult than she'd envisioned; and then there was a constant demand from Nazi officers billeted in Colmar, all of whom required discounts: discounts she could hardly afford in these hard times, yet impossible to refuse, constantly reminded as she was that they could, actually, requisition the whole lot if they so chose and that they were actually doing her a favour. Margaux had always loathed the paperwork of winemaking, yet here she was, buried in accounts, sometimes well into the night.

'Hello?' said Victoire into the receiver, and then, in delight, 'Jacques! How are you? What—'

'Can't say much,' Jacques interrupted. His voice was short and sharp, and Victoire snapped to attention. This was not a social call.

'I'm listening,' she replied.

'Uncle Louis is coming to visit,' said Jacques. 'Do you have a room for him?'

She understood at once. This was the code they had arranged for when and if a Jew needed to be hidden, in case the phone was tapped. This would be the first 'visitor' since Leah had left.

'Yes! Yes, of course! He's very welcome – I look forward to seeing him. It's been ages!'

'Good.' His tone relaxed immediately. 'And I'll come a day later. I'm bringing Juliette with me.'

'Juliette! Oh, my goodness, wonderful! I can't wait to see her!'

'And your *petit ami*.' Her heart lurched.

'You mean…?'

'Yes, of course I mean him. We'll be there in two days. Goodbye.'

Typical of Jacques: his deep distrust of modern amenities, as well as a wariness, a suspicion that German spies were hiding round every corner and listening to every conversation, meant that telephone conversations were always reduced to just the bare essentials. For Jacques, a telephone was a shortcut that speeded up the exchange of essential information, no more, no less. He disdained its use for any kind of useless exchange of pleasantries, unlike Victoire. But the curt information she'd just received was enough. She knocked on the door to Margaux's office and put her head round it.

'What are you grinning at? You look like a Cheshire cat,' said Margaux, looking up from her ledger.

'Jacques is coming, and Juliette, and Eric!'

The frown melted from Margaux's face. 'Really! When?'

'He said in two days.'

'We'll need some flour. And butter. Jacques and Juliette both have ration cards, so that's fine. You'll look after that, won't you?'

'Of course!'

'And you must be happy that Eric is coming back!'

'Oh, Maman! Yes! I'm happy!'

She skipped over to her mother, bent over to plant a kiss on her cheek. Margaux reached up, cupped a hand around her daughter's head, rubbed it, smiled.

'First love is a beautiful thing, and Eric is a good boy. I'm happy for you.'

'Oh, and Jacques said we'd have a visitor. For the cellar, I mean. A man, apparently.'

Margaux's forehead creased again.

'Did he now! Well, then, we need even more food, and whoever it is, he won't have a ration card. So remember that. It's back to walking on eggshells and alarms, and you'll be the main carer again. We can't let Pierre, Jeanette and Aimee know, so be careful. And…'

They spoke for a while on the minutiae of keeping a refugee hidden in the wine cellar, and then Victoire went out to secure the hens in their coop, still smiling. It had been weeks since she'd seen Eric. It was time.

Two days later she was in the kitchen, reading, after a long and busy day, the kitchen being the warmest room in the house. It was late, Maman had already gone to bed. The book she was reading was a medical one; she had struck up a friendship with one of the doctors she trained with, and he had lent it to her. It was called *A Textbook of Medical and Surgical Emergencies*, and she found it fascinating, inspiring and depressing all at once. This damned war! Were it not for the war she could have finished her schooling and, perhaps, gone on to be a proper nurse. Or even a doctor. One of her trainers was a female doctor. They did exist. Were it not for the war, she could have continued, uninterrupted, along that path. But war was the reality, and this course was all that was available to her at this time. Perhaps the war would end this year, and she could pick up the pieces of her life where she had dropped them, and set off on something bigger, better. As it was, this was all she could do. She sighed, and turned the page.

'Oh!' Startled, she dropped the book; it crashed to the floor. A sudden knock on the door, loud, confident, brash, like a gunshot; her heart bounced, her breath stopped and she leapt to her feet. Three sharp knocks. She waited, and then relaxed. They came again, those three sharp knocks, and then a third time. The signal. It must be Jacques. Jacques, and Eric…

She flew to the door, turned the key, opened it, and was about just about to cry his name; instead, a second *Oh* came out, surprised and disappointed. It wasn't Eric and Jacques who stood just beyond the doorway, but a tall, hollow-cheeked young man, a man she had never seen before.

He spoke: 'Monsieur Michaud would like to order three cases of Pinot Noir.'

She relaxed. The reply to the password was 'Unfortunately we have no more Pinot Noir. I can offer you a dry Riesling instead.'

They both smiled, then. She stepped aside to allow the young man to enter. He removed the woollen cap that hid his forehead and she saw that despite the pallor of his face and his haggard expression his eyes were wide and bright, and his smile was warm and embracing.

'I am Nathan,' he said. 'Jacques must have told you I would come.'

'Yes. Yes, he did. Come, sit down. Let me make you some coffee, and we have some bread, and some cheese – you must be hungry! You have come from Strasbourg, I believe.'

'Yes, yes, from Strasbourg, and all on foot. And I can only move at night. Fortunately, there are enough hospitable people who helped me on my way.'

'We have a room for you. You can stay as long as you need. Unfortunately, it is underground, behind the wine cellar, so it is dark, but for that reason it never gets too cold.'

'Underground is good. I have been in an attic up till now and that can be freezing. Of course, one must choose between them: cold and light, or warm and dark.'

'Well, it's not actually warm, just not cold. But very dark, I'm afraid. But I expect you won't be staying long. Jacques and Eric are coming and I suppose then they will help you escape over the mountains.'

But he shook his head. 'No. I am not here to escape. We have other plans, but I think it is better if Jacques explains it all to you.'

'Other plans?'

He nodded. 'I am one of Jacques' *Maquis* team. I have been working with him for many months now. And with Juliette.'

'Juliette? Juliette Dolch? Jacques' sister?'

He nodded. 'Yes. She too is part of the team. She is my friend. My close friend, if you understand.'

'You – and Juliette? And you are Jewish? Oh, my goodness! I never knew, she never told me…'

'Of course not, she has not seen you for a long time and it has all been very clandestine and dangerous. But now – well, they are all coming and you will see. Jacques is holding a meeting with all of us.'

'With me too?'

He nodded. 'You too, Victoire. You are to be part of the team. We have a plan, and you are to be part of it, and that's why we are meeting now. In a few days. When Jacques comes.'

In fact, Jacques came the very next day, bringing Juliette with him, and Eric arrived the following day. Victoire became aware of something big, something grand, something vital coalescing around her, and she was a part of it. Unaware still of the details, there was an atmosphere of conspiracy, formless yet, and optimism in the chateau. Maman, aware of it, kept a distance yet kept a protective watch over them all, like a mother hen spreading open a wing to enfold her precious young.

'I trust you,' she said. 'Do good. But don't tell me.'

Once Eric had arrived, Jacques called a meeting, to be held in Nathan's cellar, at night. And under the dim glow of the dusty light bulb, Jacques spoke.

'It's time,' he said, 'the war is not going to end this year, and probably not next year. We all thought it would be over by now but as we know now, it's worse. All of us here: we are young, and our futures are at stake, the futures of all Alsatians and all the French and all Europeans, of the whole world, because Hitler will never stop if we don't stop him. So, we have to stop him. That's what I've been working on over the last year. This has to be better organised.

'I've been working with various groups with just that aim, and now we have our own little group – this one, within the family. I'll get back to that, talk about us and what we're going to do, but first, this: we are working on many levels, in many ways, and this meeting is to let you all know what your roles are, and how we can work together and separately. For me, it started with the Black Hand, the Resistance boys in Strasbourg. Their work will continue, but I've taken it upon myself to expand, to bring it down here to the Haut-Rhin and, especially, Colmar. I am working at building up the *Maquis* here; finding young men willing and able, and organising their actions. Nathan is going to be my right-hand man in that, coordinating the action, but he cannot stay here, it is too rural. Right now, Nathan, I'm trying to find a suitable hideout for you in Colmar. As soon as I've found it, you will move there from Strasbourg.

'Juliette, you will be a courier. As a woman, you can move more freely and are less likely to be arrested. There's just one problem: your hair.'

'My hair? Why should it be…?'

'It's too conspicuous; too long, too black. You look Jewish. Didn't that soldier accuse you of being Jewish on the very first day of the invasion? Don't they keep stopping you, asking for papers?'

'Yes, but…'

'I'm sorry, we can't risk it. You can't wear it loose, and you can't spend time on hairstyles. You'll have to cut your hair, Juliette. I'm sorry. You'll be a better *maquisard* with short hair.'

All eyes turned to Juliette. She was not a vain person, but everyone in the cellar knew that her hair was her one weakness. Juliette loved her hair. Everyone loved Juliette's hair. People stared at Juliette's hair, longed to touch it, to stroke it, run their fingers through it, hold strands of it up and watch how it would cascade from their fingers, ribbons of it snaking out of their grasp to fall in satisfying silken bands. Juliette doused her hair in herbs – rosemary and nettle – to retain its strength and its shine. She brushed it steadfastly to maintain its health and that of her scalp. She carefully tended its ends, snipping them if they split and wrapping them in warm herbal poultices to keep them strong. She washed her hair with a home-made lemon shampoo that balanced the oils; not too frequently, just often enough to remove excess oil and dust. Even now, after weeks of living rough, Juliette's hair shone as if it had been pampered by a Parisian coiffeur. Beyond the careful snipping of ends, she had never cut it. And it was black, so deeply black. Its sleek blackness was the epitome of its splendour.

Juliette gulped. She and Nathan looked at each other, exchanged a silent message. And then she met Jacques' gaze with steady and steadfast compliance. The hesitation was less than a second.

'*Oui*,' said Juliette. 'I will do it.'

'Thank you,' said Jacques, and moved on. 'So, that's that. We will discuss the details later. The next area of our work – well, this is where Eric comes in. And you, Victoire.'

He looked from one to the other, and they both nodded. They were sitting next to each other on folded blankets, holding hands. Eric squeezed hers.

'You've already started, actually. This work involves the evacuation of Jews from Alsace. As we know, not all of them left early this year when they were called to do so, and those that remained are now in grave danger. We have to remove them. We've already got Leah and Estelle out of Alsace, thanks to you two. But there are more, and they are all over the place. I'm in touch with a Jewish organisation based in England that has found safe houses in France and a safe route to Vichy, and is taking care of the financing of such flights. Here in Alsace, we have to build up a network of safe houses and help them to get here. Victoire, you will look after them until their escape route is set up and Eric can take them over the mountains. You understand?'

'But—' Victoire was about to protest, but Jacques pre-empted her.

'Victoire, I know you want to do the escorting. I know you are capable. I know you know the way, even better than Eric does… but no. You are only fifteen, still a child – no, don't deny it, because it is true – and I have a responsibility towards you. I have promised your mother; so, no. Your time will come. One day you will be a hero.'

Chapter Thirty-Six

Marie-Claire

It was good to be back in Colmar, a world away from the stuffiness and stodginess of the chateau. It was good to be back at work, to know that she was useful and appreciated and admired. And now, after the mortifications of the Christmas season, it was absolutely necessary for her emotional well-being. She could look back on the last few days only with a shudder. She had almost died of humiliation – rejected by two men, and upstaged by Victoire – *Victoire* of all women! – over a third. It was beyond crushing. It was death: the death of her confidence and self-esteem, a complete devaluation of her worth. Yes, a little death. Something had to be done.

Up to now, she had lived in two spheres: one foot still firmly stuck in the past, in the old familiar orbit of the chateau, which had extended to Colmar in the form of Tante Sophie. The other foot, or rather, her entire existence, had moved on and into the future, into the Era Germanica, as confirmed by her workplace, the *Mairie*. This was the reality. Maman and the rest of the family might reject it all they wanted, but history had moved on, and they had to be on the right side of it, move on with history. They were all still stuck in the past. She was already being pulled into the present and the future, and the last little bit of her old self had to be unstuck. Yes, that dreadful book *Mein Kampf* had shocked her, but it could be dismissed as the ramblings of a madman. Other people were sane, the people actually driving this forward, like the people she worked with. The first thing she did, on returning to work, was to request to move in with the German secretaries, in the house they shared on the rue Stanislas.

'But of course!' said Ursula, a big blond girl who had always courted friendship with Marie-Claire. All the German girls were friendly towards her, unlike the Alsatian women she had worked with previously. Marie-Claire knew exactly the reasons behind her popularity: on the one hand, as the *Kreisleiter*'s chosen personal assistant, she was ranked the highest and thus had, among the girls, the most influence within the *Mairie*. It was plain that the *Kreisleiter* trusted and appreciated her, and it was in everyone's interest to be associated with her.

The second reason was more personal.

These women, Ursula in particular, lacked that certain *je ne sais quoi* that Marie-Claire exuded from the tips of her fingers to the bounce of her hair and the bow of her lips and the long sweep of her eyelashes. Ursula was big-boned and inelegant in an indefinable way. She tried so hard, too hard. Like all the German girls she had access to cosmetics and clothes, unlike the French, and yet she could not throw off the aura of frumpiness. Paris chic was the pinnacle of achievement for these women, but Marie-Claire was the only one who actually embodied it, and she knew it.

She also knew this advantage could go two ways. It could cause jealousy and antagonism. It could also go in the opposite direction: obsequiousness. In the weeks before Christmas, while Marie-Claire was working at establishing her position within the *Mairie*, she had opted for a neutral stance: neither encouraging the would-be sycophants nor giving the would-be opponents cause for alarm. She had remained aloof, courteous but distant. There was always Jacques, lurking there at the ground of her consciousness, luring her back into the family fold. Jacques, and that impossible love that somehow, some day, could be made possible. Jacques, the ultimate goal. And so Marie-Claire had kept her options open, hoping, dreaming, and at Jacques' request, even spying. For him.

No longer. Jacques had dealt her a blow from which there could be no recovery, and this catapulted her into a new life. Marie-Claire had made her choice. Alsace was now German and it was not only futile to resist, it was dangerous. Her way forward was clear.

And so, on her second day back in Colmar, Marie-Claire moved into the house on the rue Stanislas and accepted the friendship of Ursula, Gertrud, Klara and Erika. It was a new beginning, a radical new life. It basically meant a parting of the ways, the rejection of her home and family – for there could be no compromise, the disapproval from that quarter would be absolute and final – while she forged forward boldly into this new world.

The girls accepted her into their fold with not a single reservation; it was as if they had been only waiting, eagerly anticipating this new, classy member of their clan. That first evening they cooked for her, a German potato dish they called *Schupfnudeln*. Her own contribution to the meal was a bottle of Château Gauthier-Laroche Riesling she had helped herself to from Tante Sophie's cellar. (And no, it wasn't stealing. She had a *right* to her mother's wines.)

There was only enough for one glass each with a top-up, but it was enough to loosen everyone's tongue and raise the general mood, and soon she was laughing and joking with them all as if they were long-lost friends.

The conversation, of course, swirled around the obvious: the girls were eager to know how and where from Marie-Claire was in possession of such stylish Paris fashions. She told her story, and they *oohed* and *aahed* over her almost *divine* good fortune at having a father in Paris who could be of such help in keeping her up to date, through the regular delivery of *Vogue* and the coincidentally named *Marie-Claire*.

'No, of course I wasn't named after the magazine! It was named after *me*!' said Marie-Claire, and they all roared with laughter, and Marie-Claire promised to somehow get hold of her collection of copies from the chateau and donate them to the house. 'And some more wine!' she promised. 'We need more wine!'

They all agreed, of course, and Marie-Claire frowned for a minute, raking her brain for a way to get hold of said items; could she smuggle herself into the house one day, and take them? She still had a key, after all… The main problem was finding transport to the chateau; she'd need a car, as she couldn't possibly bring everything back on a bus.

'Oh, that's easy!' said Klara. 'I'll just ask Franz. He can use one of the officers' jeeps.'

All eyes turned to Klara. It was well known that she had been stepping out with a Wehrmacht lieutenant, and the other girls were curious.

'Really? He'd do that for you?' asked Gertrud. 'I mean, it's a bit frivolous, isn't it, and not *your* things he'd be fetching.'

Klara blushed. 'Well, actually, he owes me a favour, you see. I've decided to be a bit more… generous.'

All the girls tittered and teased. 'Go on, tell us more! What are you up to? Did you let him…?'

But Klara only smiled enigmatically. 'Get your own officer, girls, and don't be so nosey! All I can say is: that film on at the Gloria – *Wer küßt Madeleine?* – is – well, how shall I put it? Quite inspiring, if you get what I mean!'

They all laughed and whooped. Klara was the prettiest of the lot. She wore her long blond hair in milkmaid braids wrapped around her head, and her eyes were a charming shade of dark green. She was petite, the very opposite of Gertrud, and before Marie-Claire's acceptance into the house the acknowledged beauty among the German secretaries, as well as the one most likely to challenge Marie-Claire's own standing. She, Marie-Claire, had recognised a certain glint in Klara's eyes, which she interpreted as on the brink of hostility. She'd have to tread carefully here, but she knew exactly how to win Klara for herself.

While the other girls joked and teased Klara and discussed the officers they had their eyes on, and who was flirting with whom

(Nazi officers, they had all ascertained by now, were actually, at heart, all quite ordinary red-blooded men, no different from the farmers' sons and bank clerks of civilian life they had all dealt with adequately in their hometowns and villages), Marie-Claire remained silent and her eyes narrowed. She watched Klara, with a smile carefully adjusted to demonstrate benevolence and magnanimity. She was thinking. Finally, she spoke, and the other girls immediately fell silent and listened.

'Klara,' said Marie-Claire, 'I have quite a bit of make-up in the chateau, which I don't use any more. My father sent it from Paris – you know, bits and pieces discarded by models and such. Also, some clothes and shoes I don't wear any more. Granted, none of the latest fashions – even Papa can't get hold of those – but some quite lovely dresses, skirts, blouses. I can fetch those as well, and you – well, all of you…' (here, she made a sweeping gesture to ensure everyone was included) '…might like to have a look? I know how such things are difficult to get hold of in these hard times, and I know how lucky I am to have a father in Paris, who has connections. So, I'd love to share.'

The excitement those words produced – well, if Marie-Claire had ever doubted her admission into the closed circle of German secretaries, or feared their rejection – such doubts and fears were immediately abolished by a volley of squeals and whoops and even, surprisingly, hugs. She smiled smugly to herself. Really, vanity, she thought, is the easiest portal to a woman's heart. (But then she remembered other women she knew. Victoire. Maman. Juliette. And a slight scowl nipped at her lips, but only for a fraction of a second – those women didn't count.)

The conversation, quite naturally, progressed to the other officers, the higher-uppers, the ones beyond reach. Some of these were married, and lived with their wives here in Colmar. But some were single, and, the consensus filtered through, there was no more desirable outcome to this rather drab Colmar posting than to nab a senior officer, a military man or a political one, not just for a kiss at the back of the cinema, or a fumble against a wall in a narrow, cobbled Colmar *Gasse,* but for marriage. Marriage was the firmament, the starry sky above. And not too unattainable; after all, surely these men were lonely, and surely the whores in the *Rote Löwe* could not satisfy all their longings? Didn't the *Führer* himself recommend marriage and progeny? Surely these men were looking for wives, and surely they, yes, *they,* the ladies of number 19 rue Stanislas, were in prime position for such a promotion?

Who were the unmarried among these men? And who were the most obvious targets? And who were the opposite: the unassailable?

And of the latter, one stood out, head and shoulders above the other. The *Kreisleiter,* Marie-Claire's own personal boss: Dietrich Kurtz.

'I'm sure if anyone could win him, it's you, Marie-Claire!' That was Ursula, the most sycophantic of all the girls, who looked on Marie-Claire with glazed and adoring eyes.

Marie-Claire laughed and shook her head. 'He's not a man, he's a robot!' she said. 'He's probably even a virgin – impossible to imagine him with a woman. Just the sight of him makes you think of a machine rather than a man.'

'Ah, but that's what makes him so interesting!' said Erika. 'Me, I love a challenge, but unfortunately, I'm modest enough to know I lack the kind of allure necessary to break that armour. Now you, Marie-Claire…'

'Me? You must be joking. I wouldn't touch him with a bargepole. He's old, for one, and ugly.' Jacques' face, unsummoned, rose in her mind's eye, but she quickly pushed it away.

'He's not *that* old,' said Gertrud. 'Only about forty or so.'

The cries poured in:

'He's at least fifty.'

'He doesn't have grey hair, so that can't be true.'

'I'd bet he's around forty-five, give or take a year.'

'That's still much too old for me. I'm not even twenty-one yet!'

'But older men are more stable, reliable.'

'He's not that ugly, either!'

'*Only* forty-five? That's old enough to be my father!'

'If only he would smile, once. You can't tell if a man is really ugly until he smiles. A smile makes nearly anybody beautiful.'

'Ha! Not even a smile would make him attractive. He's got an ugly mind. He goes through life mentally spitting on everything. Everything for him is rubbish or nonsense or bunkum or humbug.'

'Oh, absolutely! He's the King of Humbug. *Bockmist. Scheisse. Wahnwitz. Blödsinn.* His favourite words, from the horse's mouth.'

Erika giggled. 'King Shit. *König Scheisse.* Let's call him that.'

'No, that's too explicit. We need to be subtle. Something else. Something funny.'

They all spoke at once, giggling and offering up suggestions. Prince Rubbish. Lord Twaddle. General Gobbledygook. But it was Marie-Claire who came up trumps. '*Graf Koks,*' she offered. 'Count Nonsense.'

Applause and giggles all round. 'That's it! Definitely!'

Marie-Claire frowned. 'But it's not complete. We need a *von*. *Von*-somewhere. He's aristocracy, remember.'

Suggestions poured in, among much hilarity. Graf Koks von Berchetsgaden. Von Mückenloch. Von Zufenhausen. But to each suggestion, Marie-Claire shook her head. 'No. It has to have that certain… I don't know. A certain *rhythm.*'

'Graf Koks von Schmerlenbach?' offered Erika.

'Yes! That's it exactly!'

'Where's Schmerlenbach?' asked Gertrud. Marie-Claire shrugged. 'It doesn't matter, does it? It sounds good.'

'It's a village in Bavaria,' said Erika. 'Where I grew up.'

'Well, it's perfect,' said Marie-Claire. Erika giggled. 'Graf Koks von Schmerlenbach. Yes! Now, let's see if he's as unassailable as you claim. I mean, I did try once, you know. Flirted with him before your promotion. He didn't react. He's immune to feminine charms.'

'I bet I could get a reaction, if I really tried,' said Marie-Claire.

Klara sniffed. 'Well, go on then, prove it! I challenge you, Marie-Claire. To find out if he's got red blood running in his veins, or ice.'

Marie-Claire swung round to look at Klara. Her eyes narrowed, and she slowly smiled. The room fell silent as everyone waited for her response. The words 'he's old and ugly' hung in that silence. But still, a challenge was a challenge. Marie-Claire licked her lips. She remembered her recent defeats where her seductive powers over men were concerned. She had largely recovered her lost equanimity, but still. Something still rankled. She smiled.

'Challenge accepted!' she said. 'Give me a month.'

They all cheered.

'But,' Marie-Claire added, 'it's only a joke, remember. All I need is a reaction. Of some kind. I don't really want him.'

Words she would one day have to eat.

Chapter Thirty-Seven

For the first time in her adult life, Marie-Claire could say she had friends. The German secretaries closed her into their fold as if she had never been outside of it. They liked her, they opened themselves to her, they respected her. There was nothing – almost nothing – she couldn't talk about with them. They were on the same – she searched for the right word – the same *frequency*. Whereas at home, at school, in the family, she had always felt like the odd one out, the alien, the one nobody understood, while they were all tuned in to each other. That's how it felt now: tuned in. Most especially, these women *understood* her. At home, everyone had disparaged and mocked her vision of a future life in Paris. Here, they shared it. Furthermore, obviously, nobody here disparaged her for working with the enemy – they *were* the enemy, after all, from an Alsatian point of view.

As promised, Klara's Franz had driven her out to the chateau last Saturday, at a time she knew Maman would be out making deliveries. There was a risk she'd run into Victoire or one of her brothers, but it was a risk she chose to take. It was quickly done. The magazines packed into a suitcase, a quick selection of dresses, skirts and blouses from the wardrobe packed into another suitcase, a drawer of make-up and perfumes emptied into a canvas bag, and *voilà* – she was ready to go. She grabbed the two suitcases, slung the bag over her shoulder and clattered down the stairs.

Just as she reached the downstairs hall the kitchen door opened and Jacques stepped into her path. She stopped dead in her tracks

– but only for a moment. She brushed past him without a word. It was he who spoke.

'Marie-Claire! Wait a moment! Where are you going?'

She marched down the hall towards the front door, not deigning to answer. He hurried behind her, grabbed an elbow, stopped her in her tracks. 'What's the matter, Marie-Claire? Talk to me!'

That's when she did talk. She glared at him. 'I have nothing to say! Let me go!'

'I will. I will, Marie-Claire but – but what about your work? You know what I mean. It's so important – when can you get the next spool?'

'Spool? You must be joking! You don't really think I'm going to still risk playing that game? Who do you think I am?'

'I think you're my friend, I think you're a citizen of Alsace, and you want to help!'

'Well, you can think again. It's over, Jacques. Goodbye.' She wrenched her arm free, and he loosened his grip to let her go. He called after her: 'Goodbye, Marie-Claire. I wish you all the best.' But he said it to her back as she put down one suitcase for a moment, opened the front door, picked it up again and fled out to the waiting jeep. She flung the bags into the back of the jeep and settled into the passenger seat.

'Whew! That's done! Let's go!'

Franz grinned at her. 'You sound like you're escaping prison!'

'I am, Franz, I am! You can't imagine!'

Nobody could imagine. They couldn't imagine the wild pounding of her heart as she made her escape, a breakneck, almost audible hammering, and it didn't let up until she was safe at home in the rue Stanislas. That was it, then. She was free. Jacques behind her, completely and forever.

A pity, though, she had not, as planned, been able to nip back into the house and down to the cellar to retrieve a crate of wine. That was her only regret. It had been good, seeing the look on Jacques' face as she'd spat out her last words.

The girls were delighted with her Parisian trophies. They giggled in delight as she raised one dress after the other, held them up to their shoulders, advised them on what suited whom and which colour dress went best with which colour hair. Ursula alone was disappointed, as everything was too small for her; but then, Ursula was the least likely to metamorphise into that vision of Paris female perfection they all strove for. She knew it and she accepted it graciously, content with admiring the others and offering opinions. 'You are all so beautiful!' she sighed. 'You will take Paris by storm! Me – well, I suppose I'll have to make do with good old Ernest in Stuttgart.' Ernest being her childhood family friend, with whom a family 'understanding' of marriage had been long arranged.

But that night, they would all – including Ursula – be going to the officers' dance at one of the larger Colmar houses, and for once, appropriately dressed, they would shine.

Now, the dance behind them, with every passing day Marie-Claire felt more at home. The cloud of boredom that had settled around her when she'd lived with Aunt Sophie dispelled forever. Here, there was never a dull moment. When she wasn't chattering with the girls she was teaching them French – they had insisted, it was preparation for their Paris debut – or they were clustered around the radio, listening to the evening news.

That was the part Marie-Claire enjoyed the least. The politics. What a pity that politics followed her wherever she went; she wished radios could be un-invented. Back at the chateau, it had been clandestine sessions with the BBC, obsessively followed by her mother and sister; she had always escaped whenever she heard those five pips introducing the news.

Here, it was the *Volksempfänger*, people's receiver, they gathered around each evening. It was almost a religious ritual, and just as with the church services she had been forced to attend while growing up, Marie-Claire knew she could not excuse herself without raising eyebrows, and even sanctions; here, the disapproval of her new friends.

They were all so enthusiastic. Marie-Claire, determined to maintain her neutral stance regarding the war and its controversial leader, found it almost impossible to shut her ears to the strident messages delivered over the air with stunting regularity and irritating pomposity. How could the girls listen to that rot? It was deadening, but she was obliged to nod and smile with them as they enthused over Germany's progress in the war. The talk was all 'when the war is over and Germany has triumphed'. Yes, she too was keen for it all to be over, for Paris to shake off the shadows of the present and emerge again, shiny and new. Paris would always be Paris, whatever government ruled France. Its spirit could not be vanquished. Marie-Claire only longed for it to be over. Talk of war and battles won and bombs and air raids seemed only to push that date into a distant future. But what could she do? The girls loved talking about German triumphs, and listening in and pretending to enthuse was the price she had to pay to be one of them.

Yet still, the subject closest to everyone's heart, the one that created the most buzz, was the immanent seduction (only in theory, Marie-Claire reminded them all) of Graf Koks von Schmerlenbach. That good man, however, was still not back from his Christmas holiday. Still, they could talk about him, and Marie-Claire could prepare and practise her tactics. She had already started, by leaving the top buttons of her blouse unbuttoned. She could hardly wait for his return.

Chapter Thirty-Eight

Victoire

Juliette closed her eyes, squeezed them tight, placed her hands over them for extra protection.

'Go ahead. I'm ready.'

Victoire, standing behind her, open scissors in one hand and a long silken strand of black hair in the other, still hesitated.

'You're sure? Quite sure?'

'Yes, dammit. Just do it. Snip snap.'

And Victoire did it. Closed the blades on the hair, and her fingers over the amputated hair, before it fell to the floor.

'It's done,' she sighed. 'No going back now.'

'Just get it over with, Victoire. I'm past caring.'

'I know you're not, Juliette, because why're your eyes still closed?'

Juliette immediately dropped her hands and opened her eyes. 'There! Happy now?'

Victoire had already cut a second strand, placing each length of hair carefully on the bed beside her. She chuckled.

'You can't see anyway, seeing as there isn't a mirror!'

'Yes, it's more hearing than seeing, isn't it! And feeling. I can feel it, you know. Feel the scissors cutting. I think my hair has nerves.'

'I know it must, the way you've taken care of it. It's such a pity. You're so brave.'

Juliette swiped the air in dismissal.

'This isn't brave. Brave is going out there, facing up to those Nazi devils, defeating them. Brave is Nathan, not running away but staying to fight them. Brave is facing the terror in your heart and going after them anyway. Nothing brave about cutting off your hair. That's just overcoming vanity.'

'I know, I know. And I know I've a long way to go. I just wish—'

'No, Victoire. You're brave too, doing what you're doing. Anyway. Let me have a look…'

She held out her hand, and Victoire placed a long ribbon of hair in it.

Juliette sighed. 'Now that it's done, it doesn't feel so bad any more. I'll keep it. Who knows, maybe it'll be useful for something.'

'I've heard they make wigs out of real human hair. You should definitely keep it.' Victoire continued to cut in silence.

At last she said, 'That's it, then. Short hair. I don't think *coiffeuse* is a profession for me, but it's done, and doesn't look too bad. You won't recognise yourself!'

'Ah well. I'll still be the same inside, and Nathan will recognise me.'

Later that evening, Jacques dropped by.

'Eric's back from Colmar,' he said. 'It's all arranged. It's a seamstress called Madame Delacroix, and she's going to put you up in her basement, Nathan. It's a bit better than this place, with a small window so you'll have a little daylight. She's happy to help. Her best friend was Jewish and was evacuated. She's furious about it. And she knows your mother.'

'Yes, I know her,' said Nathan. 'Maman was a customer from when I was a little boy. It's on the rue Stanislas, isn't it?'

'That's right. You can move in tomorrow, she says.'

Juliette frowned. 'And I? Where should I go? Have you spoken to Tante Sophie? Can I stay with her?'

'You could. But, Juliette…'

'But, what?'

'I don't want you to stay in Colmar. I need to separate you two for a while.'

'But why? Why can't I stay in Colmar, with Nathan?'

'It's because you're known in Colmar. People will notice your changed hair; they'll talk about you. It's one thing to fool the Nazis but you won't be able to fool those you've grown up with in Colmar. Besides, you're needed elsewhere. I need you to go back to Mount Mount Louise, to Natzwiller, and stay there for a while.'

Juliette and Nathan exchanged a glance.

Juliette was silent as she digested all this. Finally, she nodded. 'If you say so, Jacques. But can you tell us why? Have you found out what's going on there?'

Jacques nodded. 'Yes, we know. Thanks to Marie-Claire. You know she was working for me?'

Juliette nodded. 'I was wondering. Has she backed away? I heard she spent all of Christmas in a sulk. I haven't seen her in ages. What's she up to? She seems to have cut ties with the family completely.'

Jacques nodded. 'Unfortunately, yes. She's gone off on a tangent. She came home today to get her things, sneaked into the house and ran off with two full suitcases. In a Nazi jeep. It's very worrying.'

'Oh my! So she's changed sides? That's terrible! You don't think she'd…? She knows so much already!'

The word betrayal hung in the air, but Jacques shook his head. 'I don't want to accuse her of changing sides. She works for them, that's all – administrative work. It doesn't mean she's turned into a Nazi. It's just a job, she said.'

'But what if she tells them about us? About you? She knows you're a *maquisard,* Jacques. What if she betrays you?' There. The word had been spoken, out loud.

But Jacques shook his head. 'She won't go that far. I know Marie-Claire. She's the most apolitical person on earth – she truly doesn't care. She just does what's best for herself. And right now, that's working for the Germans in the *Mairie*, Nazi or not. Betraying us, betraying me, would not be to her advantage, so she wouldn't do it.'

'That's a horrible thing to say, Jacques! So you think she's selfish enough to betray you, if she thought it would be to her advantage? Is she that calculating?'

Jacques shrugged. 'Of course, we can't know for sure. I'll admit she's a risk – but a minor one. Her decision to work for me, for us – it was personal rather than political.'

'But what if the Nazis she works with, what if *they* offer her personal reasons? A promotion, for example, or some other perk? Would she betray you then?'

He shrugged again, and made a dismissive hand-gesture, waving her doubts aside.

'Marie-Claire is a law unto herself. I admit that I'm offering her the benefit of the doubt; I can't believe, I really can't believe, that she'd put her own family in jeopardy, and she knows very well, or suspects, that Margaux, too, is involved. If she'd wanted to betray us, she'd have done it by now. No. No, she's not that self-serving.'

'Why did she stop working for you?'

'It's complicated.'

'Was she of any use at all?'

Jacques hesitated before answering. 'She was of immense help. The information she was able to hand over – it was tremendous.' He paused again. 'It actually concerns you both – you especially, Juliette. That's where you come in. That's why I want you back on Mount Louise.' He paused again, thinking.

'Well, now you've said that much you'll have to tell us the rest.'

'Yes, I see that. It's about the Nazi activities up there, at Natz-willer. I now know what they're up to. And it's not good.'

'Yes?'

'It's for a labour camp. There's a granite mine near there, excavation work to be done, and they need workers. They're going to use political prisoners to do the work. And the terraces you saw – that's where they're going to be housed. Mount Louise itself has always been a ski resort; it was called Le Struthof, but now it's going to be called *Konzentrationslager Natzweiler*. That's the information we have.'

'A camp, so high up in the mountains? That's strange,' said Juliette.

'Well, I've done some investigation. There's method to the madness. It all started when Colonel Blumberg, a friend of Heinrich Himmler – you know who that is, don't you? One of Hitler's top henchmen – was made mayor of Schirmeck, a small mountain town near Natzwiller. They got rid of the old mayor and installed this Nazi big shot. Now that was strange. Why? All was revealed in the information Marie-Claire provided, which was mainly correspondence between himself and the *Gauleiter* in Strasbourg.

'Blumberg's mission was to find a site suitable for the construction of a labour camp near the granite quarry up there in the mountains. The goal is to extract and cut blocks of granite. Out of that granite, magnificent palaces and grand edifices are to be built all over Germany, all for the glorification of Hitler and the Third Reich. It's to be a new Renaissance, a grandiose undertaking reflecting all the megalomania our dear *Führer* is known for.

'And… to preserve precious German men for more noble causes – you can guess what those causes are – they needed cheap labour. And so, they need a so-called labour camp to provide workers for the quarry. It's a simple as that. They found this place: Le Struthof, a picturesque and charming site, 700 metres high, where the good citizens of Strasbourg can go skiing in winter and walking in summer, for a healthy, relaxing holiday among pine forests, meadows and mountains, far away from the spectre of war, beautiful scenery thrown in as an extra. Perfect for Nazi needs. Our friend Blumberg was delighted. Specialists came to measure, survey, draw up plans, excavate, expropriate, requisition everything. Struthof has become a nest of Nazis. That's what you witnessed when you were up there, Juliette.'

'So basically, a prison camp?'

Jacques nodded. 'I presume for Jews. Or anyone who crosses the Nazi regime. Political dissidents. Resisters. You and me.'

He looked from one to the other. 'We don't know yet who will be incarcerated there. We only know it's being built.'

A pregnant pause followed. Jacques had always had this sense of the dramatic. Juliette could almost hear the drum roll, the thumping of her heart. He wasn't finished. She knew her brother well.

'And…?'

'And guess what? Marie-Claire's immediate boss, a grim Nazi officer called Dietrich Kurtz, the *Kreisleiter* for this region, is headed for a top administration post when the camp is up and running.'

'Does Marie-Claire know all this?'

'No, of course not. She's just the courier who delivered the information to us. That's her only role. *Was* her only role, as far as we're concerned; looks like that source has dried up, no more information will be coming our way. Marie-Claire continues as his secretary, but she knows nothing.'

Juliette and Nathan, stunned into silence, looked at each other through the gloom. Then Juliette spoke. 'You said – you said that's where I come in?'

'Yes, Juliette. I want you to return to Natzwiller. I want you to keep a watch on the camp, and report back to me whatever you can find out. I want all the information you can get. We need to keep an eye on that place.'

Chapter Thirty-Nine

Marie-Claire

On the third day after the Christmas break, the *Kreisleiter* returned to work and summoned Marie-Claire to his office. She rose from her desk in the secretaries' room and straightened her skirt.

'Just a minute,' said Ursula and patted Marie-Claire's hair so that not a strand was out of place. Erika whipped a small compact out of her handbag and dabbed at Marie-Claire's forehead with a ragged piece of sponge. Gertrud stood before her and fiddled at her blouse, opening two buttons.

'But it's the eyes that will do it, mostly. The eyes!' said Erika.

Marie-Claire rolled her eyes, extracting herself from Gertrud's grasp. 'Don't be ridiculous, Gertrud, not *that* button; he'll think I'm a floozy or something.' She re-fastened the lower button.

Gertrud giggled. 'But maybe he needs a little nudge in the right direction. A little *encouragement*. Graf Koks von Schmerlenbach isn't a pushover, remember!'

'Stop it! If I think of that name I'll end up in a fit of giggles and ruin everything. I have to be serious.' Marie-Claire pulled a hand over her face as if lowering a grim expression. 'So… serious, yet still seductive. How's this?'

'Perfect. Now run along, don't keep the Graf waiting!'

Marie-Claire wiggled her hips and with a saucy kiss of the air slid out the door. 'Good luck!' they cried after her.

She climbed the stairs to the first floor, walked down the hall and rapped on his door.

'Herein!' came the call, and she pressed the handle, opened it and walked in. He was sitting at his desk, bent over a ledger, pen in hand, but looked up as she entered.

'Ah, Fräulein Gauss. There you are. Good morning. Come in. There are a few letters I need to dictate.'

'Guten Morgen, Herr Kreisleiter,' said Marie-Claire as she drew her chair up at the desk, next to his. Slightly closer, but not ostentatiously so, than usual. She crossed her legs, making sure that in doing so one shapely calf was favourably angled against the other. Notebook and pencil in hand, she looked at him in expectation.

He did not meet her gaze. Instead, he turned slightly away from her as he opened a desk drawer and fumbled with its contents, finally removing what looked like a small address book.

He cleared his throat. 'Ah… Fräulein Gauss. I hope you had an enjoyable holiday.'

Marie-Claire frowned slightly before answering. The question was very much out of character. Polite chit-chat was not something he engaged in, ever.

'Yes, I did, thank you, *Herr Kreisleiter,*' she replied.

'And, aaaah… did you – did you manage to finish the book?'

'The book? I don't… Oh! The book! Yes, yes, of course. I er, I enjoyed it very much.'

Mein Kampf. Oh, hell. She had never got past the first twenty pages, and had struggled even with those. She had, though, retrieved the book from the wardrobe where she'd thrown it, and packed it into her suitcase when she returned to Colmar, and it was in her room in the rue Stanislas. She would have left it at the chateau, but hadn't wanted to risk it being found by Maman. Not that she actually *cared* about Maman's opinion, she just didn't want to deliver yet more ammunition for rebuke and mockery.

The *Kreisleiter* frowned, indicating that her reply did not meet his approval.

'It's not exactly a book one *enjoys,* though, is it. It's a book that one reads for enlightenment. For self-education. I hope you gleaned more from it than mere *enjoyment.'*

'Yes! Yes, indeed. It was most *enlightening.* That's what I meant.'

'I'm glad to hear that.' He paused. She waited, pencil poised in hand. He started again. 'Um, Fräulein Gauss. I've been thinking.'

'Yes, *Herr Kreisleiter?'*

'Well… now that we are here to stay. We Germans, I mean. Here in Alsace, in Colmar.'

'Yes?' She had never known him to speak so hesitantly, so awkwardly. Usually he'd launch into a lecture or a speech and never stop.

'Well, I realise that many Alsatians don't welcome us. Don't appreciate our presence here and don't understand that we came not to conquer, but to *absorb.* To absorb *them.* We want them to know that we consider them as our *Mitbürger.* Our co-citizens. We want to do all we can to make them feel welcome, as full German citizens. This year we'll be consolidating that absorption into the Third Reich by issuing new identity cards, German identity cards, and other steps are planned. Every Alsatian citizen will have the full rights – and duties – of a German, with all the advantages that offers. We came as friends, not as enemies.'

He paused, glanced at Marie-Claire, looked away again. She had never experienced him so very fidgety – almost nervous. She waited for him to continue, controlling the urge to fidget herself.

'This is where you, as a native Alsatian, can be of enormous help.'

'Me? Me personally?' She pointed at herself in alarm.

'Yes, you, Fräulein Gauss. As a native of this district you are the connecting link. The bridge, one might say, between two cultures, the bridge through which we Germans can communicate our own culture, through which that culture can be merged into the old Alsatian identity. A new identity is to be born, the old cast aside, like a caterpillar sloughing off a cocoon. Over the holidays I have been considering ways and means by which this could be done. And I have had a very good idea. This is where you can come in, in a practical sense.'

Another pause. She waited. He glanced at her again, and she noticed – yes, his glance had been directed not towards her face, but towards her upper body. She felt an urge to raise her hand, cover that part of her chest, rebutton the open lapels of her blouse. Close it up to her chin. Accepting the dare had been a bad idea, she concluded. A very bad idea; bad, because it seemed to be working in a way she had not planned.

Even as if the *Kreisleiter* had been thinking all too favourably about *her*, and had returned to work with a completely altered approach. More familiar. *Too* familiar… Where was the carefully sustained distance that had characterised their working relationship? The distance she had been goaded to shatter?

'As you know, that book I gave you, *Mein Kampf*, is the central doctrine of the new Era Germanica. I would say it is required reading for anyone with the desire to understand what is happening to the world today. Most especially, the young need to understand. People of your generation, young men and women.'

He leaned over, picked up his briefcase off the floor, fumbled inside it, but removed nothing.

'I have thought of a way to do this in a friendly way that is not intrusive, not overpowering. I want you to be a German ambassador. You have a foot in both cultures, born Alsatian but with an open heart and mind to the German way. You, more than anyone else, are in a position to do good. And what I thought is this:

'You will go to the registration office downstairs and request a list of all couples who have recently married. You are to find out their addresses and personally visit every one of these couples with a goodwill message from the mayoral office. And as a congratulatory gift, you are to give each couple a copy of *Mein Kampf*, and encourage them to read it. We think that is the way to foster a good relationship. I have already put in an order for a hundred copies of the book. As soon as that order arrives I want you to go ahead. I think you will find this work extremely rewarding.'

Marie-Claire could only stare back at him. It was as if all words, any viable response, had been knocked out of her head. The *Kreisleiter* paid no attention. He lined up a pile of papers on his desk with the flat of his hand, moved the bottle of ink two centimetres to the right, wheeled his chair nearer to the desk, flexed his fingers, lit a cigarette and continued, almost in the same breath:

'So, Fräulein Gauss, you'll start with that immediately, today. In the meantime, please take down the letter I'm about to dictate. Are you ready?'

'J-jaaa, *Herr Kreisleiter!*' Marie-Claire found her voice. Pencil poised above her pad, she prepared to take notes.

'You mean, he *flirted* with you? It's not possible. I can't imagine it.'

'No, no. He didn't flirt, exactly. It was something different. Something – something odd. Too familiar, too intimate, as if he was no longer my superior but just another colleague – as if he had lowered himself and wasn't this high and mighty *Kreisleiter* but just someone asking a favour. He wasn't even suggestive, or in any way rude. Though I did notice he was staring at my boobs.'

They all giggled, and everyone spoke at once. 'Well, they are rather – attractive, you know, especially in that blouse. Of course he had to peep.'

'But, Margarethe, this is wonderful news. It means he has his eye on you. It means you've already broken the ice.'

'It sounds as if he was thinking of you over the holidays and decided to make a move.'

'The trouble is, what am I going to do about it? I can't encourage him, can I? Anyway, the bet is off. I can't go through with it any more.'

'You don't have to encourage him, darling. Just be your own ravishing self. A bat of the eyelids here, a Mona Lisa smile there – that's all it will take.'

'You don't understand – I don't want his interest! It was all just a game, a challenge. To see if I could cut through his armour. I'm not serious about him at all! Quite the contrary! I really don't want him to court me.'

She had to raise her voice to cut through the excited chatter, and her last words, vehement and shrill, fell into an astounded silence. It was Gertrud who finally spoke.

'But, Margarethe—why not? I mean, he's the top officer in the *Mairie*. The highest prize. If you can get him, why not?'

Klara chimed in. 'I mean, do you really want to spend the rest of your life in the secretaries' room? Marry some lowly clerk?'

'Oh, she'll never have to do that,' said Ursula. 'Not with her looks. She'll be able to choose when the time comes. But, Margarethe, you must be sensible about it all. I remember you complained he's old and ugly. Surely that's not what's putting you off?'

'If so, you're being perfectly silly!' said Erika. 'Who cares about age and looks! A woman betters herself by moving up the ladder. Aim for the highest, is what I say, and here in Colmar, you can't do much better than the *Kreisleiter!*'

'Oh, I don't know about that!' said Klara. 'There's a rather dishy major in the Wehrmacht – I met him at the Christmas dance. Major von Haagen. A lot younger and more attractive than Graf Goks.'

'Please, please don't call him that any more. This has gone beyond a joke. What can I do? I can't encourage him but how do I put him off without appearing rude?'

'I don't understand why you'd want to put him off. When you've got the biggest fish on the line, why on earth wouldn't you reel him in?'

'Because-because – what about love? What about falling in love with someone who's-who's your other half? The love of your life? The one you dream about at night?'

Klara laughed. 'You've seen too many romantic films! That sort of thing doesn't really happen. Not in real life, and certainly not in wartime. I would say grab what you can. I thought you said your big dream was Paris?'

'Yes, it is.'

'Well, how on earth do you expect to get there with the love of your life? That could be *anyone*. It could be Tobias from the supplies store, or Rudolf from Security: small fry. Many a girl's life has been ruined by choosing love above ambition. One has to be pragmatic in these things, if you have a dream for a better life. For you, that's Paris. It's always been Paris.'

'How would encouraging the *Kreisleiter* get me to Paris?'

'Are you being deliberately obtuse? You silly girl. You reel him in, marry him, and every night you whisper in his ear that he should get himself promoted to a post in Paris. It's as easy as that.'

'Klara, don't be silly. Officers don't just get posted to Paris because their wives say so. They climb the ladder of promotion.'

'Oh, it might take time. But one promotion leads to another and I know for a fact that wives can steer the direction. Clever wives, that is. And our Margarethe is clever enough to do it.'

'You all forgot one thing. It might be possible to marry out of ambition but nobody's spoken of marriage. Just because the *Kreisleiter* let his eyes roll over my bosom doesn't mean he's looking for a bloody *wife*. Maybe he just wants to… to get into my knickers.'

'Well, that's easy. You don't let him. You lead him on, tease him, make him crazy. And let him know he's getting nothing till there's a ring on your finger.'

'These men are all the same,' Klara agreed. 'Why would you buy a cow when you can milk it through the fence? You need to play your cards wisely. Let him know you're a respectable woman, a virgin, and there's only one way he can have you.'

'You *are* a virgin, aren't you?'

'Yes, yes, of course! But you're all missing the point. I don't want to marry him. Like I said, he's old and ugly and – and, well, a bit creepy. I don't like him. Why would I want to marry someone I don't even *like?*'

'Yes, he is a bit weird, I'll give you that. Old and ugly – that's nothing. Just shut your eyes and keep him sated, that's all. And anyway, we've all agreed he's not *really* old. Fifty is old. Around forty is a good age. By then, they're established in their career and they know how to treat a woman. They're *distinguished*.'

'Klara, you sound as if you're an expert on men!'

'Well, actually, I am. I've been around the block once or twice. I know men.'

'The more you all talk about it, the more depressed I feel. I don't want to encourage him. I don't want to marry him. I don't want to go to bed with him. So what shall I *do?*'

The last word came out as a wail. For the first time in her life, Marie-Claire was out of her depth with a man, and the girls weren't helping with their talk of marriage.

Ursula patted her on the back.

'Don't worry, sweetheart. Just think about it for a couple of days. Do this thing with the married couples – that will at least get you out of the office. Don't encourage him, but don't insult him either by rejecting him. Play it by ear. Play with him a little. Keep him at a distance, but not too far. Nothing's going to happen in the next few weeks anyway. Make sure he moves slowly, and play him cleverly. A man is a man; we have to look out for ourselves, we women. And he's a really, really good catch. Don't dismiss him out of hand. Let the idea work on you, and see how things develop.'

'She's right,' said Gertrud. 'We shouldn't be rushing you. It's just all so exciting.'

'Not to me,' said Marie-Claire. 'It's the most awkward situation I've ever been in.'

All of a sudden a great deep longing for home overcame her. To sit around the kitchen table with Maman and Victoire and maybe even Juliette – Juliette was so very sensible! – and talk things through with women who didn't have ambition as their primary motive in life. But she had cut all ties with home, and this was her new reality. She sighed.

'I'm exhausted,' she said. 'I'm off to bed.'

'Think about what we said!' Klara cried after her as she slipped out of the door.

Marie-Claire dressed for work the next day in her most dreary clothes, an old brown sweater with a polo neck and a tweed skirt that was unshapely around the hips. She wore a minimum of make-up: just a dab of powder and no lipstick or eyeshadow or rouge. At the breakfast table, the girls were appalled.

'You look twenty years older, Marie-Claire!' said Klara. 'What's up?'

'I've made my decision,' said Marie-Claire. 'He might be a catch but I don't want him. You all can have him – I don't care. Like I said, the bet is off.'

'So then, what will you do if it turns out he still wants you?'

She shrugged as she reached for the coffee pot.

'I don't know. I'll just discourage him.'

After breakfast they all walked over to the *Mairie* together, arms linked, in twos and threes along the pavement, a brisk fifteen-minute march. The security guards put up their usual little flirtation game; the girls flirted back, winked and blew kisses, entered the building, made their way to the secretarial office, removed coats and hats and slung them over the coat-stand, hung their handbags on the backs of chairs or set them on the floor, hiked up their skirts to sit down at their desks, removed the covers on their typewriters. The clatter of typewriter keys soon replaced the buzz of early-morning chatter as everyone set to work. Marie placed three sheets of clean paper, two sheets of carbon between them, and opened her notebook, and soon her fingers danced over the keys as she translated the shorthand symbols into a clean typewritten report. But at the back of her mind lurked disquiet – when would he summon her? What would she say, and do, should he be as familiar today as he was yesterday?

But it did not happen. She was not summoned, and soon the rumour reached them that the *Kreisleiter* had gone to Strasbourg for talks and would be there for a week or two. Marie-Claire relaxed, but her respite was brief. At the end of that week a shipment of a hundred copies of *Mein Kampf* arrived. Mayor Grötzinger summoned her to his office.

'You're to begin work immediately – those are the instructions. I've already given orders for a list of all couples who have married in the last three months to be compiled. Fräulein Bock from the *Bürgeramt* will have it ready for you. Your work is to start immediately. Today.'

'You ought to be ashamed of yourself, Marie-Claire!'

Marie-Claire bowed her head. She *was* ashamed of herself, but it was a shame she needed to keep hidden, for her own self-respect. She raised her chin defiantly, and looked her former classmate, Michelle Perreau, in the eye. In German, she said:

'That's Fräulein Gauss, if you please. I am Margarethe Gauss now. Do not use my old name. And you should be addressing me in German, not in French. I'll let it pass this time, but it's the last time. And, Fräulein Pelzer—'

'Don't call me that! I'm still Michelle Perreau! I will never submit to your nasty Nazi rules!'

'I'm going to have to report you for speaking French again, after you have been warned. It's not a joke.'

She changed her tone, dropping the brisk and bossy tenor. She continued, in German, in a more conciliatory, pleading even, timbre: 'You *must* speak German, Martina. You must use your new name. You must get used to the changes! Trust me, it's for the best and easier in the long run. The Germans are here to stay. Alsace is German now and the sooner we adapt, the better. Please. I'm asking this in your own interest. Refusing to do so will only mean trouble for you down the line. And, read the book. Please. I'm telling you, confidentially, that perhaps someone from the *Mairie* will come along to test you, and it's vital that you toe the line.'

'Never! I will never toe the Nazi line! The book is going straight into the rubbish, or rather, into the fireplace, to give us some warmth at least. I will never speak German to a Frenchwoman, to an Alsatian – and that's what you are, Marie-Claire! I don't know what's come over you. I used to like you. I don't like this person you've become, a Nazi pawn.'

'Well, I tried my best.' Marie-Claire tapped the book she'd laid on the sideboard. 'I'm leaving this here. Please read it, for your own good. And ask your husband to read it. Congratulations, by the way. I always liked Eugène— I mean, Eugen. I wish you a happy marriage. Please, consider what I told you and try to adapt. I won't report you after all. I know how difficult it is to switch to German in everything, but you *must*, and eventually, you will. Germany is winning this war, Martina, and the sooner you accept that reality, the better. Alsace is already part of Germany, part of Baden. Sooner or later, you must comply.'

'Never! *Jamais!*' cried Michelle as Marie-Claire slipped the backpack onto her shoulders and stepped out into the street.

Marie-Claire ignored her. Adjusted the weight of the backpack – it held three more volumes of *Mein Kampf* – and strode away. Three more newly-wed couples to visit in Colmar. And then it would be out into the villages. And everywhere, up to now, the reception had been the same. Some of the women – it was always the wives, the husbands being out at work – knew her from school, or through her mother, and always they threw insults at her, rebuked her for her 'disgusting collaboration'.

But it wasn't collaboration, was it? It was just a job, like any other. This was the reality, and they would all accept it in time. One had to be pragmatic in times of major societal change. Resistance was futile. There was nothing to discuss: this *was* the new reality. Marie-Claire shouldered the animosity just as she did the backpack, with stoicism. They would all come round in the end. She stopped, looked at her list and crossed the road.

Chapter Forty

Marie-Claire

Three weeks had passed. She had not seen Kurtz in that time but then, she was mostly out of the office, trundling through the Alsace countryside on old buses that huffed and puffed their way up and downhill, into the villages. She had in those three weeks delivered fourteen copies of *Mein Kampf* to newly married couples, as well as to couples about to be married. Each time, she had attempted to put on an enthusiastic face for the work – it was, after all, just work – smiling and encouraging the couples to read it; it would make life so much easier! But each attempt to push the *Führer's* doctrine down unwilling throats was met with resistance, if not blank hostility, and she had long started to hate the task, long started to dread the lonely excursions into the more remote villages, knowing full well the reception that invariably awaited her. Marie-Claire, accustomed to reaping admiration and/or envy from other females, did not at all relish this new role of public enemy, a lightning rod for furious wives who had no intention of ever reading the book, and who no doubt, like Michelle Perreau, used its pages as kindling.

But it kept her away from the office, away from *him*. That was the one good thing about it. However, the backlog of newly-weds from the last three months was coming to an end, and henceforth there would be fewer trips to be made and, as a consequence, more time spent in the office. Time she dreaded. The last time she'd seen him, there was no mistaking the simultaneously calculating and covetous look in his eyes. He *wanted* her. She could tell. She'd seen that look in many a man's eye in the past, and had prided herself on her ability to keep them at arm's length even while basking in the glow of undeclared yearning; it was good to be wanted. Just not to be wanted by him.

Her new-found friends could not understand it, and loud was their rebuke. She must, they advised and admonished her, get over her antipathy. A woman's ultimate power lay in exactly this: the power to weaken the defences of a powerful man. This placed her above him. She should rejoice, and be glad: 'Play him for all you're worth. He's your ticket to Paris. Paris is what you always wanted, isn't it? Never mind his character. Once you've got him you'll be able to wrap him round your little finger. Especially after you've had a child or two.'

That was their reasoning. Hers was simpler: she did not love him. She hardly liked him. She couldn't bear the thought of him even touching her, much less of making babies with him.

'Pffft!' said Klara. 'Just close your eyes and do it, like most women in history. He's your ticket to the world you always dreamed of, we all dream of. I can just see you swanning down the rue de Rivoli, in furs. Once the war's over, of course; as it will be soon. We're winning, and then *you'll* win. But if you really don't want him...' Her eyes narrowed. 'Then send him to me.'

Ursula, more sensitive and insightful than the others, placed a hand on hers. 'Who is this fellow you've set your heart on, Margarethe? Why couldn't you get him? Is he married or something?'

Her reply was instantaneous:

'There's no one!'

But Ursula only shook her head and smiled enigmatically. 'Well, I think I detect something there. But it's obviously not possible, whoever it is, so I suggest you just close your eyes, as Klara said, and get on with it.'

'He'll soon lose interest anyway, once you've had a baby or two and lost your figure,' put in Ursula. 'That's what men are like. He'll be after the latest model, quite literally, if you're over in Paris, and leave you in peace.'

'You can even have a lover of your own,' said Klara. 'Isn't that what French women do? They all have lovers.'

'How could you say such a thing!' Ursula's rebuke was sharp. 'That's not the behaviour of a good wife. What would the *Führer* say if he heard you! Even if *he* were to take a lover, Margarethe, you must remain faithful, a good and loyal wife.'

'Ah yes, you and your *What would the Führer say?* motto. I can imagine it even inscribed on your gravestone, Ursula: "The *Führer* said I was a worthy woman". I'm afraid I'm not so beholden.'

'If you ask me, all I care about is that she doesn't forget us, once she's sitting in her posh *maison* in Paris! You will remember us, won't you, Margarethe, and invite us over? Remember, it's thanks to us you—'

'Oh, just *shut up!* cried Marie-Claire, and fled the kitchen. She'd had enough – it was always like this, the teasing, the encouragement, the pronouncements, the advice, the predictions. It was a slow manipulation of her psyche, a tedious breaking down of her resolutions, almost a brainwashing, and there was no one there to talk it through with. No one to back her up. Sometimes she held imaginary conversations with her mother. She knew *exactly* what Margaux would say. Her horror would be off the scale; and it was only through such mental gymnastics that she was able to stay the course.

But tomorrow – tomorrow she'd be seeing him. There was no way around it, no excuse: he'd be there, and he had asked her, through a private note in an envelope, to be present at three in the afternoon in his office. He had never done this before. All her instincts told her that this was not for a simple shorthand session. There was something deeply personal in the flourish of his signature.

Dietrich Kurtz. He had signed with his full name. He never, ever, did that.

*

Is awkwardness contagious? As she walked up the stairs to Kurtz's office Marie-Claire wondered if it had started with him or with her. Surely not with him. Kurtz was the most dominant, domineering almost, man she'd ever met. The moment he walked into a room the people in it stiffened, jumped to attention, watched him. Awkwardness did not at all suit him, yet it was there. And yes, she was used to self-assured men behaving like sycophantic lumps of jelly when it came to making intelligent conversation with her. They simply didn't know what to say, because their brains seemed to melt. Turn to mush. It was a power she'd always enjoyed but never exploited – she liked keeping them at a distance while at the same time allowing them to hope, to dream, and until recently, until last Christmas, it had worked well.

She'd never actually regarded Kurtz as a *man* in the normal, human, sense, certainly not as someone to test her charms on. He was an SS representative of the highest order, a man who had probably even hobnobbed with the *Führer*, and so belonged to an entirely different stratum of humankind – more a robot with human attributes, a distant relative to what one would normally think of as a living, breathing human. And yes, he had his weaknesses: his smoking habit – definitely an addiction – and his propensity for uncouth, or inappropriate, language, words that fell just short of being vulgar, blurted out when on the phone with his obnoxious adversary. *Das ist ja Unsinn!* What nonsense! being a favourite of his, or, *Verdammt noch mal!* Damn it! Once, he'd blurted out *Leck mich am Arsch!* Lick my ass! But it must have been inadvertent, because he'd immediately looked at her and turned red, and she'd also blushed, in embarrassment for him.

She had no idea who this person was he seemed to be perpetually in heated dialogue with. It was obviously always the same person, because the belligerent, annoyed tone was always the same; the person seemed to be perpetually delivering bad news to him, the details of which remained obscure to her. He still engaged in furious

typing sessions. She was certain that, had she been still spying for
Jacques, she'd have been able to deliver gold. He'd certainly been
pleased with the three spools she'd sent to him before the Christmas
fiasco. Sometimes, she was tempted to continue; to once again check
the progress of the ribbon, observe how full it was, remove it, pass
it to Madame Guyon – but no. That episode was over.

Now, her feet dragged as she walked up the stairs. It was all so
embarrassing. He was Nazi top brass – he should not be susceptible
to female allure. She did not want or need it; she had accepted
Klara's challenge, really, as a joke, not for one moment believing
she had a chance. She'd have laughed at the end of it and said to
the girls, in a charming display of sportsmanship: well, you can't
win them all! That man's made of stone! It had been a bloody game.
But he had pre-empted her, revealed a weakness, and she had no
idea how to deal with it.

Reluctantly, she knocked on the door, waited for his bark of
herein!, pressed the handle, pushed it open and walked in.

There he was at his desk, pen in hand, writing in that eternal
ledger. He looked up as she entered. He never used to do this, and
it unnerved her. It was far too familiar. She longed for the early
days when a barrier of sheer awe, issuing from her to him, kept the
appropriate distance between them in place. Now, he even *smiled*. She
preferred not to smile back, but she couldn't afford to be rude; yet she
didn't want to encourage him. The whole situation flummoxed her.

'Ah, there you are, Fräulein Gauss.' He looked at his watch; she
knew she was five minutes late. It was deliberate. Just as, now and
then, she allowed spelling and grammar mistakes to creep into her
work. Perhaps, with some luck, he'd have had enough of her flaws
soon and would exchange her for Erika. Or Klara. Both of whom
were pretty and willing and eager for his attentions. But her lack
of punctuality seemed not to bother him.

Instead, he seemed to stumble into a pit of indecision, fumbling
for the right words, hemming and hawing. 'Aaaaahhh, Fräulein

Gauss, I was wondering if… I've had a bit of news of late – good news, in fact, and – well, we work so well together, you and I – you've been an excellent assistant and I'm very pleased with you… I thought that perhaps you might consider…'

She couldn't bear it. She lowered her eyes and stared at the floor while he stuttered and stammered, hearing without listening. She could not meet his eyes. It was awful.

This discombobulation went on for a good five minutes; he spoke without actually saying anything. He asked her to take a seat, and she did, still not looking at him. She fidgeted, prepared her notebook and her pencil, rose up when he still didn't find the point he was trying to say and threw a log onto the fire. And then he did find the point.

'Fräulein Gauss, I've just received news of a promotion, to Strasbourg. It's an important post and I intend to accept it. I am hoping you will accompany me as my personal secretary. We work well as a team and I see no reason to discontinue what is, in effect, a positive and extremely beneficial – aaaah – collaboration.'

Now she looked at him, mouth agape. It wasn't at all what she'd been expecting. She thought he'd proposition her in some way – invite her to the cinema, or a restaurant, or both. That was the way of most men, and surely… had she perhaps misjudged him? Had her vanity run away with her? Was he really only interested in her as an efficient – though slightly sloppy of late – personal secretary? But no. The glaze that sometimes flickered in his eyes: she had not imagined that. Perhaps this was his simply his method. A long, drawn-out collaboration, which would one day lead to more? She'd have to talk to the girls about it.

Now, she closed her mouth, opened it again. Words came out, the first words she could think of.

'I-I'm sorry, it's all so sudden – I don't know – I need time to think – a lot to think about… Please, let me consider…'

'Certainly. Of course you must think about it. However, I do require an answer by tomorrow. And now, let's get down to work.' It was as if he'd flicked an internal switch – now he was all efficiency, diligence and level-headed dispassion. He had donned his armour again. She much preferred him this way.

But he had placed a problem before her, and she had no idea how to solve it.

He didn't give her the promised time to solve it. He solved it for her.

Chapter Forty-One

A sudden letter that had to be dictated, today, after work, when everyone else was about to go home. She'd put away her notepad and had crouched before the fireplace to put out the last glowing embers. She picked up the poker and thrust it into the hearth, nudging the embers apart, burying them in ashes. He, for some reason, was still at his desk, fiddling in its drawers as if searching for some obscure item. That in itself was unusual. And what on earth had been so very important about that letter? It had been a perfectly routine one, one that could very well have been done the following day, the following week. She was aware of his presence at the desk as a sort of itching at the nape of her neck, a need to watch her back, look behind her.

The embers now buried in ash, the tiles before the hearth swept, Marie-Claire stood up, eager to flee the room so filled with the presence of Kurtz. She glanced at the clock; the entire building, by now, would be empty. She was quite alone with him, and that realisation made her want to hurry yet more, escape the room, race down the stairs, grab her coat and hat and bolt from the building as fast as her legs could carry her.

As she straightened up she simultaneously heard a slight puff, like an out-breath warning her of danger as he, too, rose from his padded chair. She swung round.

Too late. With two strides he was before her, his hands heavy on her waist and pulling her to him, his lips forcing themselves on to her cheeks, her neck, her mouth, a wet tongue prising her lips apart. A cry of shock rose within her but his mouth on hers muffled the sound. She struggled, but her movement seemed to incite him only further.

Dull fear overcame her then, fear of this hulking beast of a man and his overpowering grasp. She froze under his hands, her cries died in her throat, and all of a sudden she went limp, as the realisation took hold that her puny strength was nothing to him. She was a matchstick in his hands. Resistance was futile.

Stiff as the poker that had fallen from her hand, she allowed it to happen, unable to resist though everything in her screamed *no!* No to the kiss, no to the gasping and fumbling and moaning, the groping hands all over her body. But no sound came from her lips.

He pulled her down onto the carpet, right there in front of the fire, and grasped and pulled and pinched at her body. He moved his wet slobbery mouth all over her face and neck, moaning and groaning. He grabbed the hem of her skirt and, now panting, dragged it over her hips. Thick sausage fingers inserted themselves into the elastic of her drawers and pulled and fought with the material before dragging them off her body. He threw himself on top of her, pumped and heaved at her for what seemed like an eternity and then exploded into her with a shout: *'Oh mein Gott!'*

And then he rolled off of her while the fingers continued to probe her body, and he crooned at her and the words came, words spoken into her dishevelled hair, words spoken between wet kisses, words that were supposed to excuse what had just happened but instead only amplified the horror of it all.

'Fräulein Gauss – may I call you Margarethe now? – my dear Margarethe. My dear, dear Margarethe. You must, I insist, forgive me for my – um – my overenthusiasm this afternoon. I am sorry I momentarily lost control – but how could I not, with such a lovely creature as you in such close proximity? Believe me, I have over the past months done all I possibly can to control the impulse that this afternoon overcame me with such fervour – please believe me that it is your loveliness alone that incited me; you must know of the effect you have on men, the animal desire that you release in the male psyche! Look at me – no, don't turn your face away, look at me and tell me you accept my apology. Trust me, I had been hoping for a more sedate courtship, a more dignified approach, but it is plain that in the end it all boils down to this one thing: I need you, I must have you.

'No, please, don't turn away again. Why are there tears in your eyes? Why do you tremble so? Margarethe, I meant no harm. Quite the opposite. Yes, I had hoped for a kiss – come, here is another one – but you must understand me, you must realise that as a man in high position I have to remain somewhat disciplined when it comes to women and was completely overwhelmed by your charms. I am certainly not the kind of man to dishonour a respectable woman, and I know you are respectable; I know, from officer gossip in the *Rote Löwe* that you have not allowed any man to court you, though many desire you, and I greatly admire you for such restraint, for your breeding, your culture. For this reason alone I have singled you out; I abhor a loose woman, a woman who preys on the weakness of men, a weakness that, sadly, I cannot claim to be exempt from.'

On and on he talked, his fingers kneading various parts of her body all the while. She kept turning her face away, he kept turning it back, licking away the tears that escaped from her eyes, squeezing her breasts, probing the more intimate areas of her body. She let it all happen, the turning away of her face, the closing of her eyes her only defence. Her lips trembled, but she said not a word. There were just no words.

He still had plenty. Words, empty words, gushed from his lips.

Though he was plainly sorry to have moved a little too quickly, he explained, and he would have preferred a nice soft marital bed for the act, one had to understand that a red-blooded man couldn't always control himself, and that was that. A good woman would understand, sympathise.

And yes, he had asked her to accompany him to Strasbourg for *exactly* this reason. It was a ruse, an excuse. He didn't want a personal secretary – *they* were a dime a dozen. He wanted, needed, a wife. The *Führer* encouraged marriage. The *Führer* believed in happy, wholesome families with a multitude of children, and single men were less likely to be promoted, and he had chosen her, specifically. She, Marie-Claire, herself had of late been delightfully engaged with newly-weds and he hoped that this task had encouraged her to think of her own future, her own opportunities. This was what he was offering her: *opportunity.* Surely she didn't want to be stuck forever in this backwater, Colmar? Strasbourg, for him, was just a rung on the ladder of promotion. The world was open for him. Munich, Berlin, Paris. Once the war had been won, London. Open for him, and for her too. She would be privileged. She *was* privileged. It was a magnificent offer, a promotion.

Eventually he stood up and pulled her up behind him. She still had not offered a word or protest or rebuke, or even a simple no. The word simply would not come. She hung her head in shame, unable to look him in the eye. He helped her get dressed, picking up her drawers and holding them open as she stepped in, one foot, two feet, and even cracking a joke about her beautiful legs and sweet triangle of pubic hair (*Schamhaare* – hair of shame), and he tried to tidy her dishevelled chignon but advised her to go off to the ladies' room, as it needed more than a pat or two.

And then he pulled on his own drawers and trousers – yes, he'd been disgustingly half-naked all this time – and tightened his belt. He looked utterly ridiculous, striding about to pick up the strewn clothes, with his long thin hairy legs poking out beneath his shirt-tails. The girls would have roared with hilarity, had they seen him. For her it was no laughing matter. It took all her strength to hold back the tears. She could not let him see her cry. It was a matter of pride. Pride was all she had to cling to. He smiled at her fondly, patting her on the shoulder.

'I must go now. I'll go first; we don't want the security guards to jump to conclusions. Goodbye, my dear. We'll discuss the future in more detail in the coming days.'

And then he was gone. That was when she broke down, collapsed on the carpet before the dying fire as her body erupted in great racking sobs and howls emerged from her throat and all she could do, now, was pummel the carpet.

That was how Madame Guyon found her, later on, when she came to clean. And Madame Guyon cleaned not just the office but Marie-Claire too, dried her eyes and embraced her and whispered words of comfort to her, interspersed with curses and furious utterings: *they are brutes, these men!* And Madame Guyon cleaned her up in the ladies' room and made her hair respectable, and brought her a chair and made her sit in the room to regain her composure while she, Madame Guyon, cleaned the office, which happened to be her last task for the night. Returning to Marie-Claire, she said: 'Mademoiselle, this is my private opinion and excuse me if I am too forward, but this is an abomination. You must quit this job. You cannot work for this beast any more. I will speak to Jacques, if I may, and tell him you cannot—'

'No! No! You must not tell him! Please don't tell him! Jacques cannot know this happened!'

'But—'

'Promise me you won't tell him, Madame Guyon! Please! Promise me! I will deal with it myself.'

And Madame Guyon shrugged and gave that promise and together they walked downstairs and past the smirking security guards into the street, and Madame Guyon accompanied her to the corner of rue Stanislas before bidding her goodbye.

'Tell Jacques yourself,' she whispered in Marie-Claire's ear. But Marie-Claire only shook her head. Jacques must never know. The shame would be too great. 'Thank you, Madame Guyon,' was all she said.

She slunk upstairs, unable to face the girls. Crept into her bed. Tossed and turned there, churning between utter revulsion, guilt, shame, hatred, fear and sheer helplessness. What was she to do now? How could she possibly ever return to work? Where was she to go? Curled up in a ball, she silently sobbed into her pillow.

Later that night Ursula, who shared her room, came in to find her sobbing into her pillow. She felt Ursula's hand on her back, gently rubbing, Ursula's soft whisper; and, Ursula being a compassionate young woman with strong maternal qualities, comforted her and slowly, bit by bit, drew the story out of her.

'Don't cry, Margarethe; it will be all right, you'll see. Tomorrow you'll feel better. Tomorrow you'll be strong again. Many of us have to put up with that sort of thing – it's disgusting, but that's life. I'm here for you. We're all here for you, all the girls.'

Sure enough, by the next morning the whole house knew.

Reactions were mixed. Ursula called it rape, but Gertrud argued it couldn't be rape since Marie-Claire had not resisted, had not fought, had not even once uttered the vital word *no*. Erika said that Marie-Claire was anyway to blame because she had led him on, by dressing provocatively the entire time, and only recently had tempered that look by more modest and less seductive clothing.

'But-but… it was all a game! A joke! We were all involved! You were all egging me on!'

'Ah, but you went ahead, didn't you? You flirted with him – encouraged him! You should know what that does to men! You should have known what it might lead to!'

'But…' But the girls all nodded wisely. Marie-Claire must accept some responsibility.

But there was a silver lining to the whole disaster, as Klara pointed out. Klara was only interested in one thing: he had proposed marriage: 'You need to put it all behind you and move on, move forward! You must use this to your own advantage, Margarethe!'

All agreed she was in no state to return to work that day. They all persuaded her she should report sick that day; they were the witnesses.

That evening, too, they talked and talked. And the final conclusion, among all of them, was that yes, it *might,* at a stretch, be described as rape, since Marie-Claire had clearly not wanted it; *but:* a): who would she report the crime of rape to, since Kurtz was the final authority in Colmar? And, b) she had not resisted, and she had in many ways led him on, and he had apologised and even offered marriage. So it was a very *forgivable* rape; even, some said, a fortunate rape, as it cut out the whole courtship ritual and Marie-Claire had already extracted a proposal, which was, after all, the best outcome of all.

In the end they were unanimous in their final evaluation of her situation: as Klara maintained, she couldn't change what had happened, and the best thing was to see the positive side. She was luckier than most; he had proposed marriage, which was not a thing an *actual* rapist would do. She should pull herself together and use Kurtz's indiscretion to her own advantage. There was a good side to this and she should straighten her back, lift up her head and do the *right thing.* They all agreed as to what the right thing was. They advised her to put it all behind her and move on. Move to Strasbourg, marry Dietrich Kurtz. In the end, she'd wrap him round her little finger and drag him off to Paris. This was her pathway to the top. She was in an enviable position.

But Marie-Claire wished, above all, that she could go home. Back to the chateau. Tell her little sister, kind, caring Victoire, all about it. Tell her mother. Have her mother take her in her arms, express outrage and tell her to come home. *Come home, baby. This will always be your home. I will always be your mother. Put that all behind you. This is where you belong.*

That's what Marie-Claire longed for, above all. But would Maman be so compassionate? Wasn't this *exactly* what Maman had warned her about? Wasn't it all her own fault, for disregarding Maman's warning? Would Maman even, perhaps, gloat, because she'd been right?

A weekend followed. In spite of her longing for home, she remained in Colmar. She longed for Margaux's arms round her, but simply could not face her mother's *I told you so*. In spite of everything, Marie-Claire still had some pride left. She would cling to it as to a lifeline. She could not go home.

Her biggest fear, for the moment, was coming face to face with Kurtz again. She took a second sick day, this time with less approval from her friends, some of whom thought she was making too much of a drama out of the whole thing. 'Pull yourself together and move on,' was the clear consensus.

She had no choice but to follow their advice.

Kurtz was not at work on Monday, and more fruitless discussions with the girls followed her into the new week. She no longer sat with them in the downstairs *salon*, laughing and gossiping. Now, she knew, *she* was the subject of all the gossip. Resentment flared up within her – how dare they! The knowledge that they were all wallowing in her pain and helplessness, that they hid their glee under a thin veneer of commiseration, was an anathema to her. The stink of *Schadenfreude* was strong. *Serves her right,* they were all thinking, and some were almost saying it.

But then it came to her, one early dawn after another restless night: the solution, fully formed and staring at her. Why on earth hadn't she thought of it before! Maman's words, loud and clear before her: *when you're twenty-one and an adult, you can do whatever the hell you want.*

In clear terms, that meant: *you can go to your father.* In Paris.

She would be twenty-one in less than six weeks, and free to go. She'd go to Paris, to Papa, and put all this behind her... the best outcome of all. That was how one turned a disaster into victory. In the house in the rue Stanislas, she'd have the last laugh. She'd be off to Paris before any one of them could say, *Oh you poor thing but you deserved it* again.

She couldn't wait to put her plan into action. She slipped out of bed, put on dressing gown and slippers and hurried down the stairs as silently as she could. The rooms downstairs were cold, though there were some embers left in the *salon* fireplace – she presumed that the girls had, once again, gossiped deep into the night.

There was a desk shoved up beneath the window and that was where they kept their stationery. Writing paper, pens, blotting paper, ink, envelopes, stamps – it was all there. The girls all wrote home frequently, and bent over this desk was where they did so. Marie-Claire had last written to her father in November, just after the invasion, and had not received a reply. Now was the time to renew her claim on his affections – she was, after all, his favourite child, his firstborn.

It had been a disappointment that in the past he had refused to let her come without Maman's consent; a stupid inconvenience, a mere formality it would have been easy to defy. Who cared if Maman let her go or not? They surely wouldn't ask for such approval on the train to Paris – she could just go. But Papa had said no. *I don't want trouble with your mother,* he said. *If she says no, then it's no. Wait till you are of age, and then we'll see.*

Well, she wasn't quite of age yet, but it was just a matter of time and she might as well prepare him. She was off to Paris, at last, leaving behind this cursed place and awful people, forever.

Removing the writing pad from its drawer, refilling the pen with ink, she set to work:

> *Darling Papa, it's been a long time since I last wrote and I'm sorry for that, but so much has happened in the meantime I'm sure you'll forgive me! And anyway, you never replied to my last letter, did you? Anyway, I'm writing with good news. As you know, I've been waiting with bated breath for my birthday in March and finally, finally, I'm almost there so I was thinking it's time to make plans, because at last I'll be coming to Paris, at last I can be with you, at last I can leave behind this dreary province, the boring chateau, and join you in the City of Light! I hope you're looking forward to it as much as I am, though I have to say, so much has been happening in the last few months I'd almost forgotten that we'd decided I could come after my birthday. I feel as if a whole new life is about to begin, and I just can't wait!*
>
> *As for what has been happening – I don't know where to begin! You know I was able to transfer to Colmar as a bilingual secretary – well, after the Nazis moved in it turned out that people like me are in great demand, and...*

She went into great detail about her work, her colleagues the girls, making it sound, on the one hand, as if she were immensely in demand, indispensable to the running of the *Mairie*, on the other as if this was all far beneath her abilities and only in Paris could she grow wings and fly. She did not mention Dietrich Kurtz.

Not once.

By the time she had finished, signed and folded the several pages of her large, neat writing and placed them in the envelope, addressed the letter and pasted a stamp on it, it was beginning to grow light outside and footsteps could be heard on the floor above as the girls woke up and prepared for the coming workday.

Marie-Claire slipped the sealed envelope into her dressing gown pocket and made her way back upstairs to prepare for the day. She'd post it tomorrow. He'd get it next week; if she was lucky, she might have a reply by the end of that week. Maybe, even, he'd be so eager to have her he'd send a telegram. *Come at once,* it might say, *I'm waiting!*

Chapter Forty-Two

Victoire

Winter morphed into spring in an outburst of abundant, glorious nature, an overture of colour and sunshine and birdsong. At the chateau, life that year went its own placid way. It was hard to believe that out there, a war was raging, people were killing and being killed. It was even more difficult to imagine that, outside of their little Alsatian bubble of relative safety, the world was on fire. Reports of the London Blitz, delivered to them through clandestine BBC reports, rendered them heartsick. They had close friends in England – were they safe? And if Germany should defeat the Allies, what then? Poland, it seemed, was lost: the German scourge was expanding eastwards as well as westwards. North Africa, the Middle East: all seemed to be one huge battlefield. And as for Asia: Allied forces seemed exhausted, depleted of soldiers and hardware after two full years of war with Germany, and the battle-hardened Japanese seemed to be making mincemeat of them.

Here, in Alsace, war was no more than a sinister presence, a dark cloud hanging over them all, yet still far away, planting in everyone's heart a deep sense of foreboding, as if it could all erupt in the wink of an eye. Colmar swarmed with ever more soldiers. Everywhere, tanks and armoured cars and motorbikes and swastikas. In every public building, life-sized photos of Hitler. People on the street could be stopped and searched for no reason – just for fun, it seemed. Everyone had to speak German, whether they were fluent or not. All the books in the shops, all the signs, all the names of everyday objects: all were translated into German. She, too, had a new name.

Her name was, officially, Viktoria. Viktoria Gauss. All their friends and acquaintances, and Margaux's customers, had new names, and one had to be constantly conscious of using the right appellation; there were stories of people being denounced for speaking French or using the wrong name, which could result in an arrest; the Germans spoke of re-education, of ridding the population of their habitual thought processes and replacing them entirely. French-think had to become German-think, and disobeying the new rules, ordained by a few on the many, could be disastrous. One had to watch one's language, even one's thoughts, and be careful to whom one expressed even slight disenchantment with the new world order. It was as if one could deny one's entire upbringing as a Frenchwoman, and overnight become a German, just by speaking this new language and thinking these new thoughts.

A fog of gloom had settled over a once-pleasant land of rolling hills and fairy-tale villages, an ugliness in stark contrast to the beauty of the landscape and the former contentment of its people. Outside the borders, the war showed no sign of letting up. This year, it was worse than ever. Headlines in German newspapers screamed of great victories. The *Deutsche Welle* blared out exaggerated reports of every little skirmish, and always it was the Germans who were winning. *Der Stürmer*, the Nazi propaganda tabloid newspaper available at all the newsagents, waxed lyrical as it revelled in German victories in Europe and elsewhere. The only lifeline they still clung to in the Château Gauthier was Margaux's own secret wireless, tuned to the BBC. They took courage from those defiant broadcasts.

And they prayed. There was little else they could do. It might not change the course of the war, but praying brought the strength to face each new day without despair.

*

Victoire hardly ever saw Eric. His work, now, centred on the safe evacuation of Jews, who came clandestinely through the Colmar route over the Rhine as well as Strasbourg, strategically located just across the river and just minutes away from Kehl in Germany. Throughout that summer, Eric escorted four parties, individuals, couples and, in one case, a family, down from Strasbourg to the chateau and then, after a night or two, over the Vosges. Victoire longed to go with them – indeed, to be the guide over the mountains herself – but Jacques remained adamant: she was too young, too inexperienced and, most of all, too female.

'What does being female have to do with it?' she asked repeatedly, and always the reply was, 'The Nazis can do worse things to a woman than to a man. I cannot allow it.'

Her Red Cross course came to an end, and now Victoire's only contribution to the cause was caring for the refugees Eric delivered into her hands. She'd rather be out there, living rough with the other *maquisards*, risking her life. Killing Nazis.

Not that they actually fought Nazis, much less killed them, as far as she could tell. Jacques, it seemed, had already assembled a ragtag group of young men keen to do whatever they could. But, without weapons, without military training (though some had survived the French army the previous year), there was no actual fighting; instead, they indulged in small acts of sabotage. Removing or exchanging road signs, to confuse Germans; puncturing jeep tyres; throwing home-made bombs into buildings known to be Nazi lairs. So far, nobody had been caught.

She wanted to go the whole way, as Eric and Jacques did, Juliette and Nathan. Put her life on the line, *because* she loved that life so much.

Love and death. They were so closely aligned. Once you loved someone you were vulnerable, deeply so: Maman and her children. Juliette and Nathan. Jacques had warned her about Eric, not to get too attached: 'What he's doing is dangerous, Victoire. It's better to remain unattached in wartime. Love can distort our decisions, our reasoning. Keep him at a distance, if you can.'

'Did you tell that to Juliette as well?'

He shook his head. 'That's different. Juliette and Nathan have always loved each other. There was no distance to be kept. They were already as one when they finally got together. But you, Victoire, all your life is before you. Eric put his own life on the line even before I met him. I don't want you to get hurt.'

'Is that why you've never had a girlfriend, Jacques? So as not to get hurt?'

He'd shrugged it off, not answered.

Summer progressed and the grapes ripened and grew plump and sweet. The summer reached its zenith and began to recede towards autumn. The grapes swelled to their climax and the *vendange* came and went – this year a sober business, a far cry from the celebration of the pre-war years.

They were all weary, so weary of a war that seemed to dangle at the periphery of their lives, spreading its sinister net above them, holding them captive but never actually closing in. A war that was so far, and yet so near.

Chapter Forty-Three

Marie-Claire

My dear Marie-Claire,

It was wonderful, to receive and read your letter. I admit I wasn't happy to hear that you're working for the Nazis, and particularly for the Kreisleiter, yet I understand your reasoning and accept the inevitable. I am happy that you were able to be promoted, and proud that you are fast becoming a confident and independent working woman, even if I'm not so happy about your employer. But obviously I am realistic and these days one can only adapt to the unfortunate circumstances of war and hope it all works out in the end. It really is each man for himself, these days, isn't it? But in your case, each woman for herself!

Now for the bad news.

You know I would love to have you in Paris, knowing it has always been your dream. But the time has never been right, and now it is more so impossible. I'm sorry, but you cannot come right now. There is the question of accommodation: I am no longer living at the postal address you have used. It is now rented out to a friend of mine, and any post forwarded to me. I'm sorry, darling, but where I am living there just is no room for you. You would not feel comfortable here. It's very complicated and I really can't go into details, so you must take my word for it. It is absolutely out of the question. I also cannot find alternative accommodation for you right now. It's very hard for all of us and as a newcomer to Paris, looking for a job, you would be out of your depth and I am extremely busy and unable to help you. Paris is not what you think it is and I must advise you, very strictly: please do not come. Perhaps in a year or two it would be feasible but definitely not now, not this year.

I'm so sorry I cannot be more accommodating, my dear; it's a long story and one day I shall tell you what is going on, but at the moment it is all quite out of the question.

However, I am willing to help you, of course – perhaps you could move to Strasbourg? The wine trade is doing fairly well at the moment and I would be quite willing to send you some money if you'd like to move there, and also contact some friends of mine there who might be able to help you find a new job. Just let me know…

He rambled on for several more paragraphs. About wine and fashion and other matters that right now, Marie-Claire couldn't care less about. She didn't finish reading the letter. With a cry of annoyance, she scrunched it up into a ball, and pitched it against the fireplace. It missed by a long shot, knocking a vase to the floor, where it cracked apart. Several of the girls looked up.

'Bad news?' asked Erika. The commiseration in her voice was false. Marie-Claire could always tell. Could always detect the *Schadenfreude,* the barely disguised invitations to reveal more, offer more insight into her plight. Once the excitement over the rape itself had died a new topic had raised its ugly head: whether or not the *Kreisleiter* had impregnated her. A topic they worried to the bone while she silently listened.

It was, in fact, a secret fear of her own – but how did you know for sure, and how soon? Marie-Claire was woefully ignorant on such matters, and so, while contributing little to such conversations, she kept her ears pricked for solid information. She hoped Klara was right. 'You can't get pregnant the first time,' Klara had said with some authority. Klara had an older married sister who had taken months to get pregnant.

'Months!' said Klara. 'It's not so easy. It doesn't happen right away, not even if you want a baby.'

Marie-Claire had perked up at those words, but then Erika had countered, 'That's a myth. My mother told me you can. It can happen any time. It all depends on your time of the month. When did you have your last time of the month. Marie-Claire?' And all eyes turned to her, and everyone discussed her *Tage,* her 'days', and how long ago they had to be before 'intimate relations' for Marie-Claire to be safe, and how long since her last *Tage* would she know whether or not she was pregnant, and if the next one was late, how would she know for sure, and if it was very late – what then?

All of this Marie-Claire had agonised over in her own head, calculated and recalculated, trying to glean, from the titbits of information the girls offered, whether or not she was safe. In fact, she was terrified. If she was pregnant, then what?

She hadn't been keeping count, couldn't remember, but living in such close proximity to other girls, it seemed that *they* had been keeping track, watching her, calculating, and it seemed that, according to their reckoning, there *was* a possibility. Maybe a probability. And yes: then what?

In the weeks and days before Papa's letter had arrived she'd felt confident that, if the worst came to the worst, Papa would take care of it. Papa moved in circles where such things could be dealt with discreetly. Progressive circles, in which an unwanted pregnancy was a mere inconvenience, and certainly not a reason for marriage to the wrong person. Papa would help her out, without judgement, in such a case. She wouldn't even have to tell him who the perpetrator was; he'd wink and let her know that her secrets were her own, and to be more discreet next time, and even, perhaps, give her a little lecture on protection. Papa was liberal on such matters.

But now, after today's letter, if the worst had indeed come to the worst… what then? Who would help? Certainly not these girls, whose only solution was marriage. And certainly not Maman. Marie-Claire knew Maman's likely reaction. She'd rage and fume, and threaten to shoot the *Kreisleiter* for rape – Maman would have no doubts that it was, indeed, rape – and come down heavily on Marie-Claire for putting herself in such a position in the first place by working for the enemy: *she should have known! The Nazis are not to be trusted! Everyone knows they think nothing of raping women! I told you so!* would be Maman's final verdict. But she'd never, ever, countenance getting rid of the baby. Maman was a Catholic; she would want Marie-Claire to go through with the horrendous duty of bearing her rapist's child, and then either give it up for adoption, or raise it, slap bang in the face of societal censure, in the chateau. Maman cared not a whit for what society thought – she'd listen to her conscience.

Marie-Claire had a fleeting thought of returning to the maternal nest, burying herself in the warmth and safety of the chateau, burrowed away into a cocoon of maternal love. A yearning for the latter rose momentarily into her consciousness. But no! It could not be! That rebuke, *I told you so!* That was what she could not face. Anything but that.

'So what do you think, Marie-Claire? What will you do?'

She returned to the present, to the girls' gossip, with a jolt. 'Huh?' she said.

Ursula, the kindest of them all and the only one who, from the start, had seemed genuinely concerned about the pickle she was in, repeated the question.

'What will you do if you *are* pregnant? You said earlier you didn't want to marry him. Would pregnancy change that?'

'And what was in that letter? I saw it had a Paris postmark – was it from your papa? Did he say you can join him?'

'Obviously not!' said Klara. 'That's why she had a little hissy fit and tried to throw the letter into the fire!'

'And missed!' said Erika with a titter.

'Oh, leave her alone!' said Ursula. 'She obviously doesn't want to talk about it. It's basically nobody's business but her own.'

'We're only trying to help! Offer her sound advice!'

'Yes – we're all she has, and she needs support.'

'If she *is* pregnant, she really doesn't have any choice, does she!'

'You mean, she'll have to marry him?'

'It would be the best outcome. The safest for her.'

'She said she doesn't even *like* him, much less *love* him!'

'All that can change once you're married. It's normal for a woman not to be madly in love, but in time come round to caring for her husband. My mother said that's how it was with her.'

'Yes – my aunt too married against her will and now she adores her husband.'

'Especially since he – the *Kreisleiter,* I mean – practically proposed already. It's not as if it's one of those men who run off at the first mention of a child. She's lucky in that. She already has a solution.'

'Yes. There really isn't another option, is there – and she *is* very lucky. He'll step up and marry her. He's obviously besotted.'

Marie-Claire felt suddenly, violently, sick; felt the bile rising within her. They were talking about her as if she wasn't in the room, and that in itself forced her to step back, to dissociate herself from the situation, to see it all from a neutral, unemotional viewpoint. Perhaps the girls were right. Perhaps marrying him was the obvious, the easiest, solution. IF. Such a huge IF.

She stood up and rushed to the door, into the hallway, to the downstairs lavatory, where she threw up every last scrap of her paltry dinner.

Could it be? Could one have morning sickness in the evening?

No, morning sickness did not come in the evening, not only. It came in the morning, and sometimes all day, stopping some time in the afternoon. And then came the tender, swollen breasts, and oh, the fatigue, which, in Marie-Claire's case could very well be caused by the utter despair in which she found herself just a month after the definitive encounter with the *Kreisleiter.*

She had only seen him once since that day, because now, more and more, he was up in Strasbourg for, according to him, talks relating to his imminent promotion. In addition, she had – having developed a sudden keenness to do this job – several times had the excuse of delivering *Mein Kampf* to engaged couples in remote villages. It removed her from the office, from him, gave her empty time to reflect on the sometimes hours-long bus or train journeys into the countryside. The hundred copies of the first delivery were almost at an end, now; she would have to arrange for a new delivery. Anything to keep her out of the office.

On the one occasion she had been unable to avoid him, he had summoned her to his office. There she had met a completely different man to the one who had been her domineering director. It was a supremely awkward meeting, giving Marie-Claire the solid suspicion that his absence from the office was not entirely work-related, but that he had no idea how to pick up the pieces left by their last encounter.

And so he had at first continued as if nothing had happened. For the first two hours it was indeed a continuation of the formal, neutral boss-and-secretary relationship. She took dictation, closed the shutters against the brilliant morning sunshine, stoked the fire, brought him coffee, just as she had in the time before he had overstepped the mark. It was as if the rape – if rape it was; Marie-Claire still wasn't quite sure – had never happened. She had even started to hope. If there was no mention of marriage, or even of accompanying him to Strasbourg as his secretary, if they could return to normal, whatever that was, then she could, eventually, recover.

If – and that was a big IF – she were not pregnant, of course.

But then, towards midday, he had quite suddenly flung the file he was holding on to the desk and exclaimed: *'Verdammt nochmal!'* Damn it!

She looked up, and flushed. It was over, the respite. He had risen from his chair, and, his already gammon-coloured face now the shade of beetroot, was staring at her with unmistakeable purpose. He took a stride towards her, leaned over, took her hands in his, pulled her to her feet.

'Fräulein Gauss, it's imperative that we discuss the, er – the matter I broached last time. I admit that I may have overstepped the mark and pushed the, er, the – your – decision a little more to the foreground, so you must be wondering where we both stand on the little matter of – er – Strasbourg. I originally offered you a job as my personal secretary but as you may have correctly guessed in the aftermath of, er… subsequent developments, that was only an excuse for a far more intimate involvement. I had in fact already made up my mind to offer you marriage, which I subsequently did on that day, though the situation, er, rather unprecedently led to an unfortunate precipitation of the salient desired outcome, which I would eventually have made after a more appropriate courtship. I merely wanted to prepare you for the move to Strasbourg in advance of a formal proposal. You can now consider that as having been made, though in rather – er – unconventional circumstances. Please accept an apology for my admittedly indefensible and ungentlemanly behaviour as inherent in that proposal. The thing is, I shall be moving permanently to Strasbourg as of next week to take up the intended position. My promotion has been approved, subject to a few conditions that I am in the process of resolving, and shall commence with immediate effect. I only have to tie up some loose ends here so there will be little opportunity left to formalise the, er, matter, always assuming, of course, that your decision is in the affirmative; which, considering the great advantages offered to you, I am allowing myself to take for granted.'

He paused for breath, his eyes boring into hers, her hands grasped tightly in his sweaty paws. She had not the strength to tear away either hands or eyes, not the courage even to shake her head and say *no, no, NO!* She was a quivering deer, and his gape was the glaring headlight in which she was caught. Maman had almost crashed into one, braked just in time, a winter or two ago in a forest lane. The little roe had simply stood there, not a metre in front of the car, as if hypnotised, staring at them instead of plunging away into the woods. So, too, was she incapable of flight or even denial. She never even said yes. She only nodded, helplessly.

That was weeks ago. Not seeing him daily had given her a respite, a time to think and make decisions and calculate her prospects; there had been the letter to Papa and, recently, his patronising reply and now this.

Undeniably, she was pregnant. No speculation any more, no guesswork.

No options.

The girls, of course, only reinforced the sense of falling backwards into a pre-ordained future in which she had no say, no decision to make; everything was already decided, no other way out, because the one path opening to her was, logically, obviously, the best, a gilded road. She was the envy of the typing pool, her status elevated to the skies.

'And he doesn't even know you're pregnant!' exclaimed Klara, eyes bulging with envy.

'He must have made up his mind long ago, even before the Christmas holidays, and then simply lost control. I think he was planning a much slower courtship.'

'I think he *has* to get married. To get the promotion. They only like married men in high positions. Loyal party men are supposed to father four children each. Only the *Führer* himself is allowed to be unmarried. Because he is above normal human passions.'

'He chose you! You're so lucky!' was the unanimous verdict.

'He'll be so *excited* to know you are pregnant!'

Only Ursula heard her weeping at night, came to her bed to stroke her hair and comfort her. Only Ursula understood.

'I know you don't like him very much, and he *did* overstep the mark. There's no question about that. But, Margarethe, your situation is not that unusual. Throughout history, women have had to marry men they didn't really care for, have their babies. They simply got on with it, gritted their teeth and accepted it and you know, in the end they learned to even love their husbands and it wasn't so bad after all. I think, with your intelligence, you can turn this around into something positive. You can persuade him, for instance, to move to Paris, which is what you always wanted, and then do what *you* want. He'll probably get a young mistress anyway. All men do. And leave you alone. Please try to see the silver lining.'

And slowly, over time, it was Ursula who helped the most. She was right: women had always married for convenience. Even her own mother had done so; marrying her father had been a business decision taken by both their parents. And look at Margaux now, happy in her own four walls (as happy as a woman could be in wartime) and totally independent.

She, too, could go that route. But deep inside, Marie-Claire could hear her mother's warning voice: *'Run, Marie-Claire! Run as fast as you can!'*

But Marie-Claire had nowhere to run.

A personal letter landed on her desk in the *Mairie*. It was from *him,* inviting her to Strasbourg to 'make formal arrangements'.

She would have to tell him she was pregnant.

Chapter Forty-Four

Margaux

The hall telephone was ringing, and Margaux hurried to answer it. Always on tenterhooks, these days, always waiting for news of some sort. War did that to people. And as one of the only people in these parts to own a telephone, she was often the first to know, the first to find out the worst. She picked up the phone: 'Hello? Château Gauthier here.'

She listened. Gasped. And then shouted so loud Victoire, in the kitchen, could hear it: 'Marie-Claire did WHAT?'

A minute later, Margaux staggered into the kitchen. She waved towards the bottle of Pinot Noir on the countertop.

'Pour me a glass, Victoire! That was Madame Guyon – you remember her? She now works at the *Mairie*. The place is buzzing with the news: Marie-Claire has just got herself engaged to the *Kreisleiter*, the top Nazi in the building. She's getting married next week, in Strasbourg.'

The next day, in fury, Margaux shot off a letter to Marie-Claire: *Do not ever set foot in my house again! You have betrayed everything we hold sacred …*

The moment she posted it, she regretted it. It was too harsh. That *never again…* perhaps she should write another letter, explain… but no. Let Marie-Claire read it. Let her betrayal sink in.

Chapter Forty-Five

Nathan

It was euphoric, the release that came after you'd blown up a Nazi rail communications centre. Nathan wanted to shout and dance and sing and yell it out to the world. Of course, in the grand scheme of things it was only one small victory, but he'd *done* it, along with Henri, a chemist from Strasbourg, and the little band of brothers. Together, he and Henri had created the explosive in Henri's lab; they'd passed it on to Jacques' *Maquis* lads, who sneaked behind the wire fence surrounding the main Nazi communications central in Strasbourg, planted the bomb, set the timer and ran for it. From a safe distance, hidden in the back of a black van parked several blocks away, Nathan had watched the building erupt in a deafening blast of red-hot flames: he and Henri had hugged each other, laughed and gone their separate ways.

Nathan was supposed to return to Colmar, where other jobs waited, but so consumed was he by exhilaration that he decided on a small detour. It would only take two days. He had to see Juliette. It had been months, now; he had to share with her this new-found sense of certainty. That they would win; that good would triumph in the end. That it was all worth it, no price too high to pay; not even the price of one's own life.

He knew the way. He had visited her before, when she had first stayed in Natzwiller last December. He had a good map; he could make it, even in daytime, if he kept to the fields and forests, and used his compass.

Chapter Forty-Six

Juliette

Juliette's work finished shortly after midnight. Serving Nazis was exhausting and frustrating work. They were loud, uncouth and, usually, drunk, and the older the night grew, the more their legendary German discipline faded away and the cruder their behaviour became towards her. Slaps on the behind, bawdy comments, vulgar insinuations were all part of the night's work – she was used to it. The pub grew noisier and more raucous as the hours slipped by, and this was every night. It was as if the clientele, all of whom worked up at the camp – now in full operation – needed to empty themselves of whatever ugliness they had filled up on over the course of their day. Vomit it out, sometimes literally; and she was the one who had to clean up after them. Some of the faces had become familiar over the summer months; she knew many of them by name, and they her. She used her legitimate name and identification – there was no reason to hide, Jacques had said. Her new, official, German name was Johanna – Johanna Dolch.

There was one new patron who looked familiar, and she had racked her brain, while in the kitchen collecting his order, figuring out where she had seen him before – that face…

He, too, had seemed to recognise her. Since the start of the war she had had run-ins with several German officers, with or without swastikas, and they had all ended innocuously; but this man's face gave her the shivers, and that fact made her think back to the less harmless encounters, and then it came to her: Colmar, November

1940. The day the soldiers marched in. She, on her way to the post office. The ginger-haired brute who had stopped her, questioned her, and later organised the requisition of her home. How could she have forgotten?

Since that first spark of recollection she'd been on edge. He had definitely recognised her. Would he wonder what she was doing here, in a remote pub in the mountains, instead of at her studies in Clermont-Ferrand? She tried to remember – had she told him she was a student, or not? It wasn't unusual for an Alsatian girl to be working as a waitress, but a student, surely, should be studying? Would he remember? What would she say, if he questioned her? Her papers were in order, yet still. He'd been suspicious even then: eyes narrowing, the probing look, the question: *sind Sie Jüdin?*

But she was a quick thinker. She'd say she had finished her studies that summer, couldn't find a job as a vet, couldn't find a job in Colmar, had heard of a host of new vacancies in Natzwiller and Schirmeck, and applied. It was all supremely plausible. A burden of fear fell from her mind. She had nothing to worry about. There was nothing about her, nothing in her rented room, that could point to guilt of any sort. All she did was listen and make internal notes, which she then passed on to a courier who came once a week, sent by Jacques' network. She was safe.

Yet, walking home that night, up a lonely lane leading to the farm where she lodged, she couldn't help have the jitters, that sense of spiders running up and down her spine. She kept looking behind her. Was someone following her, or not? She had no proof, had seen no shadows. It was just a *feeling*. Victoire would call it an intuition, though of course that was nonsense – there was no such thing. Without evidence, there was no need to feel this way, no proof of anything untoward. And yet she was spooked, evidence or not. She put her hand on her chest, and beneath the wool of her pullover her fingers found the sapphire pendant she always wore, her only physical link to her mother. It brought luck; the touch of it brought calmness.

The night was dark, the moon just a sliver, appearing every now and then from behind banks of drifting clouds. There were no lights on the road. Overhanging trees from the forests on both sides seemed like black holes on her path – she avoided them and their shadows. She heard sounds, but it must have been an animal – foxes roamed here, she knew – and there was no need to feel fear. No need at all.

But then she heard it. Definitely. Footsteps. Following her. She gasped, and picked up her pace, but so did the footsteps. She began to run, but then a shout, an almost hoarse cry: 'Juliette! Stop! It's me!'

And she *did* stop. And it *was* him. And then he was in her arms, and it wasn't a spook but the opposite, the quintessence of love. She folded him into herself.

A whispered conversation, a temporary parting.

Later that night, Juliette opened the window of her ground-floor bedroom. She let him into her room, into her bed, into her heart. The raid came in the wee hours, before the cock's crow.

Juliette and Nathan, dragged out of bed by three, or four, or was it five, shouting screaming Nazis with pistols pointed at their faces. They were allowed to drag on some clothes, and then shoved and kicked out into the open. Her landlady, Madame Chevalier, stood looking on, stunned out of her wits, but then she, too, was overpowered. There was that ginger-haired officer, directing the others, bellowing orders. Both of them shoved into the backs of two waiting jeeps, separated once again. Shouts of: *Jews! They are both Jews! Scum! Pigs!*

It was only a short drive up to the camp.

Chapter Forty-Seven

Marie-Claire

It all happened so quickly, and had the quality of a dream; or rather, of a nightmare. It hardly seemed real; it was like an episode in one of the novels she used to read, so long ago. A formal proposal of marriage – in writing! – from Kurtz.

She knew then that she had lost. There was no way out. She sat down to reply, and kept it short and formal.

> *Sehr geehrter Herr Kreisleiter Kurtz,*
> *I am going to have a child. For this reason I accept your proposal.*
> *Yours sincerely*
> *Margarethe Gauss*

He sent a car for her the following week. She was brought to the home of a colleague of his, where the colleague's wife, Frau Baumgärtner, fussed around her, took her shopping, made sure she had a 'suitable' wedding dress (not white, of course; and nothing too festive, something practical) and hosted her for the two nights leading up to the wedding, a sober ceremony at the local *Bürgeramt,* witnessed by Frau Baumgärtner and her husband, quickly over. Margarethe Gauss became Margarethe Kurtz.

'What about your family, Margarethe?' Frau Baumgärtner had asked. 'Aren't you going to invite them? Your parents, your brothers and sisters? I know it's a just a small civil ceremony, but still…'

But Marie-Claire shook her head. She never discussed her family, her mother, with her future husband. There seemed to be a silent agreement that it was an out-of-bounds topic, forbidden. She assumed that Kurtz understood, but could live with, her mother's rejection of the Nazi infiltration of Alsace, because of the perks. Later, she was to notice that all the wine in the house was from the Château Gauthier-Laroche, and she too understood, though only vaguely. Sometimes it was better not to know the details. And so, too, at the wedding no mention was made of family, and no family member of either bride or groom was present.

It was a workaday, functional ceremony, the only nod to festivity a small bouquet of yellow roses, organised by Frau Baumgärtner. Afterwards, her new husband kissed her chastely on the cheek and whisked her away in a heavily swastika'ed black Mercedes-Benz to a reception at the Edelweiss Hotel in central Strasbourg. It seemed that the entire upper echelon of Nazi functionaries had been invited, along with their wives. Wine flowed, and beer; Herr Baumgärtner (Marie-Claire never actually found out what position he held) made a speech with several lewd references, at which Marie-Claire blushed and her new husband bent almost double with laughter, along with the rest of the male contingent. The ladies tittered behind lace handkerchiefs, and one poked Marie-Claire in the ribs.

The evening quickly morphed into a raucous singing session of embarrassingly bawdy German songs, after which Kurtz breathed a beer-infused '*Liebling*, it's time to go upstairs' into her neck. His hand crept round her waist, pulling her to her feet. 'Now, ladies and gentlemen, I have to excuse myself. It's time to exercise my husbandly duties!' he called out, raising his stein, causing yet more bawdy laughter and whistles and calls to *ride her to heaven!* Marie-Claire had herself only drunk one glass of champagne; now she wondered if it would not have been better to be drunk herself, to be numb and without care and without any conscious awareness of events, and no memory.

Up they went in the lift, Kurtz's fingers still digging into her waist.

He half-walked, half-staggered to the bedroom, fumbled with the key, almost fell through the door, then managed to pull himself to his feet and propel them both across the room to the bed.

Fumbling fingers wrestled with buttons and zips and, failing, just didn't bother; it was easier to simply rip things open, tearing garments and undergarments. Marie-Claire closed her eyes and gritted her teeth and retreated to a place within herself where it all was not happening. Where it could not happen. Where it was all just a nightmare, happening to someone else, to a body that was not hers, and she herself was untouched. It was the only way to bear it.

It was the only way, in the days and weeks and years to come.

Chapter Forty-Eight

Marie-Claire

Six months later

It was Friday once again. He'd be home tonight. She'd have him for two full days and three whole nights, smelling of death and putrefaction. Not that she'd ever smelt death and putrefaction in her real life before this, but those were the images his smell evoked. He'd tear off his clothes in the bathroom (after she'd run a warm bath for him) but not all the sweet-smelling salts and soaps in the world could remove that smell from his skin, his hair, his very breath. She could hardly bear to touch those sloughed-off clothes: she'd bundle them into a laundry bag and send them down to the concierge for the laundry service. Let them deal with it! Though even the cleaners couldn't get rid of that ingrained stench.

But worse, much worse, was the fact that his very *mind* smelt of it. Stank of it. It was like a sheath around his personality, a shell of something revolting. She had no words for it. And she was the receptacle for it. He sloughed it off, into her body, each of those three nights. She provided a mental laundry service for him, against her will. This was her entire *raison d'être* in his life.

By Monday he'd be rid of it, and she'd be rid of him. Then it would be *her* turn to slough it all off. That grim, grimy, stinking layer of whatever it was he collected at that place where he worked, doing whatever he did. She still didn't know. Not for sure.

It was only a prison, he said. A prison where enemies of the state were detained. Terrorists, he said. Bad people who were a menace to society. They were put to good use while up there. Hard work was the antidote for criminal activity, and these people worked, and *his* work was to supervise them. That was all. It was a good and necessary thing. Yes, the work itself was not pleasant but otherwise one could not ask for a more satisfying place of work. It was idyllic, he said, at the top of a mountain with far-reaching views of forested hills – a wonderfully scenic place, which made up for the contact with the vermin he had to deal with all week. Fresh air, the vast blue sky, forests and mountains – it was, really, the ideal workplace, and if it weren't for the clientele – well, one couldn't have everything.

He'd given her the choice. He could have requisitioned a lovely mansion in one of the idyllic villages on the mountainside, in Natzwiller, or Schirmeck; she could have moved there, and they could have been together all week. Or she could stay in Strasbourg and have a weekend marriage.

It was not a difficult choice. Fortunately, he had not noticed how quick she'd been to choose the latter. He'd assumed it was because she liked the shops and the cafes and gossiping with the other wives who lived in the city; a mini Paris, as it were. As if Strasbourg could ever come close to the City of Light!

He didn't know it was because of *him*. She couldn't let him know. She hid her revulsion, played the dutiful wife. She couldn't let him know how much it still haunted her, that day back in Colmar when he had asked her to stay longer, the same day he had proposed she come with him as his personal secretary to Strasbourg.

The five days between the weekends – they were given over to recovery, short respites between what was, in her view, three consecutive nights of legal rape. Friday, Saturday, Sunday.

As for her day-to-day relationship with Kurtz: nothing had changed, or very little. He had insisted that now, as his wife, she must address him as Dietrich, but that was all. She could easily have still called him *Herr Kreisleiter*, or referred to him as such when speaking of him to others (which happened seldom enough), for her role was still that of a personal assistant rather than a wife, and conversation between them continued as it always had: he asking her to do this and that, and she complying with his wishes. Occasionally, when reading an 'interesting' article in *Der Stürmer*, he would recommend it to her to read as well. And of course, he told her which visitors to expect that weekend or where he might be taking her on Saturday night (to the officers' club, to the Edelweiss, to some colleague's home) and what kind of behaviour would be expected of her there: *If Frau Schneider asks about your family, leave the answer to me; her husband is in the Gestapo and the less they know about your family, the better.* There had already been awkward questions pertaining to her family that she had managed to evade, and leave to him. *Why had they not attended the wedding? Were they perhaps anti-German? And the wine, the wine: would it be possible, perhaps, to get a friendship price on the wine?*

One can get used to everything, Marie-Claire had learned. It was possible to shut off one's mind to disgust and revulsion. Many women had done it before her. Many women had been married to monsters; throughout history, ordinary women, just like her, had married beasts, and somehow survived. She too would survive. She had never thought of herself as *docile* before this, but there it was: she was that. Exposed, and conquered. The Marie-Claire of the past: she had been a mirage; what use now, her beauty, that practised sophistication and superiority? All gone. Consumed by the beast.

And, as it turned out, not even a baby to look forward to. Three months into her marriage a gush of blood and tissue had ended the pregnancy. Just when she had started to look forward to having a little one to distract her from the horrific reality of being married to Dietrich Kurtz, just when she had put her heart forward into imagining what it would be like: a little person, all her own; the child would be her family, her only family, replacing the one she had lost. But now she had lost the child.

And lost the only friends she had. Gertrud, Ursula, Klara and Erika were long gone, left behind in the flurry of hasty wedding preparations that had excluded them; of being whisked off to Strasbourg by an over-eager Kurtz. Yet she did not lack for women in her life. Ursula and co had been replaced by new, updated, more mature, more sophisticated editions: Helga, Gudrun and Ingeborg, the wives of her husband's closest colleagues, had replaced the rue Stanislas ring of confidantes. Or tried to. Or were still trying to.

They were all in a similar position to herself: left alone during the week while their husbands did whatever they did up at the camp. They were all younger women, like herself, with the exception of Gudrun, who was past thirty and looked it. All, like her, married to older men of power. Unlike her, they were all ethnic German and, at least seemingly, women who relished their roles as the other-halves of men of Nazi power.

There were other young German women in Strasbourg, married to Wehrmacht officers and SS functionaries. There were older women, too, women in their thirties and forties and even fifties, women with long-term marriages, frighteningly superior: Frau Baumgärtner, Frau Schneider, Frau Habsburger; she met them at the social events Kurtz dragged her to every weekend, and at church, him claiming to be a devout Catholic, and church being obligatory for Catholics of a Sunday.

But it was the women of her own age that Marie-Claire hob-nobbed with. Women with whom, under other circumstances, she'd have enjoyed shopping trips and the weekly *Kaffeeklatsch*. But these days there was nothing to shop; the shelves were almost bare, even in Strasbourg. The women tried to make something of the bleakness life offered; they put a brave face to the world and laughed at their current situation, because, of course, when Germany won the war it would all be different.

She met with them during the work week, when she was left alone in the sprawling fourth-floor flat of the art deco apartment building in which she now lived. She hated it. It was all so modern, so sterile, so without character! The very antithesis of Château Gauthier. But they all admired it and came to visit once or twice a week, or she went to their homes, and she had managed to get into the swing of their chatter so as not to stand out as snobbish or boring or taciturn, and they sat in cafes and, sometimes, when the husbands were home at the weekends, went to dinner parties. She had adapted and now fitted in. Marie-Claire was now an expert at adapting and fitting in.

And then there was Silke, a young woman with whom she'd struck up a conversation quite on her own during a 'cultural evening' they had been invited to. She and Silke had met in the ladies' room during a pause in the musical programme; Silke had admired her dress, she had admired Silke's earrings, and they'd taken it from there. Now she and Silke met several times a week, mostly at Silke's home in a purpose-built apartment building just three blocks away, for, as a mother of two-year-old twins, Silke had less leisure time than Marie-Claire. Silke's husband was a fairly high-ranking Nazi in the Strasbourg administration headed by the *Gauleiter* of Alsace. Marie-Claire met him, Silke's husband, once: his name was Klaus and, unlike her own husband, he was close in age to his wife and was not only good-looking but had a charming personality. Which made Marie-Claire wonder.

She speculated, but hesitated to ask out loud, what Silke – and for that matter all the other Nazi wives – thought of the weekends. What did their husbands do to them? How did these marriages work? Did the other wives dread the weekends as much as she? Was this the lot of every married woman? Did *love* ever play a role? Certainly, every marriage was different, but Silke's was of particular interest because her husband was young and good-looking and charming, and worked in Strasbourg itself. Finally, she summoned up the courage to ask.

'How did you and Klaus meet, Silke? Did he court you for long? You seem... er, quite happy with him?'

Silke laughed gaily. 'Oh, Klaus and I have been in love *forever!* We were childhood sweethearts; we got engaged when we were eighteen and married when we were twenty-one. We've always been hopelessly in love. He's such a dear!'

That seemed to answer her question. And it was a fact that Klaus did not work up at the camp, which meant he did not bring home a veneer of mental grime for Silke to dispose of. Silke, she conjectured, was one of the lucky ones. If only she, Marie-Claire, had chosen more wisely, been less discriminating, she, too might have married a halfway decent man... but it was too late.

Dietrich Kurtz had made of her a shadow of herself. But she had made this bed, with her own hands, and had to lie in it. Literally.

Chapter Forty-Nine

Victoire

In retrospect, Victoire remembered the telephone's ring as being unusually shrill. Perhaps it was only a false memory, but the fact remained that it made her jump, and she dropped the bowl of soup she was carrying to the table, and it fell to the tiled floor and broke into many pieces, and soup spilled all over the floor. And why had her heart started to wildly thump? It couldn't possibly be because of the wasted soup?

She was alone at home; she had to answer it before it stopped ringing, so she stepped over the mess on the floor, which wasn't going anywhere, and hurried into the hallway to grab the receiver in time. Jacques' words fell over each other, rushed through the wire, a detached volley charged with a worrisome solemnity.

'Hello, Victoire. I'll make this quick. I'm on my way down, calling now from Colmar. I met your maman, she's driving me up. I'm calling an urgent meeting, this evening at eight, at Papa's.'

'At the Maison des Collines? Why there, Jacques? Why not here – surely…?'

'I'll explain tonight. I've got to go now.' And he was gone.

Victoire replaced the receiver. In retrospect, she remembered a cold hand of dread clamping round her heart. Perhaps just another false memory. That's how Juliette would interpret it. Juliette didn't believe in unscientific things like intuition, or perceptions that came from anything other than known facts. But Victoire did. Which was why she spent the rest of that day in a state of dark disquiet, nervous energy that resulted in her cleaning up not only the debris of spilled soup and cracked bowl, but the entire kitchen until the floor and surfaces gleamed, and then launching herself on the farmyard stalls, cleaning out all the rabbit hutches and the chicken coop.

She wondered if Maman would come home first, before the meeting at Max's home. Maman now worked as much in the little Colmar office and shop as here in her home office, meaning that Victoire saw less and less of her during the day. She often worked into the night, and was then distracted and not accessible for general conversations about the war, about the family, about anything except the business she was holding together. It was as if she had poured heart and soul into the propagation and sale of wine – and to the drinking of it. Luckily, Maman held her wine well and was never actually drunk. It was all distraction, plain to see.

Now, Victoire decided to pour herself a glass of Pinot Noir. Now that she was sixteen Maman had relaxed the rules a little bit; permission had been granted. One glass a week, on Saturdays. Today was a Thursday.

At seven o'clock Maman had not yet arrived home and so, unable to contain the tenterhooks that prevented her from sitting still, playing her clarinet, reading a book, she made her way over to the Maison des Collines, hoping that Maman and Jacques might already be there and the meeting could be brought forward. But no such luck; Maman's van was not in the courtyard.

The Maison was a second home to Victoire, and so, with just a quick rap on the upper half of the kitchen's split door, she entered. The kitchen was cold and empty.

'Coo-coo!' she called. 'It's me!' and walked through to the *salon*. There they were, Uncle Maxence and Tante Hélène, the latter ensconced in a comfortable old settee and knitting what looked like yet another woolly hat, and Uncle Max kneeling before the

Kachelowa, feeding it with kindling. Though the autumn had not yet properly arrived, it grew cold of an evening, and the cosy warmth was always welcomed.

Uncle Max looked up as she entered, and a broad smile lit up his face.

'Victoire!' he cried. 'How wonderful!'

He rose to his feet and approached her with open arms, folding her into one of his legendary bear-hugs, the kind of hug that seemed to wrap itself round you and made you want to nestle there forever, all burdens lifted from your soul. Even when her father had lived at home, it had always been Uncle Max who provided this sort of immersive all-embracing sense of fatherly protection, safety. Now, after the many hours of nebulous worry, an ill-defined anxiety that had nibbled away at her spirit and finally – she now realised – stripped her bare of her inherent buoyancy, his hug seemed like a safe harbour.

He seemed to sense her disquiet, for he released her from the hug, took hold of both her arms, held her at arm's length from him as he inspected her face.

'What's the matter, *chérie?* You look as if the dog's eaten your dinner!'

'I don't know – I thought you might? Haven't you heard from Jacques?'

'From Jacques? No, of course not. I never hear from Jacques. What's he done now?'

'That's just it – I don't know. But he called me at home and said I should come here at eight – he and Maman are coming too. He seems to have something to tell us.'

'I haven't heard a thing – how could I, without a telephone. Did he say what it's about?'

'No, not a hint. But I have a bad feeling, Uncle Max. I don't know why.'

He chuckled. 'You and your *feelings!* I would say we don't indulge in unfounded fears or premonitions. Come, sit down and let me get this fire going. By the time they arrive it should be nicely warm.'

Already half of her burden of dread lifted, Victoire moved over to Aunt Hélène, bent down to exchange kisses and greetings and drew up a smaller chair.

'Who's that hat for, Tante?' she said, smiling. 'I like the colours!'

'Well, then, if you like it, it's for you, *chérie!* said Aunt Hélène. 'I used one of Juliette's old pullovers for the wool – remember that red and blue one?'

'Of course! I loved that one! I'll take it!'

She settled into the chair and proceeded to answer a barrage of questions as to what she was up to these days. There was, of course, little news; now she had finished her Red Cross course, Victoire's life was once again boxed in by domestic and farm duties.

'But when the war is over I'd like to finish school and go on to be a proper nurse. Or maybe even a doctor. Juliette said there are quite a few girls studying medicine at the university. But I don't know if I'm clever enough.'

'Of course you are, my dear! And a doctor you shall be! You'll be brilliant – Juliette's right! But have you heard from her lately? I haven't seen her all year, not since last Christmas.'

'I expect it's not easy to travel up from Clermont-Ferrand,' said Victoire. Neither Uncle Max nor Aunt Hélène were aware of Juliette's involvement in the Resistance, and Victoire was aware of the need to protect them from unnecessary anxiety. It was a little white lie she was happy to keep.

Shortly after eight Jacques and Margaux arrived. They came straight through to the *salon* and immediately a chill settled into the room, despite the *Kachelowa's* radiant warmth. Grim, pale faces told the story: something terrible had happened.

Jacques did not bother to beat about the bush.

'Juliette has been captured by the Gestapo,' he said. 'Along with Nathan.'

Tante Hélène's gasp was almost as loud as Victoire's shriek and Maxence's outcry: 'No!'

In drips and bits, the story came out. Jacques' network of *maquisards* included a kitchen boy at the Black Ox public house in Natzwiller, and a baker in the same town. The entire Natzwiller area was abuzz with rumour and speculation, but in the end it had been easy to piece the story together. Juliette, already under suspicion due to a Nazi officer who had recognised her from Colmar and wondered what she was doing in Natzwiller, had been visited by a Jewish lover without papers. They had been carted off to the local prison at Schirmeck, or perhaps – speculation was rife – even to the camp at the top of the mountain. They were still there, awaiting – what?

'What? What is the crime? What has she done? What can they try her for?' Maxence's anguished questions were pitiful. His fury at Jacques, once it was revealed that Juliette was part of the *Maquis* network, was relentless.

'She is your sister! How could you! How dare you put her in jeopardy! Jacques, how could you!'

Jacques maintained a stoic and dispassionate exterior. 'It was what she wanted. She wanted to be with Nathan. She wanted to fight for Alsace. Nothing I said could have ever dissuaded her.'

'But what now? What will become of her? Where will they send her?'

'We don't know, Papa. Trust me, I am doing all I can to find out.'

'Can't you rescue her, Jacques? You and your *maquisards*? Can't you break into the camp and find her and get her out? Her and Nathan? I thought you went around bombing places? Surely this is a job for you?' Victoire wanted to know.

Jacques shook his head. 'Security there is impossible to get around, Victoire. Guards everywhere, in towers along the fence and marching around the place as if they owned the mountain. The camp's in a double enclosure of tightly spaced barbed wire, each four metres high. The inner one is electrified. There's no way we can get in. No way anyone can get out. We can't even get near, to throw in a bomb or two. It's unsurmountable.'

'But what is her crime? Was she caught spying? You said she was arrested in her bed, with Nathan?'

'That is crime enough, Papa. They call it *Blutschande* in Nazi Germany – blood disgrace. Any non-Jewish person having intimate relations with Jews is guilty of it. The consequences are extreme – it's as bad as being a Jew, according to Nazi law.'

Victoire, bent over double, face buried in her hands, let out an anguished cry. Jacques rubbed her back. She flung her arms round him, and sobbed:

'Juliette is my best friend! She is my sister!'

A knowing look passed between all the other people in the room. Maxence, Margaux, Jacques, Hélène: they all looked at each other, but in particular, Maxence and Margaux held each other's gaze, and nodded.

It is time, that gaze seemed to say. Victoire saw the look: 'What's the matter? Why are you all looking at me that way? What's going on?'

Margaux stepped across the room to Victoire, took hold of both her hands and said: 'Victoire, look at me.'

Victoire did as she was told.

'It's time we told you. It's been a secret much too long. Juliette really is your sister.'

Victoire looked up at her mother, her forehead creased in confusion.

'I don't understand… what do you mean?'

Margaux let go of her hands, turned away, gestured towards Maxence.

'Your turn, Max.'

Maxence took a step closer. 'Because I am your father, Victoire.'

'I still don't understand,' said Victoire. She looked from Margaux to Maxence and back again. 'The two of you – you…' She couldn't say the words. It was just too preposterous. Her mother and Uncle Maxence, together, making a baby, her? The very thought embarrassed her. She blushed, and said, 'You committed *adultery*, Maman? With Uncle Max?'

Maman was an upright Catholic; a rebellious and outspoken one, to be sure, but one with a deep sense of morality, which was why she so abhorred the Nazis.

'We loved each other, always have,' Margaux said now, eyes eloquent with an emotion Victoire could not decipher; for the intuition on which she so depended failed her here. 'It's all in the past, *chérie*, I promise you. We are now just friends. We slipped up, just the once, and you were the result.'

'But, Maman— That means…'

'It means that I am your father and Juliette is your sister.'

She couldn't look at the man she had always called Uncle Max. Eyes fixed on Margaux, she said: 'She's always been my sister! This makes no difference! But why? Why are you telling me *now*? Of all times, why now? Why not earlier? Have you always known, Unc…'

She couldn't say the word Papa. Not yet. But she couldn't say Uncle Max, either.

'Always,' he said. 'You've always been my daughter.'

She turned now to Maxence, met his eyes for the first time. 'But if you knew, why didn't you…? I would have liked to know! I needed a father! I missed having a real one!'

'Believe me, there was nothing I would have loved more than to claim you as my daughter. But she –' Maxence pointed to Margaux '– she didn't want it. And she's the boss around here. She told me to wait, wait until you're ten, wait until you're fifteen, and so on.'

'Does... does Papa know? I mean, I mean...' Confused, she glanced at Maxence and then away. It was so perplexing. The man she knew as Papa... was not. But Margaux understood what she meant.

'Of course he knows, Victoire. He has always known. It was pretty obvious.'

Victoire said, almost to herself, 'So that's why he never liked me.'

'Oh, he likes you all right; he just knows you're not his.'

'And that means that you, Tante Hélène, you're...?'

'Yes,' said Hélène. 'I'm your grandmother!' She held out her arms, but Victoire wasn't finished. 'Did *you* know, Jacques?'

Jacques nodded, rather shamefacedly.

'Why didn't you say! Did everyone in this family know except me? The one who most ought to know? Does Marie-Claire know?'

Margaux shook her head. 'Marie-Claire doesn't know, and Leon and Lucien don't know.'

'But why? And why now? Why are you telling me now, of all times, when we should be worrying about Juliette! My sister!' She choked. 'Why now?'

Margaux and Jacques exchanged a meaningful look. Margaux waved to Jacques to speak. He said: 'I'm sorry, Victoire – I know it's all sudden and especially now, today, it's all a bit much, first the news about Juliette and now this. But, well, I insisted.'

'Jacques always wanted you to know,' said Margaux. 'Because you're *his* sister too; he wanted you to know he was your brother. Blame me for insisting we kept it from you. But now – now he absolutely demanded we tell you, now, specifically now. *Because* of Juliette.'

'Victoire – we think you can help. We're hoping you can help. We want you to talk to Marie-Claire.'

'What's Marie-Claire got to do with Juliette being captured?'

'Well, Marie-Claire happens to be married to one of the top dogs at the Natzweiler-Struthof camp,' said Jacques. 'And almost certainly, both Juliette and Nathan were sent there. We hope that Marie-Claire can help. Help get information; but better yet, help release them. And you're the only one who can talk to her.' He turned to his father.

'I know this is all news to you, Papa, and I'm sorry. I've tried to keep it from you but now – now I've failed. Failed Juliette, failed to keep her safe.'

'I still don't understand. How can *I* help, exactly?' said Victoire.

'It's a long shot, especially as we've all cut ties with Marie-Claire, or she with us. Maman has practically disowned her, and she's not talking to me. You're the only one. The only one who's not at loggerheads with her. We – that is, Maman and I – we've been talking about it all afternoon. We'd like you to go to Strasbourg and see if you can persuade Marie-Claire to help. You're the only one of us she speaks to, the only one she actually likes.'

'Yes, but she doesn't like *Juliette*. They were never close.'

'We all grew up together. We were all friends, when we were small. Brothers and sisters; she must remember those days. She must, deep inside, *care*! I can't believe she's taken on Nazi ideology, that she's on their side. I can't believe she's heartless. I believe in her; that she'd be shocked to hear of Juliette's capture and would want to help. And if anyone can speak to that part of her, it's you, Victoire. You're the only one.'

Margaux, always so outspoken and assertive, looked at Victoire with pleading, bloodshot eyes. It was plain that she had been weeping.

'Juliette is like a daughter to me. She *is* my daughter. You know how you were all raised, it wasn't just blood ties. I was mother to all six of you. Max was father to all six of you. We are one family. Just that Max and I aren't together, as a couple.'

'Not yet,' added Maxence.

Margaux continued: 'Juliette is Marie-Claire's sister too, Victoire. You're the diplomat of the family. If there's anyone among us who can mend this rift, this horrible, horrible cleft in the family unit, it's you.'

'But Maman, surely you're the one who threw her out, because of what she did, marrying a Nazi. That letter you sent – it was harsh. Surely you're the one who should make amends, forgive her?'

'I do – I do forgive her! I just want us all to be together again! All one family! Juliette free, and Marie-Claire my daughter, once again back in my heart! But – but I can't. After the things I said, in the letter – I need a... a mediator. A go-between. You're the one to do it, the only one.'

'You'll be our ambassador,' Jacques said. 'We want you to go to her and – well, talk. Just talk to her. Marie-Claire is not evil. She's not a Nazi. She never was. She's just silly, and ignorant. We don't know why she married this Nazi. We don't know what's behind it all. We don't know if she has any influence on him. But you can go up there and try. Let's repair this family.'

'You could write her a letter, Maman, take back what you said, apologise. Tell her you love her!'

Margaux shook her head. 'It would look bad, as if I'm only approaching her because I want her to help release Juliette. She'll see right through it.'

'But it's true, isn't it?'

Margaux let out a wail of utter despair.

'No! It's not true! I want Marie-Claire, my daughter, back! In spite of everything, I want her back! Tell her I love her, I really do! Tell her I'm sorry, for everything! Tell her we're a family and have to stick together! There's nothing a child can do, nothing, to really break a mother's love. She has to know this!'

'But you still want her to save Juliette?'

'Because Juliette is her sister too. Marie-Claire is a part of us, just like Juliette. She'll want to save Juliette, once she knows. I know she will. Tell her I'll do *anything*. Bribe him, her husband. He can have my entire wine cellar. All the very best wine, the wine I hid.

Just let Juliette go. These Nazis will do anything for good wine. Marie-Claire is the key to the Nazi door.'

'And Victoire, you're the one to turn that key, to open the door,' Jacques said.

'It all sounds – well, as if we want her back in the family just to save Juliette, not for her own sake. Kind of – manipulative. She might see it that way.'

'No. It's not like that. Juliette's capture may have opened the wound in this family, but it's also the reason we can heal it, bring us all back together again. Please, Victoire. Please do it. You can find the right words, you always could. You're the family ambassador.'

Silence settled on the group as all waited for Victoire's reply. Only the trusty *Kachelowa* hummed loyally and steadily in the background, a calming presence in the fraught atmosphere. Victoire closed her eyes as if in deep concentration, or even prayer, but tears escaped and trickled downwards, across her cheek, leaving snail's trails. She sniffed, opened her eyes, caught Jacques' gaze and said, 'Very well, I'll talk to her. Of course I will. How will I meet her? Where does she live?'

Jacques breathed a sigh of great relief. Everyone did.

'I'll find out, and let you know,' he said.

Chapter Fifty

Marie-Claire

And then, out of the blue, came the letter. She couldn't help it; a frisson of excitement gripped her as she read it. *Victoire was coming!* Victoire, the only member of her family she could bear to talk to, the only one who had not condemned her, right from the beginning, and put her into the Nazi box. Who had not judged her as contemptible. There had been that one incident about that cursed book, *Mein Kampf,* but Victoire had admitted her prejudice and made amends; Victoire had been consistently sympathetic towards her, had always been considerate and kind.

If anything, it had been *she,* Marie-Claire, who had rejected Victoire, not the other way round. When Victoire was very small, very curious, very talkative, Marie-Claire had thought her a nuisance, and had constantly tried to escape the little puppy-dog girl always at her heels, asking questions, looking up at her with adoration in her eyes.

And she had deliberately palmed that little girl off on Juliette, pushed her away, sometimes with an unforgivable brusqueness. Juliette had taken Victoire in with open arms. And in the end Juliette and Victoire had become an inseparable team, and the boys, of course, had banded together with Jacques as their leader, and she, Marie-Claire, had been the outsider, the black sheep of the family.

Worst of all, Maman had rejected her. With good reason, Marie-Claire now realised. Maman had warned her, but she, Marie-Claire, had known better – thought she'd known better. She thought with a shudder of Maman's final letter to her, on the occasion of her marriage. It had been final, indeed. Maman had shut the door on her. She'd never forget that letter:

> *You are no daughter of mine. You have betrayed everything*
> *we hold sacred in this family. You have betrayed us all,*
> *betrayed your nation. How could you do this, Marie-Claire?*
> *Do not ever set foot in my house again.*

She was no longer a member of the family that had nurtured and nourished her. She was an outcast, homeless except here, in Strasbourg. With him. This brute of a man stinking of death and putrefaction. How had she got herself into this situation? How, indeed. She needed to know.

Marie-Claire, forced into an unprecedented course of self-reflection and self-criticism, was now alone in the world. Her present misery now forced her to peel away the outer layers of pride and even conceit that had protected her for so many years; she had cocooned herself away from her family and gone her own way, not ever evaluating her own behaviour. They had all warned her against taking a job at the *Mairie*, but she had pushed ahead with typical arrogance. One thing had led to another and now here she was, married to the worst Nazi of them all, with no way out.

But now! Victoire had asked to come. Victoire was coming – today! Victoire, who, in spite of having been rejected by her, Marie-Claire, as a child, had never been offended or upset; who had shrugged off Marie-Claire's snubs and still always been her natural kind self. No matter what, Victoire always reverted to kind; there was something inherently, deeply, *good* about her. She could not be anything *but* kind.

Marie-Claire had never been much of a cook and certainly had never baked a cake in her life, and so she had ordered some sweet specialities from a German *Konditorei* who baked specifically and only for the Nazi contingent of Strasbourg. Today, they had managed to fulfil her order for a *Schwarzwälder Kirschkuchen*, a Black Forest cake, which, Marie-Claire remembered, had always been Victoire's favourite back in the day. And she had *real* coffee. A treat for her little sister. In the days leading up to today a certain nostalgia had swept through her, a longing for the cosy comforts of home and family, the delicious warmth of a *Kachelowa*. A sister's love. Sometimes, even, the idea of a *mother's* love nipped at the edges of her heart— but no. Not that. The fissure there was far too deep, could not be crossed. Yet still: a longing, a yearning for female nurturing had opened a different kind of yawning gap in her being, one that longed to be filled.

The telephone rang. That would be the concierge – or rather, to give her the correct title, the *Hausverwalterin* – an absolutely terrifying ramrod-backed dragon called Frau Frank.

'Your visitor is here, Frau Kurtz. She says her name is Fräulein Viktoria Gauss.'

'Yes, yes, thank you very much, Frau Frank. I'll come down.'

She hurried to the apartment door. There in front of her was the lift-well, like a metal cage in the centre of the hall, a dark tunnel vertical through the bowels of the building, next to the stairwell. She had decided she would go all the way down to the bottom to welcome Victoire into her home.

The lift, a clanking metal pen pulled up by cranks and shafts, axles and chains, groaned and clattered into action. It was only two storeys down, and soon it had scraped itself into position on her floor. She pulled open the outer concertina doors, stepped inside and pressed the down button. The inner gridded door clanged shut and the lift shuddered and groaned and began to move downwards.

There was Victoire, standing in the ground-floor lobby, waiting. Frau Frank stood in the doorway of her own ground-floor apartment, arms folded, beady eyes watching, making sure that everything was *in Ordnung.* The metal cage of the lift ground to a halt, the doors opened. Marie-Claire opened her arms wide for her sister. Victoire, startled – for this was not the Marie-Claire she was expecting – took a step back, but Marie-Claire leaned in and drew her close.

'Victoire! Victoire! I'm so happy to see you!' she cried, and pulled her sister into a close embrace. An arm round an astounded Victoire's waist, she nudged her into the lift, pushed the button. The lift door groaned shut, the cogs and chains creaked into action, the lift rose slowly through the innards of the building.

'Oh,' said Victoire, as, a few minutes later, they stepped into the apartment. 'This is... different.'

'Oh, yes,' enthused Marie-Claire. 'It's in the art deco style, built in the thirties, very modern.'

'Really?'

'Oh, yes. We're very lucky to have found this place. We did consider a villa in the older part of town but in the end, Dietrich said this would be more convenient. We've been here since the summer.'

She chattered gaily as she showed Victoire around, small talk that would hopefully break any ice between her and her sister. She was desperate – frantic, even – to bridge the long uneasy silence that had kept them apart, and the guided tour provided a welcome frame of reference, something to hang her words on. The apartment was impeccable, thanks to the cleaning lady who came every morning for three hours to clean and cook Marie-Claire's lunch. Her name was Elke. But she was Alsatian, so Marie-Claire had taken to calling her by her French name, Esmée, and speaking to her in French – a private rebellion of her own. In fact, she preferred Elke's company to all the Gudruns and Helgas of the world. Marie-Claire told Victoire all these details, as if Victoire's sole purpose in visiting was to catch up on Marie-Claire's domestic situation.

'We also have a balcony! I really enjoy sitting out here in the summer,' said Marie-Claire, leading Victoire outside.

'Hmmm,' said Victoire, a sound that could be interpreted as either appreciative or derogatory; Marie-Claire couldn't be quite sure. Victoire had been less than enthusiastic up to now. One had to admit, though, that the balcony wasn't particularly inviting: a narrow concrete thing, with a view of the courtyard and car park below and similar buildings and rooftops beyond.

'Well, it's nice to get some fresh air and sunshine,' said Marie-Claire weakly, leading Victoire back inside. 'Come, let's have some cake. I ordered it specially for you. There's this *Konditor* who can get all of the ingredients – it's incredible!'

They sat down at the oblong dining table, already laid for the mid-afternoon snack. There was no tablecloth; the sharp-edged surface of the glass-topped table, the matching chairs with tall, perpendicular backs, were quite in keeping with the rest of the apartment's décor. Marie-Claire was anxious to know Victoire's verdict on the style – after all, she, Victoire, was the artistic one of the family – and so asked her directly. Victoire chuckled.

'Well – it's all horizontal and vertical, isn't it? I'm afraid I prefer softer, rounder shapes, a more cosy style, but of course I'm terribly old-fashioned, very behind the times, so don't mind me.' She dug into her cake with a small, geometrically formed fork and said, to mollify Marie-Claire, who had frowned, 'Mmmm! This is absolutely delicious! A real treat! Thank you so much, Marie-Claire!'

Marie-Claire chatted on for a while. Now it was all *Dietrich this* and *Dietrich that*, and *my husband this and that*. Finally, Victoire asked, in a conversational tone, 'So, what is he like, your Dietrich?'

'Well, he's very, um, very sort of – strait-laced? I'm not sure that's the right word. He likes order and… and punctuality. That sort of thing.'

Victoire chuckled. 'And he likes *you,* obviously! I do hope it's mutual. I do hope he's good to you, Marie-Claire!'

'Oh! Oh yes! He's very good. He gives me everything I want. I could not have found a more generous husband. I mean, look at this place! He does take care of me. And one day, even, we might move to Paris. You know that's what I always wanted, and—'

'But what about you, Marie-Claire? Do you *love* him? Are you *happy?*' Victoire looked around, her forehead creased, and went on, 'You know, I really don't want to lie to you, so my honest opinion? This is a bit like a gilded cage, and I wonder if it's what you really wanted. I don't know, we weren't talking much back then so you didn't tell me, or any of us, how you and Dietrich got together. I don't want to pry or overstep the mark and maybe it's none of my business, but I *am* your sister and I love you and I just hope he's good to you. I mean kind. Caring. *Good enough* for you. And that you love him.'

Marie-Claire said nothing. Victoire took another forkful of cake, another sip of coffee.

'I'm sorry. That was rude of me. It's really none of my business and I'm sure you don't need my opinion— *Marie-Claire!* Marie-Claire! What's wrong?'

She flung away her fork, scraped back the chair as she leapt to her feet, and rushed round the table to where Marie-Claire sat bent forward, her own plate with the uneaten cake pushed away, head buried in her arms on the table, back heaving with uncontrolled sobs.

Victoire managed to lift Marie-Claire's upper body so that her sister could fall into her arms, a blubbering heap of misery.

'Come, come, let's go to the sofa,' said Victoire, and, arms round Marie-Claire, led her away from the table. They sat down.

'I hate him! I hate him with all my heart! He's *horrible!*' bawled Marie-Claire, and then the whole story came out, from the beginning, between sobs and sniffs and abject wails of *I'm so unhappy! I want to go home!*

'Then come!' said Victoire. 'Come with me, now, today. Just walk out. You owe him nothing!'

'You don't understand! I can't! I can't leave!'

'But why not? Why not, Marie-Claire?'

'Because – because I'm pregnant!'

'What? I thought you said you'd lost the baby, a couple of weeks after you got married?'

'Yes, yes, I did and it was terrible. But I'm pregnant again. At least, I think I am.'

'Well, who cares! It doesn't matter. I'd love a little niece or nephew! And Maman—'

'Maman hates me! She'd never have me back!'

'Of course she would! Don't be silly. She loves you. She's your mother. She'd have you back with open arms.'

'But anyway, I can't leave him. You don't know him! He's very… very possessive. He wouldn't let me go.'

'How can he stop you?'

'You don't know him. He's a *Nazi,* Victoire! A powerful Nazi and he takes what he wants, he gives orders and people obey! He doesn't take no for an answer! If I left him, he'd – I don't know what he'd do. He just takes what he wants.'

'Just like he took you, on the carpet. Raped you.'

'No, no – it wasn't rape, Victoire. I didn't protest. I didn't fight. So it wasn't rape.'

'You don't have to fight for it to be rape, Marie-Claire. I might be young and inexperienced but even I know that. If you didn't want it, then it was rape.'

'No, but I was a tease. I used to dress up, and on that day, I was – um – provocatively dressed. Deliberately! I just wanted to play with him a little. It was a dare, the girls, the office girls, had said – you see, he was such a stone statue, and we used to laugh at him behind his back, and we secretly thought we'd see if we could arouse him, if *I* could, and I did – it was a dare! So it was all my fault to start with.'

'No, Marie-Claire. Just get that out of your head! He took you violently, on the carpet. That is so, so wrong. And then you felt guilty – am I right? – and thought you had to marry him?'

'Yes. It was obviously all my fault! And all this, this life here – oh, Victoire, you can't *imagine* what it's like, every weekend, in that bed with him!' She flung out a hand towards the bedroom. 'He's – he's like a ravenous, raving *monster!*'

She shuddered, and so did Victoire. 'Oh, Marie-Claire! If I'd only known earlier! You should have reached out—I'd have come running! You know that.'

'I was so ashamed! I felt so guilty!'

'You're lucky it's just the weekends, though. But let's get back to your leaving him. You must! Especially if you're pregnant. You must come home.'

But Marie-Claire was adamant: 'I can't. It's just not possible.'

'Everything is possible, if you put your mind to it. Within reason, of course – you can't fly to the moon or become the king of England overnight!'

'That's just it. He's beyond reason. He's like a god in his realm.' She paused, gulped and continued. 'You don't understand. I-I think he's dangerous, Victoire. If I were to run away, I don't know what he'd do. I'm afraid of him. I'm trapped, Victoire! I'm really trapped! My life is ruined.'

She wailed again. And then she blew her nose on the handkerchief Victoire had given her. 'That is… there's one thing that helps, that would help, and that's this baby. It's my one anchor, Marie-Claire. The one good thing. And I must stay with him for that.'

Victoire sighed. 'If that's really your decision, Marie-Claire, I'll accept it. I suppose a baby will be some comfort to you. Though you never struck me as the maternal type.'

Marie-Claire managed a chuckle. 'I know! It's strange, isn't it! But all the other girls here, my friends, I mean, they all have babies and children and they've convinced me it's the best thing. A baby will be something, someone to love. I can't wait!'

'Well then, I look forward to being an auntie! Now, then, wipe away those tears. If you're determined to stick it out, then you must make the best of it. Hardships make us strong. It's what we're all discovering in this bloody war.'

'How is everyone, Victoire? Maman? The boys? Jacques? Juliette?' She snorted into the handkerchief. 'It's funny, I've been thinking so much of home lately. So much. I never used to, I couldn't wait to leave. And now – now, even more than Paris, it's what I dream of. Home is home. I wallow in good memories – they keep me going. When we were all children together and we didn't have any cares at all. All one big happy family. So tell me – how are they all?'

Victoire hesitated, a little too long. She had come to Marie-Claire expecting to find the woman she had known: superior, confident, proud, a woman in charge of herself and her life. And that was the Marie-Claire who had first greeted her. Now, she knew, it had all been an act. This Marie-Claire was a broken woman, one who needed help herself. How could she now request help of her? Nevertheless, she must – how else could she save Juliette?

'Victoire? What's the matter? I'm sorry, I've been talking all about me the whole time. How is everyone? They're all right?'

Victoire coughed, awkwardly.

'Well, actually, no. They're not all right. There's... there's a problem. It's actually the reason I came, to talk to you about it.'

Marie-Claire's eyes opened wide. 'Jacques? Has something happened to Jacques? I know he's in the Resistance – it's so dangerous! Did they catch him?'

'No, Marie-Claire. It's not Jacques. It's Juliette.'

She told Marie-Claire the devastating news. And how she, Marie-Claire, could help.

'So,' said Marie-Claire, 'you didn't come here to see me. You didn't come because you wanted to know how I was doing, because you *cared* about me. You didn't come to reconcile, you came to ask me for help. Because you thought I might be useful to you.' Her face, so animated just minutes earlier, so reflective of every emotion passing through, now seemed carved in stone.

'Oh, Marie-Claire! Don't take it like that! It wasn't like that at all! I've always worried about you and hoped you were all right, but it was always so hard, knowing how to approach you…'

She reached out to take Marie-Claire's hand, but her sister pushed her away.

'No, I understand. I'm only *really* important if I can be of use to you, is that it?'

'Please don't take offence! It's not like that at all. It's just that—'

'It's just that your beloved Juliette is in trouble and you think I can rescue her. You always preferred her to me anyway. She was always your sister, not me.'

This was definitely not the time to reveal scandalous family secrets. But anyway, Marie-Claire had stood up. Her voice now was cold, distant.

'I'm sorry, I can't help. Dietrich can't help. We never, ever, talk about his work. I can't even mention it. It's as if it doesn't exist. He leaves on Mondays and returns on Fridays and I have no idea what he does in the meantime and I don't care. I would never, ever, intervene on Juliette's behalf, and if I did – well, he would probably fly into a rage, which wouldn't help at all, would it?'

'Because, Victoire, and this is something you won't understand, men empty themselves, their rage and their anger and their filth, into women. That's what they do. We are their laundries. That's their whole role in life, and it's our role in life, to be receptacles for the junk they don't want, to clean them out. It's what I've figured out, all on my own, because it's exactly what my husband does. And it's quite bad enough as it is. So, no, I won't intervene on Juliette's behalf. My own burden is bad enough; I won't carry Juliette's as well. And now I'm going to be rude enough to ask you to leave.'

The look the concierge gave her when she stepped out of the lift on the ground floor was downright venomous. Victoire even wondered if she had some kind of hidden microphone in the apartment, and had listened in to the entire conversation. Anything was possible in a house of Nazis. She walked out into the road with a deep sigh of despair.

The visit had been in vain. She was not one step closer to rescuing Juliette. And her relationship with Marie-Claire, another lost sister, was worse than ever. She had failed, dismally, to help her parents' plan to heal all that was broken.

Before she returned home she went to see Jacques, who was in Strasbourg again. He had asked her to come. 'There's someone I think you should meet,' he'd said.

She found him by following the strict directions he'd left her, and a tattered map, and using a password that made her feel that she, too, was a conspirator, a *Maquis*, a spy. She met him up in an attic room in a backstreet of Strasbourg, and reported her failed mission. Jacques was disappointed, but not angry.

'Don't blame yourself, Victoire. You did well. Marie-Claire was always difficult, always moody, and there was always a chance she'd refuse to help. That's what she's like. Unreliable.'

'You're so – so dismissive of her, Jacques! Didn't you hear what I just told you? She was *raped*, by that monster of a husband! Doesn't that upset you at all? She's desperately unhappy! Don't you care?'

'Yes, I care, and I suspected something of the kind – Madame Guyon dropped a few hints that she and Kurtz… well, that it isn't exactly a love marriage. But, you know, Marie-Claire made her bed, and now she has to lie in it.'

'You're so heartless, Jacques!'

'Maybe. Maybe I just have other priorities right now. Anyway, I didn't ask you here to discuss Marie-Claire.' He looked at his watch. 'He should be here any minute now.'

*

'Victoire, I'd like you to meet Marcel. Marcel, this is my sister, Victoire.'

They shook hands. 'I've heard so much about you,' said the young man before her. Like Eric, he was about her own age; unlike Eric, he didn't at all fit the image of the fearless guerrilla leader Victoire had built in her mind. She had heard about Marcel Weinum, of course: both Jacques and Eric had filled her head with stories of the intrepid teenager who had organised Strasbourg's youth into a force to be reckoned with. She had imagined a bearded, burly anarchist type, slightly uncouth, a bit of a ruffian, to judge by the actions of his Resistance group, the Black Hand. Instead, before her was what looked like a clean-cut, well-adjusted student, or an academic, perhaps, complete with glasses. She simply could not imagine him out there in Nazi-land, throwing Molotov cocktails over the fences of Nazi installations and slashing the tyres of SS vehicles. Perhaps it was better so: his disguise was his authentic self.

'I've heard so much about *you!*' she said. 'And I wish I could join you. I would in a flash, but...' She pointed to Jacques, and scowled.

'He's right,' said Marcel. 'Please don't be offended. The work you are doing, hiding Jews and helping them escape, is just as worthy and just as dangerous. Do not think of it as a lesser task. There is not a hierarchy of bravery in the Resistance. We appreciate what you do and honour you.'

'But I'd prefer to be out there, doing things! Killing Nazis!' said Victoire. 'I know for a fact that there are women in the Resistance. I'd love to join you.'

'One thing at a time, Victoire!' said Jacques. 'Maman would kill me if I involved you. When you're eighteen, we'll reconsider. Right, Marcel?'

'Right. It's a promise, Victoire. If we haven't won the war by then, you're in. You'll join the Black Hand.'

'Two more years! Will it really last two more years?'

'The way things are now, I'd say that's a generous estimate.'

Victoire returned to the chateau in a cloud of gloom, a cloud that settled in and darkened as the year went from bad to worse. Jacques went completely underground. Leon and Lucien moved to Colmar and Strasbourg respectively, where they both found jobs in the retail wine branch, Leon in his mother's own little shop and Lucien in a larger agency involved in shipping Alsatian wine Germany-wide. None of them came home that Christmas. Margaux and Victoire, alone in their despair, did not celebrate beyond Midnight Mass in Ribeauvillé, joined by Maxence and Tante Hélène.

Late that year, the news broke that Marcel Weinum had been arrested. The Black Hand had attempted to blow up a vehicle in which, they'd thought, the *Gauleiter* of Alsace, Robert Wagner, was a passenger. He and nine further Black Hand boys – for boys they all were – were now in the hands of the Gestapo. Victoire, distraught, wept at the thought of that fine young man she'd so recently met and admired. Nathan, Juliette, now Marcel.

She feared for Jacques. She feared for Eric. She feared for herself, and Maman. And she feared for Marie-Claire. They were all, every one of them, in jeopardy. Would it never end?

Prayer was all she had left. Her last anchor.

The year 1942 broke, and nobody cared. The war was endless, and Alsace was a sinking ship, a ship with a Juliette-shaped hole in its hull. It could hardly get much worse.

Chapter Fifty-One

1942

But it did get worse.

Marcel Weinum and the other Black Hand boys were hauled in March 1942 before the Special Court of Strasbourg. With remarkable equanimity and extraordinary eloquence, Marcel took upon himself responsibility for all the past activities of the Black Hand. He was condemned to death, and appealed. The appeal fell through.

In April, Jacques turned up at the chateau with the terrible news: 'Marcel is dead. He was beheaded yesterday, at dawn.'

Victoire could not withhold a cry of horror. She fell into Jacques' arms.

'We must be strong, as he was,' said Jacques, stroking her head. 'He paid the ultimate price, Victoire. He went with his head held high. He took Holy Communion before he went, wrote his parents a long letter – they let me read it. And before the tribunal, he said, loud and clear: *I am proud to give my life for France. I go with a pure heart.* Marcel is a hero, Victoire, and we must hold him in our hearts and take courage from those words.'

Victoire wept. She wept for Marcel, and she wept for Juliette. She wept as if all the oceans of the world were contained within her being. And yet, she refused to abandon hope for Juliette.

'Surely,' she said to Jacques between her tears, 'surely Juliette's crimes don't even come close to Marcel's? She didn't blow up anything, did she. She didn't try to kill Nazis, or anything. Surely she has done nothing at all? Surely we'd have heard, if something terrible had happened to her? I mean, she's disappeared, but she must be alive somewhere, in one of their camps, or something? Wouldn't they inform us if she was dead?'

'No,' said Jacques. 'Marcel was a prominent figure in the Resistance – they *had* to make an example of him. That's the only reason we heard of his execution. Hundreds, perhaps thousands, of prisoners are executed without a trial and without a defence all over Germany. Juliette could be anywhere. She could be dead. We just don't know.'

'I'd know,' insisted Victoire. 'I'd know if Juliette were dead. I'd feel it in here.' She placed her hand on her heart. 'I'd know.'

But Jacques only scoffed. 'You and your women's intuition!' he said. 'It just doesn't work in Nazi-land.'

'I'd know,' insisted Victoire. 'I would.'

And yet still, the agony of not knowing *for sure* gouged a hole into her being, a black hollowness that consumed her day and night. She yearned, she wept, she prayed. And all that came back was silence.

From bad to worse. In August of that year of despair, *Gauleiter* Wagner declared it official: since Alsace was an integral part of Germany, its men, like all German men, were to be conscripted into the Wehrmacht, to take effect immediately. Over the rest of the year some 100,000 young Alsatians were drafted by force into the German armed forces.

Leon and Lucien were among them.

Many of the new conscripts ran away to join the Resistance; Jacques was able to recruit several of these. But those men who refused conscription saw their entire family deported after they refused to serve. Leon and Lucien went willingly for this reason.

'To hell with this conscription!' fumed Margaux. 'I won't see my sons fighting on the German side! We will cope. Don't worry about us. I will bribe them all. I will bribe the *Gauleiter*. I'll offer him my entire cellar of prime wine.'

But her sons were loyal. They joined the host of Alsatian conscripts known as the *Malgré-nous,* the 'in-spite-of-us' forced into the German army. Like most of the *Malgré-nous,* they were sent off to the Eastern Front to avoid a conflict of interest.

Jacques was not called up. His father had had the prescience, before the war, to hand over the legal reins of his business to his son. Jacques was a winemaker, a protected trade. But he no longer practised; his *maquisard* troupe, augmented by the new horde of young men refusing conscription, needed a strong leader. This was more important than wine.

Of Margaux's four children, only one, Victoire, remained at home.

Of Maxence's two, not one remained.

Christmas that year was again not celebrated at the chateau, beyond the obligatory Midnight Mass, whatever spark of hope they had still nurtured the previous year now completely extinguished. War might not yet have arrived in Alsace, but its shadow had sunk into every heart and its heaviness was hard to bear.

Yet still, they all survived and, one day at a time, struggled on, devoid of hope and faith, merely going through the motions of survival. With Leon and Lucien fighting on the front line in Poland, Jacques as a Resistance fighter with his own life on the line and Juliette in the hands of the enemy, even prayer could not keep hope alive.

Victoire alone held up her chin. 'As long as there is breath in my body, I will not give up,' she said. And: 'Juliette is out there somewhere. I know it.'

* * *

In Strasbourg, Marie-Claire had another miscarriage. It happened during a visit to her friend Silke's house, so Silke was on hand to comfort and console Marie-Claire, folding her into her arms and allowing her to weep.

'Come, dear, it will be all right. This happens sometimes. You must mourn this lost child, but soon you will be pregnant again and one day you will hold a baby in your arms.'

'But I wanted this one! I did! It was the last hope I had! The only thing I could live for!'

'Nonsense! You have so much to live for. One day this silly war will be at an end and you will be happy with a brood of children around you. You must be strong and carry on.'

'But I can't! I just can't!' wailed Marie-Claire. 'I can't go on! I can't bear it! I hate my life! I hate *him!*'

Silke's eyes opened wide. 'You mean, your husband?'

'Yes! Him! He'll want to make another baby but I just can't do it any more! I can't do that thing! I can't make any more babies!'

'Oh, my dear, you say that now but soon you will feel better about everything.'

'No, I won't, I can't! Oh, Silke, it's not just about the baby I lost. It's about *him!* It's about everything! It's about living life with a man who is evil.'

Silke pulled away. Her brow knitted. 'What do you mean, *evil?*'

Marie-Claire could hold it in no longer. 'He is, Silke, he is! I don't know what he does in that cursed camp but I know, I just know, whatever it is, it's not good. It's a place of… of something really terrible. I can feel it, sense it when he comes home on Fridays. It's like this whole layer of rot that surrounds him. I can't describe it.'

Silke said, 'You should not be saying these things, Margarethe. You should not. You should be supportive of your husband. At least try to be.'

'How can I be supportive if I don't even know what he is doing? How can I be supportive of a bad man? What about you, Silke? Do you support your husband?'

Caught unawares by the question, Silke stuttered a reply. 'Well, um – yes, yes, of course, I mean, what else can I do? I mean, I try. I try to be a good wife and support him in every way.'

'But does he support *you*? Does he care for you, love you? I feel so lonely, Silke. My husband only married me because he had to be married and to have someone to screw at the weekend.'

'Margarethe! You should not talk like that!'

'I'm sick of not saying what I really think. Sick of it all. Sick of this war. Sick of Hitler and his damned *Nationalsozialismus*! It's terrible, terrible, and I don't know how any sane person can believe in it! This whole war, Silke, is being fought for the sake of a single madman. Hitler is mad, off his head. Have you read *Mein Kampf*?'

The question came like a shot, catching Silke unawares. 'Well, yes, yes, of course I have.'

'What did you think of it, honestly? What do you think of Hitler? Of Nazism?'

'Margarethe, please! We should not be talking of such things. It's disloyal. If anyone heard you…'

'I just don't care any more. And someone *is* hearing me – you are. Are you going to report me, turn me in for the heresy of saying what I think?'

'N-n-n-no, of course I won't turn you in, Margarethe. I do understand, in a way – I know what you mean. It's hard for me, too, and deep inside I do sometimes wonder…'

'I think we are all brainwashed. I think it's all humbug. I think it's dangerous humbug and people are being killed and Europe is one big slaughterhouse because of this one man. That's what I truly, deeply think. And I think you know it too. You're a good woman, Silke, you must know, you must feel, it's not right.'

Silke said nothing. She hung her head. After a while she whispered, 'Margarethe, I-I do know what you mean, in a way I know, but I-I can't ever say it out loud. I can't, I just... can't. Klaus would kill me if he knew some of my thoughts. I don't want to think them but they are there, and I can't help it, it's just these doubts, these questions, is it really true what they say, is it a good thing what we are doing, is it Christian?'

Marie-Claire snatched at Silke's hands, squeezed them, until at last the other woman raised her head and looked her in the eye. Marie-Claire saw reflected in those eyes the very same anguish she herself felt. 'No! No, it's not Christian at all and yet we all go to church on Sundays, and yet we support this horrible thing! Silke, you must not be afraid of your own thoughts. I think we know it's not right. I think we should be able to talk about it, about our misgivings. It's all just wrong. The camp is wrong, the war is wrong, our husbands are wrong, Hitler is wrong. We must be able to say these things, to each other, if not aloud!'

Silke pulled her hands away. She looked down again, and said nothing. Then she looked up, and whispered, 'Perhaps you're right. But it's not safe to even think these thoughts, Margarethe. Let's not talk about it any more.'

And they never again brought up the subject.

But a few weeks after this conversation, Marie-Claire rang Silke and asked her to come over. When she opened the door, Silke gasped in horror.

'What happened! Who did that to you?' Marie-Claire's right eye was surrounded by a smudge of dark purple.

'I told you he was evil, Silke. This is not the first time he's hit me. Smack in the face, because I had the temerity to fight back at... at night, when he rapes me.'

'But, Margarethe, he is your husband! It's not rape! It's your *duty!* You cannot call it rape!'

'I've been thinking about it and I choose to call it rape. Of course, it's easier if I don't resist but sometimes I just can't help myself and-and this is the result. I then just hide myself away for a few days so that it goes away. But I wanted you to see. To know. This is not a good man, Silke. And I have decided to call it rape. And I wanted you to see for yourself.'

Chapter Fifty-Two

1943

The fourth year of the decade was the turning point. The good news was that the war, like a huge ocean liner sluggishly changing course to return whence it came, slowly turned on its axle. Slowly, slowly, hope grew in the hearts of all those beneath the Nazi boot that the war could be won, the war *would* be won, this brutal Goliath was not invincible.

On the Eastern Front, the bloody Battle of Stalingrad, which had seen some of the fiercest combats of the war, came to an end over the winter, due to dwindling food and medical supplies. The last of the German troops there surrendered on 31 January. For the Nazis it was all downhill from then on.

But in Alsace there was no respite, and for the Gauthier and Dolch families, no news of loved ones; quite the opposite. Leon had been killed in Poland. Lucien was still fighting the lost cause on the Eastern Front, and they could only cling to hope for his survival.

And Juliette was still in Nazi hands, leaving a gaping hole in the joint family's heart. Certainly, they were all worried sick over Lucien; that he too might fall, any day. But at least they *knew* where Lucien was, what he was doing. For someone to be missing, to be gouged out of their midst with no hint of where they might be and what might have happened, whether they were dead or alive – that was the worst.

Just before the wine harvest, Jacques called another meeting at his father's house. Victoire's heart raced like a jackhammer – it seemed to her it must surely break. News, Jacques had said. News of Juliette? She could only imagine what it must be like for Maxence.

Over the past year the two of them, father and daughter, had forged a new closeness, a slow and tender readjustment of their relationship. For Victoire, it was a strange thing, knowing that the man who had, for most of her life, played a father's role really *was* her father, and she was, at first, awkward, reticent, towards him. But he had trod carefully, sensitively, and over time the initial discomfort had melted away, added to which the shared anxiety over Juliette had built an unshakeable bond.

Now, she sat next to him on the sofa in the *salon*, her hand clasped within his. He placed an arm round her and pulled her close; both knew that Jacques had new information, and that it could possibly be the worst.

Once they were all together – Margaux, Victoire, Maxence and Hélène – Jacques began.

'One of the Natzweiler prisoners was able to escape,' said Jacques . 'He was working on the quarry and managed it, somehow. He hid in the forest and was eventually found by one of my men keeping an eye on the area. I brought him to the Free French intelligence services I'm in contact with. They passed some information on to me.'

He cleared his throat, took a deep breath and looked up, and then away again – the pain was hard to take, the pain etched into the faces of those who waited for his words, the pleading pain of the eyes fixed on his, begging for release. Begging for some titbit of hope. Because hope was not his to give.

'First of all, let me get this out of the way. I have no news of Juliette.'

An audible sigh went through the room as everyone breathed out, the sigh of hope escaping. Jacques continued: 'This escaped prisoner has not seen her. There are no women in the camp, he says. It's all men, political prisoners, mostly, some criminals. Not many Jews, and the Jews that are there are also there for political reasons. Nathan was there. And he knew Nathan. And...' Jacques gulped audibly. '...and Nathan is dead.'

Gasps, moans, groans filled the room. Victoire's face fell into her hands and she sobbed aloud. Maxence, next to her, pulled her close, stroked her hair. Margaux and Hélène, too, arms round each other, drew closer still and wept.

Nathan was not a family member; they hardly knew him. But he was the love of Juliette's life and they, too, had learned to love him that Christmas season of 1941; they had learned to love his earnest reticence, the depth of his arduous determination to fight the Nazi scourge, the might of his love for Juliette.

'What happened?' whispered Margaux. Jacques, obviously struggling with emotion himself, continued.

'We've learned so much, now, of what goes on within that camp. It's a terrible, awful place. The men work in the quarry nearby, but are so malnourished they can hardly walk; once they are too weak to work they are executed. Every day there are executions, on the top terrace of the camp. Everyone is forced to watch. By the time a man is ready for execution he's a living skeleton, and that was Nathan's case. He could hardly walk up the terraces: to climb the terrace steps, he had to reach down and lift his thighs, one at a time. Our man knew him. He had shared one of the barracks with him. He was killed in April of this year.'

By this time, all the women in the room were openly weeping, and Maxence too visibly fighting his own tears. Jacques spoke with tears in his voice, faltering, sniffing as he spoke, but speaking nevertheless.

'I know it's hard to take but I still want you to know. I want you to know the worst of it so that we all know what exactly we are fighting. We cannot hide from this knowledge.'

He paused, took a deep breath, and continued.

'There's a building, right at the bottom of the complex, with a tall chimney poking out of the roof. It's a crematorium. It's where all the dead bodies are burned. It's where they took Nathan's body. Our man was a witness. Other prisoners have to do the work of carrying the bodies to the crematorium. You can see the smoke coming out of the chimney. You can smell it. The stench is everywhere.'

'And… and Juliette? Is there really no news at all about her?'

'Not a word,' said Jacques. 'As I said, there are no women in Struthof, or at least no female permanent prisoners. It's a transit camp, so some prisoners move on to other camps in the east, and occasionally a woman passes through. But there is no news at all of Juliette. I'm sorry. But at least we know about Nathan. The thing is…'

Jacques turned to Victoire. 'Can't you try again, with Marie-Claire? I know she refused to help when you tried last year but she's our most valuable link. I've tried everything to find out more, but it's all been in vain. If only she wanted to help, I'm sure she could.'

Victoire wiped her eyes on her sleeve, sniffed and said, 'Marie-Claire is as stubborn as she always was. She's unhappy in her marriage – desperately unhappy. But she won't help. She says she can't. She says she can't possibly approach her husband. She doesn't dare.'

'Oh, for God's sake, why doesn't the foolish girl just come home?'

'Maman, it's not as simple as that. She says her husband is dangerous. If she were to leave him to come home she'd bring that danger to all of us.'

'So what? We're family, aren't we? We should face this together.'

Jacques shook his head. 'Empty bravado isn't going to help. Her husband is Dietrich Kurtz. He's the *Schutzhaftlagerführer*. He's directly responsible for order in the camp. He assigns prisoners to the outside work details. And he assigns prisoners due for execution. He is, most likely, the one who ordered Nathan's execution. In the camp, they call him Doctor Death. That's who we're dealing with. That's Marie-Claire's husband.'

Victoire whimpered. 'Poor, poor Marie-Claire! No wonder she's so frantic, so terrified of him! But what can we *do*, Jacques? I bet he knows exactly what happened to Juliette – she was captured in Natzwiller village. Surely they brought her to him, and he knows? He *must* know!'

'I'm sure he knows. But I'm not sure Marie-Claire can help, if she's so terrified of him.'

Victoire nodded in acknowledgement. 'That's what she said. He doesn't bring his work home, and he won't talk about it to her. And – and she's terrified of him. He's a beast, and now I know who he really is – who my sister is living with – there must be a way, surely? I have to *do* something!'

It was a wail. Victoire, unable to contain her grief and her anxiety, stood up, casting off Maxence's comforting arms. 'You're right, Jacques. I have to try again. I'm going back to Marie-Claire. She must help. I can't believe we're so close, and yet so far! I'll find a way. I swear it. I made a huge mistake the last time. I was so concerned about Juliette I failed to acknowledge Marie-Claire and her own plight. Marie-Claire was right: I was using her. We're all using her, and that's not right. Especially you, Jacques.'

'I'm not...'

'Yes, you are. Jacques, you are. She loved you and you used her – oh yes, you didn't use her for personal gratification, but you used her all the same, for your political ends, and that's just as bad. You didn't really see her, and realise that she's in trouble up to her neck. And when she wouldn't be used any more you didn't care, did you? You thought you were better than her. You think you're the brave important freedom fighter and Marie-Claire is just a silly vain little girl who wouldn't do what you wanted, wouldn't spy for you. And because she wouldn't, you turned your back on her.

And even when I told you about her husband, what did you say? *Marie-Claire made her bed, and now she has to lie in it.*

'Maybe if we'd all talked to her more in the past, held her close, she wouldn't be in this horrible situation. And the very first time in her life Marie-Claire opened up to me, reached out to me, I failed her. Anyway, it's not too late. I'm going to talk to her again. I'm going to ring her – tomorrow! And I'm going to let her know I'm there for her. I'm going, not to ask her a favour, but because she needs me, needs her family. She needs all of us, but we've failed her. And continue to fail her: we see her only as a means to an end, that end being Juliette. But first and foremost, Marie-Claire needs *us*. And that's why I'll go back to her and try to make amends. I've left it far too long.

'And now, to all of you: goodnight. I'm off to bed. I need to think. I need to be alone. All this is too much for me.'

Chapter Fifty-Three

Marie-Claire

'*Bonjour,* Marie-Claire. It's Victoire.'

'Oh… Oh, *bonjour,* Victoire. To what do I owe this honour?'

Sarcasm dripped from her words. A whole year had passed since Victoire's last visit. A year, and two more miscarriages, and countless nightly violations, and bottomless despair over a situation from which there was no escape; her heart had hardened. But it was a fragile hardness; she knew it. The hardness of an eggshell on the brink of cracking open. Yet still, she clung to it.

'I just wanted to speak to you… I—'

'And ask for another favour?'

'No! No, Marie-Claire. I'm not asking you for anything – I just wanted to say I'm sorry, so sorry. I've handled it all so badly and I just wanted to make amends. Marie-Claire, all I want is to be your sister again! I want to be there for you – I want you to know I'm here if you need me. I made a mess of our last meeting. I'm sorry, truly sorry. Can we start again?'

'Victoire, it's been over a year! Not a word from you in that time. Radio silence. And now suddenly, this? There must be some reason. Why are you ringing me, now, of all times? What do you want me to do for you?'

'Nothing, Marie-Claire, nothing, I promise! I just want to repair things, mend things. I know you're hurt, and…'

'Hurt, me? Of course not. I won't let myself be hurt by the likes of you!'

'Don't be like that, Marie-Claire. Let me come and visit you again. No strings attached. No motive. Just to be your sister.'

Marie-Claire said nothing. A tidal wave of injured pride rose up within her, preventing speech, rejecting the outstretched hand. Her dignity rode on that wave. It protected the so fragile remains of whatever it was that made her herself, of which there really was very little left. Pride, dignity, self-awareness, confidence – it had all been eroded by the years under Dietrich Kurtz's thumb. And so the tidal wave had no substance, no reality. Pride had all crumbled away, and the tidal wave was a mirage, a sleight of hand, an act. It collapsed into itself.

She sighed. 'Very well. Come. Come during the week, any time, just let me know the day before. Just come!' Before Victoire could respond she slammed down the receiver. She fell to the floor, crumpled into herself, dissolved in sobs. 'I can't go on! I can't! I hate him, I hate him, I hate him!' she wailed to the empty room.

Victoire came two days later. This time, there was no awkwardness, no pretence, no playacting. Marie-Claire spoke her heart, truthfully and without subterfuge, and Victoire listened, consoled, hugged, wiped away tears, offered a shoulder to cry on; and Marie-Claire cried. She wept in Victoire's arms, and it was good.

Weeping like this, withholding nothing, was cleansing, healing, a letting-go of all the trappings she had clung to, the image of herself as Marie-Claire, that beautiful being, exalted above all others, looked up to and admired; she could just be *herself*, a woman, a sister, a friend, no shameful secrets withheld, no hurt concealed, all pain exposed and received into Victoire's huge receiving heart. Marie-Claire had always known it, but now she experienced it: a heart wide and unjudgemental, like a deep warm bath she, Marie-Claire, could simply sink into and let go. Let go of the pain and the humiliation and the despair. How could such a young person – Victoire was only eighteen – hold such power to contain and absorb and heal another? Marie-Claire couldn't understand it, and didn't try to – she only knew it was true, and let it happen.

'You're an angel!' she whispered, enclosed by Victoire's arms. Strong arms, arms that had schlepped endless logs and chopped them into firewood, mucked out endless stables, dug endless beds of stone-hard earth, stirred endless pots of soup, wiped many tears away; and now hers.

Victoire laughed. 'No, I'm not! I'm just a sister discovering what a marvellous thing it is to be a sister!'

Marie-Claire managed a giggle. 'I know! I can't believe I didn't know, all these years! I think I could have avoided a lot of the mess I'm in if—'

'Shhh!' said Victoire, placing a finger on Marie-Claire's lips. 'Don't rake over the past. It only brings guilt and shame and self-recriminations. That's no help.'

'But I was the eldest. I had a duty. To you, and the boys – Leon. I never got to say goodbye…' Once again, the tears began to flow. Victoire had told her about Leon's death. Marie-Claire had not even known her brothers were fighting on the Eastern Front.

'I locked myself out of the family. I thought I was better than you all. That I deserved better. And look where I landed. In the biggest mess ever.'

'And we'll get you out, somehow. The tide has turned in the war, Marie-Claire. I don't know what will happen, but it's not looking good for your husband and his ilk. He's a war criminal, the Allies won't be happy with him.'

It was then that Marie-Claire uttered the magic words: 'What can I do to help?'

* * *

For Marie-Claire it was the turning point. She watched and waited. Watched who came and went, asked innocent questions of her husband and waited for her chance. Played the role of the dutiful wife, but this time not as a subservient chattel but as a cat after a prey: watchful and yielding on the outside, hard as nails on the inside, stripped of self-pity. Victoire had lent her a new confidence, a new strength, and now it was all different. Yes, the weekends, those dreadful nights, were still an endurance test, but now, in the third year of her marriage, Marie-Claire was adept at playing her role: the passive wife and hostess to Kurtz's friends during the day, the internally numb recipient of his lust, receptacle of his seed, during the night. All while waiting and watching, listening to conversations she had previously blocked out, all with the intent of discovery. There *had* to be something.

Another miscarriage came in early 1944, but this time it left her unmoved. She no longer mourned the loss of those unborn children, three to date. As she told Victoire, who now came to visit regularly: 'I think his very seed is poisoned. I think my body knows it's poisoned and rejects it. Every atom of my being rejects him. I don't want his child.'

'But you would love it if one came?'

'I think so. Yes, of course; the child is not to blame for its father. But I would prefer for it not to happen.'

Victoire had nodded. 'Yes. But, Marie-Claire, if it's too much for you come home, don't let him destroy you.'

But Marie-Claire was adamant. 'I won't. He almost did, but I caught myself in time. And now there's work to do. I can do it.'

She watched and waited. Observed his friends, the husbands of her own friends. Pater Pius, the Catholic priest who often dropped by on Sunday afternoons after Mass. Robert Wagner, the *Gauleiter* of Alsace. Once, even, Heinrich Himmler, Hitler's right hand, came to Strasbourg and she and Kurtz were invited to a formal dinner.

She watched and waited and listened. But there was nothing to report. These men were careful, hiding their iniquities behind an outer façade of jovial complacency. It was if they truly believed they were winning the war.

Beyond that little clique of Nazi colleagues, tension in the city became palpable. The girls no longer giggled. Fear engraved itself on the faces, people spoke in hushed tones and nobody trusted anybody else. The Allies were closing in.

Chapter Fifty-Four

Victoire

In the late summer of 1944 Jacques called another meeting at the chateau. Victoire took one look at his face as she entered the room and her heart crashed to earth: she knew.

She took her seat next to Grandma Hélène – formerly Tante Hélène – on the chaise-longue and took her freezing cold hand. Victoire knew that her own hand was just as cold. Kneading her grandmother's hand brought a modicum of warmth to them both. Opposite them, on two adjoining settees but hands joined, were Maxence and Margaux. Everyone's face was grim: they all knew.

'Yes, I have news, and it's bad,' said Jacques. 'We must all be strong. I'm not going to waste words or use euphemisms. You all deserve the truth, as ugly as it might be. Because only in facing reality, knowing the full truth, can we be strong.'

He took a deep breath. 'There's been another escape from the camp – four prisoners managed to hijack a jeep, disguised as Nazi officers. One of them worked in the camp laundry and had managed to get hold of uniforms. Three of the escapees headed south, through France to Spain. One of them stayed in Alsace and has been de-briefed by French Intelligence. I have his full report. Right here.'

He tapped a wad of papers. 'I think I'll just read it out to you, in his own words.' He rustled the papers, took a deep and audible breath and began.

My name is Hervé Leroi. I was a political prisoner in the Natzweiler-Struthof camp since January 1942. I am 25 years old and French. I worked at first in the granite quarry and later I was promoted to work in the kitchen. The camp is built on wide terraces down the mountainside, like a giant's staircase. On the last level there is a prison block and next to it a crematorium. The crematorium has a high chimney. After a cremation it billows black smoke.

There are only males in the camp but in July of this year four female prisoners were brought in at around 4 p.m. one day. Some were carrying suitcases. As it was unusual to see women in the camp many of the men stared at them. Two of them had blond hair. One had very black shiny hair, shoulder-length. She looked Jewish.

Jacques looked up. The pain in his eyes was palpable. 'We thought this woman might be Juliette, so we showed him a photo of her. He scrutinised it for a while and confirmed that it was her.'

Jacques cleared his throat and shuddered, as if ridding himself of a cloak. He continued.

There was a rumour going around the camp that the women were sent there for 'special treatment'. Everyone knows that that means execution. This normally happened by hanging, and usually we were all forced to watch the hangings on the uppermost terrace. But some were killed by gunshot or by gas. The bodies were then cremated. You could see the smoke coming out of the crematorium after someone was killed. There was a high chimney which would spill the smoke.

These women were led down to the cell-block at the bottom of the camp by SS guards. At first they were together in a cell but then placed in individual cells, and managed to communicate with each other and other prisoners. One male prisoner who was later released said he was able to pass cigarettes to them through the cell window. This prisoner said that he later saw the women dragged one by one to the crematorium, which was just a few yards away.

It was my job to deliver food from the kitchen, which was on the topmost terrace, near the camp entrance, to the prisoners on the bottom terrace. But on that day I was not allowed inside the prison block where the women were being kept.

I later spoke to the German prisoner in charge of the crematorium. He stoked the fire that night before being sent back to his own barrack, higher up on the terraces. He was on the highest bunk and he could see out of a small window above the door. He said that each time the door of the oven was opened, the flames came out of the chimney and that meant a body had been put in the oven. This happened four times.

Here, Jacques fell silent. Dusk had fallen but nobody switched on the light, nobody lit a lamp or a candle. It was as if a spell had been cast upon the room. Nobody moved. Nobody took a breath. And then Jacques sniffed, and continued.

The next day the rumour spread quickly that the four women had all been executed by being put into the oven alive. Everybody was talking about it. There were several witnesses. One prisoner said he had heard low voices the night before and the sound of a body being dragged along the floor, and also the sound of heavy breathing and low groaning. This happened four times, but the fourth time, there were sounds of resistance. The prisoner said he heard a woman's voice say 'Pourquoi?' *and then the noise of a struggle and muffled cries, as if someone was holding a hand over her mouth.*

This woman too was dragged away, and she was groaning louder than the others.

The prisoner could hear the crematorium oven doors opening, and in each case the groaning women were shoved immediately into the crematorium oven. Alive.

By this time there was no more silence in the room. Grandma Hélène was weeping openly. Victoire, trying to withhold her own tears, failed and broke into a crying fit. Maxence was bent over, his face in his hands, his shoulders heaving. Margaux sat stock-still, her face stony and apparently unmoved.

'I think I'll stop here,' said Jacques, his own voice cracking.

'No! Go on!' cried Margaux.

'Grandma? Victoire? Papa?' Jacques addressed each one of them, and each nodded assent. Jacques continued, but his voice trembled.

I spoke the next day with the cleaner who works in the crematorium. He said that he opened the door later that night and saw four blackened bodies within. The next morning his duty was to clear the ashes out of the crematorium oven.

There had been many SS officials in the crematorium building the night of the execution, as well as the French prisoner who worked there. He did not speak German but said the officers were all discussing the women. One of them was the camp doctor and another was a medical orderly. Also present was the Schutzhaftlagerführer, *Dietrich Kurtz. We all knew him by sight and feared him; we called him Dr Death. It was clear that he was giving orders. The women had all been sedated before being put in the oven, feet first. But the final prisoner came to her senses at the last minute and struggled. There were enough men who were able to push her down and into the oven, but she was able to reach out in defence and scratched Kurtz's face. The next day we were all able to see the scratches on Kurtz's face.*

By the time Jacques finished speaking his voice could hardly be heard above the weeping. Hélène kept repeating *No. No. No. No. No.* Margaux's face had crumpled. Maxence's was buried in his hands, and his shoulders heaved. Victoire was a silent stone.

Jacques threw aside the wad of papers and kneeled before his grandmother, who leaned forward to embrace him, her back trembling with the force of her sobs.

Jacques stood up. 'Brandy,' he said, 'we all need brandy. Wine won't do it tonight.'

The next day, Victoire dialled Marie-Claire's number. 'I'm coming, today,' she said. 'Something's happened.'

Chapter Fifty-Five

Marie-Claire

A telephone ringing in the middle of the night was always bad news, and when she heard the voice screaming down the receiver Marie-Claire knew that this was *very* bad. It was shrill, panicked, so loud that Marie-Claire had to hold it away from her ear. Silke, in hysterics.

'He's dead, he's dead!' Silke screamed into the phone. 'It's over, it's over, it's over! *Es ist vorbei! Ich bin am Ende!* I'm at my end!'

It took a further few minutes before Marie-Claire could extract a coherent story from Silke. Apparently, she'd been woken in her sleep by a loud bang. She'd jolted upright, found the space next to her where Klaus usually lay empty, and rushed into the living room, then his study, then the bathroom. She found him in the bathtub, limp, covered in blood, blood-splatter on all the tiled walls. His pistol lay limp in his hand: he had shot himself in the heart.

'You're my only friend, Marie-Claire, the only one who understands! What am I to do? Where am I to go?'

'I'm coming,' said Marie-Claire, 'at once. But ring the police.'

'You can't come! The curfew!'

'I don't care about the curfew. I'm coming.'

Silke was still in hysterics when Marie-Claire arrived, collapsed into Marie-Claire's arms the moment she opened the door. Marie-Claire led her, weeping, to the bedroom. Through the open bathroom door, she could see the bathtub, the top of Klaus's head, the splatter on the walls. She shuddered.

Silke had had the presence of mind to call the police, and her nanny to take the two toddlers away. Two officers arrived half an hour later. They went about their routine procedures, called for an ambulance, arranged for the removal of the body, interviewed Silke. Both officers were native Alsatians. Both had an air almost of approval.

'A Nazi officer, eh? That's the third Nazi suicide we've had this week. They're dropping like flies.' He spoke in French, to Marie-Claire. He smirked, and mouthed some words that, Marie-Claire was certain, were *good riddance.*

'Did he leave a suicide note? They usually do, when they go like this.'

They found one, on his writing pad in his study: a letter of apology advising Silke to return to her parents with the children. That was all.

'You can come and stay with me for a while, if you like,' said Marie-Claire. 'You can't stay here!'

But Silke ran off that very day, back to her childhood home in Hamburg, taking the twins with her. 'I can't deal with this. Let the Nazis bury the body!' she said as she threw her clothes into a suitcase. Marie-Claire helped her carry luggage and twins down to the taxi, helped them all onto the train and waved goodbye to her only friend in Strasbourg.

If only, if only, she thought to herself. If only her own husband would do the same… she'd be free. In spite of the horror involved in finding a body in a bathtub full of blood, she envied Silke.

But Kurtz remained remarkably sanguine. Discussion of 'work' continued to be taboo at home, though now Marie-Claire tried repeatedly to raise the subject. After all, it was all everyone was talking about. He appeased her with virtual pats on the head. 'Don't worry, my dear,' he'd say, 'Hitler is almighty and we will win in the end. Your friend's husband was a coward. A true patriot does not kill himself, he fights to the end and dies standing. We must be strong and trust that God is on our side. At the last moment there will be a miracle that will save us all.'

'He really believes it,' Marie-Claire told Victoire at her next visit. 'He's so relaxed! Everyone else is in panic, and all he tells me is not to worry my pretty little head.'

'It's all show,' said Victoire. 'Hitler is finished. It's all a matter of time.'

But Marie-Claire knew that something was wrong. She knew her husband. And so she watched. Something was up, something sinister and terrifying. A plot was in the making. His behaviour was stranger than ever.

For instance: the men he brought into their home. He'd lock himself away with them for hours in his study. She tried kneeling at the door, peeping through the keyhole, putting a glass to the door in order to listen, but invariably there'd be a key in the inside lock and a radio blaring at the same time – as if he knew she might be eavesdropping. As if he no longer trusted her.

Suspicion grew. She noticed that the most frequent visitor was Pater Pius, who came now almost every Sunday afternoon and stayed till evening. Pius gave her gooseflesh. For a man of God he was astoundingly – well, *creepy* was the only word she could find. His eyes were pits of something so dark and terrifying. She avoided them at all costs, yet they'd bore into hers as if demanding she meet their gaze. She'd flicker a look at him, and recoil in a barely concealed shudder.

One afternoon in mid-August he was there again. Unusually, the study door was open and as she walked past, she spied the two of them, standing at the desk. As usual, the radio was blaring: military music. She stopped for a moment. Kurtz placed some papers into a manila envelope, then he handed a small leather pouch to the priest. They shook hands. At that moment Kurtz looked up and caught her in the doorway. 'What are you doing there? Go away!' he barked, and she leapt away as if bitten, ran to the kitchen and stayed there until the priest had left.

When she heard the front door click shut, she emerged and walked over to the study to inform her husband that dinner was ready. She knocked and waited for his *herein*, just as she had in Colmar. 'Dinner's ready,' she said, but her eyes immediately drifted to the wall behind the desk. The oil painting that always hung there was slightly awry. Kurtz's eyes followed her gaze and, for a fleeting moment, his face was that of a deer caught in the headlights: shock, guilt, fear registered there. And then the face smoothed out again, and anger registered instead.

'Why were you watching us earlier, Margarethe? Why did you not walk past, when you saw the door was open? Are you spying on me?'

She stammered, 'No, no, of course not, not at all, I was just waiting to ask if I could serve you both coffee...'

'Well, don't let it happen again. If we require coffee, I'll ask for it.'

Later that night, when Kurtz was in the bathroom preparing for bed, she tried to return to the study, but the door was locked. *That* was unusual. There was nothing in the room worth stealing, apart from that awry oil painting, an original by Josef Hoffmann. Something was off.

The next morning, Sunday, Kurtz retreated to his study and spent several hours in there. She brought him – at his request – a cup of coffee. She set the cup down on the table and glanced at the painting. It was no longer awry.

Marie-Claire might not be as intuitive as Victoire was said to be, but all her senses were now on full alert. It was no longer conjecture: something was very wrong. Something devious was going on, and she had to find out what. She'd have to wait till Monday.

*

On Monday, Kurtz left for work as usual. The study door remained locked. She had to get in…

At nine o'clock, as usual, Elke, the cleaning lady, arrived with her bucket and a myriad of rags. As usual, Marie-Claire chatted with her in their forbidden native language, and casually mentioned, as if in passing, 'I wonder if you have a duplicate key to my husband's study? He seems to have locked it by mistake.'

'By mistake? Madame, men don't lock their studies by mistake. If it is locked, it is deliberate.'

Her eyes narrowed. 'But yes, I do have a key. I have duplicate keys for all the rooms in the building.'

'Could you – could you perhaps lend it to me, just for a day?'

She held her breath. The reply would be a test. Elke was a native Alsatian. Most native Alsatians detested the Nazis and wanted them gone. But some had sought their own advantage, and worked for them. Elke had done so; she could not have acquired this job in a house occupied by Nazi tenants without having passed an initial intense interrogation by the concierge.

She and Elke had, up to now, enjoyed a certain camaraderie. Elke knew that she, Marie-Claire, was troubled, and that Kurtz was the cause of her trouble. She had always felt that Elke, secretly, was on her side. And besides, Elke must know that time was up for the Nazis, and if she had once sought advantage on that side of the fence, surely she would know that it was time to switch sides.

This was the test. Marie-Claire held her breath…

And then the great release. Without a word, Elke plunged her hand into her apron pocket, removed a bunch of keys, inspected them all, walked to the study door, tried a few.

One of the keys turned in the lock.

Again, not a word was spoken as Elke eased the key from the keychain and handed it to Marie-Claire. A slight nod of understanding – that was all.

'Thanks,' said Marie-Claire. 'I'll return it tomorrow.'

The moment Elke left the apartment Marie-Claire was in her husband's study. She carefully lifted the Hoffmann painting from the wall. It was as she had suspected: behind the painting was a safe, with a combination lock set into the metal door.

Marie-Claire inspected the lock. She tried it out, with the eight digits of Kurtz's birthday. Nothing happened. She tried the shortened version: six digits. Nothing happened. She tried her own birthday: eight digits, then six. Still nothing. Panic gripped her. What else could he have used as a combination? Had he written it down somewhere? Where? She dashed to his desk, looked through the drawers for some note with a number written on it. Perhaps it was a random number that he had memorised… Marie-Claire *knew*, now, she simply *knew,* that it was utterly vital for her to open that safe – but how?

She looked wildly around the room for a clue, a hint. There was a bookshelf, with only a few books on it. *Mein Kampf,* of course, and a biography of Adolf Hitler, and a few others on the history of Germany and Austria and Nazi propaganda. A flash of light went through her mind. She walked to the bookshelf, removed the Hitler biography and opened it, scanning the first pages. She found what she was looking for.

Back at the safe, her hand trembling slightly, she twisted the lock back and forth to the digits *20041889.* Hitler's birthdate. Nothing happened. Then she tried 200489. The safe clicked and sprang open. She gasped in delight.

Inside the safe were only two objects. A large manila envelope, most likely the same one she had seen in Kurtz's hand through the doorway. And a leather pouch, this one much larger than the one Pater Pius had taken.

She took both objects to the desk, sat down at it. Opened the pouch, and gasped. It was filled with jewellery. Brooches, rings, bracelets, watches, gold chains and pearls and stones that even with an amateur eye, Marie-Claire could tell were precious.

She stuffed everything back in the pouch and picked up the envelope. It was slightly bulky: there was more than paper in it.

She shook out its contents onto the desk. Picked them up, inspected them...

And then she did not gasp. She gave a cry of horror, and rushed to the telephone.

'Victoire! Victoire, you must come, at once! Today! It's an emergency!'

Chapter Fifty-Six

Victoire

It really didn't suit her to travel to Strasbourg today, but Marie-Claire had obviously been desperate. *An emergency,* she'd said. What could that mean?

It was inconvenient, because the wine harvest was just a few weeks away and, without the usual hands – all the younger males of the district had been conscripted and were somewhere in the East, or dead – it was mainly up to Victoire to recruit pickers from the surrounding villages. There was some competition between the Ribeauvillé *domaines*. Pickers this year would be mostly female, many children, older people, anyone with two working hands. But Marie-Claire was not one to unnecessarily panic: she had to go.

The concierge gave Victoire the creeps. Those beady, suspicious eyes, when Frau Frank let her in, the grudging telephone call up to Marie-Claire, the disagreeable tightening of her already thin lips – entering Marie-Claire's building was like walking into a refrigerator and closing the door behind one. Victoire nodded at Frau Frank and stepped into the lift. Slowly, the concertina-grille door clanked shut, the chains and pulleys began their creaking and cranking, and the lift slowly moved upwards.

Marie-Claire was waiting on the fourth-floor landing. Victoire saw her feet first through the grille, and then her legs, her torso, and finally her face. It was the face of a person about to be led to the gallows.

Marie-Claire yanked her out of the lift and almost dragged her into the apartment and slammed the door behind her.

'You have to help me!' she cried. 'I found him out! He's planning to flee! In two weeks' time! It's all planned! And – and to kill me!'

'Calm down, Marie-Claire, and tell me what happened. From the beginning.'

And so Marie-Claire told her all. About the visit of Pater Pius on Sunday, and the awry painting, and the locked door, and the key, and the combination, and the manila envelope, and the contents of the latter. While speaking, falling over the words, she led Victoire into the study, removed the painting, opened the safe, and showed her the evidence.

'See,' she said, shaking the contents from the envelope onto the desk, picking up the items one by one, handing them to Victoire, breathlessly explaining all the while, words tumbling from her lips. 'A passport. With his photo, Victoire, but a different name: Roland Schneider. Obviously forged! And letters, look. Correspondence with a priest, Pater Paul, in Karlsruhe, who seems to have organised the whole thing. And he – Dietrich – wanted to take me along too, but Pater Paul advised him against it as I would only complicate everything. And Dietrich said if he left me behind, I could be a danger because I knew too much, I could name names; I could name Pater Pius and also provide photos of himself, of Dietrich, identify him. And Pater Paul said, "You have to get rid of her, then." Victoire, that means, *kill* me, doesn't it?'

Victoire nodded. 'That's what it means, yes. But how on earth does he expect to flee when Germany loses? Does he think he can stay hidden forever?

'No. Victoire, look!' Marie-Claire waved a sheet of paper at her sister. 'A *list!* A list of addresses, all the way through Germany, down to south Tyrol. And names of people. Priests, Victoire! They are all Catholic priests, and they are going to help him flee! It's all planned out! He's going to stay with these priests – first in Karlsruhe, then

Nürnberg, then Salzburg, all the way down to Tyrol. And then he's to wait for a while, and then cross over into Italy, and get a ship, the *Maria Rosario*. To – to Buenos Aires, Argentina! His passage is booked already! He wants to flee to Argentina!'

'I bet lots of Nazis will try to flee, now the game is up. Rats fleeing a sinking ship. And what's this?'

Victoire picked up the pouch, loosened the fastening, upended the leather bag so that its contents spilled in a clattering, glittering heap onto the desk. She grasped a handful of gold chains and necklaces, pearl chokers and jewelled rings and brooches.

'The bastard! Do you know where this came from, Marie-Claire? From his victims. The people he killed. Jews.' She let the jewellery fall, held up one piece after the other. 'I'm no jeweller but I think some of these things must be very valuable. This necklace, for example. That looks like real diamonds. And you say the priest had a smaller pouch?'

Marie-Claire nodded. 'I saw Dietrich hand it over.'

'Payment, that's what it is. He paid this Pater Pius and he's going to pay all those other priests on his escape route with these valuables. What a bunch of murdering thieves!'

'But *priests*, Victoire? Catholic priests? Christians? How can they? Don't they see the evil? Surely it's the duty of the Church to resist?'

'Some people are corruptible, Marie-Claire. Even so-called Christians. I guess for some people there's a breaking point where temptation and greed win out. And power. And— oh! Marie-Claire!'

'What?'

Victoire was holding up a thin gold chain on which dangled a small blue pendant.

'This is – was – Juliette's! I'd recognise it anywhere, that pear shape. She always wore it – it was her mother's. She wore it in remembrance. She never wore any other jewellery. It was *hers!*'

'So that's the proof, then.'

'I can't believe it! So it *was* Juliette! She was one of the four, burned alive! Oh, Marie-Claire! I didn't, I couldn't believe she was really dead! I never believed that last report, that she'd been seen in the camp. It didn't make sense – why would they bring her back after three years? Why would she still have shiny hair after three years in prison? I clung to the hope that it was a mistake, that it wasn't Juliette. But this! This is proof! She was there, and they killed her! He killed her – your husband!'

Overcome by the reality of that little sapphire pendant, and what it meant, Victoire gave in to her grief, and this time Marie-Claire was the one to give comfort, to take her sobbing sister in her arms. But then Victoire pulled away.

'And he wants to kill *you,* too! Marie-Claire, we need to do something, quickly!'

'But, Victoire, what can we do? I mean, I know I could just run away, now, with you. But we can't let him get away with this! We can't let him escape to some paradise in Argentina, protected by friends! He needs to be tried as a war criminal! I can't just save my own hide and let him go free, he has to be punished! And if I just flee now and take all these things he'll come after me, after Maman, after all of us! The Nazis are still strong here in Alsace; he still has enormous power! He's vicious, and devious. And so dangerous!'

'No. You're right. We can't let him escape.'

'So what now?'

'I'm thinking,' said Victoire. 'Wait a moment.' She sat down at the desk, rested her head in her hands. Closed her eyes. Remained still for almost five minutes. Then she looked up, and a light was in her eyes.

'I think we – you – have to kill him.'

Chapter Fifty-Seven

Marie-Claire

It's all so simple, Victoire said, but it didn't feel simple at all. Juliette's death, and Marie-Claire's ongoing marital rape, night after night, had to be avenged, and *they* were the ones to do it. Victoire went home that same day. She had to think about it, she said, make concrete plans, talk to Jacques. She had an idea – something Jacques had once mentioned.

Victoire – dear, sweet, angelic Victoire – was transformed. It was as if some other-earthly power had taken hold of her, turned her into this new being, this avenging angel. Yes, that was it – divine wrath, a no-holds-barred knowledge that this was the thing, the only thing, the right thing to do. As if, almost, Victoire was an instrument of divine justice; she who, more than any of them, was good and kind and obedient and even as a child had never given her mother the least cause for complaint, always dutiful, always good, reliable, compassionate.

Whereas she, Marie-Claire, the black sheep of the family – she was the one worrying about sin and guilt. Victoire, who had gone home last week to 'think things through and talk to Jacques' and was now back with not only a concrete plan, but concrete means to execute it, just laughed away her qualms. Now they stood in Marie-Claire's kitchen, clearing up after a light lunch, discussing the final details of the plan – and preparing for it.

'If it really worries you, just go to confession later on, to Père Roger,' Victoire said. Père Roger was their family priest in Ribeauvillé, a gentle, kindly, grey-haired man who had known them all their lives. '*That's* a real priest. He'll understand. He'll know you had to do it. He'll grant you absolution.'

'But… in cold blood? It's murder, a mortal sin!'

'Yes. In cold blood.' Victoire paused. 'It's for Juliette, and everyone else he killed, all the thousands he's tortured and starved and worked to death and hanged and burned alive.' She paused. 'My own opinion is this: extraordinary times call for extraordinary actions. This man is murderer of thousands. He murdered Juliette, and has no qualms about murdering you. He's a monster. You are in a unique position to ensure he does not escape justice. You should use that position, Marie-Claire; I think God has given you this opportunity, and you should use it. It's almost as if, as if, almost – you are an *instrument* of God. To bring him down at last. You must, Marie-Claire. *We* must.

She paused. 'I will take responsibility, Marie-Claire. It is my decision, and I will do it, not you. I will talk to God about it, in my heart, because that is where God lives. And I know I will find forgiveness.'

Marie-Claire thought about it, and nodded. 'But what if they question the suicide, accuse me of murder?'

'They won't. Trust me.'

'I'll do it. But, Victoire – can you stay here, over the weekend, so I'm not alone? See it through with me?'

Victoire shook her head.

'I'd love to – and any other time, I would. But this is the busiest time of year. The *vendange* is just about to begin. I'm really indispensable. I want to go home tonight – well, early tomorrow, on the first train.'

'I need you, Victoire. I need you as much as the *vendange* needs you. Please! There's the whole aftermath. The police. I need support. What do I tell them?'

'It won't be a problem, I promise. Remember what the police told you when Silke's husband killed himself: they're dropping like flies. Everyone knows the game is up. It was suicide. That's all you have to say. That he's been depressed and panicky lately and killed himself. I promise you it'll be fine.'

'But he won't have left a letter. Silke's Klaus did. Apparently, most of them do.'

'Not Kurtz. Kurtz is far too proud to think of you when he commits suicide. Everyone knows that.'

'Still… Stay with me, Victoire. Please. I can't do this alone.'

Victoire thought in silence. 'You're right, I suppose. You're too nervous; I'd better stay. Maybe I can get a message to Jacques, tell him to go home for the *vendange*.'

She was silent again, and then looked up.

'I'll do it, I'll stay. It was my idea, my plan; I need to see it through with you. I can't let you do this alone.'

Marie-Claire breathed a sigh of relief. 'Thank God! I'm really a coward, when it's all boiled down.'

'No, you're not. You've been very brave, Marie-Claire, and you've gone through enough. It's too much to ask of you, especially since it was all my idea.'

'It's quite brilliant, though! So simple.'

'Brilliant in its simplicity, right? I'm quite the little devil, it turns out.'

She removed the pill box from her bag, opened it. The capsule lay in a bed of cotton wool.

'Where did you get it from?'

'Jacques, of course. And he got it from an English girl sent to Alsace as an agent to help the Resistance. Apparently, they give all their agents these deadly pills – suicide pills. They work instantly. She gave one to Jacques, and he gave it to me.'

She held it up gingerly, between thumb and forefinger. 'They call it the L-pill, lethal pill. Cyanide. The agents hold it in their gums if they get caught, and if it comes to the crunch – ugh, quite literally, the crunch! – they bite into it and it cracks open and the poison works immediately.'

'It sounds so dangerous! What if they swallow it by mistake?'

Victoire shook her head. 'No. See, it has a thin rubber hull. If they do swallow it without cracking it open, it passes through the body without releasing the poison. It's quite ingenious. Better than being tortured by the Gestapo and possibly giving away vital secrets.'

Marie-Claire shuddered. 'I don't think I could ever do that.'

'If you were an agent, you could…'

Victoire looked at her and laughed. 'You look as if you're about to go to the gallows!'

'It feels like it.'

'It shouldn't, Marie-Claire. This is the right thing to do. It's the *only* thing to do. We can't let him escape, and escape he will if we allow him to live. He's still far too powerful. It's your duty! You must see that!'

Marie-Claire gulped and nodded. 'I do see it. It's just… it's just such a big thing! Murder!'

'No, it's not. There's not much for you to do, really. Just do what you always do, like a devoted wife. So let's go through it again. You said, when he comes home he first takes a bath?'

'Yes. He has a strict routine on Fridays. He comes home late – he always has dinner before, either at the camp or in the Black Ox in Natzwiller with his colleagues. Then he disappears into his study with a stiff drink to read the week's *Stürmer*. He brings that back from the camp. An awful magazine! Full of Nazi propaganda! A real rag.' Marie-Claire shuddered, and continued. 'And then he has a bath. Thank goodness for that at least. I don't have to sleep with the smell of the camp. But you know, I swear, the smell of death is ingrained in his skin. Not even the hottest bath, the sweetest bath salts, can get it all out.'

'And then he goes to bed?'

'Yes. He expects me to be waiting there for him. And then this stiff cold statue of a man turns into a rampant beast forcing himself on me. I don't want to talk about it. No, don't look at me with pity. I've learnt to deal with it. I can handle it. I can shut myself off while it's happening. Mercifully, it's quickly over. And then he falls on his back and goes to sleep immediately.'

'And you?'

'I lie awake for a few hours more, thinking about it all.'

'But you always prepare his glass of water in advance, right?'

'Yes. He wakes up at about 2 a.m. He goes to the toilet, and then he returns, sits on the side of the bed and drinks it all down. A whole glass.'

'Always?'

'Always.'

'Bien. As I thought. Well, tonight, you will prepare a very special glass for him.'

She plunged her hand into her handbag once again and pulled out a small brown paper envelope. She handed it to Marie-Claire.

'Keep this safely. You'll empty it into the water when you prepare the glass. It's a strong but tasteless sedative. It'll put him to sleep in a few minutes. He'll nod off like a baby.'

'Victoire! Where did you get this?'

Victoire shrugged. 'I have friends who work at the hospital, a friend at the hospital *pharmacie.* I told him it was to kill a Nazi. He was only too willing to help.'

'So,' said Marie-Claire. 'I have to prepare the glass, put it on the night table. And then…' she shuddered.

Victoire's eyes gleamed with mirth. 'And then, Marie-Claire, you will perform your so-called wifely duties for the very last time. I'm sorry, but you must do it, but take comfort in the fact that it will be the very last time. He'll drop off to sleep as usual. He will wake up, as usual for his nightly bathroom visit. At about 2 a.m., you said.'

Marie-Claire, deathly white, nodded.

'When he's fast asleep, you get up and fetch me. I'll do the rest. I'll be the killer. You'll be free, Marie-Claire.'

Marie-Claire still looked as if the world was about to end. Victoire turned to her and folded her into her arms.

'I know you're scared. It's going to be all right. We have to do this.'

'Jacques knows what we're going to do?'

For some reason, it was important to her that Jacques should know, that Jacques should be there with her tonight, in spirit.

Victoire nodded. 'He knows, and he approves. Jacques said he always knew your heart was in the right place.'

'Jacques said that?'

'He did. He always believed in you, Marie-Claire, even when everyone else doubted, thought you'd turned into a Nazi. Jacques kept faith in you.'

'I suppose I let you all down. I was such a fool.'

'Don't say such things. That's in the past. We all make mistakes. The main thing is to learn from them, and grow.'

'You're so wise, for your eighteen years!'

Victoire laughed. 'That's because I'm the youngest, and able to watch you all making your mistakes! What will he say when you tell him your sister's staying for the weekend?'

'Frankly, I don't care. I've put up with his friends coming and going all these years. It's about time I had my own guest. And you're my sister. He can hardly object.'

Kurtz didn't object. He came home late that night and barely nodded at Victoire when Marie-Claire introduced her and said she'd be staying the night. He stretched out a stiff hand and shook hers. His grip was cold, hard, almost painful. His face might have been carved from stone. His eyes bored through her without actually acknowledging her. He nodded again and disappeared into his study.

Marie-Claire fussed around for a while, tidying things, placing his greatcoat on a hanger in the hall, and finally running his bath.

After that, she and Victoire sat together in the sitting room, sipping wine and chatting, the picture of placid domesticity. But Marie-Claire's heart hammered inside her as she waited, and Victoire, for once, found it hard to keep up a stream of empty chatter on a night like this, on a night when murder had been planned and the victim sat unsuspectingly just metres away. But it had to be done.

At last he emerged from his study, approached them to say goodnight, shook Victoire's hand again, and disappeared into the corridor that led to the bedrooms and the bathroom. It was time. The thing had to be done. Marie-Claire stood up. She reached out to Victoire, who clasped her hand and nodded. She walked to the kitchen, then opened the cupboard where the glasses were kept. She filled the water glass and emptied the sachet of powder into it. The water turned cloudy for a moment, but in a few seconds the powder dissolved. The water was as clear as ever.

Marie-Claire walked into the bedroom and placed the glass, as always, on the night table next to Kurtz's side of the bed. As always, she placed a folded handkerchief on top of it. Such a simple, basic task, and yet, tonight, it was the first step in a murder plot.

She walked back to the sitting room. Victoire was waiting for her.

'I'm not ready for bed yet,' said Victoire. 'I'll read a little and then go to bed in about an hour.'

The sisters hugged and went their separate ways.

Marie-Claire put on her nightdress and moved over to the washbasin in the corner of the bedroom. She cleaned off her make-up, washed her face, and brushed her teeth. And then she went to bed to wait.

He came. Her heartbeat, as ever, began to gallop as he approached the bed. He climbed in next to her, but a moment later he was on top of her, heaving, heaving, a rutting brute. As always. But, as always, it was over in less than a minute thankfully. As always, she endured it with eyes shut tight, teeth clamped and breath held. Thank goodness, over the years his needs had reduced and now it was only the one time, not all night long intermittently as it had been at the start of their marriage. She could take it now.

But this was the last time. The very last time.

She lay awake for about an hour after he had finished. A sense of calm drifted through her. It was over. The nightmare was over. She could sleep in peace. She drifted off but her sleep was light and nervous and when he got up in the middle of the night, her heart began to madly thump, so loud she was sure he could hear it. Yet all was as normal. He stood up, walked to the door, into the corridor, closed the bedroom door. This was it then. Off to have his nightly wee. The last one ever.

She waited, struggling to control her nervousness, to keep from trembling. Waited for his return. Her heart hammered palpably. She waited. And waited. The wait, tonight, seemed endless. It *was* endless. Something wasn't right, surely. Something wasn't normal. As she waited, she felt her heart thundering away within her chest, as if it knew, it understood – tonight was different.

Finally, after what seemed like hours, but might only have been minutes in her heightened state of alarm, she heard the click of the door opening. He was back. She held her breath, but then forced herself to breath slowly, rhythmically, as if she were asleep. *No break in the routine,* Victoire had said, but he had already broken the routine by this unusually long visit to the bathroom – or was that just her imagination? She couldn't tell. She must pretend to be asleep, though she was sure that he, too, must hear the hammering from inside her. She tried to breathe slowly, rhythmically. Audibly.

He sat down on the bedside. It took tremendous effort now not to change the rhythm of her breathing, yet again, not to sigh in relief. And now – she could almost hear him reaching for the glass. Yes, he had done it. He had raised it to his lips. She couldn't see, turned away from him as she was, but she heard him take a sip, and then swallow, gulping it all down. *Glug, glug, glug.* It was done.

He climbed back into bed, pulled the covers over himself. She listened to his breathing. To the rhythm, the depth of it. As each breath grew longer, so did hers. For her, it was a slow melting of her body into relief as he breathed his way into a deep, dark sleep. He began to snore. It was done. Tentatively she turned over in the bed, reached out and touched him. He did not stir. She grasped his arm and shook him, daring him to wake up, ravage her again, but he slept on, heavy as a log, unconscious, lost to the world. It was time.

She slipped out of bed, ran to the guest room, opened the door, and cried out, 'Victoire, Victoire! It's done! He's asleep! We've done it!'

But Victoire did not leap from her bed and run to the door, she did not seem in a hurry at all to complete the deed. A soft groan came from the bed, and then a sob, and then the whispered words, '*D'accord.* I'm coming.'

Marie-Claire, standing at the door, watched as Victoire slowly got out of bed, and in the darkness – for only the hallway light was on – opened the night table drawer, removed an object and closed it again.

Victoire was now at her side, in her nightdress, brushing past her into the hallway, but something was wrong. *Very* wrong. They should be exchanging hugs and words of triumph and conspiratorial grins of glee by now. They should be giggling in nervous excitement, or in exultation – Kurtz would be dead in a matter of minutes! – but Victoire was silent as she hurried ahead of Marie-Claire, her face hidden from view, her hair, a mass of tangled curls that fell forward as she hastened ahead. There was something odd about Victoire's movements, her haste: jerky, vehement, almost manic. This was not the cool, collected Victoire of earlier. Something was *very* wrong.

Victoire strode ahead of Marie-Claire into the bedroom, her face still hidden from view by shadows and by that wild mane of hair and by movements that somehow seemed unnatural, though Marie-Claire could not tell exactly how. It was a feeling more than a logical observation. Everything felt wrong, and suddenly, Marie-Claire felt a cold chill run through her, and she was terrified.

They reached the bed. Kurtz lay there, fast asleep, his face relaxed, his mouth slightly open. A dribble of spittle lay on his bottom lip. His jaw hung loose.

Without looking up, Victoire signalled to Marie-Claire and said, 'Come behind me, and hold up his head for me. Hold it steady. It's crucial.' Her voice was strangely slurred, her vocals unclear, almost muffled, and her face still turned away.

'No! I can't! I can't touch him! Not his head!' Marie-Claire cried.

'Don't be such a chicken!' cried Victoire. 'We're in this together! *Look at me!*'

Only now did Victoire turn her face and looked Marie-Claire straight in the eye. Marie-Claire gasped. Across Victoire's cheek was a huge red splodge, in the vague shape of a hand. A bruise had formed beneath one of her eyes; and yet, both eyes shone with something beyond pain, beyond anger. They shone with triumph.

'Yes,' said Victoire, her eyes meeting Marie-Claire's. 'Yes, he came to me. And yes, I fought him off, but in the end he won the fight, and had his way with me. Or so he thought. Because he is about to breathe his last. Hold his head up!'

She opened her hand to show Marie-Claire the thing she had retrieved from the drawer: the tiny cyanide capsule.

And again, stunned with the realisation of the unplanned horrors of the night, Marie-Claire did as she was told. She held Kurtz's head steady. Victoire pulled latex gloves over her hands. She held the capsule carefully in the fingers of her right hand while gently pulling open his jaw with her left. She placed the capsule between his back teeth and pressed his jaw together.

'For Juliette,' Victoire whispered. 'And all the others.'

The glass crunched as it broke between his teeth.

'Now you can let go,' she said to Marie-Claire, who did so with a shudder of revulsion.

Kurtz's head fell back, and now lay heavy against the pillow. They watched in silence, arms wrapped tightly around each other. His breathing stuttered, his body gave a slight jerk, and then there was stillness. Victoire let go of Marie-Claire, bent over him and pulled a sheet over his head. She then picked up the glass from the night table and handed it to Marie-Claire.

'Wash it out thoroughly, and put it back on the night table, full of water. Your story is: he must have woken up in the night as usual, gone to the lavatory, lay down again and taken the capsule, and bit into it, without water. They'll find splinters from the crushed capsule in his mouth; they'll know it was a suicide pill. You heard nothing; as always, you slept like a log. You only found him when you woke up this morning. You screamed in horror, tried to wake him, shook his head, his body, but he was dead. All you did then was pull a sheet over his head. That's your story, Marie-Claire, and you must stick to it. It's vital.'

Marie-Claire nodded. She started to speak. 'But—'

'But listen. I can't stay with you as planned. I can't let them see me like this. It will raise questions.' She pointed to her face. 'We have to avoid questions. So, in a few hours I will slip out of the house, before dawn. You will tell them I had to catch the first train back to Colmar. For the vendange.'

'I... I can help a bit,' said Marie-Claire. 'I have some make-up, concealer. I... I sometimes used it, when he got rough and my face was bruised the next day. It doesn't hide everything, but it helps.'

'Good idea, thanks. We'll do that in a while. I'll take the stairs down, so as not to wake the concierge with that clanking lift. I'll let myself out the front door. Perhaps you can come down, and lock it behind me?'

Marie-Claire nodded.

Victoire continued, giving instructions as if ticking off the programme, as if, in the minutes after her assault, she had simply rescheduled the night. 'Right. Then, at about eight o'clock, you will call the police. You will be in hysterics – you just found your husband dead in your bed! But your story will ring true, and they will believe you.

'But now, we will both go back to bed and try to get a few hours' sleep. No, Marie-Claire; don't weep. You don't have to stay with him. You can come and sleep in my bed; this one's polluted. Remember, when you were very small, how I would crawl into your bed at night and you would throw me out, and then I would crawl to Juliette's bed and she would let me sleep with her?' She chuckled wryly. 'Now it's the reverse, isn't it! You'll come into my bed. Come on, big sister, come with me. Everything's all right. Everything's going to be all right. Leave that piece of scum behind.'

She placed an arm around Marie-Claire, who was could hardly stand for the sobs that shook her body, and led her out of the room. She shut the bedroom door behind them, turned to Marie-Claire, white as a ghost, her face a grim mask, eyes wide open with the horror of the night.

'Because in the end *we* won. Just as we will win the war. See, Marie-Claire. We both paid the price. Your nightmare is over. Tomorrow, you will ring Maman, and then you will come home. The Nazis might have torn this family apart, and now it's time to mend the wounds. Stop the bleeding. As a family, Marie-Claire, we have won.'

Their eyes met. At last, Marie-Claire's face relaxed, and she smiled as she spoke. 'What about a glass of champagne, *petite soeur*?'

Epilogue

1945

It all came out in the end. Kurtz's last plan, to empty the Natzweiler-Struthof camp before the Allies came, succeeded. Even without him, all the prisoners were evacuated by 1 September of that year: sent to camps in the East, in Germany or Poland. Some were sent on a death march. By the time the Allies arrived it was a ghost settlement.

Kurtz's 'suicide' was accepted without question by the police; he was one of many who, knowing the game was up, chose this final solution for themselves. Marie-Claire, the grieving widow, verified that yes, he had seemed very depressed and frantic towards the end – and of course she knew nothing of his evil deeds, and only wanted to return to her family home to mourn. Which she did, leaving the death rituals to the remains of the German administration. She told her story, truthfully except for the final chapter, and it was believed by those who mattered.

Victoire destroyed the passport and letters pertaining to Kurtz's escape plans; it was better that no suspicion of a murder plot should ever fall on Marie-Claire. Why would Kurtz have committed suicide if he had been planning to escape? But the list of Catholic priests willing to harbour escaping Nazi criminals – that, she passed on to Jacques, who passed it on to Allied Intelligence, not naming his source. Those priests, too, should find justice…

Margaux, on hearing of the dastardly plan, and of the Church's collaboration with the Nazis, immediately did as her husband had begged her for years: filed for divorce. She could no longer respect the rules of a Church that could so readily break the very first tenet of Christ's message: *love one another, and your neighbour as yourself.* Yes, she was ready to divorce, and to remarry, with or without the Church's blessing. Preferably *without;* but with Christ's. A different matter altogether, she said.

Strasbourg fell to the Allies in November 1944. Hitler, determined to hold Alsace, launched a final defence on 1 January 1945. Operation Nordwind, as it was called, was the final, furious flailing of a dying beast. The Colmar Pocket became a vicious, bloody battle that turned the snow-covered rolling hills of the countryside from pristine white to red – red with the blood of Allied and German soldiers equally. Civilians took shelter in their cellars as their villages became battlegrounds, some reduced to piles of rubble, homes left behind as hollow ruins.

Eric, Victoire's Eric, bled to death in a mound of red snow outside the decimated village of Jebstown. Jacques brought the news to Victoire, who now worked as a nursing aide in a school taken over by the International Red Cross to do what little they could for those injured and dying who could be brought back to Colmar.

Victoire, by now no stranger to grief, had not the time or space to mourn Eric, busy as she was day and night with her patients, who lay side by side on the frozen ground as there were no beds, no cots.

'This is what Eric signed up for, Victoire,' said Jacques. 'All of us knew we could be the next to go, that every day could be our last. He died a hero. Be proud of him; proud that such a man loved you.'

'I am,' said Victoire. She turned away. She had wounds to dress. Her own wounds must wait their turn. After Marcel's death, after Leon's and, most of all, Juliette's, grief had become her permanent state of being, a substratum of herself that could not be added to.

But then it was over. Colmar, France, finally free. Church bells rang out, citizens came out of hiding. 'La Marseillaise', their anthem of triumph, rang out from jubilant throats. Hitler commited suicide. The war in Europe was finally over after almost six long weary years. The Allies crossed the Rhine and advanced into Germany, to find not only a nation ravaged, its defeated citizens dazed and unbelieving – for this was never meant to happen! – but new horrors, untold horrors, of which Natzweiler-Struthof was only the beginning.

Ravensbrück, Bergen-Belsen, Theresienstadt, Auschwitz. Synonyms for a horror whose like the world had never before seen. One by one, the death camps were discovered, their emaciated survivors freed. The International Red Cross was once again to hand.

On 29 April 1945 the 42nd U.S. Infantry Division liberated Dachau. They found 67,665 registered prisoners in Dachau and its sub camps, around 32,000 prisoners in the Dachau camp itself, crammed into 20 barracks designed to house only 250 people. Most of them were dying; Dachau's prisoners had been used as subjects of medical experiments. Thousands had been deliberately infected with typhoid. Thousands had already died, and been cremated.

Victoire was sent by the Red Cross to help with the evacuees of Dachau.

In yet another makeshift ward she stepped between bodies that were little more than skeletons covered in skin, kneeling down to offer a bottle of water, leaning over to offer a useless word of comfort, to hold up the head of a half-starved stranger.

And then, this. A twinge of recognition. A second look, a step nearer. She knelt down beside the still-living, half-dead (it was impossible to tell from appearances) woman; her head was little more than a skull covered in skin, the eyes buried in sunken hollows, the cheeks caverns clinging to bones. A few grey strands of hair still clung to the bald bony scalp.

Hair that had once been black. Eyes buried in hollowed-out canyons; eyes that once shone with life and love and the promise of a future, now closed. Kneeling beside the woman, she cupped a hand beneath the head, raising it slightly, gently. With the other

SHARON MAAS

hand, she turned the head to face her. Had there been hair, thick, luxuriant, shiny black hair, she would have brushed it aside in a so-familiar gesture, but there was none. Not a single black strand, just a few grey wisps on a bald head. She leaned nearer, placed her face before those eyes' seemingly empty depths.

'Juliette?' she whispered. 'Juliette, it is you? It's me, Victoire.'

She reached for one of the woman's hands, felt for a pulse. The hand was as thin and fragile as a bird, but the tiny flutter it gave could not be mistaken, the flutter of a butterfly's wing. The woman was alive, and had heard.

'Juliette!' she whispered again. And again: 'Juliette! It's me! I'm here!'

And somewhere, deep within those dark sockets, eyelids twitched and then flickered open. 'Juliette! It's me, Victoire!' Victoire whispered again. She cupped the head in her hands, stroked the almost transparent skin with her thumbs and came closer, repeating the name, calling to life. No response. She kept calling, calling into the emptiness within those sockets. A blink, another blink. And then from deep within, two tiny lights of recognition flickered. Fireflies in the darkest night.

'Juliette!' whispered Victoire again, slightly louder this time. 'Wake up, Juliette! Wake up! I've come to take you home.'

A Letter from Sharon

Dear Readers,

Thank you so much for reading *Her Darkest Hour*. I do hope you enjoyed it; that would be my greatest reward! Should you care to tell others of your enjoyment by word of mouth, or on social media, or in a review, that would be even better! You might also enjoy my previous books, *The Soldier's Girl* and *The Violin Maker's Daughter*, which are also set in Alsace and feature a few of the same characters. If you would like to keep up to date with my latest releases, please do sign up at the following link. Your email address will always be confidential and you can unsubscribe at any time.

www.bookouture.com/sharon-maas

Writing a novel is a solitary occupation. I lived with the characters and the story for many months, but once that work was done, many others gave their wisdom and their expertise to helping this work make its entry into the big wide world, and into your hands. I would like to thank, first of all, my wonderful editor, Lydia Vassar-Smith, who with her sensitive and skilled touch helped to create the very best version of the story. Many other members of the Bookouture family played their part in the book's release: Jacqui Lewis, Jane Donovan, Ami Smithson, Alexandra Holmes and Radhika Sonagra; thank you to them, and to Kim Nash, Noelle Holten and Sarah Hardy for their dedicated work in promoting it; and not forgetting a big thank-you to all the bloggers and social media readers who've taken the time to review and write about it; word of mouth is a silent but powerful helper!

I'd also like to thank my fellow authors for their unwavering support, advice and encouragement, in particular Debbie Rix, Renita D'Silva and Laura Elliot, as well as the wonderful authors in the Facebook groups Second World War Authors and the Savvy Writers Snug, and also members of the AbsoluteWrite Water Cooler.

Last, but not least, I'd like to thank Oliver Rhodes, who, by creating the publishing phenomenon that is Bookouture gave my faltering writing career a new lease of life back in 2014. *Her Darkest Hour* is my tenth Bookouture novel! I couldn't be more delighted to have reached this milestone, but I couldn't have done it without you, my readers. Just knowing you are out there, reading words I've written, entering worlds I've created, is the best encouragement ever, and hopefully there'll be many more books to come. So once again – thank you!

To my children, Saskia and Miro, the biggest thank-you of all, for standing by your mother through all the years and your good humour at her sometimes scatty and absent-minded behaviour. I really do, sometimes, live in another world, but all for a good cause!

Historical Note

Of course, if you are writing a historical novel, it is not about dumping all that knowledge and research into the text. That's the last thing you want to do. Your aim is to entertain readers with a riveting story, not bore their socks off. Elizabeth Chadwick

Her Darkest Hour is a work of fiction; its main aim was to tell the story of a fictional family living through World War Two and torn apart by certain events of that war. It was never intended to be an account of the war itself, but only of how it affected that family. But it is my duty, as a historical novelist, to get that war background as accurate as possible, and weave fact and fiction neatly together so as to retain the historical details without jeopardising the story, and vice versa.

My task while writing it was, I felt, to do my research as thoroughly as possible, and then use my imagination to fill in the details; and now I owe it to you, my readers, to pull apart the woven tapestry of fact and fiction and let you know which is which.

The facts are: the Nazis did march into Colmar in early November 1940. They did claim the annexation of the French province of Alsace, which was separated from Germany by the River Rhine. They did initiate a thorough Germanisation of Alsace, which meant that the spoken and written language had to change, almost overnight, from French to German, French names had to be changed to German, schools had to adopt a German curriculum and so on. They did take over the Colmar *Mairie*. The misguided attempt to woo newly-wed couples by distributing copies of *Mein Kampf* to them: that indeed happened. Later on, Alsatian young men were indeed conscripted into the Wehrmacht, and if they refused or absconded, their families were targeted for reprisals.

However, *how* this all took place is in its entirety a figment of my imagination. The figures of Otto Grötzinger and Dietrich Kurtz and all the *Mairie* staff members – the giggling secretaries, the guards, the keeper of the storeroom – are all invented. I've used creative licence to describe the internal workings of the *Mairie* during this time, and the pressure Marie-Claire felt as she continued to work there, and her eventual rape, is all a part of that.

Finally, though, this novel was inspired by two little-known (in the English-speaking world) historical realities. One was the heroism of Marcel Weinum. The very thought of this brave young man, a teenager, moves me to tears, and it's a crying shame that, in doing my research, I found nothing at all in English about him. Yet just as Sophie Scholl was guillotined for her role in resisting the Nazis, so too was Weinum. He is only a minor character in *Her Darkest Hour,* and obviously his cameo appearance in the novel is fiction, but he was a real person, a genuine hero, and should not be forgotten but rather be remembered and honoured as one of the outstanding unsung heroes of the Resistance. His letter to his parents, written the day before he was beheaded, is a tragic and very moving testament to his faith, courage and compassion, and can be found on the many French-language sites recounting his life and untimely death.

The second little-known historical fact that inspired this book was the horrific existence of one of the worst Nazi concentration camps, high up in the spectacular Vosges mountains: Natzweiler-Struthof. Situated in Alsace, where my story unfolds, it was the only such camp on French territory. Until fairly recently, I myself knew nothing of its existence, in spite of my long connection with Alsace.

As a student in Freiburg, Germany, and over the following years, I often crossed the border into Alsace to visit my much-older friend, Trudel Elsässer. Trudel had been born in the village of Ribeauvillé, not far from the town of Colmar, which features in a few of my novels. She spent the war years in Berlin, and she is in fact the only person I know who lived through the war who actually spoke of her experiences. As her mother had been Jewish, her stories were both riveting and heartbreaking. The man she married had the surname Elsässer, which means 'Alsatian' in German, and when he retired, they both moved back to her beloved Alsace, to their beautiful house in the hills beyond Colmar.

That's where I listened to her anecdotes, and in fact it is she who first alerted me to the myriad of untold personal stories that would inevitably die out with her generation. To this day, I feel sadness that I never questioned my father and his brothers about their own war experiences: they had volunteered from British Guiana, a colony in South America, and crossed an ocean to fulfil their duty. My father had been in the RAF, but I know not a thing about what he did and what he went through. Why didn't I question him more? Listen to his stories? I'm pretty sure he would have talked, but as a young woman I just wasn't interested in what went before.

That's a crying shame, because whereas the history books can reveal the recorded facts of what happened during the war, it is the personal stories that can really grab us, awaken us, move us, change us. So it was with me, listening to Trudel's stories. Trudel died, mentally still sharp as a pin, aged 102, just when I started to write historical fiction and to research Alsace in particular. And so, belatedly, I learned of the existence of Natzweiler-Struthof.

Very little is written in English about this camp, but then I was graciously allowed access to a translation by Diana Henry of testimony for the camp (see below). This testimony, coupled with a personal visit to the camp in October 2019, revealed all I needed to know. It was a visit so disturbing that I changed my initial plan to set some of the scenes of my novel there. To do so felt somehow disrespectful to those who had been its victims – how could I ever fictionalise their agony? How could I ever come close to reproducing what they went through? At best, I could just hint at it. And so the novel's action remains outside the camp walls, and the horror is revealed only as reported by others.

Here, now, are some of the facts:

Natzweiler-Struthof was planned as a very small camp for about 2,000 inmates. Yet it contained at least 7,000 during the summer of its evacuation in 1944, with 450,000 prisoners registered in total. From the start it was classified as a Category III concentration camp, the toughest camps for the 'incorrigible political enemies' of the Third Reich. As such, its prisoners were mostly dissidents and Resistance fighters, anyone the Nazis considered an enemy of the state, and they came from all over Europe. It was also a labour camp and a transit camp. There were no female prisoners.

When I visited the camp, I found very few other visitors. In fact, I was alone in the two barracks situated on the lowest terrace, the prison block and the crematorium, which allowed me time and personal space to truly absorb what had occurred there, and to feel the utmost revulsion. In particular, I was moved by the story of four female British Special Operations Executive (SOE) agents who were executed and cremated there, and I have incorporated that event into the story of *Her Darkest Hour*.

And yes, these women were indeed still alive when shoved into the oven, feet first, according to first-hand reports. And yes, one of them woke up and fought back. And yes, one of them was dark-haired and mistaken for another; first reports revealed that she was Noor Inayat Khan, who was half-Indian, to the dismay of her family. In fact, she was Sonia Olschanezky, a member of the SOE's network of agents known as the Juggler circuit in occupied France. The other three agents were Andrée Borrel, Vera Leigh and Diana Bowden. There is a commemorative plaque naming all four in the crematorium.

The real-life *Kommandant* of Natzweiler at the time that the four female SOE agents were executed was Fritz Hartjenstein.

Tried by a British war crimes court at Wuppertal, from 9 April to 5 May 1946, he was found guilty and sentenced to death. Hartjenstein's death sentence was commuted to life imprisonment on 1 June 1946. Later sentenced to death by a French court, he died of a heart attack in prison in 1954.

And so, my fictional avengers Marie-Claire and Victoire were obviously quite right to kill Hartjenstein's fictional counterpart, Dietrich Kurtz. Left to the Allied courts, he could very well have escaped justice.

As many have said before me: let us never forget. Let the stories keep coming, whether in fact or fiction. They inspire us to do better. Or should...

Sources

Thanks to Diana Mara Henry, www.natzweiler-struthof.com for her translation of *L'Enfer d'Alsace* by Eugène Marlot, which is soon to be published in English.

Further reading on the Natzweiler-Struthof camp: www. scrapbookpages.com/Natzweiler

The official camp website: www.struthof.fr/en/the-kl-natzweiler

Quote: Chadwick, E. (2017, Jul 23) 'Beyond the Dressing Up Box: How I Write Historical Fiction'. Retrieved from http://elizabethchadwick.com/blog/beyond-the-dressing-up-box-how-i-write-historical-fiction/

CPSIA information can be obtained
at www.ICGtesting.com
Printed in the USA
LVHW011645150520
655693LV00003B/548

9 781838 886646